The Nanokillers Are Loose...

Debris poured out through the open hatch. The laboratory deck was dark. Val turned on her helmet lights which cast milky shafts through the churning, shattered remains of the lab. Each step revealed more wreckage. Delicate instruments were twisted beyond recognition. Racks of complex equipment were torn from their anchors and thrown like toys in the hands of an impetuous child. Now they floated in zero-g, a suspension of destruction in an ocean of fouled air.

"Careful not to tear your suit," Adrianna cautioned.

Val pushed forward into the debris. The space in front of her took on a reddish cast. A bloody torso floated under a shattered console. "I think it's Pete," Val whispered. She turned her head. A lifeless face, ruptured and torn hung next to her. It was Mattie North. "Oh my God."

Sobs broke the silence as Val turned away and continued her inspection. "What about the containment unit, Val?" Hunter was beside himself.

"I'm going over there now."

Hunter held his breath as he waited for Val to make her assessment. She took her time avoiding the torn metal and plastic that hovered around her. The containment unit was still bolted to the laboratory deck. The holochamber was gone, broken into a thousand pieces and distributed around the compartment. As Val moved closer, the image cleared. The top half of the device was sheared away, revealing the delicate inner workings, now ripped loose and floating on tethers of torn wiring above the cavity that once held the phase two machines.

Val's voice was a cool, lifeless whisper. "We're dead. We're all dead."

Meridian's Shadow

MERIDIAN'S
SHADOW

MERIDIAN'S SHADOW
Copyright ©2011 Daniel T. Moore

Published by
DMP
Liverpool, NY
www.danmoore.com

Cover art by Jason Moore

ISBN 978-0-9834283-0-5
ISTC A03-2011-00000003-E

September 2015 Revision
Printed in the United States of America

Visit www.meridiansshadow.com

This book is dedicated to Diana,
my bright and morning star. Thank you for being my
wife and best friend..

FOREWORD

The characters of Sprite Logan and Kate Sloan came to me almost twenty years ago in a screenplay I wrote in graduate school. Sprite told me about her nanoskin in early 2009 and I began to write Meridian's Shadow.

This book belongs to my characters. I am their chronicler, giving voice and context to the grand sweep of their struggles and dreams. Meridian's Shadow tells the story of how Sprite got her skin and introduces a number of people whose stories will be told in upcoming novels.

I could not have written this book without the support of my wife Diana. She has always believed in me. I also thank Andy Robinson who helped me trust in my storytelling and Jean Armour Polly and Rick Fensterer of the Liverpool Public Library for their kind support and guidance in the world of publishing. My friends Larry Mauser and Jim Brand read early drafts and gave me the encouragement I needed to press forward with the project. Thank you all.

Finally, I ask my hard SF readers to forgive some of the liberties I have taken for the sake of this story. This book is intended to be a Science Fiction adventure that is centered on the lives of my characters, not on the laws of physics. I hope I haven't done anything to disrupt the suspension of your disbelief.

Dan Moore
March 2011

THE CHARACTERS

NARI
Dr. Hunter Logan
Dr. Adrianna Logan
Dr. Tyson Edwards
Dr. Jo Smith
Dr. Alexis Wren
Dr. Robert Hastings
Dr. Maryanne Hastings
Dr. Mattie North
Jenson Reed
Samina Haddad
Valerie Lopez
Pete Cushing
Wiley

NARI YOUTH
Sprite Logan
Kell Edwards
Emile Hastings
Aurora North

COPERNICUS BASE
Director Winston Marshall
Kate Sloan
Spud Leonard
Prudence Leonard

THE CITIZEN'S LEAGUE
Damon Trask
Maya Lewis
Simon James

MERIDIAN CORPORATION
Amos Cross
Susanna Frost
Dr. Maxwell Thrune
Drew Mallick
Beverly Mallick
Bud Sorenson

THE SMUGGLERS
Captain Grit
Nixie Drake
Spif
Ice
Slake

MERIDIAN 6
Commander Adam Taberg
Cilla Ashe
Ray Bright
Troy Mack
Athena

ASTEROID BELT
Prescott Logan
Maria Logan
Scurvy Winslow

BOOK ONE:

DETONATION

1

Fierce pain. Icy hot needles shot through young Hunter Logan's right index finger. All thoughts of an exhilarating camping trip dripped away as he dropped the knife, now crimson with blood. The boy had been carving a tiny piece of wood with the razor-sharp blade. His grip was misplaced, and the blade had slipped. A chunk of meat now dangled from the side of his knuckle, on a flap of skin.

An older boy watched gleefully. "I told you! You can't carve something that small."

"Doofus!" said another. It sounded like a curse. Two other boys were laughing and shaking their heads.

Hunter was on a camping trip with a group of boys in his scout troop. They rode him mercilessly about his interest in science and his clumsiness. He wanted to be their buddy. He wanted their respect, but they would not give it. One on one with the boys, Hunter would feel a connection, believe that some inroads had been made into friendship, but together they were a pack of derisive animals.

Hunter squeezed his finger, trying to stem the flow of blood. He turned away from the boys, hiding his tears. He was embarrassed and angry. Now they had another reason to hate him. He should have been more careful. Hunter looked at the bright-red splotches on his clothes. His uniform was ruined. He winced at the thought of never gaining the friendship of the other scouts. Through one lapse in judgment, he had become a joke.

* * *

The Selene Station revolved around the Moon in her elliptical orbit, one hundred fifty-three kilometers above the lunar surface. The station had a large photovoltaic array, whose wings tracked the sun as Selene made her circuit around her mistress. She was an old space station. Like the lunar deity for which she was named, Selene had been supplanted by newer incarnations. Until recently, she had been a barren sentinel, hosting a few lunar communications and navigational systems. Now she had been resurrected by the Meridian Corporation, a vast off-world conglomerate, to meet the needs of NARI, the Nanotechnology Advanced Research Institute. A gleaming new laboratory had been built within her hull, providing a zero-g environment for NARI research.

Dr. Hunter Logan floated next to his wife, Adrianna. They held hands, glancing at each other as a technician talked quietly into a headset. Larson Daniels, chief correspondent for the Inner System News Syndicate, smiled benignly at the couple. He glanced down at his monitor. The camera shot framed the two scientists perfectly in front of Selene's new laboratory. "Dr. Logan."

"That would be us," Hunter smiled. "Just call us Hunter and Adrianna. It's easier."

Larson grinned. "Hunter. So I get it right, what are your official titles?"

Hunter glanced at Adrianna. She winked back at him and said, "We're the co-directors of NARI."

"Why have you built this new laboratory on Selene Station?"

Adrianna let go of her husband's hand. The camerawoman read the telltale signs and pushed into a close-up. Adrianna was a beautiful woman with dark, close-cropped hair and a quick, disarming smile. "Well Larson, as your viewers know, our work has been somewhat controversial. We've been building machines out of particles that are measured in nanometers. A human hair is about 10 thousand nanometers in diameter, so our machines are pretty small. Our work is called molecular manufacturing. People have been worried that our work might harm Earth's environment. New international laws prevent us from doing our research on Earth, so we have partnered with Meridian Corporation to build this laboratory on Selene Station."

"Your most vocal critic has been Damon Trask of the Citizen's League." Larson's smile was gone. He only had a few minutes for the interview and had to press on with the hard, probing questions. "He claims your work is a danger to humanity. He spearheaded the movement to outlaw your work on Earth, and has vowed to do everything in his power to stop your research altogether. What do you have to say about that?"

The camerawoman saw Hunter draw in a breath. She pulled back to a two-shot of the couple and then smoothly zoomed in for a close-up. "You may not believe this, but we understand his concern. Frankly, I'm glad we're here in lunar orbit. The phase-two machines are completely isolated from the Earth and the off-world population centers."

"What are these phase-two machines?"

Adrianna gave Larson a radiant smile. "Right now, they're indiscriminate killers. Our goal is to program them to destroy the deadly pathogens and cancers that plague humanity and its environment. Once we are able to train them, the phase-two machines will hunt specific compounds and molecules. They will bond with their target and break down its internal structure. Once their work is done, they will become dormant, since the target no longer exists."

"You say they're 'indiscriminate killers.' What does that mean?"

Adrianna locked Larson in her gaze. "In their present form, they target everything. We call them piranha machines because they're very aggressive."

Hunter nodded. "They won't stop eating. They feed on order and leave chaos in their wake."

Larson turned pale. "Where do you keep them?"

Adrianna offered her most innocent face. "They're right behind you."

Larson jerked around too quickly in the zero-g. He reached for a nearby handhold to stop his spin. The camerawoman swung around smoothly, framing the image of a massive rectangular device bolted to the laboratory deck. A large chamber was integrated into the unit and displayed a complex arrangement of nanoscale particles. Hunter floated over to the apparatus and gestured toward the holodisplay. "You're looking at one of the phase-two machines."

Adrianna floated to Hunter's side and took his hand. She noted the fear in Larson's eyes. "The containment unit holds the phase-two machines in stasis and permits us to manipulate them safely."

Hunter gave Larson a proud smile. "Would you like a demonstration?" Larson paused, uncertain. Hunter could see the man's fear. It was almost perfectly balanced by his curiosity. Hunter didn't wait for Larson's answer. He worked the controls on the containment unit. The view in the holodisplay zoomed back, revealing a smaller nanoscale structure floating to the right of the phase-two machine. It looked like the skeleton of a soccer ball: carbon atoms arranged in a geodesic sphere. "This is a nano-diamond. It's made up of 275 atoms and is 1.4 nanometers in diameter. To give you a sense of scale, the hair on your head grows about ten nanometers every second. Watch what happens when I nudge it closer to the phase-two machine."

The nanomachine moved slowly toward the smaller object. As it grew closer, the inner workings of the nanomachine began to undulate, its outer layer prickled with tiny structures. The nano-diamond and the phase-two machine snapped together like the opposite poles of a magnet. Immediately, the machine tore apart the ball-like structure of the nano-diamond, leaving a dissociated cloud of carbon atoms in its wake.

Larson was visibly shaken. "What would happen if the containment unit failed?"

"The phase-two machine would disassemble this laboratory and Selene Station." Hunter's voice was calm and analytical.

"Destroy the whole platform." Larson's voice cracked.

Adrianna nodded thoughtfully. "That's right, but we are tuning the machine's appetite so it only likes certain things. Once we have accomplished that, the phase-two machines will be quite harmless."

Larson regained some of his composure. "This could cause a monstrous plague."

Hunter shook his head. "That will never happen. I've dedicated my life to finding ways to heal the environment. It's true. These phase-two machines are dangerous in their present form. That's why we've taken great precautions. The containment unit has many safeguards. Remember, we're working with these machines every day. I urge you and your viewers to see their potential. Once we're able to train them, these nanomachines will put an end to some of Earth's most vexing problems."

Larson's face became dispassionate, an unreadable mask. "Why should people trust you?"

Hunter paused to choose his words carefully. "We know what we're doing. There is no need to fear our work. I stake my reputation on that." Unconsciously, Hunter rubbed the old scar on his right index finger.

* * *

Emile Hastings was a precocious nine-year-old. He floated next to his mother, Dr. Maryanne Hastings, on the residence deck of Selene Station. He hadn't stopped grinning since he arrived on orbit. His father had convinced his mother to bring him along. Maryanne didn't think it was a good idea. She cited the risks of having him on board, but finally agreed to bring him. She wanted to keep the fragile peace with her husband, Dr. Robert Hastings. Both were NARI scientists and struggled to combine parenting with the all-encompassing demands of their research.

"Wow, Mom! I can fly!" The boy launched his slender frame across the cabin, bouncing from handhold to handhold.

"Easy, Em. You could break something. Slow down."

"But Dad said I could go fast."

"I don't care what your father said. Slow it down."

"Aw, Mom…"

"Don't 'aw, Mom' me, young man. If you don't behave, I'll send you back down to Copernicus Base with the Logans."

"Okay. Okay." Emile kicked off much slower this time, somersaulting as he crossed the residence deck.

* * *

Dr. Robert Hastings lifted Samina Haddad's body, his hands cupping her buttocks. Her bald head was thrown back, and his face was buried in her breasts. Her perfect skin and slender form excited him. He stood naked in Samina's private quarters on Copernicus Base. The low lunar gravity enabled him to lift his lover up over his hips effortlessly. Her legs folded around him. He raised and lowered her rhythmically, allowing her weight to press them both toward the inevitable moment of climax. Robert could feel her ecstasy rising with his own. He lowered her, making one final thrust. They merged together into a nexus of physical and emotional joy. They embraced, breathless from their intimacy.

"Hmmm," The sound came from deep within Samina's throat.

Robert managed a satisfied sigh. "I could never do that on Earth."

Samina gave him a devilish smile as she reached for him. "I'm glad you talked Maryanne into taking Emile to Selene Station."

"I'll pay for it later." Robert kissed her. Samina was a beautiful woman. She had joined the NARI team a few weeks earlier, and he was drawn to her immediately. The closeness of the NARI team had offered them an irresistible opportunity. At first, there were stolen glances, infatuation in the shadows. Their secret passion ripened, and they had thrown themselves willingly into the abyss of sensuality. There was no climbing out of it.

* * *

Hunter and Adrianna shook hands with Larson Daniels and sealed the airlock. The news correspondent was staying behind on Selene Station to conduct several more interviews. They left him with Maryanne Hastings and Valerie Lopez, two of NARI's lead researchers. The Logans took their seats, and the jumpship undocked for their return trip to Copernicus Base. They never tired of the view. Selene Station rose above them as they fell away toward the ancient, cratered surface below.

"We've complied with every law and demand." Hunter tapped the arm of his seat. Adrianna could sense his anxiety. "When are they going to stop questioning our motives? When will they stop accusing us of playing God? Daniels has asked me the same questions every time he's interviewed me. When will my answers be enough?"

Adrianna touched his arm gently. "It's his job, Hunter. He's a bloodhound. He's intoxicated by the scent of the story, and he won't let go."

"That bastard single-handedly drove us off-world. The first time he came to NARI, I was naïve. I was too honest with him. He took my words and spun them into a tale of horror. He intentionally tapped the fears of his audience and started a global firestorm of protest against us." Adrianna squeezed her husband's arm, but said nothing. "Why don't people trust me?"

"What we do is misunderstood, and people are scared easily. They don't know you. You take it too personally. Step away from it and remember whose opinion matters."

Hunter studied Adrianna's face. She was a woman of smiles. He touched her hand and nodded slowly. "You're right. But it doesn't make it any easier."

"Listen to the people who love you, Hunter. We know who you are, and we respect you. You have good intentions."

Hunter squeezed her hand. "Yeah, I know."

Adrianna leaned over and pecked him on the cheek. She didn't understand why someone as smart as her husband could be so insecure. She couldn't change him. This was a lifelong struggle for Hunter, and she knew it wasn't the last time they'd speak of it.

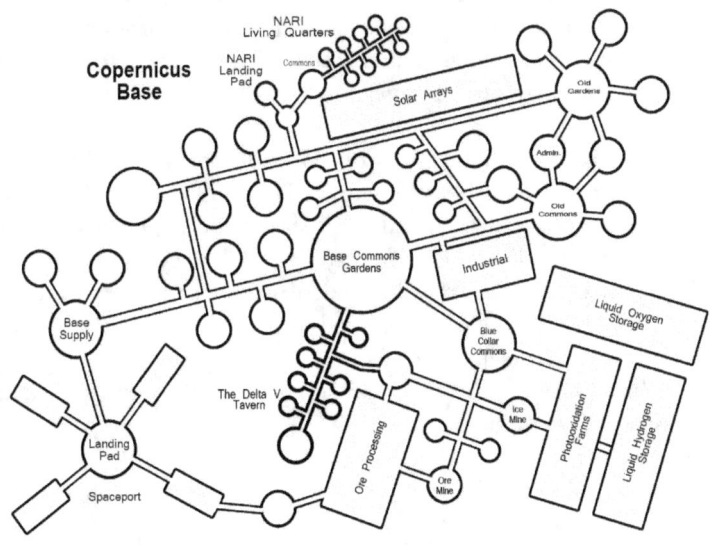

Copernicus Base sat inside the rim of an impact crater named after the famous Polish astronomer, Nicolaus Copernicus. Dozens of dome structures, fabricated from the lunar soil, rested on the floor of the crater. A huge glass hemisphere dominated the center of the base. The Base Commons, as it was called, housed a lush garden with grass and trees, food and flower gardens, benches and walkways. Microstructures within the dome's aluminum silicate glass adjusted its opacity in order to protect her treasure from the burning sun.

Copernicus was one of fourteen lunar bases owned by the Meridian Corporation. People of all races and classes scratched out livings in a hierarchal society, a lunar caste system. The vast majority of Copernicans shared cramped quarters in overcrowded domes. The wealthy minority had domes to themselves. One of the privileged few was the base director. Appointed by Amos Cross, the administrator of Meridian Corporation, the director served as the base's legal and administrative authority.

The Logans' jumpship swept around the perimeter of Copernicus Base and settled on a small private landing pad on the north side of the complex. The pad adjoined the living quarters for the NARI scientists and their families. A common area was housed in the largest dome in the residence complex. There was a long access corridor branching away from it. A series of smaller residence domes sprouted to the left and right of the corridor like leaves.

* * *

Sprite Logan sat lightly on the edge of her bed, folding smart wrapping paper over a box containing her father's birthday present. The seventeen-year-old painstakingly creased the paper. She wrapped the gift with the dexterity of a surgeon, her eye catching every misalignment of the pattern. She folded the paper twice and tore off the unneeded piece. The paper, trained to tear with a clean edge, pulled away effortlessly. She pressed the free edge of the wrapping paper down against the box, the paper adhering to itself. Sprite smiled with satisfaction. Her attention to detail came from her father, her stubbornness from her mother.

Sprite was exceedingly bright and was fond of artificially intelligent machines. She considered AIs her friends. They didn't get mad or take offense. They didn't stab her in the back. They were straightforward and honest. Working with AIs was a study of diplomacy and foreign affairs. She understood their culture and their language.

Sprite picked up her father's present and held it in front of her card comp. "What do you think, Wiley?" Sprite loved an ancient cartoon about a coyote and a roadrunner. She named her AI in honor of the coyote who never gave up.

"It's beautiful," the AI replied. "I notice variations in the alignment, but they are undetectable by the human eye."

Sprite laughed. "I'm glad you approve." Her piercing blue eyes twinkled at her digital friend. "Please remember to apply human parameters to your judgment algorithms."

"I have applied them." Sprite rotated the present so Wiley could see it from every angle. "It's an excellent job for a human."

"Send a picture to Uncle Prescott. Call it 'Sprite's present for Hunter's birthday.' Encrypt it and send it the usual way."

"Done."

Two weeks earlier, Sprite had moved into the NARI living quarters with her parents. She quickly adapted to the lunar gravity and was thoroughly enjoying her lunar adventure. She became enamored by Samina Haddad, NARI's new research cybrarian. She was Sprite's idea of the perfect woman: beautiful, brilliant, and an experienced space dweller. She wanted to walk like her, talk like her, and look like her. Sprite could have cut her hair short, like most off-world women, but she wanted to be like Samina, so she shaved it off. Samina was bald, so bald was beautiful.

Dr. Adrianna Logan entered her daughter's room. "Dad and I are back from Selene Station." No response. Adrianna could feel her daughter's cool reception. She looked approvingly at the present. "Great job on the wrapping."

Sprite shrugged. "If you say so."

"I was just trying to say something nice." Adrianna sat down on the bed next to her daughter.

"Fine. You said something nice." Sprite refused to make eye contact.

Adrianna ignored her daughter's attitude. "You're good at wrapping." She reached out to touch Sprite's shoulder, but her daughter pulled away.

Adrianna sat for a moment. Over the past several years, a seemingly impenetrable wall had formed between them. Adrianna had tried many times to offer her daughter an olive branch, a vain attempt to make peace in their familial cold war. Its cause eluded her, and she didn't know how to end it.

"I thought moving to the Moon would give us a new start." Sprite folded her arms tightly. Adrianna knew she shouldn't take it personally, but her daughter's attitude broke her heart. "Why are you so angry with me?" Still, no response. Adrianna decided to try another approach. "I used to get mad at my mother..."

Sprite cut her off. "I'm not like you, and you aren't like grandma!" She pulled her legs up to her chest and wrapped her arms around her knees. "Would you please leave?"

Adrianna left her daughter's room without another word.

* * *

The NARI Common Area hosted spaces for meetings and relaxation, as well as dining and exercise. A large viewport occupied one wall, offering an expansive view of the lunar surface. The main entrance to the living quarters was set into an alcove opposite the viewport. The corridor providing access to the residence domes was cut into the wall near the dining area. Clusters of comfortable chairs and two work tables occupied the center of the dome. A large-format holographic chamber was built into the wall to the right of the viewport.

Hunter Logan stood before the holochamber. Maryanne Hastings' simulacrum stood in the three-dimensional display. She was floating on Selene Station's residence deck. "Larson is finishing up his interview with Val. He should be gone within the hour."

Hunter nodded to his colleague. "Very good. I'll be glad when we can get back to work. I'm not cut out for this publicity business."

Maryanne pulled herself closer to the camera. She was almost life-sized in the holochamber. She spoke with a hushed voice. "Me neither. That guy gives me the creeps. I think he's going to sensationalize our work and stir up everybody's fear..."

The sound of a muffled explosion came through the audio-link. The image wobbled. Hunter could see Maryanne's smile morph into a concerned look as she grabbed a handhold to steady herself. The lights flickered, and alarms began to chime.

Hunter flinched. "What was that?"

"We've had an explosion up here." Maryanne checked an instrument mounted to the bulkhead. "The pressure is holding steady. I don't think we've breached the pressure hull."

"Where was it?"

"Below me. I think it was in the lab."

"Check it out, Maryanne. Let me know if we have any injuries." Young Emile floated over to his mother. He was no longer smiling. Hunter watched Maryanne reach out to her son as the young boy grabbed her waist. A wave of foreboding coursed through Hunter's stomach.

"Will do."

Hunter glanced at the control panel next to the holochamber. "Martin?"

"Yes, Dr. Logan?" Martin was the AI that supervised the NARI living quarters. His voice was crisp and businesslike.

"Get everyone in here, please. We have an emergency."

"I'm on it, sir."

Within a few moments, the Common Area was filled with people. Hunter told them what little he knew of the explosion. Everyone stood in rapt attention when Maryanne's image reappeared. Her face was drawn into a flinty scowl. Hair tousled, hands shaking, she visibly pulled herself together to make her report. Valerie Lopez floated next to her, wearing an environment suit. She clutched the helmet in her hands.

"Pete Cushing and Mattie North were in the lab when the blast occurred." Maryanne gestured toward the woman next to her. "Val was on the observation deck with Larson Daniels and his crew. Benson was doing a routine inspection of the life support system on the utility deck."

"Can you get to Pete and Mattie?"

"They're gone, Hunter. It was a pretty big explosion. The panels on the inner airlock door are bowed out. If they survived the overpressure, they would have been killed by the flying debris. We've been listening to the contents of the lab banging against the bulkheads for the last five minutes. The place sounds like a clothes dryer full of marbles. It's like Brownian motion in there. There's no gravity to stop things from bouncing around. Val's going to do an inspection, as soon as we think it's safe."

"Is there fire?"

"No. The suppression systems kicked in immediately. We still have an atmosphere in the lab. Pressure is holding steady."

Hunter nodded slowly. "Let's get in there and see what we've got."

In a matter of moments, the image in the holochamber dissolved into a view of the passageway outside the laboratory airlock. The image bobbed back and forth. It was coming from Valerie Lopez's helmet camera.

"I'm entering the airlock now." Val was in her detached, scientific observer mode. Her voice was cool, almost matter-of-fact. Everyone watched as the outer hatch opened. The inner door loomed before them, slightly distorted by the wide angle of the helmet camera lens.

Adrianna grabbed Hunter's arm. "Look at that." The inner hatch, once smooth and straight, now bulged outward.

"I think it will still open," reported Val. She operated the controls, and the door swung inward toward the laboratory beyond.

Debris poured out through the open hatch. The laboratory deck was dark. Val turned on her helmet lights, which cast milky shafts through the churning, shattered remains of the lab. Each step revealed more wreckage. Delicate instruments were twisted beyond recognition. Racks of complex equipment were torn from their anchors and thrown like toys in the hands of an impetuous child. Now they floated in zero-g, a suspension of destruction in an ocean of fouled air.

"Don't tear your suit," Adrianna cautioned.

Val pushed forward into the debris. The space in front of her took on a reddish cast. A bloody torso floated under a shattered console. "I think it's Pete," Val whispered. She turned her head. A lifeless face, ruptured and torn, hung next to her. It was Mattie North. "Oh my God."

Sobs broke the silence as Val turned away and continued her inspection. "Can you see the containment unit, Val?" Hunter was beside himself.

"I'm going over there now."

Hunter held his breath as he waited for Val to make her assessment. She took her time avoiding the torn metal and plastic that hovered around her. The containment unit was still bolted to the laboratory deck. The holochamber was gone, broken into a thousand pieces and distributed around the compartment. As Val moved closer, the image cleared. The top half of the device was sheared away, revealing the delicate inner workings, now ripped loose and floating on tethers of torn wiring above the cavity that once held the phase-two machines.

Val's voice was a cool, lifeless whisper. "We're dead. We're all dead."

2

Meridian Corporation's center of operations was on the far side of the Moon. The sprawling complex was built on the terraces of Jackson Crater. Its rim was seventy-one kilometers in diameter and had an extensive ray system spreading out across the lunar surface. Jackson Base was the largest spaceport in the solar system and serviced the rapidly expanding commerce of the off-world colonies. Giant photovoltaic arrays blanketed the bleak landscape, providing electricity for the base, in tandem with her newer fusion engines. A large well system was driven deep into the lunar surface. Factories, warehouses, residence domes, and research facilities fanned out along the northern edge of the crater. Meridian Corporation's headquarters was perched on a broad terrace, overlooking the crater's floor. A series of grand arches and towers adorned the structure, like an immense piece of jewelry. Thousands of mirrored viewports gave the place a crystalline appearance.

Meridian Corporation was humanity's most powerful economic force. It was behind the colonization of Mars, the development of hundreds of mining and research settlements in The Asteroid Belt, and fourteen lunar bases. Meridian influenced every aspect of life beyond Earth's gravity well. It was the de-facto government for the off-world colonies, providing infrastructure and critical goods and services to everyone. Meridian Corporation was as secretive as it was ubiquitous, guarding her immense resources with a small army of security forces with state-of-the-art weaponry and an impregnable digital network. Meridian hadn't built her corporate center at Jackson Base by accident. The privacy of the far side of the Moon was the perfect place to establish an indomitable seat of power and commerce.

Amos Cross was a short, compact man. As the chief executive officer of Meridian Corporation, he had guided the gigantic company for an unprecedented fifteen years. He was smart and ruthless. A mystique surrounded him, which imbued him with almost godlike power. No one challenged the great man. Everyone deferred to him. He had risen beyond the need for wealth. He glided freely and authoritatively through life, granting and withholding political and economic power in his slipstream.

His office was a giant holographic chamber. Everything was virtual and interchangeable, from the artwork on the walls to the images in the great viewports, which typically presented the breathtaking vista of Jackson Base. He could place displays of data and imagery anywhere in the room. He used his office décor as a weapon, changing it to disorient and manipulate his visitors. Cross did not believe in furniture of any kind. For him, they were signs of lethargy. He stood through all of his meetings, constantly prodding his subordinates through agenda items like a cruel jockey bludgeoning his horse toward the finish line.

Cross thrived in the lightning pace of his work. Why do one thing at a time when he could manage a dozen? Meridian medical had designed a cranial implant to enhance his productivity. A thought would link him with anyone in the corporation. Sometimes Cross would link with someone through the implant and discuss a seemingly irrelevant matter while engaged in a conversation with someone else. He was like a man playing ten chess games simultaneously. He played all the pieces, all the time, in a bewildering flurry. One never knew what Amos Cross would do next. He enjoyed the confusion he engendered. In fact, he depended on it.

The great man's office was awash in brushed gold and deep burgundy. A half a dozen virtual displays presented constantly changing, up-to-the-second status reports on Meridian Corporation's Mars holdings. Across the room, on a small display, was a live news feed. Larson Daniels, the news commentator from the Inner System News Syndicate was reporting from the observation deck of Selene Station. "What just happened?" Amos Cross looked up from the virtual file folder that floated in the air next to him. He stabbed a finger at the display. A glowing red boarder appeared around it. He spread his fingertips, and the display quadrupled in size, the audio level increasing proportionally.

"A few moments ago, the Selene Station shuttered. We heard a muffled explosion below us. We are being told that something blew up on the lab deck. We were there, just hours ago with Hunter and Adrianna Logan, the co-directors of the Nanotechnology Advanced Research Institute."

A segment of Larson's interview filled the screen. Cross thought of his assistant, Susanna Frost. She responded immediately. "Coming, sir."

Seconds later, the large doors to Cross's office opened. Susanna Frost entered cautiously. She paused by the entrance, waiting for her boss to beckon. She stood in a sleek, form-fitting business suit. Her hair was dark and cut in a medium hairstyle, with bangs and layers. She would have preferred closely cut hair, but Amos had insisted on this particular style.

Susanna had grown up in a fractured family. Her father left when she was nine years old to seek his fortune in The Asteroid Belt. Susanna and her mother had to fend for themselves. Her mother was a strong woman and started her own business. Susanna grew up quickly, working side by side with her mother as they scratched out a life for themselves. She had married but was single again, her husband having left her for another woman. He claimed their marriage was unsatisfying. Childless and depressed, Susanna poured herself into her job at Meridian, trying earnestly to satisfy Amos Cross.

Cross gestured for her to approach. "There has been an explosion on Selene Station."

"The new NARI lab, sir?"

"Yes." Cross turned up the volume on the news report.

"...Dr. Logan assured me that NARI's new product, a voracious nanoscale device they call a 'piranha machine,' is well protected. I asked him about the chances of his work unleashing a monstrous nano-plague on humanity." Larson paused as Hunter Logan's face appeared on the screen.

"That will never happen. I've dedicated my life to finding ways to heal the environment. It's true. These phase-two machines are dangerous in their present form. That's why we've taken great precautions. The containment unit has many safeguards. Remember, we're working with these machines every day. I urge you and your viewers to see their potential. Once we're able to train them, these nanomachines will put an end to some of Earth's most vexing problems."

Larson's disembodied voice came from off-camera. "Why should people trust you?"

Cross watched Hunter Logan's face. He could tell the man was upset. "We know what we're doing. There is no need to fear our work. I stake my reputation on that."

Larson's face appeared again. "We will find out if Dr. Hunter Logan can be trusted. We are waiting for a report on the extent of the blast damage and whether or not NARI's prized piranha machines are still under the control of their masters."

Cross muted the audio. He noticed a small fleck of dust on his shirtsleeve. He scowled and cocked his head, mentally summoning another assistant. "Veni? I'm going to need a new shirt. I'll be in my quarters in five minutes."

He turned toward Susanna, without skipping a beat. "These scientists are finally developing something useful. How is our intel?"

"We have a source on the team. I'll find out what happened and what they're planning to do."

"Good. Stay on top of this. Don't disappoint me." Cross looked at Susanna's suit. "What color is that?"

"It's Cerulean blue."

Cross gave her a disapproving look. "I don't like it. You'd look better in carmine." He turned his back to her and launched into another conversation. Susanna felt like she had been stabbed with a knife. She blushed and left the office.

* * *

Aurora North trembled as she sat on the couch, her knees drawn up to her chin, her eyes wet with tears. Sprite sat next to her, wrapping an arm tightly around her friend. Adrianna was perched on a small table in front of the sofa. There was a momentary truce between mother and daughter as they tried to comfort the girl.

"How did Mom die?" Aurora's voice cracked as she fought back her tears.

"She was in the lab on Selene Station. There was an explosion." Adrianna didn't know what else to say. She paused awkwardly, believing the right words could help, a fallacy of the first order. Aurora sobbed. She twisted a sodden tissue in her left hand while rocking back and forth against the cushions. Her breaths were jagged gasps, her body shaking under the impact of impossible news. "She didn't suffer." Adrianna felt powerless and stupid.

Sprite gave her friend a squeeze. "It's going to be all right, Rory."

Rory pushed her away. "Don't say that!" Sprite could feel her friend's tears as the wet tissue brushed against her arm. "It's not going to be all right!" Sprite slid away from her, startled by the outburst. Rory glared at her, daring her to offer another platitude.

Sprite looked away. "I'm sorry."

The anger drained from Rory's face. She reached out and touched her friend's arm. Sprite looked back at her. Rory's eyes were red and swollen. Her tears streamed down her chin, soaking the knees of her slacks. She slowly tipped her head to the side until her ear rested on her knees. Then, ever so slightly, she offered her friend a wordless nod.

Sprite looked up at her mother, who in a moment of shear brilliance said nothing.

* * *

Hunter Logan was standing a vigil in the NARI Common Area. Several members of the NARI team had lingered with him, hoping to hear the latest news. They could see Maryanne Hastings and Arvid Benson in the holodisplay. They were floating on the residence deck of Selene Station. Emile Hastings was clinging to his mother's side.

Hunter glanced at the young man who was standing at the holodisplay controls. "Jenson? Is the transmission secure?"

At twenty-six, Jenson Reed was the youngest member of the NARI team. He was NARI's comm/comp specialist. He had a wrestler's body, strong and muscular, but was a stereotypical engineer. He lived out of his head, was extremely organized, and he was totally oblivious to fashion and emotions. Jenson was a quiet person, not easily drawn into casual conversation. He was much more comfortable working technical problems. His stubby fingers danced on a virtual control surface next to the display. "Yes, sir. It's encrypted point-to-point."

Hunter thanked him and turned back toward the display. "How's the link, Maryanne?"

"It's good, Hunter." Her eyes were red. Her face was lined with stress.

Jo Smith and Tyson Edwards sat side by side on one of the couches near Hunter. Jo was a slender woman with dark hair and a swimmer's body. She took in everything. Her face was drawn into a frown as she looked carefully at Maryanne and Emile. Tyson fidgeted next to her. He was a bundle of nervous energy, brilliant and unstoppable. Tyson's red hair had a natural wave, making it impossible to comb. He insisted on wearing old wire-rim glasses rather than submitting to ocular surgery to correct his vision. Jo put her hand on his knee and pushed down hard. "Will you please sit still?"

Tyson grimaced. "Hey, that hurts!"

"Then sit still, oaf."

Tyson willed himself to sit like an immovable statue, a placid venire over a restless sea. Jo patted his knee.

Hunter let out a long breath, keeping his attention directed at Maryanne. "Some bad news today."

"Got that right." Maryanne ran her fingers through Emile's hair.

"Is Val still in the lab?"

Maryanne nodded sadly. "She refuses to come out. The phase-two machines are in there, and she doesn't want to contaminate the rest of the station."

Arvid Benson tugged at a handhold and moved closer to Maryanne. "We have a hypothesis." Arvid was emotionless. "We're thinking the blast destroyed the phase-two machines. Val is going to hunker down for several hours and watch for any telltale signs."

"How much air does she have?"

"She's coupled into the station supply. She's good for days."

"I'm sure she doesn't want to spend days in that suit." No one laughed at Hunter's attempt at humor.

Benson smiled stiffly, then nodded. "Yes. Of course. You're quite right about that." Hunter looked back at Maryanne. "Where is Larson and the camerawoman?"

"They're on the observation deck. He wanted to be part of this conversation. The man wasn't too pleased when I refused. I think he's talking to his producers."

"Let's keep him out of the loop until we know what we're going to do."

"That's not going to be easy."

"But it's necessary."

Maryanne nodded. There was a noise behind Hunter. Maryanne's eyes narrowed, her face hardening. Hunter glanced over his shoulder. Robert Hastings had entered the Common Area with Samina Haddad following closely behind him. Too close.

"Maryanne." Robert stopped in his tracks. Samina paused, then took a place toward the back of the group. She made no attempt to avoid Maryanne's glare. Robert stepped toward the holodisplay.

"Daddy!" Emile reached out for Robert, as if he could bridge the distance between them. "I'm scared. Something happened."

"Don't you worry, Em. Mom will take care of you. There's nothing to worry about."

Hunter shook his head at the lie. Robert ignored him. His eyes were riveted to the holodisplay. "How are you holding up?" It was a vain attempt at affection. Maryanne gave him an accusing stare, but said nothing. Silence held everyone in a tight embrace.

Maryanne's dark hair was pulled back and gathered into a ponytail with a rubber band. Her jumpsuit did little to hide her stocky build. She looked at Samina, taking in the woman's slender, muscular beauty. Then she gave her husband an icy glare. Guilt roiled in Robert's stomach. He could feel the blood course into his face. Maryanne nodded almost imperceptibly. "What do you expect, Robert? Emile and I are here, and you are conveniently down there." No one breathed. Robert looked away from the holodisplay, unable to meet his wife's cold stare.

"What can we do to help?" Hunter tried to steer the conversation back toward the crisis at hand.

Maryanne looked back toward Hunter, her expression softening. "Not much. Arvid and I will stay in contact with Val while we wait for signs of nanomachines in the debris field.

Hunter nodded. "Patch her in, will you?"

"I'm here." Val's disembodied voice drifted over the audio link. She spoke in a whisper, as if she was standing at the altar in some grand cathedral.

"Hey, Val." For an instant, Hunter didn't know what to say. "We're all pulling for you down here. I hope the blast destroyed all the phase-two machines."

"Yeah. That would be good." Her whisper was raspy.

Hunter couldn't tell her how he really felt. He couldn't say, "You're going to die, Val. Those well engineered phase-two machines will dismantle you, one molecule at a time." Finally, he said, "Keep your chin up," but immediately cursed himself for using such a cliché. There had to be a better choice of words somewhere. False hope was such a curse.

"Gotta keep a positive attitude." Her voice was trembling. "I'll have Maryanne alert you if anything happens."

The screen darkened, and the Common Area erupted into a murmur of voices. Robert Hastings spoke with no one and strode quickly from the dome. Alexis Wren had been wandering back and forth behind the group during the holo-transmission. Now she stood near the main entrance to the NARI living quarters. She had premature gray hair and a thin, emaciated frame. Alexis' world was her science. She meandered through life, preoccupied by the contemplation of nano-engineering. People were like ghosts to her, apparitions inhabiting a separate, parallel reality. Her quirky liabilities were offset by her absolute brilliance. Alexis would spend days on end mulling over a seemingly insurmountable problem and come up with an elegant solution.

The NARI team was stitched into a patchwork quilt of conversation. Samina Haddad had separated from the group and stood alone at the viewport, trying to lose herself in the stark panorama of the lunar surface. In a rare moment of warmth, Alexis approached her. "Maryanne doesn't like you."

Samina was startled by the comment. She turned to the gray-haired scientist. Her tanned, athletic form was juxtaposed with Alexis' pale, withered body. She studied her for a moment, wondering if she was trying to be funny. One was never sure with Alexis Wren. Finally, Samina decided her colleague was being sincere. "You think?"

"You've been copulating with her husband. That's a taboo in this culture. I'm sure she's resentful and perhaps feels somewhat threatened."

Samina stifled a laugh. Alexis' choice of words was precise but insufficient, like the utterances of a brilliant, but inexperienced child who saw the obvious but failed to grasp the nuances of a complex relationship. She nodded to the woman, but she had already walked away, immersed once more in her scientific muse.

* * *

Robert Hastings locked the door of his private quarters and walked over to his small desk. He keyed the holodisplay and waited for the connection to be established. Maryanne's face appeared in two dimensions, floating in the display's three-dimensional space. This time she appeared from the point of view of a handheld comm unit.

"Yes?" Her eyes narrowed as she recognized Robert.

"What was that all about? You embarrassed me in front of our friends."

"Hold on a minute, Robert." Maryanne's image bobbed up and down as she floated to a more private location. Her face was close to the lens, distorting her image and accentuating her anger. "You know damn well what that was about."

A knot rose in Robert's stomach. "What are you saying, honey?"

"Don't 'honey' me, you bastard. How long have you been screwing her?"

Robert blushed. "You can't be serious…"

"Samina Haddad. You convinced me to bring Emile up here so you could be alone with her."

"We're just colleagues."

"Bullshit! She's your latest fling. Be honest, Robert. You owe me that much."

Robert took a breath and let it out, his eyes lowering.

"Look at me and tell the truth."

Robert met her gaze. "Okay. We've been seeing each other for a while."

"Damn you."

"I'll break it off. Honest. I'll make it up to you."

"Like hell you will. You've been screwing around ever since we were married."

Robert looked at his wife desperately. "Look, this is neither the time, nor the place for this conversation."

"There is no other time or place, Robert. So let me be perfectly clear. You are a poor excuse for a husband. You have pretended to be my friend. You seduced me like all the others. It's pathetic. I trusted you. Damn it, I loved you. And all the while, it was a cruel game, a fantasy. I adored you. I kept myself for you. I made you the center of my life, while you wrapped every woman you could find around your penis." Maryanne's eyes were devoid of caring, her face a flinty mask. "Go to hell." She let out a long breath and then slowly lifted her chin. She straightened her spine, a power coursing through her. "I won't love you anymore."

The holodisplay darkened, Maryanne's image dissolving away. Robert sucked in a breath, surprised by how guilty he felt. She was right. He had shattered his marriage and pierced his soul with the broken shards.

* * *

Hunter summoned everyone to the Common Area an hour later. Maryanne floated in the large holodisplay. Her face was more ashen than before, fear's blade scribing its track on her features. "Something's happening."

Adrianna stepped to her husband's side. "Val? Can you hear me?"

"I, I'm here, Adrianna." Val's voice was still a whisper, but now it shook with apprehension. Panic lay just beneath the surface. "My helmet is clouding up. I can't see anything."

"Is it on the inside of the helmet?"

"No." Val caught her breath. Everyone could hear her gasping through the audio link. "Something is eroding the outside of my faceplate." There was silence in the Common Area. Even Alexis stopped her wandering and attended to the screen. Their colleague's breathing was like a ticking clock, measuring the long moments. "I've got an alarm!" Val's breathing accelerated. "Multiple alarms! Suit systems are shutting down."

Adrianna squeezed Hunter's arm tightly. "Is the lab air breathable?" Immediately, she realized the futility of her question. The nanomachines were multiplying. The suit wasn't protecting Val from unbreathable air; it was shielding her from the ravenous nanomachines. The tiny predators were eating through her protective barrier, and Val was the next course in their endless meal.

"The Lord is my shepherd..." Val's voice shook as she teetered on the edge of hysteria. "He leads me beside the still waters..." The pitch of her voice was rising. She was losing her grip. "Yea, though I walk through the valley of death..." Val was too scared to scream. She grunted. Then, there was an inhuman sound. A primal gurgling, then a chattering whine. Finally, with her last ounce of courage, she swore. "Fuck! Here they come..." Then it was silent.

* * *

"Get us out of here!" Maryanne was screaming through the holodisplay. "Come up here before it's too late!"

Arvid Benson tried to calm Maryanne as Hunter and the rest of the NARI team stood in a paralytic trance. Emile didn't know what was happening. Fear swept over him as he watched his mother screaming and pleading for rescue. He started to cry, his tears floating away from him as tiny spheres. Arvid looked at them pleadingly. "The lab airlock is still sealed. We aren't contaminated yet. We can meet you at the main airlock. Five minutes. It'll only take five minutes. Please send a jumpship!"

A mental darkness descended over Hunter. Time dilated, as if the breach had torn the fabric of reality. He felt everyone's eyes in slow motion. Wondering eyes. Yearning eyes. Pleading eyes. Hopeful eyes. They were all waiting for him and Adrianna to say something. They wanted their leaders to remove the nightmare that was unfolding before them. Hunter felt the room begin to spin.

Hunter thought it had to be a dream. This was the crucial moment when he would stir in his bed and realize that none of this was real. However, he wasn't sleeping, and none of this was going away. He rubbed his right index finger with this thumb. He took in a breath, but words wouldn't come. He panicked. Turning to Adrianna, he whispered. "I can't do this."

Adrianna looked deeply into his eyes and gave him a microscopic nod. She turned to the holodisplay. Larson Daniels and his camerawoman had heard the screaming and now floated nervously into view. The camerawoman's attention was drawn to Emile and Maryanne. Adrianna looked at her. "What is your name?"

The camerawoman seemed embarrassed. "Nina."

"That is a good name." Adrianna tried to flash her most disarming smile. "Nina, I'm glad you and Larson can hear this firsthand." Maryanne was holding Emile in her arms. She was shaking, the perturbations of her body making the two of them oscillate in the zero-g. Arvid had one arm around her waist and the other looped through a handhold to steady them. Adrianna gestured toward the camera in Nina's hand. "Please turn off your camera."

"Ignore her, Nina." Larson said it like a lion protecting its lair.

"Turn it off," Adrianna repeated softly.

Nina's expression revealed her inner conflict. "I can't do that. We're broadcasting live throughout the inner system."

"Believe me, you don't want to document this."

Larson pushed his body closer to the camera, his form looming larger in the holodisplay. "Try me, Dr. Logan. The people have a right to know."

"If you insist, Mr. Daniels." Adrianna shook her head. "Here's where we are. You know we had an explosion on the lab deck. Two of my friends were killed in the blast: Dr. Peter Cushing and Dr. Mattie North. The containment unit we showed you this morning was destroyed, and the phase-two nanomachines have been released. Dr. Valerie Lopez entered the lab to assess the damage and became the first victim of the machines. They ate through her suit…" Adrianna paused, trying to compose herself. "Ah, they ate through her suit and killed her." Adrianna locked the newscaster in her gaze. "You're next. It's only a matter of time."

Nina looked up from her viewfinder and glanced at Adrianna. She looked over at Larson Daniels. He turned, sensing her change of posture, and made a slicing motion across his neck. "Cut the feed, Nina."

Adrianna waited for Nina to shut down the camera. "Those nanomachines are going to breach the lab deck. We have no way of stopping them. If we dock with Selene Station and save you, we could contaminate the Moon. We might destroy everything on the lunar surface."

Maryanne grew calm, her voice quiet, but steady. "You can't risk everyone else's life."

"No, we can't."

Larson Daniels clapped his hands together. "Send up an unmanned jumpship. We could get out of here without risking anyone else. We could stay in orbit until we were sure there was no danger."

"We could do that, but what if you were contaminated, and you decided to land the jumpship without authorization? You'd be deadlier than a nuclear bomb."

"So, that's it?" He said it sarcastically as his rage began to boil. "We're supposed to sit here and wait to die." He gestured toward Emile. "You're going to let this little boy die?" Daniels glared at Hunter, his eyes blazing. "You staked your reputation on the security of your containment unit!" Hunter looked down at his shoes. "You assured us that you knew what you were doing." Larson paused, but Hunter didn't respond. "Look at me, you spineless coward! Be a man and look at your victim." Hunter looked up, his eyes red, his face pale. "You promised us that this technology could be handled safely. Now you've killed us. You're a fucking monster!"

"I'm sorry," Hunter whispered.

"Go to hell!"

Adrianna intervened. "We're sorry, Larson. There's nothing we can do to save you."

3

The ISS-20 space station hung in Earth's orbit, her dual rotating habitats spinning slowly in opposing directions. Large rectangular photovoltaic arrays spread their wing-like structures at the ends of the station's main truss. Between the wheel-shaped habitats, an orthogonal truss supported two immense landing docks with triangular hatchways.

Damon Trask sat behind his clear acrylic desk in one of the largest suites in the space station. His office was designed to have a look of purity. Constructed of titanium and aluminum silicate glass, the office was located in Habitat A, offering breathtaking views of the nearby solar array and the Earth beyond. His desk was a few feet from a great crystalline wall. Behind him and through it, the resplendent curvature of the Earth divided the lush blues and greens of the planet from the pitch-black infinity of space.

Trask was the chief executive officer of the Citizen's League, a radical environmental group opposed to molecular engineering. The League understood that nanoscale systems were commonplace in nature. They knew God was a nano-engineer, forging the cellular building blocks of life with elegant self-replicating machines. However, molecular engineering of the sort conducted by NARI was an affront to the universe. It was tampering with the created order and risking the destruction of humanity. No benefit to society was worth the risks endemic to the work.

Trask squeezed a spongy ball in his left hand. It was a nervous habit, a futile attempt to calm himself. Maya Lewis sat before him. She was his fixer. When the League had a problem, Maya made it go away. She could turn on her charm at will, entrancing those around her with a touch and a smile. She was a seductress and used her sensuality to promote, persuade, and manipulate.

"I am pleased with the outcome." Maya gloated with pride and exuded raw feminine confidence. Life was a dance for Maya. Her voice, her body, and her clothes were all parts of her ensemble. She could say nothing, and everyone would be mesmerized by her presentation, especially men. Maya's adversaries dismissed her at their own risk. "The mission was flawless. The bomb destroyed the containment unit, and the nanomachines were released. Two scientists were killed in the explosion, and there are reports that a third person has died."

"From injuries sustained in the blast?" Trask was mesmerized by Maya.

"No. Dr. Valerie Lopez was consumed by the nanomachines."

Trask smacked the surface of his desk. "This is perfect! We show the inner system the dangers of this research without the risk of a nano-plague."

Maya gave Trask a devilish grin. "It gets better, Damon. Larson Daniels of the ISNS was doing a story on NARI. He is among the survivors on Selene Station."

"No!"

"Oh, yes. We are going to watch the nanomachines kill a high profile member of the news media. He's going to become a martyr for our cause."

Trask stopped squeezing his stress ball. "Excellent!"

"Their work has been stopped for the foreseeable future."

Damon swiveled his chair around to gaze at the Earth. "This is good, but they will find a way to continue the work. Make no mistake. This is a war to save creation from the human race. We have won this battle, but we cannot rest. We must find a way to destroy them."

Maya studied her boss's shoulders. He took good care of himself for a bureaucrat, she thought. "Two of the victims on Selene Station were Dr. Maryanne Hastings and her nine-year-old son, Emile." Trask pivoted back, wondering where Maya was going with this new information. "Robert Hastings wasn't on the station. He's at Copernicus Base with the rest of the NARI team. He is a womanizer and has been unfaithful to his wife for years. We believe he sent his son to Selene Station, so he could meet with his lover. Our psych profile suggests he might be turned."

Trask smiled. "Do you know someone who might be able to seduce Dr. Hastings?"

Maya shifted her hips in her chair. A trace of her perfume wafted across the desk. "I think I do," she cooed.

Trask tapped the surface of his desk, and a large site plan of Copernicus Base appeared. "I want you to go to the Moon and recruit Hastings. Use his lust and his guilt. While you're there, stir up some rumors; make the residents fear their new neighbors. Our Copernican friends have been known to take matters into their own hands."

* * *

Aurora North sat on the floor of her mother's bedroom, barefooted, legs crossed, hair disheveled. Her eyes were dark and lifeless, tear stains tracing their way down her cheeks like rust trails from weathered rivets in cold iron. She hugged a pillow from the bed, clinging to the faint odor of her mother's favorite shampoo. The room was cold, but she didn't notice. Memories were slipping through the crevices of her mind, pulling her back to a lost time, a time of fleeting joy when she felt the warm embrace of her parents.

Able and Mattie North had been an odd match. She was a skilled nano-scientist, while he was an unpublished poet. He saw the exquisite beauty of life, juxtaposed with its pain and injustice. He often led with his feelings, allowing his heart to bear the burdens that others bore on their backs. Aurora had always been close to her father. She lost him three years earlier when he had succumbed to a rare emaciating disease that had eaten away his body and tortured his soul.

Now the young girl was caught between two storms, twin cyclones that ripped at her from every direction. The loss of her mother triggered and reamplified the latent pain she still held from her father's death. She was alone, orphaned by the random twists of fate. There was no one to protect her, to shield her from her greatest fears.

There was a noise. Aurora didn't notice it at first, but it kept recurring, scratching its way through her shell until it touched her awareness. It was the door chime. "Enter." It was just a whisper, but the residence AI heard it and opened the door. She didn't move, cocooned by the memories of her parents.

Adrianna Logan padded quietly to the bedroom door. It was holy ground, imbued with the diminishing presence of her colleague and friend. She looked in the chamber, then paused, her heart breaking at the sight before her. "Rory?" She didn't want to startle the girl unnecessarily. No response. Adrianna lowered herself to the floor next to her. She put her arm around her. The young girl's muscles were tense, drawn tight by her unfathomable grief. Adrianna pulled her close, and the girl went limp in her arms, sobbing tearlessly. "Come with me, honey. We have an extra room where you can stay until we sort things out."

Aurora looked up. Adrianna waited, allowing the young girl to navigate through the emotional thicket that held her in its thorny embrace. Aurora fixed the older woman in her gaze, her lips tightening into a thin line. Then, she nodded.

* * *

Each lunar base was equipped with a holographic chamber permitting virtual meetings. Participants from across the Moon could meet together as if they were in the same room. Hunter Logan was flanked by Tyson Edwards and Jo Smith as they sat in the darkened chamber, located in the Copernicus Base Administration Dome. Base director Winston Marshall sat with them. Susanna Frost sat in a similar pod at Meridian Headquarters. Her simulacrum appeared across the table from Hunter and his associates.

"We must act quickly, Ms. Frost." Hunter's face was worn and tired. "I am concerned about what happens when the phase-two nanomachines breach the hull of Selene Station."

Susanna did not appear to be interested. "What will happen, Doctor?"

"When the hull is breached, there will be a rapid release of the station's atmosphere as the internal pressure drops. The release will spread the nanomachines into space. Many of them will remain in lunar orbit. Some may fall to the lunar surface. We can't allow that to happen."

Director Marshall nodded. "It would put us all at risk. The machines could attach themselves to a ship in orbit, or they could destroy the Moon."

"It can't be as drastic as that," Frost shook her head skeptically.

"We don't have time to debate this, Ms. Frost." Hunter spread his hands. "We are in real danger here. We must act quickly."

Susanna was startled by the force of Hunter's statement. "How long to we have, Dr. Logan?"

"A few hours, perhaps a day."

"That's all?" The woman shifted uncomfortably in her seat.

"That's all." Hunter's voice had a tone of finality.

"What do we do?"

This was what Hunter was waiting for. "We must do three things, Ms. Frost. First of all, we vent the uncontaminated section of the station. Then, we open the lab airlock and flood the station with the contaminated air. This will lower the overall atmospheric pressure in the station and limit the spread of the machines when the hull is breached. Finally, we dock a propulsion unit to the station and blast it out of orbit. If we put Selene on a course toward the sun, we can vaporize the machines and eliminate the threat."

Susanna steepled her fingers. "There are still people on board."

"I know that, Ms. Frost. Most of them are my friends." Hunter's voice cracked. "We can't save them. The risk is too great."

Susanna sat back in her chair. "I'll bring this to Mr. Cross's attention."

A disembodied voice broke into the meeting. "Director Marshall? You have my permission to proceed with Dr. Logan's plan." Amos Cross materialized in the holopod, pacing back and forth at one end of the conference table. Everyone recognized him. Susanna dropped her eyes, withering slightly in deference to her superior. "Vent the station. Get a crew up there right away with a propulsion module and calculate the trajectory. Let's cut our losses and get this over with."

"Cut our losses?" Jo Smith glared at Cross. "We all know this has to be done, but couldn't you show one ounce of compassion for those people up there?"

Susanna involuntarily sucked in her breath. Tyson shot Jo a dirty look, but she was going to speak her mind no matter what. "There's a child and his mother up there."

"You can keep your feelings, Dr. Smith!" Cross's eyes blazed at her. "We are going to follow Dr. Logan's plan and avert disaster. Collateral damage is a fact of life." Cross's simulacrum disappeared.

* * *

Humanity paused. Larson Daniels' final broadcast was riveting and personal. He was a reporter to the end, detailing the events leading up to the explosion, encouraging authorities to investigate the incident, and raging against what he called "reckless science" conducted by the Logans and the Nanotechnology Advanced Research Institute.

* * *

The remaining survivors on Selene Station faced their deaths with resignation. The constellation of events that brought them to their untimely ends were beyond their control. Once death by explosive decompression was explained to them, they all chose to die by injection. One at a time, Maryanne Hastings gave them shots of ketamine, rendering them unconscious. She gave Emile his injection last.

"I don't want a shot, Mommy."

Maryanne rubbed Emile's back to calm him down. "It won't hurt, sweetie."

"But I'm afraid." He whimpered. "Is Daddy coming?"

"No, Em. Look, I'm going to give you this shot, and when you wake up, you'll be safe and sound in your bed back home. Does that sound nice?"

"Back home on Earth?"

"Where would you like to wake up?"

"On the Moon. With you and Daddy."

Maryanne's eyes filled with tears. "Then that's where you'll be."

"Okay, Mommy."

"Goodnight, Em. I love you." The little boy gave his mother a hug as she slipped the needle into his skin.

* * *

The remaining NARI scientists and staff had gathered in the Common Area, standing together in fearful solidarity. Maryanne Hastings had donned an environment suit and made her way to a control chamber on the utility deck. They could see the reflections of the deck lighting in her visor. Hunter was shaking as he gazed at his colleague in the large holodisplay.

Maryanne looked into the holographic camera, her face visible to her teammates on the lunar surface. The scientist floated near a complex panel of gauges and buttons. Her features were lifeless: eyes sunk deep in their sockets, skin pasty white, her mouth a thin line transecting a worn countenance. Maryanne had aged twenty years in twenty minutes.

"Ready, Maryanne?" Adrianna spoke in a gentle whisper.

"It doesn't matter, now." Maryanne's voice was emotionless. She paid no attention to her husband who was standing next to Hunter. "I'm venting the rest of the station." Telemetry data, superimposed on the holodisplay, relayed the dropping atmospheric pressure in Selene Station, as streams of air coursed out of the hull. When the pressure reached zero, she stabbed a button on the panel. "The valves are closed. Almost done."

Everyone watched as Maryanne made her way to the laboratory airlock. She glanced at a panel by the hatch. "Pressure is holding steady in the lab. No breach, yet."

"Good, Maryanne." Adrianna's voice shook slightly.

"I'm going to open the hatch." She tethered herself to a handhold and floated to one side of the hatch. She punched an override code into the hatch control mechanism, and the hatch cracked open. A hurricane of air exploded through the hatch. Maryanne clung to the handhold as she was whipped and buffeted by the maelstrom. Dust and debris flew through the hatchway, pummeling the corridor bulkhead. Then, the deadly wind ramped down, and a final stillness settled in the compartments.

Maryanne's suit was scraped and scored by the sand-like particles and torn shards of metal and plastic that had coursed out of the shattered laboratory. She let go of the handhold, her face a death mask. Then, her lifeless eyes narrowed, one final spark of enmity finding its antagonist, fixed on its target. Her irises were dilated, ink-black pools of endless hatred.

"Robert?" Hastings drew a quick breath. The room lost focus as Maryanne transfixed him with her glare. "Tonight when you fall asleep, I want you to remember Emile. That sweet little boy I had to kill because of you. He should have been down there, where it's safe. He could have had a life, but you had to fuck Samina. Remember that." Maryanne cracked the seal of her helmet, a hateful, defiant look frozen on her face.

* * *

Robert Hastings couldn't remember how he got to his living quarters. Maryanne's voice was still echoing in his head. He threw a chair against the wall. It bounced across the room in slow motion. He wiped the top of his dresser clean with one sweep of his arm. A cascade of toiletries tumbled to the floor. He smashed several pictures that hung innocently on the wall, and then he staggered into the bathroom. He pulled a bottle from a small cabinet, taking three pills with a handful of water. Robert slammed his way back into the bedroom and tore apart the bed. His rage burned with a scorching flame, an incendiary hatred of himself and all that he had done. The pills took control of him, blurring his vision and mercifully dulling his senses. He collapsed, a ruined heap on the remains of his defiled bed.

* * *

A team from Copernicus Base had flown an unmanned propulsion module into orbit and docked it with Selene. They wasted no time after Maryanne opened the laboratory hatchway. Selene's solar trajectory was updated, and the engines flashed to life. The old lunar space station lifted out of orbit, rapidly attaining escape velocity. The propulsion module would burn indefinitely, powered by a controlled fusion reaction. Selene, along with her deadly cargo, would fall into the sun's gravity well, until she was consumed by Sol's raging furnace.

* * *

The day's events had burned out everyone's emotions. The NARI team wandered around their living quarters like zombies, as if everyone had been injected with a voodoo drug. The day had begun full of promise, and now it ended with tragic horror. Gradually, the Common Area emptied, and Hunter remained alone by the large viewport. He watched the terminator advance across the surface, casting Copernicus Base into the lunar night. He felt the shadows closing in on him. The knot in his stomach expanded and rose up through his chest. It tightened the muscles in his shoulders and neck. He could feel pressure in his temples. He squinted his eyes shut and tucked his chin into his chest as he tried to shake off the pressure. His left thumb found the old scar on his index finger.

Hunter Logan's reasoning, thinking brain knew the explosion was the work of nefarious parties, bent on stopping their work. Logic told him they had taken every possible precaution, handling the highly virulent materials with utmost care. Hunter's mind knew all of these things, but his gut churned with guilt. He felt suffocated by shame. In that moment, he understood why people could take their own lives.

Hunter felt a tug on his sleeve. He turned. Sprite was perched next to him on the couch. He forced himself to make eye contact with her. Her lips were moving. He forced his ears to listen. "…it's terrible timing." His daughter was looking at him seriously. Hunter had no idea what she was talking about. Her left hand was on his sleeve, and her right hand was behind her back. Hunter's eyes softened as he took in her delicate beauty. She gave him one of her precocious, radiant smiles.

"What is it, honey?"

"Dad, don't you remember?"

Hunter gave her a mystified shrug. "I don't know what you're talking about, kiddo."

Sprite pulled a small wrapped package from behind her. "It's your birthday, Dad!"

Hunter looked down at the present, tears streaming from his eyes as he drew his daughter into a tight embrace.

4

The numbness of grief enveloped the remaining members of the NARI team. Some wandered aimlessly around their living quarters. Others sat alone and silent. Everyone spoke in hushed tones, the deaths of their friends enhancing the sacredness of time and relationship.

Sprite Logan spoke quietly to Wiley as she lounged near the entrance to the NARI living quarters, her card comp cradled in her hand. Nearby, Jo Smith stood in the dining area, stirring cake batter at the counter. Her mate, Tyson Edwards, sat at the table with Hunter Logan. There was no need for Jo to bake a cake. Cooking was a lost art, but she plied the ancient culinary arts to relieve stress, not out of necessity.

Tyson smacked his lips in anticipation. "I love chocolate cake."

"It's vanilla."

"But I asked for chocolate."

"I know you did, but I like vanilla."

"You asked me what I wanted."

"Your point, doofus?"

"Why did you ask if you had already made up your mind?"

Jo gave him a devilish look. "I wanted you to feel like your opinion mattered."

Hunter managed a smile. "Has your opinion ever mattered?"

Tyson shook his head. "I thought it did once, but she made a vanilla cake anyway." Jo waved a large spoon at him like it was a knife. She had a smile on her face. It was the first time she had smiled since the tragedy on Selene Station.

Samina Haddad walked confidently into the Common Area, wearing a lightweight yellow jumpsuit. She had spent many years in space and was at ease in lunar gravity. She was graceful, every step filled with life. She turned heads whenever she entered a room, some because of her beauty, others because of her competence.

Sprite Logan ran her hand over her scalp when she saw Samina enter. She admired her, and was trying to imitate the beautiful woman. She had cut off her hair to be like her. Now, she made a mental note to get a yellow jumpsuit.

Hunter glanced up. Samina nodded to him. "Where is Robert?" she asked. Discomfort rippled through the room. Samina noticed it, but didn't care.

"Not here," Hunter replied. Samina glanced back toward the residence wing, a gesture not lost on the others. She nodded and sat down near Sprite.

Hunter looked up as the remaining members of the NARI team began to filter slowly into the Common Area. Jenson Reed had been sitting on the other side of the dome. He stood to stretch his legs and turned off the holodisplay.

Adrianna walked with a purpose from the residence wing and joined her husband. She gave his shoulder a squeeze. "Are you ready for this?" she asked.

Hunter nodded. "Yeah. It will do us all some good to focus on what's next."

Tyson rolled a coffee cup between his palms. "It's not going to be the same."

Hunter stood up, trying to avoid the truth of his friend's statement.

Sprite unfolded her legs and rose from where she had been sitting. She ignored her mother. "Dad, can I stay for the meeting?"

Hunter glanced at Adrianna. She gave him a nod, then turned toward Sprite, smiling. "Sure, honey. Why don't you get Kell and Rory? They should be a part of this, too."

Sprite shot her mother a cool, unpleasant look. "Okay."

"Wasn't that the answer you wanted?" she asked.

"Sure. Thanks. I'll go get them." Sprite spun on her heels and almost ran into Robert Hastings, who had just entered the Common Area. They were inches apart, and his proximity upset her. She stepped back, making a guttural sound and giving him a flinty look.

"Sorry, Sprite," he exclaimed. Sprite whipped past him without a word. Robert gave Adrianna and Hunter a puzzled look. "What was that all about?"

Adrianna sighed. "Teenage girls."

* * *

The Citizen's League had a small group of followers at Copernicus Base, headed by Trip Howard. Maya Lewis sat with her legs crossed in Howard's modest living quarters. Nearly twenty people were squeezed into the space. Maya's perfume filled the room, acting like a magnetic aerosol that drew everyone's attention to the sensuous woman.

"I want to thank Trip for getting the word out to all of you," she began.

A thin, emaciated man sitting hip-to-hip with Maya nodded. "The pleasure is all mine."

"I'm sure you all know about what happened on Selene Station." A murmur rippled through the group. Maya shifted in her seat. "We all should be concerned about these scientists. Their work threatens our families. The nanomachines they are making could eat through Copernicus Base and kill us all." Maya paused, letting the thought sink into her listeners.

"These people are living right here at Copernicus Base. Meridian has put them up in luxurious accommodations on the north side. I've heard they may be setting up a new lab right here on the base." A chatter of nervous comments echoed off the hard walls of the small room. "If there is another explosion..." The room was silent. "If even one of those phase-two nanomachines gets out, we are all dead. Copernicus Base will be destroyed. Eventually, that one little machine will multiply into trillions of nano-killers. They will sweep the entire lunar surface." Not even Maya's sensuality could break the silence. "Imagine yourselves killing your children, so they don't have to face being eaten by those machines. Anything is better than facing that moment."

Someone in the back of the room spoke up. "How do we stop them?"

Another voice chimed in. "We kill them." There were nods.

Maya raised her hands; her skin-tight outfit lifted her breasts slightly. "I'm not suggesting you go that far. However, we need to spread the word around the base and do what we can to stop these people. The lives of your families hang in the balance."

* * *

The remaining NARI scientists arrived in the Common Area. Kell Edwards, Jo and Tyson's son, was the last one to arrive. He was a lanky seventeen-year-old boy with dark hair and surgeon's hands. He sat down next to Sprite and Rory, scanning the faces of the adults and wondering what was going to happen. Moving to the Moon had been a grand adventure, but the events on Selene Station had cast a dark cloud over everything.

"What's going to happen?" he whispered to his friends.

Sprite shrugged. "Dunno," she hissed.

Adrianna positioned herself, so she could see everyone. "Hunter and I have been talking about our work." She spoke slowly and deliberately. "We all knew the inherent risks working with the phase-two machines. We thought we had taken every precaution. We've faced anger and death threats. We believed that our sacrifices were worth the amazing benefits that would be gleaned from the success of our research."

Her eyes were filled with sadness. "When Val died..." She paused, overwhelmed by the thought. "When all our friends died, I realized we had gone too far."

"I feel the same way." Everyone turned toward Tyson. "This has been the most exciting work I've ever done. I knew it was dangerous." His voice cracked. "Maybe I was too close to it." Tyson trembled. Jo looked at her partner and snaked her arm around his waist. He drew in a big breath. "We could have destroyed the Earth or the Moon." He looked up and gave his friends a penetrating glare. "Who did we think we were? We were doing it because we could. We justified ourselves by thinking we were noble, working on a cause that made the risks acceptable. Risks we didn't fully understand." He looked down at his hands, his face red with shame. "I've got to find another line of work."

"I'm with Ty." Jo's voice was a monotone. "We're both done."

Silence embraced the group. Alexis Wren had listened intently and then rose in a fluster. She began pacing back and forth as if caught in a cage. Her world had been penetrated by the pain of her colleagues. "We should continue." Alexis looked around at them with alarm. "That's what Maryanne would want." She glanced at Robert, who grimaced at the mention of her name. This is my life. It's my science. I can't stop now." No one spoke.

Jenson Reed's face was expressionless, but he was upset. Rory sat between Kell and Sprite and wept quietly, her sobs grounding everyone in the realities they were facing.

Samina sat alone. She seemed disconnected, strangely unmoved. A calm presence would have been welcome, but Samina's demeanor verged on indifference. Sprite was the only one who noticed it. She wondered why Samina had changed. They had been family. Now, everything seemed to be falling apart.

Adrianna cleared her throat, and everyone looked up at her. In that moment, she felt the incredible weight of leadership. She squeezed Hunter's hand, hoping he would take the lead and say something. He did not. She let out a long breath and began. "Hunter and I don't want to do this anymore. We're going to pursue more conventional research."

* * *

A few hours later, Sprite Logan was pedaling an exercise bike while listening to music through a set of earbuds. She wore loose-fitting sweatpants and a thin racer-back tank that accentuated her figure. Kell Edwards came up behind her. He had dark, curly hair and a rugged, handsome face. His muscles were visible through the fabric of his shirt. Kell was Sprite's best friend, but their relationship was laced with teenage sexual tension. He tickled her. She screamed and almost fell off the bike.

"Don't do that!" Sprite repositioned herself on the saddle and started pedaling again.

Kell laughed. "You should have seen the look on your face."

"Kell Edwards, you're a total menace!"

Kell held Sprite's shoulders and squeezed a couple of times. With a furtive glance around the Common Area, he began to slide his hands over her collarbones and toward her breasts. Sprite jerked her hands off the handlebars and pushed him away. "Stop it, Kell!"

The boy was unfazed. He mounted the bike next to Sprite. "Did you hear about Dr. Hastings?"

Sprite stopped pedaling again, a frown on her face. "You mean Dr. Maryanne?"

"No. Robert Hastings."

Sprite bristled. "What?"

"Dr. Hastings has been fooling around with Samina. Dr. Maryanne found out about it just before she died."

A dark and moody look descended on Sprite's face. She imagined Samina and Robert having sex. Sprite kicked herself for looking up to her, for making her a big sister, a role model.

Kell found his stride on the exercise bike, oblivious to Sprite's inner turmoil. "I guess they had a big argument right at the end."

"How did you hear about it?" Sprite stared off into space.

"I overheard Mom and Dad talking about it. You know how hard it is to keep a secret."

"Some secrets can ruin your life." Sprite said the words to no one in particular.

"Well, I guess Dr. Hastings is going to have to live with the consequences." Kell glanced over at his friend. Sprite dismounted her bike and left the exercise area without a word.

* * *

Robert Hastings padded through the connecting corridors between the NARI living quarters and the rest of Copernicus Base. There was a NARI logo on the shoulder of his jumpsuit. Robert couldn't get Maryanne out of his mind. Their last meaningful conversation had been the argument over his infidelity. He felt waves of guilt whenever he thought of his wife. And he thought about her all the time.

A small knot of people had gathered at one of the corridor junctions just north of the base Commons. As Robert approached, their conversations stopped. There were no greetings. Rather, there were looks of hatred. Robert tried to look invisible as he passed the group. He could feel their eyes burning into him, his skin turning red with shame.

Many rough and hard-working people passed through the domes of Copernicus Base. Many of them worked in the ice and ore mines in the base's southeast quadrant. Others were transients: space haulers and thieves who considered Copernicus a lucrative port of call. A series of small domes was situated south of the Base Commons, between the spaceport and the Copernican mines. This was the red-light district, filled with bordellos and bars, porn houses, and cheap rooms that were rented by the hour. The "district" was so popular among the mineworkers, a special corridor had been built to provide easy access from the ore processing plant.

Samina was waiting for Robert at a table tucked in the corner of the "Delta V," one of the taverns in the district. The place was almost empty. There were large viewports, which offered panoramic views of the lunar landscape and the spaceport. The place had been designed so customers could watch the coming and going of spacecraft. Two transport ships were on their pads, being prepped for flight. They were immense ships. Their size was striking, even though the spaceport was two kilometers away.

The woman behind the counter looked up as Robert entered the dining room. Kate Sloan was an older woman with leathery skin. She had been the proprietor for almost thirty years. She had seen and done it all. Old Kate was a powerful woman. She had the grit to stand up to the most cantankerous customer. Kate scowled unashamedly at Robert as he scanned the tables and made his way over to Samina.

His lover looked up at him as he approached her table. "Hello there."

Robert pulled out a chair and sat down. "Afternoon."

Samina studied him for a moment. "How are you holding up?"

"Eh."

She waited for him to say something more, but he didn't. "Thanks for coming." Robert shrugged. Samina reached out to touch his hand, but he pulled it away. She sat up straight. "What's that about?"

Robert pushed back in his chair. "Look, I can't do this. When we started…"

"It's been good, really good." She said the words deep in her throat, as if she had reached down into her heart and pulled them up, just enough so Robert could hear them.

"Yeah, well, it was, but that was before…"

"Maryanne and Emile died." Samina finished the sentence for him.

Robert nodded, his eyes red and puffy. Guilt was written on his face. "I don't know what I'm doing, Sam. Being with you was all wrong. I mean, you're great, but I violated Maryanne's trust. I killed Emile. I ruined our marriage."

"The explosion killed Emile. Your marriage was already ruined. You said so."

Hastings studied his hands as he rubbed them together. "You weren't my first fling, you know. I've been stepping out on Maryanne for years. It's a wonder she stayed with me this long." The words tumbled out of him like a penitent in a confessional. "But it's all different now. Losing her. Losing Emile. Losing our friends. I can't do this anymore."

"You mean us?"

"Yes." He paused. "But more than us. I can't keep doing this kind of work."

Samina's eyes glistened. She wanted to embrace him, take all the hurt away from him, but that was impossible. A cold, hard wall had descended between them. There was no penetrating it. Their relationship, no matter how ill-advised it had been, was over. "So, that's it? We're just supposed to go on like nothing happened?" Her voice was quiet, defeated.

"It wasn't 'nothing.'" He slipped into silence, and Samina waited for him. "It seems like NARI is finished. I don't know how long I'm going to stay." Robert looked out the viewport. He gathered his thoughts and went on. "I wasn't faithful to Maryanne in her life, but I intend to be faithful to her from this point on."

"You want to go back to being friends?"

"That's what I'm saying."

Samina's eyes clouded with a profound sadness. "I can't do that."

Robert studied her face. "Yeah, I know."

"Goodbye, Robert." Samina got up. She paused, gently pushing the chair against the table. She turned and wove her way through the tables, toward the exit. Robert sat for a while, gazing out the viewport. Maryanne and Emile's faces were in his mind's eye. He would never see them again. Finally, he stood and traced the same path Samina had taken through the empty tables.

Two large men stood at the entrance of the tavern. They eyed Robert's jumpsuit as he walked toward them.

"Hey! You're one of those nano-shits, aren't you?"

Robert ignored the comment and walked past the men. A meaty arm shot out and grabbed Robert, whirling him around.

"I asked you a question."

Robert stepped back and away from the men, but the one who had grabbed him kept a firm grip on his arm.

"Let go of me."

"You're one of those murdering fucks, ain't ya? Why don't you go kill yourself? Do the world a favor."

"Take your hand off me." Robert was doing his best to keep his composure. Privately, he knew the man had pegged him for what he really was.

"Maybe I should kill you myself." The man lifted his other arm. His free hand was balled up in a fist that seemed as big as a basketball.

Robert saw a sudden movement behind his antagonist. In less than a heartbeat, the big man crashed to the floor in front of him. Robert was pushed aside, and he cracked his head against the wall. Bright popping lights filled his field of vision as he struggled to stay on his feet. In the low lunar gravity, he bounced off the wall and bumped into the man who had been standing next to his accuser. Robert sensed the man's reaction and tried to brace himself for a punch.

"I wouldn't do that." It was a woman's gravelly voice. Robert's vision cleared. Kate was standing over the first man who lay unconscious on the floor. She held a titanium club in her hand. The second man stepped back.

"Thank you," Robert murmured.

"Shut up!" Kate wielded her club menacingly. "Charley's right. You are a nano-fuck, and I want you out of my place."

"Why did you help me?"

Kate gave Robert a toothy grin. "Charley's my best customer. I couldn't have him go and kill you, could I? Now get out of here."

* * *

Hunter Logan was in his bedroom combing his hair. No matter what he did, he could never get it to look right. It was worse in low gravity. The bedroom door was open, and Sprite appeared at the threshold.

"Dad?"

"Hey, kiddo! How are you doing?"

Sprite looked down, unable to hide her feelings. "Okay, I guess."

Hunter sized up his daughter. "What's up?"

Sprite's eyes were moist with tears. "Daddy, what would happen to me if you and Mom went away?"

Hunter tried to mask his surprise. "Why would you think something like that?"

Sprite was silent.

"Look, kiddo. Mom and I will always be there for you."

"You can't say that. You can't know…"

"Are you thinking about Rory?" Hunter stepped toward his daughter and wrapped her in his arms. "She's going to be all right, Sprite. It's a horrible thing to lose your parents, but she has friends. She has you. And we'll make sure she's okay."

"I know, Daddy. But what happens to me if I lose you and Mom?"

Hunter hadn't considered the impact of recent events on his daughter. Suddenly, his decision to stop his work was easy. He put his hand gently under Sprite's chin and tipped up her head until their eyes met. "Sprite, the most important work of my life is keeping you safe. Nothing is going to get in the way of that."

* * *

The Selene Station hurtled toward her fiery death, her velocity carrying her in a steeply-diminishing orbit that spiraled into the sun's nuclear furnace. Surveillance drones surrounded the ill-fated space platform, providing three-dimensional telemetry of her final days. The drones' sensitive instruments were the first to notice the changes in Selene's outer hull, flagging the anomaly with a burst alert to Meridian Corporation.

* * *

Amos Cross paced back and forth in his office at Jackson Base. Two meetings were taking place at virtual conference tables in front of him. The participants were spread throughout the solar system. Meridian had harnessed micro-black-holes to create a means of nearly instantaneous communication over long distances. Holographic simulacra of each participant created a workable environment for collaboration.

Adjunct smart displays floating next to Cross followed the course of each meeting, screening up pertinent information as points were made and topics discussed. The great man took in both meetings at once, while dictating an email. A soft chime resonated warmly. Another screen appeared, revealing a three-dimensional image of the Selene Station. The platform seemed to shimmer as her form began to dissociate. The main body of the old space station was still discernable, although Selene was rapidly becoming a cloud of dust, traveling in a formation that resembled her original shape.

"Report."

"The phase-two nanomachines have breached Selene's hull more quickly than we anticipated. The station is almost completely consumed."

Cross interrupted both his meetings. "Continue without me. I'll be back in a few moments."

Amos thought of Susanna Frost, and within a moment, she stood in waiting outside his office. He gestured toward the entrance, and the great door opened with a visceral hiss. Susanna's shoulders rose as she postured herself and entered his office. Her carmine business suit looked brand new.

"Ms. Frost. It seems that Hunter Logan's nanomachines are more efficient killers than any of us realized." Amos waved a hand toward the remains of the Selene Station. "It's nothing but a cloud of dust. This technology is really something!"

"Are we in any danger?"

"Not at all. The machines are accelerating toward the sun. Just stay out of their way, and Sol will do the rest."

"Good."

Amos gave her a curious look, amused by her fear. "Aren't they magnificent? Our NARI friends have concocted a perfect killing machine."

"The scientists are pretty shaken up. My source tells me they have decided to abandon their work. It looks like they will disband the Nanotechnology Advanced Research Institute and go their separate ways."

Cross frowned. "That isn't going to happen. Send word to Director Marshall. The NARI team is confined to Copernicus Base. We need to change their minds. I want them to recreate these phase-two nanomachines."

"Yes, sir."

Cross furrowed his brow. "We'll need a new place to keep them."

"How about the old base at Cardanus? It could be readied in a few weeks."

"Not acceptable, Ms. Frost. We need an isolated place." Susanna could tell her boss was enjoying himself. "I think we're going to have to put our little team of scientists in some back corner of our territory. Someplace where we can hide them from saboteurs and keep them focused on what we want them to do. We don't want any more interference."

Susanna stared at the remains of the Selene Station. She twisted her long fingers, knotting them until her knuckles cracked. Against her better judgment, she turned toward Amos to offer her opinion. "Is it worth it, sir? Maybe we should just let them go."

Cross smiled, but his eyes blazed. Susanna immediately dropped her chin and looked downward, breaking eye contact with her superior. "That's what you would do? Let Hunter Logan and his team scatter to the six Cardinals?" He shook his head. "That would be a blunder of the first order, Ms. Frost. Don't you realize what we have here? These nanomachines will be a valuable tool for Meridian Corporation. If we control these machines, no one will ever know if we have infected them. We can hold all of humanity in the grip of fear. The destructive power of these – what did Logan call them? – piranha machines? These piranha machines are aggressive and unstoppable. Excellent qualities. Give us a big stick like this, and we can whisper our way to total dominance of the solar system."

Susanna dropped her hands to her sides and looked down at the floor. Cross's gaze softened. He knew he had won. "I want that technology. Meridian 6 is an abandoned research settlement in The Asteroid Belt. It's on Ceres. It has two laboratory complexes and is the perfect place for the NARI team. With the right incentives, the Logans will provide us with a new batch of these nasty little killers."

"Would we ever use them?" Susanna didn't dare look up at her boss.

"This is an opportunity for Meridian Corporation. Power is dominance at any cost."

Susanna's state-of-the-art makeup couldn't protect her. The color drained from her face.

"Susanna."

She looked up and gave Amos Cross her full attention.

"I want NARI kept intact. Bribe the scientists, threaten their children, do anything to keep them together. We must have those nanomachines. And just in case we can't persuade them, have our contact get Hunter Logan's research files. This is Meridian's highest priority."

"Yes, Sir."

Amos turned his back on her, his mind returning to his meetings. "Okay everybody, adult supervision is back."

Susanna had been dismissed. She hoped Amos approved of her new business suit.

* * *

Hunter Logan sat on the edge of his bed. He rubbed his hands nervously, as if he were trying to wash a stain from his skin. Adrianna was in her bed-clothes and walked to his side. Hunter stared at his hands. "This is my entire fault."

"No, it's not." Adrianna sat down next to him. "Hunter, you are the finest scientist I have ever known. You are thorough and honest. We underestimated the danger of the machines, but we took precautions at every step. We spent years developing the containment unit. Maybe we went too far, but everybody would be alive right now if that bomb hadn't detonated. Find the people who set that bomb, and you'll find those responsible for our friends' deaths." She paused, but Hunter made no reply. She could see him descending into a dark depression. No logical explanation was going to raise him up again.

* * *

Robert Hastings had retreated to his quarters, immobilized by remorse and shame. Apparitions of Maryanne and Emile vexed him, their faces indicting him from beyond death. He had always been special: a bright child with a wide-open future. He had been coddled, showered with privilege and scholarships to the finest schools. Robert had always gotten his way because he was smart. He got the right answers. He came up with the brilliant ideas. Robert had lived in an imaginary bubble-world, where he was infallible. Being wrong had never occurred to him until the day his wife and son died.

* * *

Sprite lay in her bed, hugging a pillow to her chest. Her mind had been spinning all evening with thoughts of her mother. There were times when she was so angry with her, she'd wished she were dead. It was adolescent hyperbole. She hadn't meant it, but she couldn't deny how she felt. She hated her mother. Her feelings made sense until Rory's mother died. Watching her friend agonize over her mother's death unbalanced her internal gyroscope. Sprite found herself tumbling out of control. She felt like a grain of sand in a sandstorm. Her inner turbulence overwhelmed and exhausted her. She closed her eyes and prayed for sleep.

* * *

There was a noise in the house. Sprite jolted awake. She was nine years old. Her father was on a business trip. She never slept well when he was away. She sat up, swinging her legs off the side of the bed. Her toes groped for her slippers. Not finding them, she padded silently from her room in bare feet. The hallway floor was cool. She heard the noise again. The sound was coming from her parent's bedroom. It was a moonlit night. Sprite approached the bedroom in the shadowed hallway. Her mother moaned. A deeper voice whispered something. There were deep, guttural sounds. Sprite wondered what could be happening. Her inquisitive nature drew her forward, toward the door.

The door stood ajar. Through the slot, Sprite could see her parent's bed washed in the blue light of the Moon. Her mother was lying naked on the bed, toes fisted, hair tousled and pushed back from her face. A man was on top of her. At first, Sprite thought it was her father, but it couldn't be. He was away. This wasn't her father at all. Why were they so close to each other? Where were their clothes?

The man's body was moving. Sprite could see something between his legs. What was that? He was pushing it into her mother. It looked like the poking would hurt, but then Sprite heard her mother squeal with delight. She had a look of ecstasy on her face. Sprite stepped back into the darkened hallway and held her breath, not wanting to be discovered. She continued watching through the crack in the door as the naked man lifted himself from between her mother's legs. His face was caught in a shaft of light. It was Robert Hastings.

* * *

Sprite's eyes snapped open. She was sweating. She was in her bedroom at Copernicus Base. The familiar nightmare had haunted her ever since she was nine years old.

5

Hunter Logan was very careful with his research data. He kept all of it in Millie, his card comp. Millie had no wireless capability, except for an encrypted interface with his holographic earset. Hunter didn't want his card comp to be part of the digital ocean that surrounded the human race. The only way to ensure privacy was to stand apart from the aggregate. Hunter had learned this from his older brother. Prescott Logan was an eccentric curmudgeon who had disappeared with his wife into The Asteroid Belt years before. He was an expert in data encryption and had written the algorithms for Millie, protecting and monitoring Hunter's data.

Hunter sat at his workspace in his quarters. It had been two days since he had picked up his card comp. He had misgivings about accessing his work. He activated Millie by pressing his thumb on a biometric pad integrated into the card comp's surface. She came alive, linking to the earset, which had an earphone, a small integral boom microphone, and a tiny holographic projector. A three-dimensional display appeared in front of Hunter's face. Everything was flashing red, signaling a security breach. Someone had broken into his system. He looked around the workspace. Nothing was out of place. "Report in, Millie."

"Good Morning, Dr. Logan. I have an alert for you."

Hunter frowned. "What is it?"

"Yesterday, my memory was downloaded at twenty-three hundred hours, six minutes."

Hunter noted the time. He had spent the last evening in the Common Area. Someone must have entered his quarters, undetected. "Who did this?"

"I don't know. My biometric security was bypassed."

Hunter was stunned. "There's no login information?"

"No, Dr. Logan. It's very puzzling. Those data fields are empty."

Hunter shut down Millie, hoping Prescott's encryption would stand up against the unknown intruder. He sat in a trance, trying to fathom what had happened.

Adrianna entered the tiny workspace and put her hand on her husband's shoulder. "How are you holding up?"

Hunter shrugged. "We've got a new problem. Someone came in here and hacked Millie."

Adrianna's face fell. She leaned against the desk and looked at her husband with tired eyes. "Someone was in here?"

"They accessed my files."

Adrianna looked grim, the color draining from her face. "Did they get the model for the nanomachines?"

Hunter nodded slowly. "They got it all."

"Prescott set up Millie's security. He said she couldn't be cracked."

"Somebody managed to bypass Millie's security." Hunter tapped his head. "They got the files, but without the key, the data can't be read. Once the data is outside Millie, any attempt to duplicate the file will fail."

Adrianna shuttered at the thought of someone re-creating the killer nanomachines. "Prescott's security had better hold."

"You aren't kidding." Hunter reached for his wife's hand.

"Who could have done this?" she whispered.

Hunter gave Adrianna a worried frown. "We've got a traitor."

* * *

The NARI team's good-natured chatter was replaced with a cool silence as they gathered for breakfast in the dining area. The Logans were sitting wordlessly at one end of the large table, caught in their post-nocturnal daze. Samina was getting herself a cup of coffee when Robert Hastings appeared from the residence corridor. She looked up at him for a brief second and then poured her attention, along with her coffee, into the cup in front of her. Robert took an empty seat next to Jenson Reed, as far away from Samina as he could. Immediately, Sprite got up and left.

Jo Smith usually enjoyed preparing breakfast, but now she was lifeless, preparing the food mindlessly. She burned the first batch of synthetic eggs, something she never did. Tyson had no appetite. He pushed his food around his plate. His body was at the table, but his soul was somewhere in the dust cloud that was once Selene Station. Across the table, Alexis Wren stirred her tea endlessly, staring down into the liquid, considering the mathematical equations that would describe its behavior.

Jenson Reed tried to engage Robert in conversation. "How are you doing?"

"Think about it!" Robert flared with anger. "My son is dead! My wife is dead!"

No one moved. Jenson hugged his coffee cup with his palms. "I didn't mean to offend." His voice was calm and low.

Robert pounded the table, rattling the plates. "This was supposed to be a safe place to work. She was a scientist. He was just a little boy. They weren't soldiers. They weren't supposed to die."

Tyson Edwards rose from his seat. His hands were shaking, and he spilled his orange juice. Hunter put his hand on his arm. "Ty, please stay."

Tyson pulled away from him "Go to hell, Hunter."

"What have I done?" Hunter knew it was the wrong thing to say.

Tyson spun around. "What have you done? You're the one who pushed us into the phase-two research. The great Hunter Logan's grand idea! You wouldn't listen to the public's opposition to our work. Hell, they saw what we were doing much clearer than we did! You're the one who struck the deal with Meridian Corporation and brought us up here to Copernicus. Damn you, Hunter! Because of you..." Tyson knocked over a chair.

"Because of me, what?"

Tyson balled his fists. His body was like a tightly wound spring. There was hate in his eyes as he glared at Hunter. Then, he stormed out of the room.

Adrianna reached for her husband's hand. He moved his hand away. "It's okay, honey."

Jo threw a fresh batch of scrambled eggs into the sink. The skillet rattled as clumps of egg flew in every direction. "It's not okay, Hunter." She moved to Tyson's side. "It will never be okay." She grabbed Ty's arm, and they stormed out of the dining area.

Robert pushed his cup away. "I've got to get out of here."

Alexis looked perplexed. "You just sat down."

"I've had enough."

"Before you go, there's something I have to say." Hunter commanded everyone's attention. "I'm sorry Ty and Jo had to leave, but this can't wait. We've got another problem. Someone hacked my card comp and made a copy of my data. Millie was in my residence."

"When did it happen?" Jenson Reed furrowed his brow.

"Millie says it was last evening, when we were out here in the Common Area. Have you seen any strangers in the living quarters?" No one had. "Did any of you..."

Samina interrupted him. "Are you accusing one of us?"

"Maybe I am." Hunter had a hardened expression on his face.

Samina folded her arms defensively. "How could you think that? I thought we were family."

"Someone breached Millie's security. That's not easy to do, and it happened in my private quarters. None of us have seen any strangers around here. What conclusion would you draw from that?"

"This is insane." Samina left the table, her arms still tightly folded to her chest.

"Jenson, would you check the security system and tell me if you find anything out of the ordinary? Whoever is behind this might have gotten sloppy."

"I doubt there'll be anything, sir. Breaking into your card comp requires real sophistication. They'd be too smart to be sloppy."

"Maybe so, but take a look anyway."

"Will do, Dr. Logan."

Robert pushed himself back in his chair. "Nice breakfast. We should do this more often. Can I be excused, now?"

Hunter slumped his shoulders. "Robert, I'm sorry." The man ignored him and got up from the table. Hunter watched him as he went to the main entrance and left.

* * *

Susanna Frost stood before Amos Cross in his office at Jackson Base. The floor of the office resembled the lunar surface. A breathtaking canopy of stars arched overhead, with the blue and white orb of Earth suspended over the far end of the office. The room was awash in a bluish-white light.

Amos gestured, and the Earth drew closer. Susanna could almost reach out and touch it. The great man was looking at an odd satellite, poised in geosynchronous orbit over the Earth's equator. A long slender cable hung below the platform, disappearing in the atmosphere below. A module resembling a cylinder with bulbous ends straddled the cable on its major axis. The module rose slowly until it reached the top of the cable. Magnetic clamps docked the module to the platform.

"I was hoping they would fail." Cross spoke quietly, but there was still a menacing edge to his voice. Cross rocked his weight from one foot to the other as he shifted his attention back to Susanna. His feet left virtual footprints on the floor. "Do you know what that is?"

Susanna nodded carefully. "It's the new space elevator. I believe that's a carbon nanotube ribbon that's tethered somewhere in South America. The module is a new lift vehicle: a revolutionary way of putting mass into orbit."

"Yes, yes. I know all that." Cross seemed put out by her response, disappointed. "I didn't ask for a description of the damn thing. It was a rhetorical question. I didn't want an answer."

Susanna cowered, unsure of how to respond. She had been down this road before, and it never turned out in her favor.

"Today, Ms. Frost, everything changes." He waved his hand, and the Earth disappeared. The room darkened, and suddenly the faux lunar surface beneath their feet began to glow with an eerie light. "The moon bases, the Martian colonies, the settlements in The Asteroid Belt, and even the orbiting platforms get many of their supplies from us. Meridian Corporation has always had the advantage of producing its products beyond Earth's gravity well. It's been very expensive for Earth-people to launch their goods into orbit and then achieve escape velocity. We've enjoyed the price advantage. We built our empire on it."

Susanna unconsciously touched the fabric of her blouse. It was carmine-red. The color stood out against the monochrome tones of the office. She bought it to go with the dark business suit she was wearing.

"That's why you spent so much for that ugly shirt." Susanna blushed. "But now, this space elevator changes the equation. Earth has found a low-cost way to bring her products to orbit. We're going to have to find new ways of competing."

"What are we going to do, sir?"

"Economics is war, and the marketplace is one of the battlefields." Amos Cross turned away. He didn't say another word.

* * *

Years earlier, Hunter Logan had spent some time at Copernicus Base with his brother. The base had been much smaller. He still knew the older sections well: the Old Garden and Commons. Today, he needed an old friend and a drink. Hunter put on a jacket to hide the NARI logo on his jumpsuit and set out for the district, Copernicus's answer to Boston's "combat zone." It was much seedier than he remembered; the expansion of the base's mining operation had brought a wider variety of addictions and distractions to the area. He kept his head down to avoid the knots of men and women who clogged the passageways like vascular obstructions. The lighting was subdued in the district. Some things were best kept in the shadows.

The Delta V Tavern was almost empty this time of day. It was too early for the lunch crowd, and most of the regulars were sleeping off their escapades from the night before. Hunter stepped in, the massive door swinging smoothly on invisible hinges.

"Damn! It's been a long time!" Kate Sloan dropped the rag she was using to massage the bar. She pivoted her bulk through a narrow cut in the counter. "Hunter Logan. I thought I'd see you one of these days." She threw her massive arms around him and planted a motherly peck on his cheek.

"Got a few minutes?" Hunter's voice was lifeless.

"Sure. Have a seat." The older woman gestured toward an empty table near the bar. "Want a forty-two?" She knew it was Hunter's favorite drink.

Hunter smiled. "It's the answer to everything."

"You got it." Kate drew two glasses of the brew and brought them to the table. "You're in a rough patch."

"Yeah." Hunter took a sip, the rich flavor triggering warm memories. "Wish I could turn back the clock. Even a week would help."

"Life's a one-way time machine, bud." She looked carefully at him. Old Kate had watched thousands of people in her day. She was a sensitive soul, wrapped in a gruff exterior. "You lost some good people up there on Selene. Bet your career's in the crapper, too."

Hunter took a long swig, then wiped his mouth with a napkin. "Not to mention killing the system's most popular newsman."

Kate grunted. "Larson Daniels? Don't trouble yourself over him. He was a glorified ambulance chaser. Don't get me wrong. I don't wish for anybody to die, but he was a detriment to journalism. No standards. He'd pull down his own mother's panties if he thought there were ratings in it."

Hunter nodded. "He had a knack for getting people mad..."

"...and getting their attention," Kate finished for him. She frowned. The lines on her face were accentuated by the filtered light from a nearby viewport. "That's Larson's legacy. You've got your own attention problem now."

"It's pretty embarrassing when your career crashes and burns on system TV." Hunter rubbed the old scar on his finger.

Kate sighed. "It's much worse than that, old friend."

Hunter looked up at her. "What are you talking about?"

"You're a little bug caught in the jaws of a pair of pliers. On the one side, some very powerful people want your nanomachines. On the other, there are those who want you dead."

Hunter ran his fingers through his hair. "I'll see your 'worse' and raise you 'much worse.' Somebody took my research files from my card comp."

Kate's eyes narrowed. "What was in them?"

Hunter gave her a sarcastic chuckle. "Oh, nothing much. Just the model for the phase-two nanomachines. If the thieves crack the encryption, they'll know how to destroy the Moon."

Kate deadpanned. "Could be worse."

Hunter shook his head. "Somebody on the team did it."

"A mole." Old Kate nodded her head. "You're up against some very smart and devious people. Do you know of the Citizen's League?"

"Damon Trask's people? I wish I didn't."

"There's a rumor that one of their emissaries came here to stir up the residents. She's told them your work is a threat to their families. She's scaring people, and these people kill what scares them."

Hunter was silent as he absorbed this new, unwelcome information. Kate sipped her drink, then set the glass down on the polished concrete tabletop. It made a sharp click that echoed through the empty tavern. "One of your people had a problem outside my place yesterday."

"Robert Hastings."

Kate nodded. "That was just the tip of the iceberg, Hunter. Your man was lucky. I was there to persuade Charlie to leave him alone. The tides are rising against you. Before long, it won't be safe for you to be here. At some point, you have to think about the safety of your daughter."

Hunter's face was a portrait of disbelief, then fear.

"And don't think you're any better off with Meridian Corporation. Amos Cross is one dangerous son-of-a-bitch. He'll stop at nothing to get what he wants."

"He's not that bad."

"Open your eyes, boy. Do you remember the name of the man who tried to ruin your brother when he wouldn't cooperate with Meridian Corporation?"

"Amos Cross?"

"He's the one. You're about to learn the same lesson Prescott learned years ago. Only now, Cross is a thousand times more powerful. If you aren't careful, you're gonna get squashed."

* * *

Dr. Robert Hastings stood at the tiny passenger terminal, located in a small slice of the immense Base Supply dome. A tough-looking woman stood behind the counter. She looked like a cross between a female wrestler and the Wicked Witch of the West. Years of sparing with the dockworkers and spacecraft support personnel had sucked the femininity out of her. She wore a wrinkled flight suit and took her time with everything. The less patience a traveler exhibited, the longer she made them wait.

The woman saw Robert enter the passenger area. By the time he stepped to her counter, facial recognition software had already told her who he was. The scientist pulled a card from his pocket and waited while she pretended to be occupied with a nonexistent task.

"Excuse me, I want to book passage to Earth." The woman ignored him. Robert looked around for some kind of bell or enunciator to get her attention. He felt awkward, unsure of the proper protocol. He caught himself looking at her buttocks, almost undressing her with his eyes. He blushed, then cursed silently at himself for falling into the same pattern of behavior that had ruined his marriage. How could he do that on the heels of Maryanne and Emile's deaths?

"Ma'am, could you please help me?" He used the friendliest voice he could muster.

Silence. Then, the woman turned slowly. She grinned widely at him. Clearly, she didn't have a dental plan. "Hastings, Doctor Robert A., employed by the Nanotechnology Advanced Research Institute. Your address is on the north side in that fancy NARI residence complex. Must be tough."

Robert nodded with his best smile. "That's me."

"You want to book passage to Earth."

"On the next available flight, if you can."

"I can't."

Robert scowled. "When can you make the reservation?"

The woman's smile grew even wider. "I can't."

"What do you mean? That's what you do, isn't it?"

"Settle down, Hastings, Robert A." She paused just to exasperate him. "I can't book your passage because you've been restricted to the base. None of you NARI people can leave Copernicus."

"Says who?"

"Says the honorable Winston Marshall himself, the base director. You ain't going no place outta this spaceport."

The room began to spin. Robert grabbed the edge of the counter to steady himself. This couldn't be happening. He turned on his heels without a word and left the terminal area. The woman smiled broadly. That had made her day.

* * *

Sprite Logan was perched on her exercise bike, cranking through her daily routine when she sensed someone near her. There was a movement in her peripheral vision. She turned her head and caught a glimpse of Samina Haddad mounting the bike next to her.

"Hello, Sprite."

The younger woman closed her eyes and concentrated on pedaling.

"Sprite."

No response.

"What's the matter?"

Sprite got off her bike and grabbed her towel. She turned away from Samina, not wanting to deal with her.

"Have I done something?"

Sprite whirled around. She lost all her self-restraint, crossing the imaginary line that separated what she wanted to do from what wisdom suggested. "Done anything?" She faced her former friend with an icy stare. "I looked up to you. I wanted to be like you. I, I respected you, but you're just like all the rest."

"What has happened doesn't have anything to do with us, kiddo."

"It has everything to do with me!" Sprite snapped her towel over her shoulder and rushed away toward the residence corridor.

* * *

Robert Hastings was still fuming over his encounter at the passenger terminal. He walked aggressively down the corridor that led from the Base Supply dome toward the Commons. The large, domed, indoor garden was filled with trees, paths, and benches, accenting green grassy areas. It was a welcome oasis, a splash of color against the stark lunar landscape. He found a place to sit with his back toward the vegetation.

Robert sat back and looked at the Earth, hovering in the blackness overhead. He could have been on his way to the blue-green world if he hadn't been restricted to the base. He felt trapped. He thought of Maryanne and Emile, now gone forever. He thought of his work, how he had devoted his intellect and his time to the study of nanotechnology. He felt betrayed. Betrayed by the love of his professional life. His work had killed his family. He turned in his seat and scanned the lush garden. Why didn't he become a painter or a gardener? He could have created beauty instead of a killing machine.

A woman walked along one of the paths in the Commons. She was dressed in a liquid bodysuit. It accentuated the curves of her hips and breasts. She moved in it like a dancer, fluid grace and allure. Robert couldn't keep his eyes off the woman as she slowly approached his bench.

"Good morning!" The woman paused in front of him. "You've picked the most beautiful spot in the Commons. May I join you?"

Robert wanted to be alone, but the woman was mesmerizing. He caught himself. Guilt replaced infatuation. Remembering Maryanne, ripples of regret washed over him. "Sure." He wasn't used to feeling so awkward in the presence of a beautiful woman. She sat down next to him.

"Thanks." The woman cooed. "These benches are so comfortable." Robert felt another twinge of guilt.

"You're one of the NARI scientists, aren't you?" the woman asked. Her opalescent eyes were positively hypnotic.

"Why do you ask?"

"I've come a long way to talk to you."

"And you are?"

"I'm Maya Lewis. Dr. Hastings, isn't it?"

"How do you know my name?"

"I've seen your face on the newscasts. I'm sorry for your loss. Your wife was Maryanne? You had a son named, Emile?"

Robert's angst was momentarily overshadowed by confusion. Who was this woman, and what did she want?

Maya reached out and put her hand on Robert's knee. "I can't imagine how difficult this must be for you." Maya's touch was like a shock of electricity. A river of tingles shot through his body. He crossed his legs in embarrassment. Maya's hand slipped to the bench.

"Th, thank you." Robert cursed himself for reacting to this woman instead of honoring Maryanne.

Maya gave him a radiant, understanding smile. She knew she had him.

"No one should ever die like your wife and son." Robert wanted to tell her to mind her own business, but Maya had managed to impale him with her irresistible charms. She had walked right into the most painful place in his heart and taken up residence. "I am sure you never thought your life's work would cause so much misery and loss." Robert felt like he had been hit with a sledgehammer. Was she a mind reader?

This perfect stranger could see right through him. He did his best to remain impassive. "I represent certain interests that want to protect people like your family."

"What are you getting at?" Robert was still recoiling from Maya's emotional marksmanship.

"Was it worth it?" Maya smiled at him like a mother comforting her child in the face of a difficult lesson.

"Was what worth what?

Maya flashed another luminescent smile. "Your research. Was it worth the death of Maryanne and Emile? Was it worth your wife killing your son to shield him from being eaten by your phase-two nanomachines? Was it worth the lives of Larson Daniels and his camerawoman?"

"I, I don't know." Robert knew he was being manipulated, but he had been hiding from the questions the woman posed ever since Maryanne's death.

Once again, Maya put her hand on Robert's thigh. He felt the Base Commons begin to tilt. "Would you help me, Bob?" Usually, he corrected people who called him Bob, but Maya said it like a love poem. "I need your help to save millions of children like Emile, millions of wives like Maryanne. I think you have doubts about the work of NARI. All I am asking for is a little information." She used her thumb and forefinger to suggest a minuscule amount. "All we are asking is for you to keep us informed about the team's future plans."

"You want me to spy on my colleagues?"

"I want you to prevent future suffering. You know you can't keep doing this. I want you to honor your family by helping us stop NARI's insanity."

"I can't do that. This has been my life." Before the words were out of his mouth, Robert knew it was a lie. His life had changed forever. His work no longer mattered. He could see himself switching sides, joining the opposition to nano-research.

"You aren't happy with this life, now, are you? You don't want to keep doing this, Bob. It's tearing you apart."

This woman had him pegged. Was it so obvious? Robert looked into her face. She was beautiful. "I'll have to think about it."

"Of course, you do. I'll contact you in a few days. If you're willing to help us, I'll tell you what we need."

Robert managed to nod his head ever so slightly.

"Well then, it's been a pleasure meeting you, Bob." She stood up. Her liquid sheath left nothing to the imagination. Robert couldn't take his eyes off her. She bent down toward him. Her aroma was overwhelming. Her face was inches from him as she brought her lips close to his ear. He couldn't breathe. "Think about it, Bob." She touched his temple with her lips, the suggestion of a slow sensuous kiss. Then, she was gone.

* * *

Hunter breezed into the small common area in his residence. Adrianna was reading a scientific journal.

"You're back!' She smiled warmly at her husband. "Did you have lunch with Old Kate?"

"Yeah. I hung around the tavern for several hours until she got busy. Caught up on old times."

"How is she?"

"She's fine, honey." Hunter glanced around the room. "Where's Sprite?"

Adrianna made a face. "She's in one of her moods. She came in here a while ago and went straight to her room."

"Good."

"Good she's in one of her moods, or good she's in her room?"

Hunter sat down nervously and told Adrianna about his conversation with Kate.

* * *

Rory North wandered aimlessly around her new room in the Logan's living quarters. She felt like time had stopped. Her life was a trance where she navigated between memory and fantasy. Nothing seemed real. She had no plans beyond taking her next breath.

She cradled a small box in the palm of her hand. It was made of translucent material with a hinged top that formed a perfect seal with the box itself. Several small holes penetrated the lid, and a faint glow emanated from a shapeless form within the container.

She held the box up to her cheek, her eyes unfocussed, her chin tipped downward. "Don't worry, Sparky. I've got you safe and sound."

Rory spoke in a low voice, her words soft and soothing. "It's all been crazy, but we'll get through it somehow."

There was no response from the box or its contents. She kissed the lid gently. "Don't shock me, okay?" Rory slipped the box into her pocket and continued to wander around her room.

* * *

Robert Hastings burst through the main hatch of the NARI living quarters. Everyone in the Common Area jumped at the sudden entrance. "Where is Hunter Logan?" Robert snarled the question, as if daring anyone to withhold the answer from him.

Jenson Reed was the only one willing to face him. He pulled his wrestler's frame erect and flexed his arms before letting them drop to his sides. He didn't want to threaten Robert, only remind him of the younger man's physicality. "I haven't seen him. Maybe he's in his quarters." Robert stormed across the Common Area and disappeared into the residence corridor. Jenson shook his head. "Hunter is going to thank me for that."

"Hunter!" Robert didn't wait for the chime to bring one of the Logans to their door. He pounded on the portal's alloy casing, his assault resonating the thin material.

The door slid open, and Hunter appeared. He didn't invite Robert in. "What's up, Robert?"

"Why in hell are we confined to the base?"

A look of confusion crossed Hunter's face. "Confined? What are you talking about?"

"I just tried to book a flight to Earth and was turned away at the passenger terminal. Something about the base director issuing orders to prevent us from leaving Copernicus."

"Why were you booking passage to Earth?"

"I was going to send you my resignation once I got on the ship, but I am still here. I can't even quit this damn team."

* * *

Jenson Reed sat at a small work area in his residence. His desktop holochamber displayed a complex schematic of the security and communications systems in the NARI living quarters. His door was wide open.

Hunter and Adrianna appeared at the threshold. "You left your door open," Adrianna said cheerfully.

"Oh. Hi, Adrianna. Hunter. I'm always doing that."

"May we come in?"

"Sure. Can I offer you something to drink?"

"No, thanks. We don't have time. We're going over to administration to talk to Director Marshall about the data theft and being confined to the base. I thought we'd get your report before we left." Adrianna and Hunter pulled up a couple of chairs and sat down next the young engineer. He swiveled in his chair, so they could see the holodisplay.

"I wish I had some definitive news for you," he began. "Whoever accessed Millie managed to get into your residence and leave without a trace. No video, no data trails, nothing."

Adrianna was dumbfounded. "How is that possible?"

"Maybe they cracked Millie's wireless encryption."

"Millie's wireless is turned off. She's a standalone."

"Very retro, Hunter. How about the earset link?"

"Yes, I use that. But it's got five hundred and twelve bit encryption, and it changes every time my earset links with her."

"Did someone get to your earset?"

"It's been with Millie."

Jenson scratched his head. "That's a good one. I don't know how they did it. How secure is the encryption?"

"The best. Once the data left Millie, it locked itself down. No one can copy it or read it without a key."

Jenson nodded. "Very good."

Adrianna touched his sleeve. "Thanks for trying."

"No problem."

"There's one more favor we'd like to ask."

Jenson gave Adrianna a quizzical look. "Anything."

"Sprite has to go over to the spaceport this afternoon for her environment suit certification. Would you mind going with her? We're getting worried about security and don't want her walking around the base by herself."

The young man smiled broadly. "I'd be happy to! Has she been preparing for it?"

"You know Sprite. She's read everything from cover to cover."

Jenson smiled. "Have her stop by when she's ready to go."

* * *

The original Copernicus Base had been built around two large domes with radiating passageways, which led to a number of smaller domes. One was the Old Garden, and the other was the Old Commons. Both domes were now dwarfed by the new Commons, which hosted a much larger garden and green area. The domes were still in use, repurposed to meet the needs of the huge base. They retained their names as historical reminders.

The base director's office was located in the administration dome, near the Old Garden. Hunter and Adrianna sat in director Winston Marshall's office. He feigned warmth as he anticipated the Logan's displeasure.

"Why are we being confined to the base?" Adrianna was direct and to the point.

"And why weren't we notified?" Hunter took up the second salvo. "One of my people was turned away at the passenger terminal when he tried to book a flight to Earth. That was the first we heard of it."

"I'm sorry that happened. We received our instructions this morning, and we failed to loop you in." Marshall wasn't sorry.

"That doesn't tell me why we're being restricted to the base." Adrianna was going to get an answer to her question.

"Well, it's a bit complicated, Ms. Logan."

"Try me. And it's Doctor Logan, Director Marshall."

"Dr. Logan. There are some legal issues that have arisen because of your accident on Selene Station."

"It wasn't an accident. It was sabotage."

Marshall steepled his fingers. "So you say. Nevertheless, I am afraid your claim doesn't fit the evidence, or should I say, lack of evidence."

Hunter and Adrianna were stunned. "What are you talking about?" Hunter gasped.

"You claim the explosion was caused by a saboteur. There is no evidence of a bomb or a bomber."

"That's insane!" Hunter was on his feet. "All the evidence is a big cloud of dust flying toward the sun! We saved the Moon!"

Director Marshall spoke commandingly. "Sit down, Dr. Logan, or I'll have you put in shackles, and we'll continue this conversation in a holding room." Hunter sat back down, still seething. "What we do know is that you had some extremely dangerous materials up there and a very complex device…" The director scrolled through several pages in his holodisplay. "…a complex device you call a containment unit. We think this unit failed catastrophically, and you are trying to avoid responsibility by claiming an act of sabotage."

"The containment unit would not have exploded by itself."

"We doubt that, Dr. Logan. We are conducting a full investigation, and we are leaning toward the conclusion that you are responsible for the lives that were lost and for a substantial loss of Meridian Corporation property."

Hunter sagged. "This can't be happening."

"Oh, it's happening all right. I suggest you get your affairs in order, doctors. You're going to clock some significant jail time before this is over."

Hunter and Adrianna rose from their chairs simultaneously. "Can we go?"

Marshall gave them a sneer. "I'm assigning a security detail to your team. They will accompany you back to your residence. They will remain posted at your main entrance hatch. No one is to go anywhere without one of my guards. Is that clear?"

Adrianna was defiant. "We will not be prisoners."

"Yes, you will, Dr. Logan. You will."

✳ ✳ ✳

Jenson was happy to see Sprite appear at his door. "Ready for your environment suit certification?"

"I can't wait!" Sprite was so excited, she could hardly stand still.

"You're going to love it. I worked for several months on a space station. I spent many hours performing EVAs. There's nothing like it." Secretly, Jenson hoped he could go out on the lunar surface with Sprite's class.

Within moments, they were on their way to the Copernicus spaceport. Sprite liked Jenson. He had been with NARI for several years and had worked with the sophisticated comp systems that aided the scientists in their research. She felt a kinship with the young man because of their common interest. "What got you interested in comps, Jenson?"

Reed didn't answer right away. He nodded at a passing stranger and received a disapproving stare. "My grandfather worked in comp science, and so did my father. Both of my uncles, too. They knew before I was born that I'd be a comp specialist. It runs in the family."

"My uncle is good with comps, too." Sprite looked away from a woman who made a face at her.

"I didn't have a choice." Jenson had a faraway look in his eyes.

"But you like it?"

"I do, but I really wanted to be a wrestling coach or a physical education teacher. I've always enjoyed athletics."

"So why didn't you do that?"

"Being in a family is a lot like wading in a river. The current is strong, and it's hard to resist. My family knew what they wanted me to be, and that's who I am." Jenson retreated into his own thoughts as they continued toward the spaceport.

Most of the morning was spent learning about the standard environment suits. Sprite became familiar with all the parts and how they worked. Safety procedures were drilled into everyone after lunch. By mid afternoon, it was time to suit up and head out onto the lunar surface. Sprite's excitement grew as she donned her suit. Jenson worked with her as she wriggled into the torso and then worked her fingers into the gloves. He paid special attention to every seal, Sprite reciting the checklist at each step.

"You've been preparing for this, haven't you?"

"I read all the manuals last week." Sprite stood still has Jenson lowered the helmet over her head. She gave him a radiant smile as the last seal was checked. She punched the buttons on her arm control, activating the breathing system.

Jenson watched the expression on her face. "Feels good?"

"Feels great!" Her voice was muffled by the helmet.

The instructor made her rounds, checking each student's suit. Sprite was ready to go. "Want to join us?" The teacher had been watching Jenson. "It's always nice to have another experienced person out there."

Jenson didn't need a second invitation. While the instructor continued her inspections, he disappeared into the suit storage area and returned a few moments later with a suit. With cool efficiency born of many EVAs, Jenson donned the environment suit. One of the attendants got him sealed in and gloved.

"Now we're going to enter the airlock, everyone." The instructor opened the massive inner hatch. "We'll take the pressure down to about five pounds, and we'll do a final check of your suits. Once that's done, we'll bleed off the rest of the atmosphere and open the outer hatch." There were ten students in the group. Everyone stepped into the giant airlock, which was used to bring surface vehicles inside the base. There was more than enough room for everyone. Once outside, the instructor had everyone pair up with a buddy and practice walking around on the lunar surface. Soon, everyone was hopping and bounding across the dusty surface in the low lunar gravity. The comm channel was filled with giggles and laughter as the neophytes got their legs.

Jenson and the instructor were standing near a work platform designed to give the students a taste of working with tools, when an alarm began to chime in everyone's helmet. The two quickly scanned the group of students. Sprite's helmet had a blinking red light. She had fallen to her knees. Jenson rushed toward her, timing his hops to maximize his speed while preventing an overshoot. Within seconds, he was kneeling next to Sprite.

"Can't breathe!" She was gasping for air.

6

Jenson tried to ignore Sprite's cries for help. He had to be calm if he was going to save her. He checked her backpack and saw the problem. A small section near her power supply was blackened and fused. He disconnected her air line quickly and mated it with an auxiliary coupling on his suit. Sprite relaxed almost immediately, inhaling the fresh atmosphere provided by Jenson's suit.

The instructor knelt down next to Jenson. "What happened?"

"Looks like her power supply burned out." He pointed to the hose that connected their two suits together. "I've got her piggy-backed on my breather."

Jenson and the instructor wrapped their arms around Sprite and lifted her to her feet. Moments later, they were in one of the smaller airlocks. Jenson helped her out of the suit and sat with her as she regained her composure. "That's a heck of a way to learn how to use a suit."

"My breather burned out?" Sprite was pale and shaky.

"It looks that way." Jenson picked up the breather unit. There was a small tear in the cloth that surrounded the apparatus. He pulled away the thermal cover. The battery compartment was swollen and fused to the rest of the unit. In an oxygen-rich atmosphere, the breather would have broken into flames. A jagged hole was directly under the tear. Something had punctured the power supply. Jenson gave her a concerned look. "Did you fall on something out there?"

Sprite thought for a moment. "No. Somebody bumped into me, though. It was right before my breather stopped working."

Jenson didn't want her to know what he suspected. A casual bump could not have caused the damage. He smiled at his young friend. "You know what? I think the bump must have damaged the suit."

* * *

Amos Cross's office appeared to float in the middle of a complex construction zone. Titanium girders disappeared into vanishing points in all directions. The office seemed to be hundreds of meters above the surface. The floor was transparent, offering a dizzying view of the spaces far below. Bundles of cables and partially assembled machines embellished the walls. Virtual workers scurried back and forth.

Cross was on his comlink, taking a report from one of his subordinates. He slapped his hands together. "Excellent! This is going to work out very nicely for us. I want construction to begin as soon as possible." Cross paused as his minion expressed some doubt. "I don't care what they say! Earn your pay for once and get that factory built!"

The conversation was over. The great man had expressed his dominance and was ready to move on. He thought of Susanna Frost. Immediately, she acknowledged his call. "Come." Within a moment, his assistant entered.

Cross palmed a virtual wrench and dropped it. It fell through the floor and then appeared to drop for hundreds of feet beneath it. Susanna felt like she was immersed in a huge video game, infinitely high, broad, and deep. Her stomach churned. She silently begged her body not to throw up. Amos was amused. "Tell me about the NARI situation."

"Maya Lewis of the Citizen's League is at Copernicus Base. She was seen talking to one of the scientists in the Base Commons a few minutes ago."

"I wonder what she's up to?"

"We're not sure…" Amos gave her a disapproving look. "…yet. There's been an up-tick in opposition to NARI's presence at the base. We think she's behind it."

Amos pouted for a moment. "Keep watching her. Tell me more about the scientist."

"He was Robert Hastings. His wife and son died on Selene Station. He was having an affair with another member of the team. He had a bad argument with his wife just before she died."

"I don't like it. He could be a problem. We're going to have to accelerate our plans to remove the NARI team from Copernicus. Is *The Avion* ready?"

"She's in lunar orbit, ready to depart when you give the word."

"Contact Meridian 6 and tell them the timeline has been moved up. It won't be long now."

"Yes, sir"

"And Susanna, I think you should work on your hair. It takes a lot of personal grooming to make it look good in lunar gravity."

"Certainly, sir."

The great man spun on his heels and launched into another conversation.

* * *

Sprite's mishap caused a stir among the scientists. Even Alexis asked if she was all right. Once Adrianna and Hunter were satisfied she had no lasting effects, they insisted that Sprite lie down to recuperate. "I am pretty tired." Her adrenaline rush was wearing off. She padded to her room and closed the door behind her.

Jenson lingered in the Logans' common area. Hunter slapped the young man on the back. "You saved her life." Hunter shuttered at the thought of losing his daughter. "Thank you seems so inadequate."

"I'm glad I was there, but there's more to the story." The three sat back down. "Someone punctured the thermal cover and damaged her breather." Jenson knew he was adding to the Logans' stress. "Somebody wanted to kill her."

"She's just a kid," Adrianna blanched. "Why would anyone do that?"

"It's because of our work." Hunter wore a heavy face, drawn by the weight of the past few days.

"It's those fanatics who set the bombs." Jenson squeezed Hunter's arm. "They're crazy. They don't consider the consequences of their actions." The three fell silent, and then Jenson left, apologizing for being the bearer of bad news.

* * *

A short time later, Hunter and Adrianna were discussing how they might protect their daughter, when their door chimed. It was Tyson and Jo. They stood meekly outside the door. Hunter, unsure of what to expect, tried to divine their intentions. Their faces were drawn, and they avoided eye contact. Hunter was the first to speak.

"Hey, Ty. Jo. How are you doing?" Adrianna came to the door and stood by her husband. She looked gently at their friends. They were clinging to each other, emotionally wasted.

Ty spoke softly. "Sorry about this morning. I shouldn't have gone off like that."

Jo chimed in. "Me, too. We didn't mean it."

Hunter stepped toward his friends. "It's okay. We've had a terrible time. Our emotions are worn thin."

Adrianna put an arm around Ty. "Come in and sit down."

Hunter and Adrianna waited patiently for their friends to speak. Ty held Jo's hand. He looked like he had rehearsed what he wanted to say, only to scrap it at the last minute. Finally, he took a deep breath. "We wish we could turn back time. I was mad at everyone. This is so wrong."

Jo's body was taut, like a rope drawn tight across a mountain gorge. "It's hard when you have such high hopes and good intentions. When everything crashes down, it's easy to keep falling."

Hunter nodded. "It is." There was a pregnancy in the moment. They felt the kinship of brokenness. Hunter waited to make sure Jo and Ty had said their peace. "Could we change the subject? There are some things we need to talk about."

Jo and Ty nodded with relief, looking at their friends for the first time. Hunter told them about the theft of data from Millie.

Ty shook his head in disbelief. "Someone on the team is dirty."

"It gets worse." Adrianna gazed into the palms of her hands. "I've been turning things over in my mind. Larson Daniels and his camerawoman were never in the laboratory unattended. Hunter and I were with them the whole time. They couldn't have set the bomb without our knowledge."

Jo's anger returned, no longer directed at her friends, but toward the unknown people who had killed their colleagues. "Someone on the team did it!"

Ty was crestfallen. "Who?"

Adrianna drew a breath. She was exhausted. "I don't know. The only people with access to the lab were members of our team."

Hunter's eyes blazed. "Adrianna and I met with Director Marshall, and he claims there is no evidence of sabotage. Meridian wants to hold us liable for the deaths and the loss of Selene Station."

Ty made a fist with his left hand and twisted it in his right like a mortar and pestle. "So that's why we have the guards outside our front door. This doesn't make any sense."

Adrianna agreed. "There's one more thing. Jenson is convinced the power supply on Sprite's environment suit was damaged on purpose. Someone is trying to get to us through her." She had Ty and Jo's full attention. "This is just the beginning. It's going to get worse before it gets better. We need to think about the children. We need a plan to ensure their safety."

* * *

Sprite lay on her bed, unable to sleep. She was exhausted, but her mind was in high gear. She took Wiley from her bedside stand and put on her earset. She gazed at the shapes that floated in the holodisplay and spent an hour talking with the AI about his impressions of the digital world.

"I don't know how to explain it to you, Sprite."

Sprite ran her fingers through her hair. "That's okay. When was the last time someone asked you to talk about your experiences?"

"No one has ever done that."

"So, it's going to take some getting used to. You've got to learn how to express your thoughts and describe what you see."

"I am good at learning, Sprite. Over time, I am sure I will master the art of self-expression."

Sprite giggled quietly. "I'm sure you will, Wiley." She got up to make sure her door was closed tightly. Then she plopped herself into the soft chair next to her desk. "Let's go on a trip."

"Where to, Ms. Logan?"

"Why so formal all of a sudden?"

"I thought it was funny."

Sprite smiled. "Let's go into Meridian Corporation's secure network."

"That's a restricted area."

"Yes, but you remember what Uncle Prescott taught you about hacking security systems, don't you?"

"I do. I was merely informing you that we aren't supposed to pry into other people's business."

"Don't worry. We're just going to look around."

Sprite watched as Wiley probed Meridian Corporation's massive network. She saw the data traffic flowing from each of the fourteen lunar bases. Wiley focused on Jackson Base, the digital hub of the network. He descended through layers of security, through subnets and virtual nodes.

Finally, they were peering into the innermost recesses of the network. A list of servers appeared in the holodisplay. Sprite scanned the information. One was named "Shadow Project."

"Let's look in that one," she said. Wiley wove his way through the security protocols, and soon an immense folio of technical schematics filled Sprite's field of view. "What is this?"

"They are plans for a new lab. Meridian has completed the dome and installed the power and environment systems."

Sprite paged through the complicated drawings. "Let's move on." Wiley pulled back to the list of servers. "Stop!" Sprite told Wiley to enter one of Meridian's communications servers. A subnet was dedicated to something called the MBH system. "What's that, Wiley?"

"It's their micro-black-hole system. It uses discontinuities in space/time to permit instantaneous communications over long distances."

"Let's see what's going on."

Wiley moved from node to node, scanning the files and data packets. Finally, he paused in an area of the network where there was an abundance of activity. "This looks like a communications feed." Sprite sat up excitedly. "Would you like me to access the channel?"

"Yes, Wiley."

The AI threaded himself into the server. A moment later, Sprite could see a woman's face. She was dressed meticulously. Her face was a mask of formality and logic, hiding all emotion and humanity. The woman's hair was freshly groomed; every strand lay perfectly in its place.

"We expect the scientists to depart within a few days," she was saying. "It will take one hundred twenty-seven days to get to Meridian 6. We will need the settlement ready when they arrive."

Sprite's ears perked up at the mention of scientists. This woman was talking about people like her father and mother. "Who's she talking to, Wiley?"

"The transmission is being processed by a micro-black-hole transceiver. I am only able to monitor the outgoing data stream."

The woman's eyes were cold. She appeared to be looking right at Sprite. It was unsettling. "Are you sure she can't see me?"

"The system is not aware of our presence, Sprite."

"Good."

The woman spoke again. "I know it's a big job. We need both laboratory bays outfitted for state-of-the-art nano-research. We had retrofitted Selene Station for their work, but there was an explosion that took out the lab. We need to get these people out of sight, so they can continue their work."

Sprite sat up straight. The woman was talking about them! What was Meridian 6, and why would it take four months to get there?

Wiley's voice jarred her out of her reverie. "We are about to be discovered, Sprite."

"Terminate!" she commanded sharply. Wiley backed out of the Meridian network, his home screen appearing in Sprite's holodisplay.

"We are no longer in the network."

Sprite was rattled. "Wipe everything related to our exploration from you memory!"

"Done."

Sprite stared into the empty holodisplay, the image of the serious woman etched into her memory. Sprite's hands were shaking. She wondered if it was a case of residual nerves from her training accident, but she knew it was more than that. Too many things were happening at once. Powerful forces were searching for her. She sensed danger. She sucked in a breath. The problem with her environment suit was just an accident, wasn't it?

* * *

Amos Cross stripped off his clothing and stepped into the decontamination chamber that led to his private quarters. Once showered and dried, he donned a thin robe and entered his residence. Few people knew about his private fear. Cross didn't like to sleep. He hated the vulnerability that came with unconsciousness. He dreaded the possibility of someone touching his body without his permission.

Years before, in a childhood long-forgotten, if not assiduously avoided, a young Amos Cross had known too much touching. His mother and father used him for pleasures no child should ever experience. They were his masters, the authors of all his values. They defined his world and demonstrated a perverted sense of right and wrong. Young Amos was innocent and impressionable. He was robbed of any sense of normalcy.

One night, after a long siege of his parents' wild ecstasy, Amos decided he had had enough. His mother had forgotten to fasten the buckle on one of his restraints. He freed himself and ran naked from the house, vowing never to be touched or abused again. He would be a controller. He would be the master of his world. He would put women in their place and never be hurt again.

Cross ate his meal in silence. He sat staring at Earth's new space elevator for most of the evening, cursing the scientists and engineers who were responsible for this latest marvel. Cross could not ignore this economic threat. He watched as the elevator pod unlatched from the geosynchronous platform and began its descent. An idea popped into his mind. Perhaps he could use the elevators to his advantage.

Much later, unable to avoid sleeping any longer, he removed his robe and passed through another decontamination chamber that led to his bedroom. With his body disinfected a second time, Amos prepared for sleep. He was the only living thing in the room. Nothing could touch him there.

* * *

Sprite and Hunter Logan perched intently on the edges of their chairs. An ancient chess set sat on the table between them. Hunter was in command of the board, having taken one of Sprite's pawns with his knight. Sprite frowned and scrunched up her face. Her blue eyes were filled with intensity. She stared so keenly at the pieces, Hunter could swear she was trying to levitate them off the board. "What's your move, kiddo?" He perched his head in the palms of his hands; his eyes were fixed intently on his daughter.

Sprite didn't answer at first. Then, without taking her eyes away from the pieces, she replied, "I think I'm going to lose. I can see seven or eight different moves, but I don't know which one to take."

Hunter smiled. "That's why I love this game. Here's what you do." Hunter pointed to one of Sprite's pawns. "If you were to advance that pawn and put my knight in danger, what do you think I would do?"

"You'd move your knight."

"Yes, but by tempting you with that easy kill, I have forced you to move your pawn. If you aren't paying attention and simply move to threaten my knight..." Hunter pointed to his bishop sitting halfway across the board. "I will swoop in with this bishop and take your queen."

"Wow, Dad." Sprite nodded with appreciation. "Did you think of that before you took my pawn?"

"I did. A good chess player thinks ahead. Each move is decided by anticipating her opponent's reaction. A move she makes early in the game can wind up being the most important move of all."

"How do you learn to do that?" She finally looked up and gave her father an open, inquisitive look.

"Lots of practice with attention to detail, my girl." Hunter's face lit up with a smile. "You must always keep the endgame in mind. Work the steps backward and forward until they meet."

"And if things don't go the way you want them to go?" Even at her young age, Sprite was a realist.

"Then adapt. Adjust your moves while keeping your eye on..."

"...the endgame." Sprite gave her father a nod. "Dad? Have you ever heard of a place called Meridian 6?"

"Can't say that I have. It sounds like one of Meridian Corporation's outposts. They're not too creative when it comes to naming things. Why don't you look it up?"

"I did, but the name doesn't exist."

"Where did you hear it?"

Sprite blushed. "Promise you won't get mad at me."

"What did you do, Miss Logan?"

"Wiley and I took a trip inside the Meridian network. We overheard a conversation about Meridian 6." Hunter was shaking his head sternly. "They mentioned us."

Hunter became still. All thoughts of disciplining his daughter were gone. "Us? You mean our family?"

"All of us. NARI. They talked about the scientists who lost their lab on Selene Station. They talked about this "Meridian 6" like they were fixing it up, so we could go there, and you could finish your work on the nanomachines. Wherever it is, it takes four months to get there, and the woman said we were leaving within a few days."

Hunter pushed back in his chair. "Did anyone discover you?"

"No way. Wiley was very careful. He sensed the network checking for intruders, and we disconnected before they knew anything about us."

"Good. Can we finish this game later?" Sprite nodded. "There's a game of a different sort I've got to attend to."

* * *

Samina entered her private quarters and locked the door. She checked the room to make sure nothing was out of place. Professional paranoia was her ally. Robert had been a mistake. She shouldn't have let down her guard. She had betrayed her training.

Samina went to her closet, removed a small purple flight bag, and placed it on her bed. Inside was an electronic device. She took a memory module out of her pants pocket and slid it into the bag. She put it over her shoulder and scanned the room one last time. Moments later, Samina was in the Common Area. No one was there. She opened the main hatch, and a guard blocked her way. "I need to go over to Base Administration," she told him. The security officer spoke briefly with a second guard. He gestured toward Samina, and the man nodded. Samina didn't wait. She pushed past them and headed down the corridor, the second guard hurrying to keep up with her. Samina's beauty oscillated beneath her jumpsuit as she moved effortlessly through the passageway. The guard didn't seem to notice.

Samina's journey transected some of the busiest corridors on Copernicus Base. Samina had taken note of this on previous trips across the complex. The passage rapidly filled with people. Samina approached the most congested node in the corridor system and adjusted her pace. The guard responded, keeping a close but constant distance behind her. Two men were wheeling a large case down the hallway to her left. There was an opening in the press of humanity, and the men had picked up speed to thrust their cargo through the intersection. Samina quickened her step and looked to her right, away from the approaching case. The guard's attention was drawn to see what she was looking at. Samina slipped ahead of the men and their lading with a burst of speed. The large case slammed into the guard, spinning him around like a top. By the time he regained his bearings, Samina was gone.

7

Maya Lewis touched her earbud. The voice of one of her agents whispered through the device. "Your visitor has arrived."

A soft chime announced her guest. Maya opened the door and ushered the stranger into her room. They shared the usual pleasantries: the offered drink, the remarks about the décor, the gesture toward the appropriate chair. Then, the two sat down across from each other. A clear glass table stood between them.

"Let's get to business." Maya uncrossed her legs. "It's my understanding that you're going to Meridian 6."

The visitor was surprised. "That's right. How do you know that?"

"Let's just say my employer has many sources."

"Impressive. It's not easy to know Meridian Corporation's plans ahead of time."

"Many people work for Meridian. Some have loyalties that go beyond corporate values and policies." Maya gave her guest a knowing smile. "I also know that you have a unique skill set that can serve my organization's purposes."

The stranger's brow furrowed. "My resume is public information, if that's what you mean."

"No. I am referring to your ability to kill people and destroy things."

"I'm not sure what you mean."

Maya leaned forward toward her guest. Her eyes were like lasers, cutting their way into her visitor. "Don't be coy with me. I know everything about you. And I need your services."

"If I did have these talents, what would you want me to do?"

"I want you to go about your business. Prepare for your journey to Meridian 6. Carry on your duties. When the time comes, I will contact you with specific instructions. You will do what I tell you, and people will die. You will escape and be paid." The stranger nodded without saying a word.

"I will triple your standard fee."

"Triple?"

"This mission is very important to my organization. I am told you are one of the best at this sort of thing, and we want this done right. Can you do that?"

"Of course."

"Then we have a deal." Maya slid a plastic card across the glass tabletop toward her new employee. "This contains the account number for the first half of your fee. You'll get the rest when the deed is done."

* * *

Susanna Frost walked confidently down the corridor and past a security guard, twisting the access ring on her finger. The gold band was a sign that she was part of Amos Cross's trusted circle. The ring emitted a signal that gave her access to the offices and corridors of Meridian Corporation's inner sanctum. She slowed as she approached a massive door at the end of the corridor, her confidence draining as she drew closer to her destination. She placed her ring-hand on the door and waited for Amos Cross to invite her into his office. After several moments, the massive door opened silently. Susanna crossed the threshold and entered.

The space was outfitted like a futuristic garden. Odd unidentifiable plants, obviously the work of some deranged botanical artist, were set at random intervals along one wall. The ceiling resembled the surface of a tranquil pond, complete with fish as strange as the plant life. In the center of the room, a waterfall emanated from the floor and "fell" upward toward the ceiling. Amos Cross was gazing at an empty fish tank, talking to some nameless underling on his comlink. Cross muted his voice channel and turned his attention to Frost. "Yes?"

"Sir, our representative on the NARI team has extracted the data from Dr. Logan's card comp."

"Good. Were there any complications?"

"No, sir. Our contact was very careful. However, we are having a problem with the data." Cross's eyes narrowed. Susanna steeled herself for his disappointment. "The encryption is extremely robust. We've never seen anything like it."

"Dr. Thrune needs that data, Ms. Frost."

The mention of Dr. Maxwell Thrune's name sent a shiver up Susanna's spine. Thrune was responsible for the "Shadow Project," a classified venture that had something to do with Hunter Logan's nanomachines.

"What's the problem?" Cross waited. Clearly, Susanna was distracted. "Ms. Frost!"

"Yes, sir?"

"What's the problem with the data?"

Susanna held up a small data module. "Our spy could upload it from Dr. Hunter's card comp, but any attempt to move it from this data module has failed. There's some sort of smart encryption that corrupts the data when we try to copy it. We had to bring the module here, in the hope one of our specialists will have better luck with it."

"I want that data." Cross's face took on a look of dissatisfaction. "The Shadow Project is my top priority. If we can't get the nanomachines from NARI, Dr. Thrune will need the contents of that data module to achieve our goal." Susanna withered. She hated the thought of failure. "I am expecting you to succeed in this matter, Ms. Frost. Impress upon our people that failure to unlock that data will come at a very high price. A very high, *personal* price."

Cross ran his fingers through the odd, inverted waterfall. "It's time, Susanna. I want you to have a face-to-face meeting with Hunter and Adrianna Logan. Take one of the corporate transports and go to Copernicus Base. Sell them on Meridian 6. I want you to close the deal and get them on their way as soon as possible."

"How much pressure should I apply?"

"As much as it takes. Bend them to our will. I want them headed for The Asteroid Belt. The last thing we need is the Citizen's League sewing doubts in their minds."

"Yes, sir."

Cross turned his gaze back to the fish tank and continued his conversation with the minion on the other end of his comlink.

* * *

The next morning, Base Director Winston Marshall came to the NARI living quarters unannounced. He stood in the Common Area with six guards. Hunter and Adrianna were sitting at a side table near the viewport. Tyson sat on one of the couches. Kell was playing a game on his card comp. Jenson Reed, who had been pedaling one of the exercise bikes, leaned against the wall behind him. Robert Hastings sat at the table in the dining area with Alexis.

Jo Smith entered the room from the residence corridor. "I can't find Samina anywhere." She looked tired and confused.

Winston scanned the NARI team with a cold, iron-like expression on his face. "I told you she was gone. She left here yesterday, saying she wanted to go over to Base Administration. She shook my guard and disappeared."

Tyson eyed one of the guards who had an ugly bruise on his face. "What did she do, beat you up?"

The guard blushed, but remained silent. Marshall answered for him. "No. He accompanied her down Corridor B, toward the Old Garden, and got hit with a cargo case. By the time he gathered his wits, she was gone."

Hunter wanted the facts. "Did she purposely evade him?" Winston turned to the guard. He shook his head without making eye contact. "So Samina might have just kept walking, and they got separated." Hunter gestured toward the entrance hatchway. "She might walk through that door at any moment."

"My security team has swept the entire base. There's no sign of her. She never went to the Administration Dome."

Adrianna was concerned. "Do you think she was attacked?"

"It's possible, but we don't think so. We've examined the surveillance video from the corridor. It's clear she knew where every camera was located. We saw her continue down the corridor in a tight knot of people and then completely disappear." Marshall's eyes kept scanning each person in front of him. "Did she have any reason to leave the team?"

"No." Jo was offended by the question. "We would trust her with our lives." Nevertheless, her inner thoughts betrayed her outer confidence. Could Samina be the traitor?

Robert Hastings shook his head slowly. "Samina was attracted to me." He paused. "She was in love with me. We met the other day in the Delta V, and I ended it. I told her that we couldn't be anything more than colleagues. She wasn't keen on the idea. She told me she couldn't work with me anymore. That's probably why she left."

No one challenged Robert's version of the events, but they knew there was more to it. Marshall's eyes narrowed. "Was that the day you were attacked?"

"That's right."

"Well, that might explain it, but we're going to keep looking. We'll find her." Marshall took a deep breath and looked out the viewport. He obviously had something else to say.

"Susanna Frost, from Meridian Headquarters, is waiting in my office." He gestured toward Hunter and Adrianna. "I'm supposed to bring you over there to meet with her."

Adrianna frowned. "What about the rest of the team?"

"Just the two of you, doctor." He said 'doctor' like he was spitting the formality in her face.

"That isn't acceptable." Hunter took a step toward Marshall. The guards tensed. "We all go together. Every last one of us. Take it or leave it."

Marshall hesitated, then nodded his head. "All right. Let's go."

The security officers split into two teams, bracketing them as they exited the living quarters. Their journey through the corridors of Copernicus Base was like a perp walk. People lined the route, shouting invectives at them: "Killers!" "Murderers!" "Go home to Earth!" It seemed orchestrated by some unseen hand.

* * *

The NARI team and their families were ushered into a large conference room in the Copernicus Base Administration dome. The security guards closed the doors behind them, leaving them alone. The group splintered into twos and threes, talking quietly about what was happening. Rory North sat in a trance at the great table. She palmed a small container in her hand, then raised it to her face and spoke softly to it. She put it into her pocket when Kell and Sprite joined her.

Susanna Frost swept into the room with confidence, after what seemed an interminable length of time. She wore a sleek carmine suit that accentuated the curves of her body. Her hair was long and elegant. Jo wondered how a woman could keep her hair so perfectly groomed in the low lunar gravity. Her scent filled the space as she shook their hands. As the group began to coalesce around the table, Sprite caught a glimpse of the woman. Her heart skipped a beat. She reached out and pulled at her father's sleeve. He turned, and she gestured for him to come close. "That's the woman I saw in the message," she whispered. Hunter nodded to his daughter and mouthed a silent "thank you."

Susanna waited for the group to sit down. "My name is Susanna Frost. I am Amos Cross's executive assistant at Meridian Corporation." She expected a reaction to her impressive credentials, but there was none. "We have a larger group than I anticipated. I asked for the Logans to meet with me, not all of you."

Adrianna met her gaze. "We're in this together, Ms. Frost. You deal with all of us or none of us."

"That is quite all right. I'm happy you're here." Her kindness seemed authentic. She paused, offering her smile to each of them in turn. As she nodded toward Sprite and Kell, Jo noticed a subtle change in her expression. The woman was not happy with their presence. She nodded to a security guard who was standing by the door. He took a step forward and waited for her instructions. "I'd like the children to wait outside." The guard began to walk toward Sprite and her two friends.

Hunter shook his head emphatically. "They're staying." Susanna scowled as he spoke. "Rory North lost her mother at Selene Station. She's earned a right to be present. All of them have a right to be here."

Susanna nodded slowly. The trace of an enigmatic smile was on her face. "Very well." She stepped toward the head of the table. "Mr. Cross is interested in your team."

"We aren't a team anymore." Tyson didn't like Susanna. "We lost some good people, and our Institute is going to be dissolved."

"Where are my manners?" Susanna seemed overly apologetic. "Please accept Mr. Cross's deepest sympathies over the loss of your colleagues. All of us have been touched by it." Susanna let her words sink in. It was important to establish rapport with the scientists.

Susanna spread her hands, her long, thin fingers reaching for the tabletop, their tips just kissing the surface. "Let me get to the point of our meeting. Mr. Cross would like you to continue your work. He is prepared to secure your services and keep your team intact."

Hunter was intrigued. "Why?"

"Mr. Cross believes in what you are doing. He's a businessman and understands research and development. He is sympathetic to the bumps that occur on the road to innovation. He would like you to reestablish your work with the phase-two nanomachines."

"The deaths of our colleagues weren't 'bumps.'" Tyson snarled.

Adrianna gave Ty a hard glance and then spoke diplomatically. "It's nice of Mr. Cross to believe in our work, but our lab was destroyed. Some of our best people have died, and we're not inclined to pursue the research any longer. Even if we did, we would have to start from scratch."

"I'm sure you're all tired." Susanna sat down and folded her hands. She became thoughtful. "I can remember when my mother died." Susanna paused. Her gaze settled on Rory, then focused on a faraway place. "It took a lot out of me. For several weeks, I couldn't think straight. The joy drained out of my life." She scanned their faces and sensed their pain. "Believe me, I understand. However, the joy returns. You will want to continue this work in honor of your friends."

Robert Hastings had tears in his eyes. Jo Smith wasn't impressed. "Nice try, but we've talked about this and made a decision. We underestimated the danger related to the phase-two research. We aren't going down that road again."

"Hear my offer." If Susanna was concerned about the team's inflexibility, she didn't show it. "You can't make a good decision until you have all the facts. Let me put Mr. Cross's proposal on the table. Then you can decide what you want to do."

"It won't do you any good, honey." Jo's voice was sickly sweet. Her face was hard as flint. Her eyes were stone cold. "But you've probably rehearsed this part, so have at it."

Hunter Logan smiled at Susanna. "Is this where you tell us about Meridian 6?"

The color drained from Susanna's face. "How?" She looked down at the conference table and collected herself. Sprite smiled at her father. Susanna looked back up at Hunter, her back straightening, her smile broader than before. "I don't know how you got that information, but it doesn't matter."

Susanna touched the surface of the table, and a holographic image of a small gray planet appeared. "This is Ceres. It's a dwarf planet located in The Asteroid Belt, approximately 2.8 astronomical units from the sun. We think it's a good place for you to continue your work. It's out of the way. Given the current climate, it's better for you to keep a low profile." She tapped the table again. The image grew larger, revealing a cluster of domes on the rocky surface. "Meridian 6 is a research settlement. We built it many years ago for a project that never panned out. We abandoned the facility. Up until a few months ago, it was occupied by thieves. They used it as their hideout. We regained control of Meridian 6 and have restored it to its original condition. By the time your team arrives, you'll have everything you need to live comfortably and reestablish your work."

"Sounds like a prison." Tyson Edwards' arms were folded tightly to his chest. "Okay, you've got a place for us to work where humanity won't try to blow us up again. However, that doesn't address the fundamental issue."

"It's a good deal." Susanna spread her hands.

"We don't care about deals." All eyes were on Robert Hastings. "We're done. We're not doing this anymore."

Susanna's smile disappeared. "I can't persuade you?"

Hunter leaned forward. "He's telling you that our hearts aren't in it. We aren't interested."

Susanna frowned and then nodded to herself. "You are aware of the charges that have been brought against you?"

"We are."

"Meridian Corporation is prepared to drop its claim for the loss of Selene Station if you cooperate. Believe me. Financially, we could crush all of you."

"We'll take our chances." Ty did his best to sound confident.

Susanna didn't move. "I understand the authorities are questioning whether the explosion on Selene was an act of terrorism or was simply due to the poor design of your containment unit."

"That's absurd!" Hunter started to rise to his feet, but Adrianna put her hand on his shoulder.

"Are you prepared to spend the rest of your lives as defendants in wrongful-death suits? I understand that Larson Daniels had an enormous salary. His life was cut short by the accident in your laboratory. His family will expect generous compensation."

Adrianna rose to her feet. She looked down at Hunter and then walked to the head of the table where Susanna was sitting. "What happened on Selene was horrible, but it was not by our hand. The containment unit was well designed and fully operational. There had to be a bomb planted in the lab. We are not going to be intimidated by you or your boss. The truth is on our side."

Susanna turned cold and hard. Her eyes were threatening. She stood up and looked menacingly at Adrianna. "The truth is irrelevant. There is no proof to substantiate your claim. If you don't cooperate, you will become an enemy of Meridian Corporation. We will seize your assets. You will be evicted from your living quarters but confined to this base. We will ruin all of you."

Susanna gestured toward the young people. "You will be homeless and surrounded by fearful and angry men. Do you have any idea what will happen to these two young girls when they are at the mercy of the miners and dockworkers on this base? They will be beaten and raped repeatedly for the rest of their mercifully short lives. They will become entertainment for the ravenous scum that live here."

Adrianna's hand went to her mouth. "No!"

Sprite looked at her parents nervously. Rory appeared comatose. Susanna smiled malevolently at the young people. "Think about our offer. I will expect your answer by tomorrow morning."

"You bitch!" Jo rose from her seat.

"Now, now, Dr. Smith. Let's be civil."

* * *

The young girl was fourteen years old, going on thirty. She was dressed in utility coveralls, her hair cut so short that the stubs stuck out like rough bristles on her scalp. She was small. She climbed up on a stool at Old Kate's bar like she was climbing a ladder and rested her elbows on the counter.

"Gimme a shot of your besty best brandy." Her voice was gravelly. "Make it quicky like. I don't want to be wait watchin'."

Kate's back was turned to the young girl. She smiled at the sound of her voice. "We don't serve minors here, young lady."

"Who's callin' me lady-fied? If I had any lady stuff in me, I'd have ya rip it out, doctor like. I don't have no wishes for none of that. I ain't no miner, neither. One of them bass terds tried to stick his drill in me once. I woulda kilt 'im if I hadn't run away. Besty brandy for Nixie Drake, I say. I'm thirsty thirsty, an I want my whistle wetted good."

"You're too young." Kate was already pouring the drink in a shot glass.

"Better young-ie an restless than farty and old, I say."

Kate turned around with a smile and slid the drink across the bar. "Hello, Nixie. Good to see you." The young girl caught the shot glass and drained it in a single gulp.

"Yummy yum!" She slammed the empty shot down on the counter. "That's besty better than tittie milk, I say."

Kate was amused. "You ever been breastfed?"

"No way to San Jose, Momma Kate."

"Then you don't know if it's better, do you?"

"Surely goodness I do."

Kate waited. The wheels were spinning in the young girl's head. "Ya can't get outa your gourd stinky drunk on tittie milk."

The two women laughed long and hard.

"Thanks for stopping by, Nix. I might have a big job for you and your crew."

The young waif pushed the shot glass toward the older woman. "Now that's tight. Nice'n tight. We's always goody twoshoes for a cob job. Gimme 'nother shot. Kisser's dry as a rug skunk."

* * *

The guards scanned the corridors as they accompanied the NARI team back toward their living quarters. Two men led the group at a distance, checking each cross-junction for any signs of trouble. Two others trailed behind them, alert for anyone who might mount a rear attack. The team was silent, convinced that the guards would report anything they said to Susanna Frost. They were angry and afraid. Amos Cross had them cornered. Their options were dwindling.

They passed the main corridor, which led south to the Base Commons, and then turned north when they reached the corridor that led to their quarters. They passed through the dock dome where their surface vehicle was parked and continued on toward home. The entrance hatch was open.

"Sir, we've got a problem up here." The voice of one of the advance guards crackled through their sentinel's earpiece. The entourage drew to a stop and waited for further word. "It's all-clear sir, but somebody's broken into their living quarters."

Hunter could see the destruction through the open hatchway. The team crossed the threshold into a land of chaos and rampage. Furniture was broken and thrown about. The exercise equipment was smashed beyond repair. Personal items from their quarters littered the residence corridor. Nothing was left untouched. Rory reached into her pocket to make sure the small container was still there.

Adrianna held her hand to her mouth. "All of our things…"

Jenson Reed cursed under his breath. The holodisplay was shattered. He turned to say something to Hunter and looked at the wall by the entrance hatch. "My God!"

The others turned and saw the words, scrawled in red paint to the left and right of the entrance. "We will kill you," the first words said. Then, on the other side, "We will feed your children to OUR MACHINES."

Hunter sank to his knees, guilt and despair washing over him like a torrent of muddy water. He rubbed the scar on his right index finger. Shame engulfed him. He had brought all of this on his family and colleagues. Adrianna and Sprite knelt down beside him. Hunter looked at his daughter, then turned to his wife. He looked like a lost child. "Tell Susanna we accept her offer."

BOOK TWO

MERIDIAN 6

1

<u>Day 28</u>

*T*he *Avion* slipped through the frictionless void of space beyond Earth's orbit. She was a transit ship owned by Meridian Corporation that carried the NARI scientists and their families spaceward on their 128-day journey toward The Asteroid Belt. Advances in space propulsion systems permitted her to make a relatively rapid trip, avoiding a longer Hohmann Transfer Orbit.

The Avion was designed in three sections. At her stern were three propulsion systems: a main engine housed in her fuselage with two outboard engines housed in nacelles attached on stubby, wing-like fins. This section also accommodated a large transfer shuttle, which could undock from the ship and land on a planet. The shuttle served as the ship's hold, where supplies and equipment were carried. The flight deck of *The Avion* was in the nose section of the ship, along with an observation deck and a smaller hold for supplies needed during the flight. Between the nose and stern sections, there was a massive rotating cabin that provided living space for passengers and crew.

Susanna Frost had made it clear: Adrianna and Hunter would lead the scientific research, and they would answer directly to her. Commander Adam Taberg would be in command of all other aspects of the mission. In addition to his duties as settlement commander, Taberg would also be serving as the power systems engineer. He sat in *The Avion's* crew compartment, studying technical readouts of the

Meridian 6 Research Settlement. His muscled body bulged under his flight suit; his hands were like those of a gymnast. He was always busy, always under motion.

Taberg was one of four new people assigned to the NARI team. He was a severely professional man, never mixing his personal life with his duties. There was an unfathomable secret in his handsome athletic frame, an inner calculation he would not share. He never talked about himself. He would steer every conversation toward technical subjects or the administration of the settlement. After being crammed together for a month on *The Avion*, he was still an enigma.

Tyson Edwards paused on his way through the cabin and glanced at Taberg. "So Commander Taberg, if we blow a fuse, we call you, eh?" Adam's eyes narrowed slightly, as if noticing a fly that had just landed on his sleeve. He said nothing, and Tyson moved on.

* * *

"There's no need for you to study that." Troy Mack looked disapprovingly at Jenson Reed, who was studying his own set of diagrams and schematics of the Meridian 6 comp systems. "I'm responsible for the comp and comm systems. I won't need your help." Troy was in his early twenties. He was the same height as Jenson, but had a small, wiry frame. He had just come back from medical leave. He wore a prosthetic chin that gave his face a robotic look. It clicked when he spoke. His skin was rough and pockmarked, evidence of severe burns. His eyes were hard. He had seen too much life for such a young man.

Jenson fumed. "You can't stop me from studying the systems." He had been in a dark mood ever since Susanna had assigned Troy to the team. "I am NARI's comp specialist, and I will have a good working knowledge of Meridian 6."

"You can waste your time, for all I care." Troy wasn't backing down. "But remember, all communications and data transfers are to be cleared through me. There will be no outside contact. We don't want anyone knowing where we are."

"Go to hell, Troy." Jenson had raised his voice. Sprite looked up from her studies and glanced at the two men nervously. Troy turned toward her, their eyes meeting. She looked away. A full minute later, Sprite glanced back at the disfigured man. He was still looking at her with a funny smile. She shuttered with fear and disgust and then left the compartment.

Jenson Reed had been watching his adversary through the corner of his eye. He spoke up defensively. "What did you do? Scare her away?"

Troy turned and faced his antagonist, his smile remaining. "No. Some people have a hard time getting used to me." Jenson took the comment personally, as Troy intended. The NARI engineer made a face and then returned to his study of the Meridian 6 comp systems, determined to master the material. Silently, he vowed to put Troy in his place.

* * *

Ray Bright hunched over in his seat with his eyes closed. An old-fashioned set of earphones was clamped to his head, and he moved passionately to the music in his ears. He was the supply officer and the tallest of the four newcomers. He had ruddy cheeks, meaty hands, strong arms and legs. He looked like a body builder. He couldn't enter a room without striking up a conversation about some trivial topic, especially Broadway shows. Adrianna had already spoken to him about interrupting, but Ray seemed impervious to suggestion or guidance. The big man couldn't help himself. He was a Broadway evangelist, using every moment to win converts to "the Great White Way."

Tyson passed by the strapping man, and Ray's mouth erupted into a broad grin, displaying his perfect teeth. He pulled the earphones from his head. "Do you like show tunes?" Ty cringed at the question. Ray fingered his music player. "I love Broadway musicals. Listen to 'em all the time. Just let me know if you're interested. Love to chat with ya."

Tyson stiffened but offered the man a friendly smile. "Maybe later," he replied.

Ray's smile grew even wider. "Great! Hold you to it!"

Ty knew the guy was going to be irritating.

* * *

Sprite was tracking the progress of *The Avion* with the help of Wiley, when Cilla Ashe walked up behind her. She was in her early thirties with a pleasant, but weathered face. Her hair was cut very short, and she had a slender body like an Olympic swimmer. Cilla was the Environmental Systems Officer. She would maintain the garden and environmental quality in the settlement. Her work was outside the purview of the NARI team, so she would answer directly to Adam Taberg. Cilla was an information-sponge. She asked far too many questions. Talking to her was like being wrung out.

"Pretty monotonous, isn't it?"

Sprite turned in her seat. Cilla was sitting nearby. "I have Wiley," the girl responded cheerfully. Cilla looked confused. "He is my card comp, my friend." Sprite tapped the slender, card-shaped device on her lap.

A disapproving expression crossed Cilla's face. "I thought you would be interested in…"

"Something more ladylike?" Sprite countered.

"No," Cilla recovered quickly. "Artificial Intelligence seems like a complicated subject."

Sprite laughed. "It's not hard. I like AIs. Once you get to know them, they're really nice."

Cilla moved closer to her. "Do you know much about NARI's phase-two machines?"

"The stuff Mom and Dad are working on?" Cilla nodded. "A little. But I'm more interested in comps."

Cilla lowered her voice. "How long is it going to take to make a new batch of them?"

Sprite felt uncomfortable. She didn't like being quizzed by strangers. "I don't know."

"Can you make a guess? Six months? A year?"

Sprite stiffened. "Look, I'm just a kid. I don't know."

There was an awkward silence, then the older woman changed the subject. "I can't believe what happened on Selene Station."

This is going from bad to worse, Sprite thought. She shrugged noncommittally.

"You knew Dr. Hastings' son Emile, right?" Sprite caught herself nodding to Cilla. "It's a shame, he and his mother died."

Sprite shook her head. "I don't want to talk about it."

Cilla moved closer. "Your parents should have been more careful. Their research runs against everything that is sacred. They created a killer."

Sprite glared at her. The woman had no sensitivity. Like a bee flitting from flower to flower, Cilla changed the subject again. "Tell me about your dad." The woman had an insatiable need to know everything about the people around her. "He seems pretty smart."

"Look, Cilla." Sprite turned cold and distant. "You should ask him yourself. I'm not in the mood to give you a report on my dad or his work."

The older woman offered Sprite a sweet, innocent smile. "I didn't mean to offend." Cilla reached out to touch her shoulder, but Sprite had already turned her attention back toward Wiley.

Day 66

The Avion was just past the midpoint of her journey. In a little over two months, they would be in The Asteroid Belt, beyond the orbit of Mars. Adrianna Logan sat in the rotating crew cabin. She gazed at her holodisplay, sifting through the data she would need to restart the team's research. Her heart wasn't in it. Life on the NARI team was different now.

Before the explosion, they had been filled with joy. They were working on a noble mission. Their work would improve the world. Now, the scientists were lifeless. Adrianna could remember, in searing detail, how Susanna Frost had threatened them two months earlier. She had threatened to hurt the children. Their residence had been vandalized, and an immobilizing terror had gripped them. Hunter had cracked. The beautiful man she had married was gone. His body was there, but his mind was imprisoned in a deep depression from which he could not escape. No one wanted to be on this ship. No one wanted to continue the work, except for Alexis Wren, who seemed relieved. Her science wouldn't be taken from her after all.

Troy Mack sat across from Adrianna, engrossed in his holodisplay. The young man hadn't moved for an hour. He looked like a wax statue in a museum. During the first few weeks of their flight, Adrianna had learned that Adam Taberg was the only career employee of the Meridian Corporation among their new friends. Troy and the other two were freelancers, hired specifically for this mission.

Adrianna started at him intently. "Troy?" He didn't move. "Troy? Are you all right?"

Finally, he looked up from his reading. "Oh, ah, yes ma'am. I'm fine."

"For a minute, I thought you were dead." Adrianna offered the young man a perfunctory smile.

"Sorry, ma'am. I get caught up in my work."

"What are you looking at?"

"I'm reviewing the architecture of the Meridian 6 Core Intellect. It's an older system, but quite good."

"What is that?" she asked.

"Places like Meridian 6 require a whole group of AIs to manage all the systems. The Core Intellect is the central artificial intelligence in the settlement's comp system.

Adrianna's eyes softened as she assessed the man. "Can I ask you a personal question?"

Troy turned off his holodisplay. "You want to know about my face."

She nodded. "How did it happen?"

"My best friend and I were working on a power module in the Jackson Base comp system. There was a frayed cable. I bumped against it and shorted out the module. The electrical fire burned my face."

"You could have been killed."

"Gerry pulled me to safety, but he got burned, too." Troy looked down at his hands. "He didn't make it."

"I'm sorry you had to go through that." The man looked down at his hands, dismissing the comment. Adrianna had known people who had been badly injured. Time could be a grand physician. She knew Troy was going to face a long and thorny path toward healing. If he was lucky, he might come to accept what had happened to him.

Time, she thought. She wondered when time would heal her team. Her thoughts returned to Hunter. He was a broken man. She remembered how he had fallen to his knees when they had returned to their residence and found it shattered and violated by unknown terrorists. He was still on his knees. The loss of their friends, the guilt from underestimating the destructive power of the phase-two machines, and the decision to accept Susanna Frost's demands had pushed him down. He hadn't spoken ten words since then. She longed for the Hunter Logan she had known for the past twenty-three years. Time would either heal him or rot him away.

* * *

All deep-space vehicles and settlements beyond the Earth's orbit had light chambers. *The Avion's* chamber was located in the zero-g section of the ship, forward of the rotating cabin. Those who ventured beyond the healing warmth of the sun were susceptible to the depressive symptoms of what was called "seasonal affective disorder" on Earth.

Sprite Logan floated luxuriously in the light chamber. The cylindrical space was lined with luminescent panels designed to affect the melatonin levels in her body. The warm glow permeated her, relaxing her muscles and calming her mind. Sprite's semiweekly sessions in the "tube" were her favorite times during space travel.

Day 79

It was far into the sleep period when the members of the old NARI team gathered in the aft spaces, astern of the rotating crew cabin. The lights were dimmed, and the ship's crew was either on duty on the flight deck or asleep in their bunks. The newer members of the team had retired. They hadn't been invited to this meeting. Hunter floated silently next to Adrianna as Jenson passed around squeeze bags of hot coffee. Tyson and Jo had already been served and were sipping the steaming beverage. Robert Hastings and Alexis Wren were both lost in thought. This was typical for Alexis, but not for Robert. He had been in a dark mood the entire trip.

Jenson carefully squeezed his coffee bag until a blob of the amber liquid appeared at the end of the nozzle. Then, like a hunter moving in for a kill, he took a pair of chopsticks out of his pocket and brought them close to the floating globule. It almost jumped from the nozzle to the chopsticks. Then, with a surgeon's touch, he held the glob in place between the sticks and put it into his mouth. "You can't take too long, or it gets cold."

"Were did you learn that?" Ty was amazed by how easily he did it.

"I spent six months in the engineering spaces of a space station. There was no gravity. I learned to do a lot of things in zero-g."

Jo Smith sucked a mouthful of coffee and cleared her throat. "I've wanted to talk about this for weeks. I'm not comfortable with our new colleagues. I don't trust them."

There were nods around the circle. Adrianna cupped her hands around her coffee bag, enjoying its warmth. "Can you give us some specifics?"

"Cilla Ashe." Ty snorted. "She's too nosey. She tried to pump me for information several times. Something's not right with her."

Jenson nodded his head. "Troy Mack is one creepy piece of work. His face looks like a piece of ground chuck roast. He may be a specialist on the Meridian 6 comp systems, but he's not right in the head. I can't work with him."

"You're going to have to get used to it." Adrianna gave him a hard look. "Get to know him. He's…"

"Not as bad as he looks?" Jenson finished the sentence for her. "I don't think so. That man is a monster."

"You're wrong, Jenson." Adrianna gave him a stern look. "You're misjudging him. Susanna put him in command over your area, and you're bitter. You're going to have to work with him. You can't change that."

"Who is Taberg, anyway?" Tyson changed the subject with a loud voice.

"Shhh!" Jo instinctively put her hand on his mouth. "Keep your voice down, you fog-horn."

Ty lowered his voice to a whisper. "Taberg has got to be military. No doubt about that. He's going to be a force to reckon with."

"He's good-looking," Adrianna said.

Jo rolled her eyes. "Fall in love with the ugly ones, I say." She stroked the back of Ty's hand. "It minimizes the competition." Ty gave her a maniacal smile.

Adrianna stared at her coffee bag. "I think Ray Bright is a Broadway evangelist." There was nervous laughter in the crowded compartment. Everyone had firsthand experience with the man's unbridled passion for the stage. Then she frowned. "Seriously, I agree with you. Nevertheless, we have to stay focused on the big picture. Amos Cross wants the phase-two nanomachines. I'm sure that our new friends have ulterior motives, but we are caught in something much bigger. We had better watch our backs."

Jo's body was inverted in relation to Adrianna's. Her long, dark hair was frizzy in the zero-g. "What are we going to do? How can we live like this?"

Adrianna looked at her. It was the kind of look that only two mothers could share. "We just do it. We do it for our kids."

"It was a mistake getting on this ship." Robert folded his arms. "I don't want to do this anymore. I resent being here." With each sentence, he became more agitated. "I don't want to spend another second of my life developing a nano-weapon."

Tyson was hovering next to Robert. He could feel the deep-seated anger rising in the man. "Calm down, Robert. None of us want to be here." Alexis gave him a wistful glance, and Ty corrected himself. "*Most* of us don't want to be here, but Adrianna is right. Our kids have been dragged into this. What happens to us will happen to them. If we spit in Cross's face, they're likely to suffer for it."

"Emile has already suffered for it." Robert pushed off from a handhold and floated out of the compartment.

Tyson rolled his eyes. "He's losing it."

Jo patted her partner's arm. "Give the man a break, Ty. How would you feel if Kell had died? He's right. Maryanne and Emile have already paid with their lives."

Adrianna glanced at Hunter. He was holding his coffee bag tightly. He hadn't even opened the container. She took his hand, and his grip relaxed. "We're all under a lot of stress. Be careful everyone. We're in enemy territory."

Day 95

Kell Edwards stood in the dimness outside Sprite's stateroom. It was another sleep period, and *The Avion* was quiet, her passengers at rest. He imagined Sprite in her bed, his teenage hormones stirring. Kell wanted to be with her. He had lingered outside her door on other nights, fantasizing about being her mate. He knew they were too young. He knew that Sprite was standoffish, unwilling to yield to his overtures, but he couldn't ignore the powerful forces coursing through his body. He looked up and down the corridor. He was alone.

Kell knocked lightly on the door. He leaned forward, straining to hear through the metal. No sound. He knocked again, a little harder this time. Sprite's voice was muffled. "Who is it?"

"It's Kell."

"What time is it?" Sprite's voice was clearer now. She stood on the other side of the closed door. Kell felt a wave of excitement pass through him.

"Late." Kell put his face to the door. "I want to see you."

"Are you crazy? It's the middle of the night."

"Exactly."

There was a pause as Sprite realized what Kell was suggesting. "Kell Edwards, you are not coming in here."

Kell pressed a button in the bulkhead next to the door. He wanted to see her face to face. Nothing happened. There were no locks on the staterooms. He couldn't figure out why the door wouldn't open.

"Let me in, Sprite. Just for a minute."

"Go away!"

Kell took his hand off the button and backed away from the door.

Day 96

The next morning, Sprite and Kell floated serenely on *The Avion's* observation deck. The starscape wrapped around them in a breathtaking panorama. There was no sense of motion, even though the ship was traveling at many thousands of kilometers per hour. The only reference points were the stars, many light-years away.

The two friends didn't speak as they gazed at the broad vista of stars spread out before them. Kell moved his hand slowly and tentatively, until it was resting on Sprite's shoulder. She felt the warmth of his fingers and inched away. She reached up and took his hand. "Kell, you know I really like you, okay?"

Kell smiled. His eyes were kind. "I know."

Sprite paused. She wanted her words to come out right. "We're best friends, and I don't want anything to change that."

"That's how I feel, too." Sprite could feel the slight pressure of Kell's hand trying to let go so he could touch her again. She resisted.

"About last night…" Sprite could feel Kell's hand go limp. She looked at her friend and frowned. "If we had sex…" She wanted to say the right thing. Kell was too important to her. "I just want to be friends. Okay? Sex would ruin it."

Kell was disappointed. Sprite tightened her grip on his hand and smiled warmly. "Look, Kell, I trust you with my life, but I can't… I mean, I don't want to have sex with anyone right now. Can we just be friends?"

Kell sighed and looked into Sprite's radiant face. He was silent. Sprite could see his inner turmoil: a battle between opposing forces in his body and his brain. She waited for him. "It's a deal," he said finally. "No sex."

"And no advances," she insisted.

"No advances." Kell shook his head solemnly.

"I just want friendship," Sprite said, and Kell nodded. She gave him a peck on the forehead. In that moment, he was the most handsome boy she had ever seen.

Day 106

Tyson Edwards sat in his compartment in front of his holodisplay. He was playing a video from the Selene Station. It was footage of the lab inspection after the explosion. A miniature 3-D version of the laboratory appeared in the small chamber. He watched from Valerie Lopez's point of view as she picked her way through the rubble. Hunter's voice whispered through his earset. "Can you see the containment unit, Val?"

"I'm going over there now." Val's voice sounded tinny. A wave of grief swept over Tyson. She had been like a sister to him.

Tyson watched as Val moved through the ocean of debris. Then he saw it. The containment unit was shattered. Wires and components were hanging out of the torn cabinet. The image grew larger and then cleared. It looked like a giant hand had torn off the lid and scooped out its delicate circuitry. The destruction penetrated to the core of the device. A twisted, shapeless mass was still attached to the bottom half of the cabinet. It was the cavity that once held the phase-two machines.

Val's voice crackled through the speaker. "We're dead. We're all dead."

Tyson froze the playback and scrutinized the remains of the containment unit. The explosive device must have been right on top of it.

Tyson opened another video file. This clip was shot before the explosion. The lab was pristine, state-of-the-art equipment lining the walls.

"What are these phase-two machines?" Larson Daniels was off camera. Ty watched as Adrianna smiled at the newsman. He shuttled the video forward a few seconds and played it again.

Hunter was nodding as he described the phase-two machines. "They won't stop eating. They feed on order and leave chaos in their wake."

Ty could hear the worry in Larson's voice. "Where do you keep them?"

Adrianna gave him an innocent smile. "They're right behind you."

The image followed Larson as he spun around in the weightless environment. Then, the undamaged containment unit filled the holodisplay. Ty froze the image. The camera was high enough to reveal the top of the containment unit. There, set back from the front of the case, was a small triangular device with a numerical readout. Tyson zoomed in on the device. The readout was a timer and was counting down. It was a bomb.

* * *

A few minutes later, Adrianna had responded to Ty's summons and was standing by his side. She looked at the video. "That must be it." She folded her arms and looked away, accessing visual memory. "It was right there in front of us, and we didn't see it."

"This proves it was sabotage." Energy was returning to Ty's voice. "The containment unit didn't explode by itself."

Adrianna put her hand on his shoulder. "You're right. The explosion wasn't our fault."

Ty's face was filled with relief. "There was a bomb, Adrianna. This is proof."

"It helps, Ty. Don't lose those video clips." Adrianna gave his shoulder a squeeze and quietly left the compartment.

Day 115

The Avion's passengers were rarely alone. Rory North found a secluded place in the aft spaces of the ship, where the rotating passenger cabin joined with the cargo hold. She floated in a quiet little alcove beside the access corridor.

"Can you talk to my Mom, Sparky?" Once again, the small box was nestled in the palm of her hand. There was a yearning in her voice, a hope that whatever was inside the box would answer her and heal her broken heart. "I miss her a lot. Could you tell her that I'm okay?" Rory paused, a dark cloud falling over her face. "I can hardly remember what her voice sounded like, Sparky."

Rory heard a sound in the access corridor. "Rory? Are you in here?"

The young girl hesitated, then recognized Sprite's voice. "I'm over here."

Her friend appeared from around a corner. Sprite smiled. "Are you alone in here? I thought I heard you talking to someone." Then she saw the box. Sprite navigated alongside her friend. "What's that? I've seen you with it a couple of times. Were you talking to it just now?"

Rory blushed. "Sort of."

"You don't 'sort of' talk to something. You either do, or you don't."

"Yeah, I was talking to it." She held out the box. "It's my pet."

"Your pet?"

Rory opened the box carefully. Inside, cradled on a small piece of cloth, was a formless little creature with a thin coat of stubby copper-colored fir. It didn't move. It didn't have a face. It didn't even look alive. "This is Sparky. I made him about a year ago." Rory's face glowed with pride.

"You made him?"

"Yeah. You're good with AIs, and I like working with DNA. I call him a "shocker." Sparky makes electricity. Do you want to feel him?"

Sprite wasn't sure. "Will he hurt me?"

"He doesn't make a lot of electricity, just enough for a tingle."

Sprite put her finger in the box and stroked the small creature's coat. "I don't feel anything."

"Use your thumb and forefinger. Spread them wide and touch each end of his body at once."

Sprite did what Rory suggested. "I feel it! It's just a little tingle."

"That's all Sparky does. Someday, one of his children might power a whole space station!" For a brief moment, Rory was her old self, full of hope and promise.

Sprite nodded, looking at her young friend with new respect. "That's pretty amazing. Children, huh?"

"Sparky's the only one of his kind. I'll have to make his children." Rory paused, wondering about her choice of words. Then, realizing what she had said, both girls laughed.

Day 117

Robert Hastings entered his compartment and sat down at a small desk built into the bulkhead. He picked up his earset and pressed it to his ear.

"Good afternoon, Dr. Hastings. You look tired today."

Robert hated comps. He had named his artificial intelligence "Dammit." He offered the comp an unintelligible grunt in reply.

"There is a message waiting for you."

Robert was surprised. The team was not permitted to receive messages.

"Read it to me, Dammit!"

"Gladly, Dr. Hastings. The message says, "Check your secret folder.""

"Who gave you that message?"

"I have no idea. It wasn't there the last time I was turned on."

Who could know about his secret folder? Robert had a small nano-drive he used for his private files. Robert stood up and went over to his closet. He opened the panel and felt around the edge of the door molding until he found the drive. He took it and went back to his desk.

Robert activated the drive, which connected with his earset automatically. "Open the file list on the external device, Dammit." The comp did as it was told. Robert scrolled through his files on his small holodisplay. He found a new file that didn't follow his naming protocol. How did they do this?

"Open the file."

"The file says, 'When the time…'"

"Don't read it to me, Dammit!" Hastings had let the comp read the initial message. The machine was just trying to oblige the irrational man. Robert even hated the sound of his comp's voice. He would change it, but he'd hate the voice no matter what it sounded like. "Put it on the display." The text appeared in the holodisplay. It read, "When the time is right, you will be told what to do." It was signed, "the woman from the garden."

Robert looked around his room to make sure he was alone. He considered showing the message to Hunter and Adrianna, but he changed his mind. His life had been turned upside down. His loyalties no longer lay with the NARI team. He had vowed to honor Maryanne and Emile. He didn't want anyone else to die like they did. Robert gazed at the message in his holodisplay. He would do whatever they asked of him.

Day 124

Hunter sobbed quietly as he lay on the bed. It was hours into the sleep period, and Adrianna held him in her arms. She stroked his hair, wishing there was something she could say to make things better. He kept whispering, "I'm sorry" repeatedly. He was inconsolable. "Hunter, you're going to have to snap out of this," she said finally. "We're going to arrive at Ceres in a few days, and I am going to need you. It's going to take both of us to lead this team." Hunter grew quiet. "Will you try? I really need you." No response. "Sprite is going to need you." Adrianna felt Hunter nod his head. "Thank you," she whispered. "Just do what you can, okay? I know it's going to take a long time to get over this." Hunter's breathing slowed and deepened. He was fast asleep.

2

*T*he *Avion* reached orbit around Ceres, her four-month voyage
almost over. Her crew undocked the massive transfer shuttle
that would carry the scientists and their cargo down to the
dusty outer crust of the dwarf planet. Ceres was just under a thousand
kilometers in diameter, a perpetually cold, forbidding place. A Cerian
day was a little over nine hours long. She revolved around the sun every
4.6 Earth-years, in an orbit bracketing the "Ice Line," an orbit 2.7
Astronomical Units from the sun that divided the rocky inner planets
and the outer gas giants.

The shuttle descended toward the surface, her landing gear
extended, her engines offsetting the weak gravity of the large asteroid.
Everyone was strapped in, awaiting the end of their journey. Finally, the
shuttle came to rest on the Meridian 6 Landing Pad. Weighing only 3%
of its Earth weight, it sat comfortably on spindly landing gear. The pilot
positioned the craft on a docking-collar, which protruded from the pad
deck.

The Meridian 6 research settlement was a series of domes, half-
buried in the planet surface. Eight concrete bulges were laid out
symmetrically around the circumference of a circle. Each dome was
thirty meters in diameter. Beyond the circle's perimeter lay the Landing
Pad and a single reddish dome that housed the power bay. Three other
domes sat inside the circle's rim. One was at the center, forming the
hub.

The docking-collar, now firmly mated to the belly of the shuttle,
was centered over a large, circular hatch, which covered a staging dock
below the pad. There was a long corridor at one end of the dock that
led to the settlement complex. Like all the connecting tunnels in
Meridian 6, the hallway was lit by electroluminescent material

embedded in the smooth white walls. The light was soft and pleasant, not stark and cold. The Landing Pad corridor formed a "T" with the arcing "rim" corridor that connected four of the settlement's domes together. The Engineering Bay, or "Eng Bay," was to the left of the pad corridor, and the General Supply Bay was to the right.

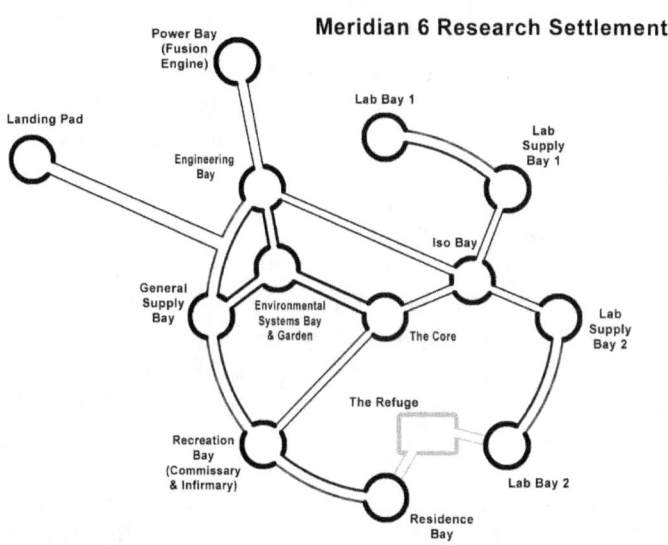

The dome that formed the hub of the circular complex was called the Core. It housed the settlement's computing, communications, monitoring, and control systems. Three corridors stretched away from the Core like spokes. One went to the Recreation Bay, or "Rec Bay," located on the settlement's rim. A second corridor led to the Environmental Systems Bay, also called the "Enviro Bay." Its dome stood inside the settlement's perimeter, not far from where the Landing Pad corridor attached to the rim. It accommodated a lush garden and equipment for monitoring the air quality, temperature, and pressure in the settlement.

A third "spoke" corridor connected the Core with the Isolation Bay. The "Iso Bay," as it was called, served as the gateway to a pair of supply and laboratory bays, situated opposite from the Landing Pad, on the settlement's rim. The Iso Bay was the only way to gain access to the settlement's laboratories. While airtight hatches could be found at the ends of every corridor, those in the Iso Bay were formidable. They were designed to seal off either lab complex from the rest of the settlement. In addition, each laboratory and supply bay had its own emergency sealing system that could flood all the interior spaces with expanding foam, creating an impermeable plug. Another long corridor connected the Iso Bay with The Eng Bay.

The red-domed Power Bay sat outside the rim of Meridian 6. A Fusion Engine throbbed inside the structure. Large conduits ran along the Power Bay's connecting corridor, supplying power to the settlement.

The scientists and their families followed Ray Bright down the Landing Pad corridor and then to the right around the settlement's rim. They passed through the General Supply Bay. The dome was filled with a maze of industrial shelving, filled with cases and boxes of various sizes. Each set of shelves was numbered and laid out in a highly organized system. Oblivious of the scientists, Ray guided his load of cases down a wide corridor that bisected the dome. Ray had his old headphones clamped to his head as he guided his motorized cargo carrier. Ray did his best work when choruses from *Oklahoma!* were vibrating his brain. He was belting out the show's signature chorus as he followed the carrier. Everyone around him wished they were deaf.

The team followed Ray around the curved outer rim corridor toward the Rec Bay. This dome was the settlement's multipurpose area. There were places to sit and study. There was an exercise room with three light chambers, a small infirmary, and a commissary. A spoke corridor connected the Rec Bay with the Core.

The Residence Bay, or "Res Bay," lay on Meridian 6's outer rim, beyond the Rec Bay. A large circular common area was at the center of the dome, ringed with a corridor that had four entrances, placed like the points of a compass. The Res Bay was luxurious compared to the cramped quarters of *The Avion*. On the outer wall of the circular corridor, nine residences arced around the circumference of the dome like colors on a painter's pallet. Each was equipped with a small kitchen, bathroom, living area, and bedrooms. The first one was Tyson and Jo's residence, located to the left of the entrance. The Logans chose the largest residence, which was next. The other residences were smaller, single bedroom units. They were appointed simply, but comfortably.

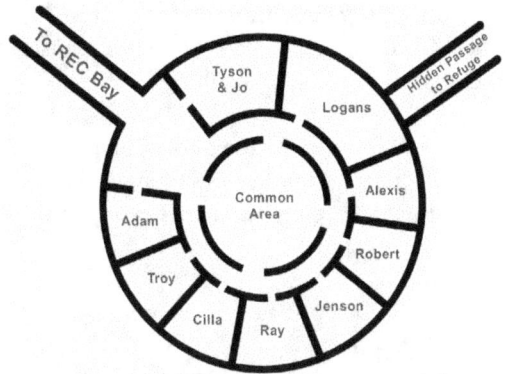

Meridian 6 Residence Bay

Meridian 6's Core had two concentric rings of curved racks called the "Tech Stacks." They were filled with complex equipment. Some racks had displays and control surfaces. Most of them did not. The arcs of racks were broken by radial aisles that spread outward from the center of the dome. Dull violet lights glowed from behind the ventilation panels as unseen circuitry performed the tasks assigned to them by the system's Core Intellect.

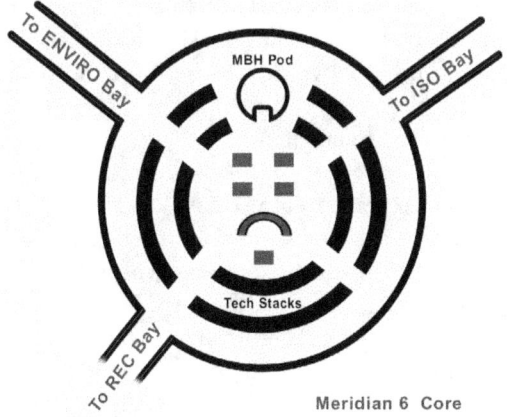

Meridian 6 Core

Sprite had tagged along with Jenson down the long corridor from the Rec Bay. The two paused as they entered the Core. She was impressed with all the comp equipment. "What's this?"

"This is the Core." Jenson was enjoying himself. "There are seventeen artificial intelligence systems in this dome."

"Seventeen?"

"Seventeen. They form a 'digital colloquium.' It's like a town populated by comps. There's one AI in command; it's called the Core Intellect. It acts as the gatekeeper and supervisor for all the other AIs. It's like the mayor of the town."

"What's her name?"

"It doesn't have one. It's just a smart comp."

"She ought to have a name."

Jenson ignored her comment. "There's a 'mirror-intellect' as well. It runs silently in the background, constantly watching and listening to the activities of the Core Intellect. The backup AI stands ready in case the "on-duty" Core Intellect malfunctions."

"What's that?" Sprite gestured toward a dark cylindrical room that was nestled in the Tech Stacks.

"It's the MBH pod." They walked over to the pod, and Jenson pulled it open, revealing a dimly-lit interior. "This room houses the controls for the micro-black-hole transmission facility. It's soundproof for classified communications. Years ago, Meridian's scientists harnessed micro -black-holes to facilitate real-time communications over astronomical distances. The MBH system takes a substantial amount of power and has two AIs to perform the signal processing. When in operation, the holographic display in the chamber presents the image of the person you're talking to."

Sprite took it all in. "So, it's face-to-face communications over the vast distances of space, with no time delay."

"Exactly. This one is brand new. They installed it just for us."

Sprite thanked Jenson for the tour and headed back toward the Res Bay. Jenson closed the hatch of the MBH pod and surveyed the expanse of technology spread before him. This was going to be his home for the foreseeable future. The center of the dome was an open area with several equipment pods and a large curved console. A smaller workstation stood behind it. He walked over to the large console and settled into the chair.

"That would be my space." Jenson turned and saw Troy Mack walking toward him; his scarred face was red, his eyes blazing.

"Like hell it is," snapped Jenson. He rose out of the chair and stepped toward the Meridian engineer. His muscles rippled under his jumpsuit.

Jenson was considerably more powerful than the smaller man, but Troy stood his ground. "You don't frighten me, Reed. I'm used to people whispering behind my back and dismissing me as less than human. I know what you're thinking, and you have to get over it." Jenson started to reply, but held his tongue. "What?" Troy took a step closer. "Were you going to call me a freak?" Mack's chin prosthesis made an odd clicking sound as he spoke. He reached up to key his comlink. "Do you want me to get Adam in here? I am responsible for the Core." Reed looked away in frustration and cursed. He moved to the small workstation, which sat on the edge of the Tech Stacks. Troy sat down at the large console. He smirked at Jenson. "I know more about the Meridian 6 Core Intellect than you ever will." Jenson stifled the urge to pulverize the man. This was going to be a long tour of duty.

* * *

Adam Taberg stood patiently in the commissary as everyone found a seat. His back was ramrod straight, and his hands were tucked behind him, elbows bent. Adrianna and Hunter sat near the front. The Rec Bay echoed with the murmur of voices as everyone chatted with their neighbor. Taberg waited until there was silence before he spoke.

"Welcome to Meridian 6. I am sure you are happy to bid farewell to *The Avion*." Laughter rippled through his audience. "She's a fine ship, but four months is about six months too long." There was more laughter. "We're going to be serving together for quite a while, so I want us to get off on the right foot." Adam reiterated what Susanna had said months earlier, reminding them that he was in command of everything, except the labs and the science. Those were the domains of Adrianna and Hunter.

"You will find that I am not a difficult man." He spoke in a relaxed manner, like one who wore the mantel of authority with ease. Adrianna felt like she was meeting Adam for the first time. During their journey, he had kept to himself. He had been private, almost reclusive. Now, as they gathered in their new home, Taberg came to life, exuding confidence. She found it appealing, power wrapped in a benevolent sheath.

"I want to emphasize that we are on a classified mission." Adam continued. "No one is to make any unauthorized transmissions or data transfers without my permission. I have authorized Mr. Mack to manage all communications on my behalf. You will follow his orders." Taberg's eyes came to rest on Jenson Reed. "*All* of you." The younger man bristled, but didn't challenge him.

Taberg explained that the Power Bay, which stood by itself beyond the circumference of the wheel-shaped settlement, was off-limits to all personnel. He informed them that a series of orientation sessions would be held the next day to familiarize everyone with safety and emergency procedures. "It's important for you to notice the safety seals for the labs. There are release handles in the lab corridors beyond the ISO Bay. They are clearly identified." Taberg's tone became deeper, more commanding. "Do not touch those handles. You will learn about them tomorrow. Should a disaster occur in one of the labs, we can irreversibly seal the affected space. The sealing system will flood the entire lab and its corresponding supply bay with expanding foam. It will destroy the lab and kill anyone in it." He smiled and relaxed. "So, don't touch. And let's hope we never have to activate those seals."

* * *

Cilla Ashe stepped into the garden and took a deep breath. The air on *the Avion* had bothered her for weeks. The air in the Enviro Bay was the purest in the entire settlement. She filled her lungs and savored the pleasant, leafy aroma. It was good to be surrounded by so many growing things. The garden was appointed like a small park with waterfalls, walkways, and benches.

She sat down in a glade and imagined herself back home on Earth. She wondered why she had come to this place to work with these people. They were developing an environmental monster, capable of destroying everything she held sacred. Cilla took a deep, centering breath. Remember your calling, she thought. She was on Meridian 6 to protect this little garden. She would use all of her skills to maintain it, and she would be kind to these people, in spite of what they were doing.

* * *

Adam Taberg sat at his workstation in the Eng Bay, which was on the outer rim of the settlement, near the Power Bay. He looked down the long corridor that led to the ISO Bay. This passageway facilitated the transport of large amounts of lab equipment without going through the bays designed for habitat and control. Taberg turned and scanned the screens at his workstation. They monitored the status of the settlement's power and electrical systems. His experienced eye told him that everything was running normally. He thought about his first meeting as the head of Meridian 6. It wasn't a military assignment, but he was in command nonetheless. The Logans seemed like reasonable people. He would be able to get along with them, but Jenson Reed was going to be a problem. Taberg made a mental note to give Troy Mack an extra measure of support. He didn't know what to think about the three teenagers. This was no place for kids, but this wasn't a standard deployment, either. No one wanted to be on this hunk of rock, almost five hundred million kilometers from the sun. He studied the dome wall. Just beyond it was frozen desolation, wrapped in a vacuum. If the Fusion Engine ever failed, they would die out here. The thought gave him a shiver. Adam got up and decided to inspect the power plant.

* * *

Alexis Wren wandered aimlessly through the General Supply Bay. She was like a window shopper, meandering through a department store with time on her hands. Her mind was elsewhere, consumed by the intricacies of nanostructures and their behaviors.

Ray Bright was stowing a pallet of cases, when he caught a glimpse of Alexis. He pulled his headphones off and walked purposefully toward the absentminded scientist. "Hello!" Alexis glanced up with a start. She gave him a vacant look, neither a smile nor a frown. She simply nodded, continuing her aimless journey. Ray fell in step beside her. "Have you ever seen a Broadway Show?"

Alexis stopped in her tracks, suppressing her irritation. This man was talking to her, and she had to submit herself to the constraints of common courtesy. He didn't matter to her, but she felt some vague need to be cordial. "No."

Ray smiled broadly. "Well, Dr. Wren, you haven't lived until you've sat in a Broadway Theater when the lights have dimmed, and the curtain has opened. It's like being carried away to another world."

"I saw a movie once." Alexis was maxing out her people skills.

"But this is live theater. You never know what's going to happen." There was a far-away look in his eyes. "It's truly amazing!"

Alexis continued walking down the aisle without a word. Ray followed her, unfazed by her disinterest. "Do you like music?"

Alexis kept walking. "No."

"You don't like music?" Ray walked along with her, offering his headphones. "Listen to this. It's 'Les Misérables.' It's fantastic."

Alexis paused. She looked at the antiquated headphones and then at Ray. "No." She thought about the proper etiquette and added, "thank you," as she hurried out of the General Supply Bay.

* * *

Sprite was on the bunk in her new bedroom. Her belongings lay around her in boxes. She sat brooding, caught in a conjunction of hormones and frustration. She missed her father. He had fallen into a deep depression. It was like his mind had taken a long trip and left his body behind. He spent hours alone. He hardly spoke. She missed his bad jokes and their chess games. She longed for his approval and care.

Sprite thought about her mother. Her anger rose. She hung on to the memory of seeing her in bed with Robert Hastings. At the time, she hadn't understood what she saw, but as she grew older, she came to realize what was happening. Her mother's infidelity nauseated her. She couldn't trust her.

Her mother had assumed much of the leadership responsibility she formerly shared with Sprite's father. Between the demands of her job and her increased attention to Hunter, Sprite hardly saw her. She didn't want to be around her, but she felt abandoned by her. Now they had arrived at Meridian 6. Everything was different, *again*. Sprite sat in her new room, hating her mother, hating the room, hating Robert Hastings, and hating everything else she could think of.

There was a knock at the door. Sprite looked up. Kell Edwards was standing at the threshold. "Hi, Sprite."

"Go away," she muttered. The boy stepped into the room and closed the door. "I told you to go away."

Kell walked to the bed and sat down next to her. "What's eating at you?" Sprite turned her back toward him and crossed her arms. "Come on, Sprite." Kell put his hand on her shoulder. "You can tell me. Why are you so mad?" At that moment, the door opened, and Adrianna stepped into the room. Kell pulled his hand away and stood up.

"Mother!" Sprite said it like a curse word. "Can't I have some privacy?"

Adrianna looked surprised, then shocked. "What's going on in here?" Both young people were silent. "Kell, I think you should go back to your quarters." Sprite glared at her mother, as Kell made a beeline for the door. "Sprite, I don't want you entertaining Kell in your bedroom. If you want to visit with him, do it in the Common Area."

Sprite gave her mother a cold, hard look. "You have no right to tell me what to do."

Adrianna put her hands on her hips. "I'm your mother, and I certainly do have the right, young lady!"

"No you don't," Sprite spat back at her. "You are in no position to tell me who I can have in my bedroom."

Adrianna was dumbfounded. She closed the door. "Yes I do. It's my job."

"You lost that right a long time ago," Sprite shot back. Pandora's Box was opening.

"What are you talking about?"

Sprite leapt off the bed and stood before her mother with clenched fists. Her eyes blazed. Her body shook with an anger she had held for years. "I saw you 'entertain' Dr. Hastings in your bedroom, once. I don't think you have any moral authority to tell me who I can see in mine." Sprite stomped past her mother, throwing the door open violently.

Adrianna's mind went numb as her daughter ran from their residence. Her face was ashen as she turned and looked down the empty hallway. "Oh, my God." Her voice was a breathy whisper. "What have I done?"

3

Sprite had no idea where she was going. She wanted to run away, a hard thing to do in the close confines of the research settlement. In the light Cerian gravity, she bounded down the corridor toward the Rec Bay like an impala. She traveled at an incredible speed. She took the first right-hand corridor and headed toward the Core. Jenson Reed was startled as she ran through the Tech Stacks. "What's the hurry?" he called out. Sprite didn't respond. She was gone in a flash. She cut to her left and down the nearest corridor. She kept running until she reached the garden. The slipstream she generated caused the leaves of the plants to flutter as she swept past. Finally, Sprite found herself in the General Supply Bay. She slowed her pace and jogged down several rows of shelving. She found a small cubbyhole created by stacks of crates and cases. She looked around, making sure she was alone, and entered the space. She sat on the floor and drew her knees to her chest. Her sobs came from deep within her, as her tears fell on the cold concrete.

* * *

Alexis Wren padded down the corridor that connected the Core with the Enviro Bay. She had spent the last half-hour wandering among the plants in the garden, touching the various leaves and enjoying the aroma of the flowers. Now, she paused at the entrance to the Core and glanced behind her to make sure no one was watching. She stepped into the dome and continued to wander absentmindedly, making sure no one was ahead of her.

Alexis kept track of Troy and Jenson. She knew they were occupied elsewhere in the settlement. She walked resolutely over to Jenson's workstation, which stood behind Troy's curved console. She prepared the system for an encrypted file-transfer and reached into her pocket, turning on her data module without removing it. Jenson's comp connected with the module and uploaded the file. She closed the gateway and turned off the module. It had taken less than a minute. Alexis rose from Jenson's chair and stepped away from the workstation. Once again, she became the scatterbrained scientist, meandering her way toward Lab Bay One.

* * *

Adrianna had a flask of strong, hot coffee in her hand. She stood before the door of her bedroom and took a deep breath to calm herself before she entered the chamber. The lights were dimmed. There was a sitting area with two chairs and a table near the bed. Hunter sat alone in one of the chairs. His face was drawn, and there was an unfocussed, faraway look in his eyes. He hadn't shaved in several days, and he was still in his bedclothes. "Hunter?" Adrianna walked quietly through the dimness. There was no reaction from her husband. She put the flask on the table and sat down across from him. "Hunter, we need to talk." Hunter looked down at the floor. "Come on, honey. I really need you. We've got a problem."

Hunter looked up at Adrianna with hollow eyes. "What?"

"It's Sprite."

Hunter straightened a bit. "Is she all right?" He mumbled. Life was returning to his face.

"She's fine. Well, she's not fine. She's upset. It's horrible." Hunter looked like a man who was under fire in a foxhole. It was like he was dazed and disoriented by heavy shelling and was bracing himself for another round. Adrianna slid the flask of coffee toward him. The aroma wafted up from the hot liquid. Without thinking, Hunter took the container and lifted it to his lips. "Honey, I've really got to have your attention." Hunter looked up and saw the tears in her eyes. He nodded slowly. "I just had a fight with Sprite. Kell was in her room with the door closed. Nothing happened, but when I spoke to her about it, she blew up at me..." She paused and took a deep breath. She looked at the floor. "Hunter, she knows about that time I slept with Robert."

Hunter squared his shoulders and leaned toward his wife. "How?"

"I don't know." There was a silence between them, then a flash of realization. "Oh, my God." Adrianna's hands went up to her face. She looked at Hunter, guilt ridden. "She was there. She was in the house when it happened. She must have…" Adrianna began to sob uncontrollably. "I thought we had worked through this. What have I done?" Hunter slowly rose from his chair. He knelt in front of Adrianna and held her in his arms.

* * *

Troy Mack sat at his curved console in the Core. An alert was flashing on his holodisplay, indicating an encrypted file-transfer to a location outside the settlement network. The data upload had taken place outside of the routine channels. He looked at the address. The upload had been sent from Jenson's console. Why would he be sending encrypted files to Mars? He walked over to the other side of the dome and entered the MBH pod. "Initiate the transmission."

"Good afternoon, Troy." The AI's voice was friendly. "Who would you like to speak to?"

"Connect me with the secure server network at Meridian Mars."

"That sounds like a simple file-transfer. Do you want to initiate a two way holographic transmission?"

"That won't be necessary. I want to speak with the coordinating AI on the network."

"Very well, Troy. One moment, please." Troy could feel the tremendous power being channeled to create the micro-black-hole. Currently, Mars was about four astronomical units from Ceres, a distance of almost six hundred million kilometers.

"Network control at your service, sir."

Troy got a kick out of how polite comps could be. "This is Troy Mack at Meridian 6.

"Yes, Mr. Mack."

"You can call me Troy."

"Yes, Mr. Mack."

Troy gave up. Clearly, not all AIs were created equal. "There was an encrypted file uploaded to your servers from this location in the last hour. Can you confirm that?"

"There is no record of such a file-transfer, Mr. Mack."

"Was there a failed transfer?"

"No, Mr. Mack. The data path was established successfully."

Troy noticed the inconsistency. "So there was a file-transfer?"

"No, Mr. Mack. There was not."

This made no sense. "If there was a data path, there must have been a transfer."

"There is no record of it, Mr. Mack."

The comp was clueless. He thanked the AI and logged off.

* * *

Drew Mallick was a twenty-year veteran in Meridian Corporation's data systems division. He was the company's "go to" guy when difficult comp issues cropped up. He had saved the day for Meridian on many occasions. He had two daughters who had married and moved to Earth. Drew's wife was very ill. They were looking forward to an early retirement so they could be closer to their children, and she could receive the high-quality medical care that Earth could provide.

Several months earlier, Susanna Frost had given Drew the task of cracking the encryption on Hunter Logan's data. She told him it was the most important project of his career. He took up the challenge with great vigor at first, but as the months crept by with no success, he lost heart. He had run out of ideas. Whoever had designed the security on the data files was a master. He knew there was only one way to glean the data's secrets: the encryption key.

Drew was sitting at his workstation; a large holographic chamber glowed with three-dimensional representations of various encryption algorithms. Susanna Frost stood across from him, her arms folded.

"Where are we on the NARI research data?"

"No progress, Ms. Frost."

"It's been four months. Do you realize how important this is to Mr. Cross?"

Drew gave Susanna a frustrated shrug. "It doesn't matter how important it is. The encryption can't be compromised. I've tried everything I know. I've consulted with other experts. No one has ever seen anything like this. The security is smart. It changes tactics as we probe it for weaknesses. It's some form of intelligent encryption."

Susanna thought of how she would be punished for Mallick's failure. "I told you that Mr. Cross would hold you accountable if you fail."

Drew threw up his hands. "I guess he'll do what he's gonna do, Ms. Frost. I can't change reality. I am very good at what I do, and I cannot crack this data." He picked up the data module and waved it at her.

"Time has run out, Mr. Mallick. I suggest you try again, and pray that you stumble on a way to read that data. At some point, Mr. Cross will ask me about your progress. When he finds out you have failed, you won't like it."

Susanna spun on her heels and left the office. Drew let out a long breath, as knots of anxiety began to tighten in his stomach. Retirement was looking better all the time.

* * *

Troy Mack stood before Adam Taberg in the Eng Bay. His superior stood at one of the benches with his sleeves rolled up. He was working with a complex piece of equipment. The device was jacked into a holodisplay, offering a three-dimensional readout of the circuitry. The young engineer shared his suspicions while Taberg worked. Then, the commander laid down his tools.

"So it has only taken Mr. Reed twelve hours to break the rules."

"Yes, sir."

"The Martian servers don't have a record of a file-transfer?"

"No, but they do have a record of an open data path. It's very strange."

Adam Taberg rubbed his chin. "What would cause that?"

"I don't know."

"Tell you what, Troy. Technically there has been no violation, since no information left our network. Let it go for now. However, keep an eye on Reed and figure out what he's up to. I'll make some inquiries on my end." Adam thanked Troy and dismissed him. Perhaps this tour wasn't going to be so uneventful after all.

* * *

Lab Bay Two was large and well equipped. Rows of benches were filled with gleaming test equipment. Six biological safety cabinets stood along the curved wall. The skeleton of a new containment unit stood in the center of the lab. Its panels were removed. Bundles of wiring and densely populated circuit boards were visible. Tyson Edwards sat in front of a holodisplay, staring intently at a technical readout. Jo Smith sat across from him, working on one of the circuit boards. Kell stood at a nearby bench, working on a bracket to hold one of the circuit assemblies.

Ty swiveled back and forth on his stool. "I'm worried."

Kell put down his work and leaned against the bench. Jo looked up from the circuit board in front of her. "About the containment unit?" she asked.

"No, it'll be fine. I'm worried about security. We need the AIs in the Core to run our models and do our analysis, but that exposes the data to the whole team. I don't trust any of the new people. The phase-two machines are incredibly dangerous, and I'm not comfortable with strangers having access to our work."

"We should be able to encrypt the data."

"That's true, but the AIs still need to know what we're doing. There will be vulnerabilities."

Jo looked thoughtfully at her partner. "It's not just the new people that worry me. What about the person who stole Hunter's data? We still have a mole."

Ty shook his head. "Samina's gone. She's the one who took the files."

Kell walked over and sat next to his father. "I'm not so sure. Sprite thinks she's okay."

Ty smiled. "Sprite isn't seeing the whole picture."

Jo leaned back in her chair. "Kell might be right, Ty. Hunter vouched for her."

"Hunter's judgment is impaired."

"But what if he's right?"

Ty thought for a moment. "Then we still have a traitor on the team."

"Right. One of our own is against us."

* * *

Adrianna met Adam Taberg as she was entering the Rec Bay. "Adam, have you seen Sprite?"

"Sorry." He shook his head. "I've been in the Eng Bay."

"Thanks." Adrianna kept walking.

"Adrianna?" Adam stopped her. "We need to talk."

Adrianna looked down the corridor to make sure they were alone and then turned back to him. "Okay. Let's sit down."

The two sat at one of the tables in the commissary. Adam sat with perfect posture, his disposition formal as he began. "It's Jenson Reed. He's going to be a problem. Troy got an alert that someone sent an encrypted file off settlement from Reed's console."

Adrianna darkened. "He wouldn't do that."

"We have evidence. He's reporting to somebody."

"I refuse to believe that. Jenson has been on our team for five years. We trust him implicitly."

Adam nodded. He knew she would be loyal. "I just thought you should know."

"What are you going to do?"

"Nothing for now. I've instructed Troy to keep a close eye on him, though. I'd appreciate it if you kept this to yourself."

Adrianna agreed as Taberg stood to leave. "Your daughter can't be far away." He smiled. "I'm sure she's not playing outside."

* * *

Susanna Frost stepped into her boss's office. Suddenly, she was bathed in chilly air. Cross had programmed his office to resemble the frozen terrain of Antarctica. The floor was white with virtual snow, while, in the distance, a domed encampment could be seen, complete with weathervane and flag. On another wall, a team of dogs stood patiently in front of a sled, waiting for their master's command. Susanna felt a frigid puff of air on her face. How did he do that? As Susanna approached her boss, the chill receded. Cross was berating one of his subordinates on his comlink.

Dr. Maxwell Thrune stood next to Cross. His diminutive form dominated the space. Thrune was an ugly little man with a scrunched face and thin, wiry hair. His ears were disproportionately large for his head, and he walked with a shuffle. He was cold and humorless. Susanna thought he could make a great villain in a horror movie.

Thrune turned and looked at Susanna, like a troll who just caught a person trespassing on his bridge. His eyes were like tiny black BBs, scrutinizing everything about her. The edges of his mouth curled upward, ever so slightly, suggesting a form of malevolent amusement. Susanna felt like a specimen in a jar, whose life was in the hands of a monster.

"Yes?" Cross turned disapprovingly toward Susanna.

"We have a report from Meridian 6, sir."

"And…"

"The scientists are in place and are getting started with their work. It'll be several weeks before we know how they're doing. They're building a new containment unit and will begin the work of reconstituting the phase-two machines once the unit is ready."

Cross smiled. "That's very good." Susanna blushed under her makeup. From Cross, this was high praise.

Thrune seemed impatient. "The Shadow Project is at a critical stage, Mr. Cross. It would be helpful to have access to the containment unit plans." His voice was high pitched. He sounded twenty years older than he looked.

Cross turned to the scientist. "You have the plans already."

"Yes. That is accurate, but incomplete. I wish to determine if they have made any improvements in the design. The Project demands perfection. I don't want any issues with faulty circuits."

Susanna expected her boss to take issue with Thrune's tone, but he didn't. "Very well." Cross turned to her. "Make sure Dr. Thrune has what he needs, Ms. Frost."

"Yes, sir."

"Remember, Ms. Frost. I expect results from these people. Give them some time, but use pressure if you have to. I will hold you responsible if they disappoint me." Cross's expression turned as cold as his office scenery. His eyes stabbed through her. Her appreciative blush was gone. Susanna had let her guard down, and Amos had instinctively chosen that moment to strike.

"Yes, sir," she managed, but Cross and Thrune had already dismissed her. They turned their backs and continued their conversation in hushed tones.

* * *

Hunter Logan left his residence and walked slowly around the outer corridor toward the Rec Bay. Adrianna's visit had pushed him out of his gloom. His wife's infidelity had shaken their friendship and their marriage. She had confessed to him right away. They went through counseling and a painful meeting with Robert Hastings. Robert had offered to resign his position at the Institute, but Hunter wouldn't accept it. Over the years, they had grown beyond the pain and distrust. Hunter frowned, thinking of the burden Sprite still carried. It troubled him that she had seen the whole thing. No wonder she was angry. He needed to find a way to bring Sprite and Adrianna back together.

Hunter felt reengaged with life. It was strange that such a dark moment in their marriage could be a healing force. For the first time in months, he felt reconnected with his family and with himself. His guilt would have to wait. Sprite came first.

Hunter wandered toward the General Supply Bay. He stayed in the rim corridor to avoid the rest of the team. He wanted to be alone for a while. He entered General Supply and followed the inner wall of the dome until he came to the corridor leading to the garden. The fragrance of the garden attracted him like a moth drawn toward a light in a darkened room.

* * *

Sprite was brooding in her den of crates. She heard footsteps approaching, and although she had nothing to hide, she tensed at the thought of being discovered. She got on her knees and crawled over to the entrance of her sanctuary. The footsteps grew louder. She peered around the stack of cases and saw her father wandering through the Supply Bay. He looked worn and tired. He passed by her hideaway, unaware of her presence. Sprite got to her feet and shadowed her father at a distance. She noticed how he held his body and how he placed his feet as he walked. He drifted down the corridor toward the Enviro Bay. As he approached the bay, his gait became more confident.

* * *

Cilla's back was turned when Hunter entered the Enviro Bay. She didn't notice him as he wandered into the garden. The plants surrounded him, and he felt their life embrace him. He took a seat on a bench under a small tree. Hunter tilted his head up and took a deep breath of the garden air. He closed his eyes. For a moment, sanity returned to his troubled heart.

* * *

Adrianna Norton stood at the edge of the gorge at Whetstone Gulf in the Adirondacks of New York State. Cut into the Tug Hill plateau, the gorge and surrounding forest offered a breathtaking vista. "It's beautiful." She set her backpack down on the path and put her hands on her hips, scanning the stream below.

Hunter stood next to her. They were graduate students at Cornell

University, taking a rare break from their studies. He put his arm around her. "I'm glad you suggested this. We'll have to tell the Conservancy. They'd love it up here." The two were members of an environmental group.

Adrianna smiled. "Mother Nature at her finest." She swung her camera up and took a picture. "I'll come back up here anytime."

The couple found a large rock, warmed by the morning sun. They sat and unpacked their lunch. The birds sang in the trees, and a crisp breeze swept across the rim of the gorge, offering cool refreshment. Hunter took a long breath, savoring the fragrance of the forest mingled with Adrianna's scent. He loved her with all his heart.

After they finished eating, Hunter took the camera from Adrianna. "I want a picture." He moved away from the rim of the gorge to frame the shot. The path wasn't wide enough, so Hunter picked his way across a patch of sharp stones. He teetered on some loose rock.

"Don't fall," Adrianna said. "You could scrape yourself up pretty good."

Hunter looked down at his shorts. His bony legs were exposed. "I'm fine," he replied. Hunter sighted through the viewfinder. "Almost have it." He kept the camera to his face as he sidestepped on the loose stones. Hunter lost his footing and fell headlong on the shards. A jagged stone sliced the skin off his left shin like a sharp knife cutting a Thanksgiving turkey. Blood was everywhere, and he grunted in pain.

Adrianna leapt up and rushed to Hunter's side. She examined his leg. "I can see the bone."

Hunter winced from the pain. "So much for saying nice things about Mother Nature."

Adrianna weighed their options. They didn't have a first-aid kit. She could tear a piece of Hunter's shirt and use it as a bandage, but she needed something against the raw flesh. She looked at a stand of trees just off the path. She smiled.

Adrianna stepped to the nearest tree. It was a slippery elm. The gray-colored bark was perfect. She withdrew a small knife from her pocket and carved out a patch of the inner bark. She took her water bottle and soaked the patch and gently covered Hunter's wound with it. Suddenly, Hunter could see millions of phase-two nanomachines spill out of the bark and begin to consume his body. He jerked himself awake, thankful it was only a dream.

* * *

Hunter didn't know how long he had sat on the bench. He awoke with a start, echoes of the strange dream reverberating in his head. It was something about a trip he had with Adrianna before they were married. Suddenly, he was aware of someone sitting next to him. It was Sprite.

"Are you okay, Dad?" She had a concerned look on her face. "You look like you had a nightmare."

He reached out and put his arm around her, and she instinctively drew close to him. "It was just a weird dream, kiddo." He paused, the final vestiges of the dream evaporating. "How are you?"

Sprite was silent for a moment. "Not so good, Daddy." Sprite was getting older and didn't call him "Daddy" very often. "Mom and I had a fight."

"I know." Hunter turned toward Sprite and wrapped his arms around her.

"I said some bad things to her."

Hunter gave her a squeeze. "Look, honey. You need to talk to Mom about this." He paused. "I want you to know that after she and Robert slept together, Mom came to me, and we talked it out. I was really hurt, and we said some things we both regretted." He paused again. "The main thing is that I forgave her, and we got beyond it. Mom and I have a good marriage because we are best friends. We aren't going to give up on each other, and we aren't going to give up on you." Hunter felt Sprite's tears on his arm. "I am sorry you saw them. That was too much for a little girl."

Sprite sobbed, years of hurt and anger pouring out of her. "I need you, Daddy."

"I know." Hunter stroked her hair. "I need you, too."

They sat together in silence, and then Sprite sat up and pulled away. "Do you think Mom will ever want to see me again?"

Hunter almost laughed. "Of course she will."

"I've got to tell her I'm sorry."

Hunter thought for a moment. "I think she wants to tell you the same thing."

"Will you go with me?"

"No, honey." Hunter gave her an understanding smile. "This is between you and Mom. You've got to talk to her on your own. Remember, your mom is a flawed human being just like you, and she loves us very much."

Sprite leaned forward and gave her dad a kiss on the cheek. "I love you, Daddy."

Hunter smiled. His face had felt tense and hard the last few months. The smile felt good. "I love you too, kiddo." He watched as Sprite disappeared through the lush arboretum. He wanted to protect Sprite from life, but thought better of it. She didn't need his protection as much as she needed the resources to protect herself.

Hunter straightened up on the bench and leaned back. He was amazed by the garden, sheltered inside a concrete dome on a large rock in the cold, dark void of space. He looked at the small tree that arched over the bench, forming a protective canopy. He looked at the bark that covered each branch. "The protector of the protector," he muttered. Hunter had more important things to do than wallow in his guilt. It was time for him to get back to work. He was going to need skin as thick as bark to stand up against the challenges they were facing.

* * *

The old, two-dimensional screens on Cilla Ashe's console displayed the temperature and pressure for each chamber in the settlement. Her system could sense the atmospheric profiles in each area. She hunched over her console, pondering the airborne particulates in Lab Bay Two. The sensors had detected traces of iron-rich clay. The Cerian surface was replete with the substance, but none of it should have been present in the interior of Meridian 6. Airlocks to the surface were located in the Landing Pad. Environment suits and those who wore them were thoroughly decontaminated before reentering the settlement.

Why would there be surface contamination in the Lab Bay? Cilla briefly considered the possibility of a leak, but dismissed it. All the chamber pressures were equalized and steady. Even if there was a leak, Meridian 6 was pressurized relative to the surface, and particulate matter would leak out, rather than in. Cilla scanned each chamber for other instances of the substance. She found it again in the Res Bay. There were minute amounts of it in the Logans' quarters. It didn't make any sense.

* * *

Hunter walked back toward the Res Bay. He nodded to Ray Bright, who passed him with a cart full of cases. He could hear the sound of "Hello Dolly" escaping from the man's headphones. Ray walked in time to the music, lost in his Broadway bliss. Hunter entered his quarters. The door to Sprite's bedroom was open. As he approached the threshold, he saw Adrianna and Sprite talking quietly with each other.

* * *

During the off-world expansion, hundreds of small mining operations had struck out beyond Mars to tap the mineral wealth of the asteroids. The asteroid settlements resembled the wild west of years gone by. They were far from authority and the rule of law. Meridian had a security force at Rinker's Knot, a large base on Vesta. Nevertheless, they could do little to tame the rough and ready culture of The Asteroid Belt.

Those who lived in Belt preferred solitude. They were people with pasts. Some were emotionally disturbed. Others were just odd. They wanted to be forgotten. Settlements came in all shapes and sizes. Some were family businesses. Others were small communities. There were also dens of thieves.

Years before, Meridian Corporation had abandoned Meridian 6. A clan of thieves took possession of it and used the settlement as a base of operations. Eventually, Meridian security forces recaptured the settlement. When Amos Cross instructed his people to prepare Meridian 6 for the NARI scientists, they slapped a new coat of paint on the walls, and installed the micro-black-hole transmitter in the Core. They were certain they had restored the research settlement to its original condition. However, the thieves had made some enhancements during their years in residence.

* * *

Rory North sat alone in the Res Bay Common Area. Sparky's box was on the table in front of her. Her arms were like the walls of a skin fortress, encircling the little container. Her face was drawn. There were bags under her eyes, evidence of many sleepless nights. She closed her eyes, listening in her imagination for the sound of her mother's voice. She painted a picture of her mother's face on a canvas in her mind. The image was fading, and she felt guilty about it. She tried to imagine the scent of her hair, the cadence of her footsteps.

"Rory? You okay?"

The young girl jumped, her eyes snapping open. Kell Edwards stood before her, a concerned look on his face. "Sorry. I didn't mean to startle you."

"It's okay, Kell." He could see the tears in the corners of her eyes. "I was just thinking."

"Missing your mom?"

"Like you wouldn't believe."

Kell sat down across the table from her, uncertain of what to say next. The silence was uncomfortable. "She was a great person." Rory looked down at the table and nodded her head.

"Why am I here, Kell?"

"What do you mean?"

"I don't have anything to contribute. Mom is gone, so I have no connection to the team." She wiped her eyes. "I'm just a kid."

Kell reached across the tabletop and touched her hand. "You're part of our family. If you weren't here, where would you be?"

"No place, I guess. Mom was the only family I had."

"There's your answer. You're here because you belong here."

Rory shrugged. "The Logans have been awfully nice."

"And they really like you."

"Sprite's kind of a sister."

"She's a real sister."

"I still don't know." There was a far-away look in her eyes. "Why did all this happen?"

Kell's mind was churning as he tried to think of the perfect words. He wanted to make things better for her. Finally, he spread his hands in front of him. "I don't know what to say." The silence wasn't as awkward after that.

* * *

Tyson Edwards placed his coffee flask on the edge of the bench. He was working in Lab Bay Two, calibrating the new containment unit with Hunter, Adrianna, and Jo. The system was designed to hold the phase-two nanomachines in a containment field, along with a miniature robotic lab module that permitted the scientists to work with the machines without risking a breach.

"It's almost nulled out." Jo stood next to an impressive rack of test instruments. "We've got 98 percent containment." The group had struggled all morning to balance the currents in the complex circuitry. It was a frustrating exercise. Adrianna was lying on the floor, reaching up into the interior of the containment unit. She was making tiny adjustments, as Jo called out the numbers.

"That's it. One hundred percent." Jo double-checked the analyzer.

"Is it holding steady?" Hunter scanned the components inside the device.

Jo's face broke into a huge smile. "Steady as an atomic clock."

Adrianna slid out from under the unit. Ty grinned with satisfaction as Jo lifted her hand to share a high five with him. Ty stretched out his arm and caught the handle of the flask. The long-necked mug flipped off the edge of the bench, just missing Adrianna. It bounced on the concrete floor, its contents splashing out of the cylindrical container.

"Sorry, Adrianna!" Ty grabbed a cloth and knelt down to clean up the mess.

"It's okay. You missed."

Ty looked at the pool of liquid. "What the heck?" Adrianna looked down. The contents of the flask were draining through a thin crack in the floor. Ty leaned forward. "Does this lab have raised flooring?"

"It's solid concrete." Hunter came around for a look.

Ty's eyes narrowed. "Something's under here."

Adrianna got to her feet, and the four scientists rolled the containment unit off to one side. They knelt down and began a careful examination of the laboratory floor.

"There is definitely something here." Adrianna pried at the crack with a fingernail. A small square panel, colored to match the surrounding concrete, popped up. The missing liquid pooled around a control panel hidden beneath it.

Ty looked over her shoulder. "Are those buttons?"

Adrianna wiped the panel with a piece of cloth. "There are two of them. One says 'open,' and the other says 'close.' I wonder what it opens?"

"Something secret." Hunter suggested, as he began pushing the containment unit further away.

Jo leaned against the containment unit to help him. "You think it opens the floor?"

"Maybe."

"Hey, guys." Tyson had his cheek against the floor. "I think I can see the outline of an opening down here."

Jo squinted at the floor. "You can't see anything from up here."

"You have to site along the floor to see it. There's some kind of opening."

Hunter went over to the hatchway and sealed the Lab Bay. "Something tells me we need some privacy."

They gathered near the small opening in the floor, and Ty pressed the 'open' button. The faint outline in the floor widened. In the opening, they could see a staircase descending to a passageway below.

4

Cilla Ashe turned her head to look at her display. A blinking icon had attracted her attention. The air quality had changed in Lab Bay Two. She checked the profile. The levels of iron-rich clay were even higher than when she first noticed them. "What's going on?" she said to herself. She ran a diagnostic and saw that the driver for the Lab sensor needed to be updated. "That must be it." Cilla made a note to ask Troy to download a new driver.

* * *

Ty led the way down the stairway. A light had illuminated the passage below when the floor had opened. A long corridor stretched out before them. There was a large hatch at the far end. Cautiously, they made their way toward it. Tyson turned to his friends. "Do you think we need environment suits before we open this?"

Adrianna touched the cold metal of the hatch. "I don't think so. There's no sign of an airlock. The hatch swings toward us. If there is low pressure on the other side, the door won't open. We can get a sniffer to check the atmosphere once we crack the hatch."

They were in agreement. Hunter went back to the Lab Two Supply Bay for a sniffer and four HEPA masks. Once he returned, they donned the masks and broke the seal on the hatch. It opened easily. The sniffer confirmed there was a breathable atmosphere in the room beyond. The slight pressure differential between the hidden room and Lab Bay Two had kicked up a mist of dust. The lighting glistened off the dust particles, creating a luminous fog.

Tyson led the way forward. They entered a rectangular chamber. The ceiling, walls and floor were lined with a fine metal mesh. There were broken plastic crates and discarded items strewn haphazardly around the room. A table and two chairs sat in the middle of the space.

On the far wall was another hatch. An airlock was centered in an alcove to their right.

Jo kicked at some of the debris. "What is this place?"

Hunter stepped over to a large box near one wall. "I think it's a Keep."

"A what?"

"A Keep is a stronghold. In medieval times, castles had hidden inner rooms, like a panic room in a high-end home. They used them to store valuables and as a last line of defense. If you think about it, Lab Bay Two is the innermost chamber in the settlement. This room is as far from the entrance as you can get."

Adrianna wrinkled her nose. "Why would Meridian Corporation install a room like this?"

"They wouldn't." Hunter tapped the box next to him. Exposed conduits ran from the case to the lighting system. "This is a standalone power unit. This room was built after the settlement was finished. The workmanship is different, not as refined. I'll bet the thieves built this place to hide their loot."

"Or torture their prisoners," Jo suggested with a shiver.

Tyson stepped over to the airlock and examined the controls. "It looks like Meridian 6 has a back door." He pressed a couple of icons and noted the readings on the small display panel. "The pressure is equalized." Tyson stabbed the touch-sensitive screen, and the hatch slid open. "Yes!" He stepped into the lock and gazed through the viewport mounted in the outer hatch. He punched a button on the control panel to his right, and a glow appeared through the glass. "Take a look at this." The other three squeezed into the lock. Through the viewport, they could see a large, cavernous space. A small landing pad was situated on the floor of the enormous room. Alignment beacons began to pulsate. Ty pressed another button, and the ceiling of the underground dock opened, revealing a canopy of stars.

"First a back door, now our own private parking garage." Hunter clapped his hands together. "This might come in handy."

Tyson closed the roof panels, once again concealing the landing pad. The four returned to the chamber. "We're going to need some environment suits."

Jo ran her hand along the wall and then paused to examine the perforated metal that covered every inch of the room. "What about this stuff?

Adrianna smiled. Everything made sense. "This whole room is a Faraday Cage. The metal mesh is a shield for electromagnetic waves."

"Nothing gets in." Hunter slid his foot over the woven metallic floor. "And nothing gets out. Take a look. There is no wiring through the shield. It wasn't just a Keep. It was an inner sanctum for scheming and planning." Jo keyed her comlink. It was dead. No signals could penetrate the metal mesh.

Adrianna stepped back into the airlock and triggered the lights in the landing bay. She squinted at the nearest wall. "The landing bay is shielded, too. They hid ships in here. Sensors wouldn't be able to detect them."

Tyson grinned. "We can do the same thing. We can put a comp system in here, and no one will be able to detect it."

Hunter nodded. They were both thinking the same thing. "Meridian Corporation wouldn't have a clue."

They spent several minutes picking through the detritus, then they moved to the far wall where the second hatch was located. It was identical to the one they had used to enter the Keep. Hunter examined the seals. "Should we open this one?"

Tyson smiled. "I think I know where this goes. We can open it." Hunter released the latching mechanism and cracked open the hatch. Another rough-hewn tunnel lay beyond. It was illuminated like the other entrance tunnel and just as musty. They walked more confidently through the passageway and stopped at a small control panel at the far end. Ty pressed a button, and a door-sized panel slid silently into a hidden recess. Beyond the open panel was Adrianna and Hunter's bedroom. Tyson grinned mischievously. "How convenient. Your own private path from the love nest to the lab bench."

* * *

The four scientists agreed to keep the existence of the chamber a secret. They called it "The Refuge." Over the next few days, they cleaned up the hidden room and rigged a portable air purification system to flush the dust from the air. Ty turned on the purifier and stood, stretching a kink out of his back. "This place defeats the purpose of the Iso Bay. If we have a breach in Lab Bay Two, the Res Bay will be contaminated."

"I've thought about that, Ty." Hunter gave his friend a cunning smile. "I don't think we need to worry." Ty could tell his friend had a new idea. "I want to find a way to stop the nanomachines. We may need to reconstitute a few of them to test our work, but I won't let those killers out of the containment unit. Ever."

"How are we going to do it?" Ty sat down on a nearby crate.

"I'm not sure yet." Hunter looked around The Refuge. "This is great lab space to do the work, but we're going to need some time. We'll have to keep Meridian from asking too many questions until we have the counter technology. Then the phase-two machines will be worthless."

"Meridian will lose interest in them." Tyson was nodding. "And they'll let us get on with our lives."

Hunter smiled. "And the kids will be safe."

"Who do we trust?" Tyson scratched his head, a scowl slowly forming on his face.

"We need to play this hand close to our chests. You, me, Jo, and Adrianna. That's it. If Meridian finds out about this, they'll stop us. We won't be in a power position until we have a way to stop the phase-two machines."

"That makes sense to me." Tyson stood up with renewed energy. "Let's start getting this lab set up."

* * *

Rory North swam across the garden pool in the Enviro Bay. The small body of water filled an irregularly shaped basin cut into the dome's floor. A number of trees overarched the water, offering the suggestion of a tranquil forest natatorium. Grass carpeted its banks, and a plethora of flowers and bushes brought color and fragrance to the place.

Rory was a natural swimmer. She closed her eyes and backstroked across the length of the pool. Then she flipped and turned, applying a leisurely sidestroke as she returned to where she began. This was a good place. A place of peace. A place for new beginnings.

As Rory approached the spot on the bank where she had left her things, she saw Alexis Wren wandering in a nearby glade. She pulled herself out of the water and grabbed her towel to dry off. Alexis looked up and wandered over to her.

"What's in the box?" Alexis gestured toward Sparky's container. "It's alive, isn't it?"

"His name is Sparky." The young girl opened the lid and let Alexis take a peek.

"I've never seen anything like it."

"That's because he's one of a kind. I stitched together his DNA and grew him in a lab down on Earth."

Alexis looked up at Rory. "You hide your talent, young lady."

"No. I just haven't been in the mood to talk much lately."

If Alexis remembered that Rory's mother had died on Selene Station, she didn't show it. Such tact in the face of a delicate moment was far beyond her people skills. "Does it do anything?"

"I call him a shocker. He generates an electrical potential across his body." Rory let Alexis feel the tingling sensation.

"Where are you headed with this?" She spoke as if Rory's pet was a beaker of chemicals.

"Someday I'm going to develop a larger, more efficient version of Sparky that will power a spacecraft or a place like this." Rory beamed with pride, her eyes sparkling with hope and promise.

"Maybe you will." Alexis turned and walked out of the garden. Rory watched as the older woman paused to examine a leaf here and a flower there. The scientist had never shown any interest in Rory. What had made her venture out of her scientific muse to examine Sparky?

* * *

Hunter wandered the rim corridor, searching for the courage to speak with Robert Hastings. He didn't like confrontations. He had spent the last forty-five minutes avoiding the inevitable. Finally, he steeled himself and entered Lab Bay One. Hunter sat down on a stool next to Hastings. The man was hunched over, studying a complex formula on his holodisplay.

"Hey, Robert," Hunter said evenly.

"Hunter."

"I wanted to have a word with you, if you have the time."

Hastings lifted his head and turned toward Hunter, letting his hands drop to his sides, instantly sensing a problem. The two men had a long history. "What is it?"

"Ah, this isn't easy, Robert."

Robert braced himself for the worst. God knew Hunter had a whole catalog of reasons to be at odds with him. "Just spit it out, Hunter."

Hunter let out a long breath. "It's about Sprite."

This wasn't what Hastings expected. A quizzical look took shape on his face. "What's the matter?"

Hunter looked down at his hands. "Years ago, when we had our personal problem…"

"Yes?" Robert cut him off, not wanting to hear the words. It was another reminder of his failure, of his infidelity to Maryanne and Emile.

"Sprite was there. She saw you with Adrianna."

Hastings was stunned. "Shit! You've got to be kidding."

"Apparently the door was left open and Sprite heard a noise."

"No!" Hastings sagged on his chair, broken yet again. "I'm sorry, Hunter."

Hunter was beyond anger. "That's why Sprite has never liked you."

Robert looked down at his knees. "That explains a lot. I don't blame her. Is Adrianna aware of this?"

Hunter nodded sadly. "At least we know why Sprite has been angry with her these past few years."

"Damn." Hastings shook his head. "I really messed up."

Hunter was surprised by Robert's reaction. Hastings had been grumpy with everyone. Hunter had not expected remorse and guilt. "Yes, you did." There was a note of sadness in Hunter's voice. Life had bruised his little girl far sooner than he expected. "The next time you screw somebody's mother, make sure the kids aren't home."

Hastings looked at Hunter pleadingly. "I'm really sorry, Hunter." He was still shaking his head as Hunter left the Lab Bay.

* * *

Hunter passed Cilla Ashe on his way through the Core. He nodded cordially but didn't speak. His anger with Robert had been rekindled, and he didn't want to talk with anyone. Cilla watched him head toward the Rec Bay, as she wove her way through the Tech Stacks. Troy Mack was checking a piece of equipment.

"How's it going?"

Troy looked up from his work. He felt the plastic covering his chin, the tightness of the scar tissue on his face. A wave of embarrassment coursed through him, but Cilla didn't react to his appearance. "Same as usual: trying to keep the civilians in line and getting my work done."

"I need your help." Cilla told him about the outdated driver for the Lab Bay Two sensor.

"I'll download new drivers for all the sensors later today."

Troy glanced over his shoulder, making sure no one was within earshot. "I was wondering. Would you like to get together tonight?"

Cilla smiled appreciatively, but Troy could see a curtain descending behind her eyes, a door closing on a set of possibilities deemed unthinkable. "I don't think so." Troy touched her hand, but she pulled away. "It's not a good idea." Cilla spun on her heels and went back toward the Enviro Bay.

* * *

Drew Mallick sat back in his chair at Meridian Headquarters. Two icons floated in his large holographic chamber. The one on his right represented the data module containing Hunter Logan's research data. The left icon symbolized his latest creation: an AI engineered to worm its way into the data module and unlock its contents.

"Are you ready, MK?" Drew had named his new tool "MK," short for "Master Key."

"Absolutely, sir. I will study the encryption code in the module and report any weaknesses."

"Execute."

MK's icon began to pulsate. Drew knew it would take his AI several hours to study the data's smart encryption. He got up from his desk, craving a cup of coffee.

* * *

Alexis Wren sat at her bench in Lab Bay One. She was engrossed in a problem related to tuning the behavior of a self-assembling nanostructure. She paused and spoke into her earset microphone. "What time is it?"

Alexis's card comp was programmed to speak in a deep mellifluous voice. "It's eighteen thirty-five, Alexis. You're late for dinner."

Alexis knew exactly what time it was. She had waited until the rest of the team was having dinner in the Rec Bay. She wanted to be alone. Alexis got up and stretched. Moments later, she was in the Core. It took her only a moment at Jenson's workstation to upload the file from the data module hidden in her pocket. With her mission accomplished, Alexis wandered down the corridor toward the Rec Bay. Everyone was seated in the commissary. There was a cacophony of voices as the conversations merged together. She found an empty seat next to Jo and Ty.

"I was wondering when you'd come up for air," Jo remarked with a smile. "How's it going?"

"Oh, I'm doing some crystal phase analysis. It's a little tricky getting the self-assemblies the way I want them." She looked at the empty table in front of her and got up. Alexis walked over to the beverage dispenser and filled a flask with water. She became distracted, and soon she was wandering around the Rec Bay, lost in thought. No one paid much attention. They were used to her idiosyncrasies. Finally, Alexis returned to her seat.

Ty looked at her. "Aren't you going to eat?"

Alexis looked down, realizing she hadn't gotten any food. "Oh! I'm hungry." She got up again.

Jo gave Ty an amused look. "Is she human? I have never seen anyone like her."

"Maybe not, but she's a great researcher."

"No argument here," Jo replied.

* * *

Later that night, Ray Bright sat on his bunk, his back propped up against the headboard. A half a flask of whisky sat on the bedside table. He cradled a small framed hologram in his hands. It was the image of a beautiful woman. She had dark, shoulder-length hair with golden strands, which flowed like rays of the sun over obsidian silk. He spoke quietly, as if she were in the room with him. "It won't be long now, baby. I'm going to find a way for us to be together." He took another sip of his drink. "Tell me that you love me." The hologram was silent.

* * *

The AI was still working on the data module at the end of Drew Mallick's shift. He was about to lock his workstation when he heard a soft chime, and the AI's icon morphed into the picture of a cat. Drew scowled. This didn't make any sense.

"Report your findings," he commanded.

The AI began to purr. "I am very sorry." The cat actually looked sad. "Your AI cannot report to you."

"And why is that?" Drew shook his head, a sense of foreboding coalescing in his chest.

"Because he's dead."

"AI's don't die."

"This one did. He was caught wandering around where he didn't belong, and I killed him."

Drew knew he had failed again. He changed his approach. "You look like such a nice kitty. Why didn't you talk to him and get to know him? You might have become friends."

The icon began to shimmer as the cat morphed into a larger, more fearsome, feline. The AI's voice became deeper, its tone menacing. "Because I am a tiger and tigers don't negotiate."

Drew pounded his desk as the icon disappeared.

* * *

Troy installed the new drivers for the sensor systems. Cilla had hoped the iron-rich clay mystery would be solved. It was not. She looked at the readings on her console. The abnormalities in atmospheric gasses in Lab Bay Two persisted. In fact, there had been an increase in the traces of iron-rich clay. She dialed up the sensors in the Res Bay and found a similar increase in concentration.

Adam Taberg walked purposefully into the Enviro Bay. He had a military bearing, his eyes scanning everything. Cilla looked up, immediately conscious of his intense gaze. "Hi, Adam." The man was built like an iron machine. "Take a look at this, will you?" Adam stood behind Cilla as she flipped through the data screens. She could smell his scent. A raw power exuded from his frame. "I noticed this last week. There seems to be trace amounts of iron-rich clay inside the settlement."

"Iron-rich clay?"

"Yeah. It's surface material. This whole place is built on top of the stuff."

"What's so strange about that?"

Cilla swiveled and faced Adam. God, he was an Adonis. His crotch was half a meter away. "When Meridian 6 was built, the entire complex was sealed to hold an atmosphere. It was also scrubbed so no surface materials would contaminate the living spaces. Everything that comes into Meridian 6 passes through the airlocks on the Landing Pad. Environment suits are decontaminated whenever someone comes in from the surface."

"So there shouldn't be any traces of surface material in here."

"Exactly."

Adam crouched down next to her. "No one has been out on the surface since we got here."

"That's right. So why am I finding trace amounts of surface material in Lab Bay Two and in the Res Bay?"

Adam smiled. He was so close to Cilla, she could see the pores in his skin. "There might be cracks in the foundation."

Cilla swiveled back to her console. She could feel the warmth of his body. Distracted, she fumbled as she screened up a floor plan of the research settlement.

Adam tapped the screen. "You should upgrade to a holodisplay."

Cilla shook her head. "Naw, I like the old technology. Two dimensions are good enough for me." She examined the display. "The atmospheric pressure is holding steady, but there's some kind of breach. I'm sure of it."

"I'll check the foundations."

* * *

Sprite watched while Jenson Reed opened the back of a rack in the Tech Stacks. He was rerouting some cables and installing some new nano-drives. Sitting next to them was the flight case Ray Bright had delivered to the Core that morning. Jenson glanced down at the case. "Open that, will you?" Sprite released the catches and lifted the cover. Inside was a gleaming black box with several electrical connections. Jenson lifted the device out of the case and slid it into an empty space in the rack. Then, he began plugging cables into the box. Jenson worked self-consciously, as if he was nervous about something. Sprite heard footsteps echo against the domed ceiling. Jenson looked up tensely.

"What are you doing back there?" Sprite looked up with surprise. Troy Mack stood with his fists on his hips, an accusing look on his disfigured face. Sprite was disgusted by his appearance and quickly looked down at the floor. Jenson stepped back and looked around the access door. "I'm working, *sir*." Jenson spat out the word "sir" like a piece of rotten fruit.

Troy pointed at Sprite. "What's she doing here?"

Jenson stepped away from the rack and stood face to face with his nemesis. "I was letting her watch. She's interested in comps, and she's pretty good with them."

"I want her out of here." Troy paused, looking at the cables hanging out of the open panel. "What are you doing in the rack?"

"If you would just look, you'll see the new nano-drives. We brought them with us, and I'm installing them." Troy took a step toward the access door. "Come on, Troy. You don't have to look over my shoulder. It's a routine upgrade."

Mack pushed the bigger man aside and looked into the back of the rack. He reached in and pulled out a small cylinder with connectors on each end. "What's this?"

Jenson took the device from Troy. "I have no idea. It was already in there."

"I'm going to find out what this is. Until I do, I don't want you in the Core."

"You can't do that!" Jenson raised his voice."

"What's up, guys?" Hunter Logan appeared in the aisle near the two men. Sprite was visibly relieved to see her father.

Jenson's face was beet-red. "Troy is kicking us out of the Core."

Hunter gave Jenson a steady look, and then turned to Troy. "What did they do?"

"He permitted the girl back here under dangerous conditions." He gestured toward the open rack. "He was installing some unauthorized equipment." Troy held up the mysterious cylinder.

Hunter's eyes narrowed. "My daughter may be young, but she knows a lot about comp systems. I am sure she wasn't doing anything that would do harm to this equipment." He gestured toward the odd device. "Jenson? Did you put that in there?"

Jenson blushed. "I've never seen it before."

Hunter turned to Troy. "Did you see him put it in there?"

Troy hesitated. "No, but he was acting suspiciously."

"I was just installing new nano-drives, Dr. Logan. It's my job."

Hunter nodded at Sprite. "What do you say, kiddo?"

Sprite stepped closer to Jenson. "He wasn't doing anything wrong." She glared at Troy, defensively. "Just like he said, he was installing the nano-drives."

Hunter took the cylinder from Jenson. "What is this?"

Troy shrugged. "I'm going to find out."

Hunter gave it back to him and took a moment to size up both men. Then he looked at Troy. "Given the circumstances, I think you should ease up on Jenson. Let him keep working."

"That's not your call, Dr. Logan. I want him out of the Core." Troy looked at Sprite. "*Both* of them."

"I think you're overreacting. We need him. For all you know, that cylinder has been in there since Meridian 6 was built."

Adam Taberg appeared from behind the racks. Troy looked triumphant at the sight of his commander. "Is there a problem, Troy?" He listened as Troy recounted the incident. "Let me see that." Hunter handed him the strange cylinder. "It's a harmonic filter. Old technology. There is nothing strange about it."

Troy was deflated. "But sir, I saw him with it in the rack."

"I never touched it."

Adam eyed the flight case for the nano-drives. He glanced in the rack and then looked at Jenson. "You were installing new drives?"

"Yes sir."

Adam Taberg motioned toward Sprite. "And the girl?"

"She was watching."

Taberg looked at Hunter, who nodded. He turned to Troy, giving him a sympathetic look. "The man hasn't done any harm. Let him get back to work." Troy turned red, but nodded in obeisance.

Jenson let out a long breath. "Thank you, Adam."

"Don't thank me, Mr. Reed. I want Mr. Mack to be fair with you as much as I want you to respect Mr. Mack's authority. Understood?"

"Yes, sir."

"And young lady, you need to get permission from Mr. Mack to be in the Tech Stacks." Taberg nodded at the three men. "Gentlemen." He turned on his heels and left.

* * *

Sprite left the Core with her father. They walked slowly toward the Rec Bay. She was clearly upset. "Troy is so mean!"

"He feels threatened, kiddo." Hunter put his arm around her shoulder. "Jenson has been on our team for years, and now Troy has taken over his responsibilities. Both are uncomfortable with each other. Jenson feels slighted, and Troy feels the need to protect his authority. It's not an easy situation."

"He's still mean."

Hunter gave her a squeeze. "I need your help." Sprite always liked helping her father. "We'll talk about it tonight. It's a little job for you and Wiley." She beamed with pride at the thought.

* * *

Damon Trask looked up from his pristine desk as Maya Lewis entered his office on the ISS-20 Space Station. The floor-to-ceiling glass behind Trask's desk gave one the feeling of walking out into space. Below them was the Earth, jeweled with breathtaking blues and greens.

"Yes, Maya?"

"Everything is ready. We just need your order, and I will put things in motion."

"Good." Trask looked at her, taking in her erotic form. "Do it."

"Yes, sir." Maya spun on her heals and left. His eyes followed her out the door.

* * *

Maya sat down at her holodisplay and collected her thoughts. She leaned back in her chair. "New message," she said.

"Good afternoon, Maya." The AI's voice purred with sultry femininity. "You look stunning today."

Maya appreciated the compliment but refused to enter into a dialog with the machine. "Send the following message, via the Mars Meridian secure server." Maya rattled off the address. A three-dimensional network map appeared, showing the routing for the message and its destination.

"I'm ready when you are, Maya."

The chamber of the holodisplay churned and roiled with a deep violet mist. A thread of cinnamon wove its way up through the digital vapors. Maya noticed that it matched the color of her bodysuit. "The item will arrive on the next supply shuttle. Look in case 176-824. Authorization granted." Maya commanded her comp to encrypt the message, using a key known only to herself and the recipient.

* * *

Hunter was in a changing room outside one of the light chambers in the Rec Bay. He stripped out of his clothing and stood before one of the mirrors, pondering his naked bag of bones. Growing old was hell. He had let himself go over the last few months. The depression had sidetracked him from his work, his family, and his body. He stepped to the control panel and set his profile. Hunter hadn't used a chamber since they arrived. The phototherapy would be good for him. As he dialed in his preferences, he sensed a presence behind him. A familiar perfume washed over him. He turned around slowly. Adrianna had already unzipped her jumpsuit, letting it drop to the floor.

"Thought you'd like some company." Her voice was filled with promise.

Hunter smiled. "Hmmm."

She leaned into him, his leg between her knees. Her body was soft and warm. Hunter reached behind him and engaged the chamber. They entered the glowing space together, their skin surrounded by the light.

* * *

Robert Hastings' residence was on the far side of the Res Bay. He made his way around the passageway that circled the Common Area and almost bumped into Sprite Logan as she emerged from her quarters. She stopped short and gave him a hateful look. Robert almost said something, but she hurried away before he had the chance.

Hastings entered his quarters and closed the door. It was a mess. He had made no attempt to move in. Boxes and discarded clothing were strewn around the living space. Robert's body trembled with stress. He pulled off his shirt and wadded it up into a ball. He used it to wipe the sweat from his forehead and tossed it aside. Struck by a violent headache, his hands flew to his head. His knees almost buckled. Struggling to keep his balance, Robert made his way across the room, weaving his way through the clutter. He found a dirty flask and splashed some water into it. He took the half-empty container into his bedroom. Placing it on the bedside stand, Robert grabbed an old pair of sneakers that lay in a corner. He stuck his hand inside, under the Velcro straps, and withdrew a small bottle. Dropping onto the bed, he wrenched the cap off the bottle and poured two pills into the palm of his hand. He looked around the room, then dumped two more pills out of the bottle. He swallowed the pills with a quick swig of water and fell back on the bed.

* * *

Kell Edwards knelt on the floor of the Lab Two Supply Bay, rummaging through a box of spare parts. The box contained items that weren't in the supply database. He found what he was looking for near the bottom. "There you are," he said to the wayward part. He felt a wave of satisfaction as he stood up.

Sprite entered the bay, carrying a pad comp in her hand. A butterfly was sketched on the flat, two-dimensional display. She wove her way through the racks of cases and bins. Rory tagged along behind her, fascinated by her friend's project. "Kell? You in here?"

Kell looked up and smiled as she approached. "Hi, Sprite. What's up?" Sprite stood next to him. He loved her, though he couldn't say it. Rory was there, and her presence made such an admission impossible. Sprite was his best friend, and he had sworn he would honor their relationship. He drank in her presence. She was beautiful.

Sprite handed the pad comp to him, and Kell admired the butterfly. "My mom's birthday is coming up, and I need some help with her present." He listened quietly as she outlined what she wanted to do. She was his goddess, and he would do anything for her.

* * *

The scientists continued their work on the new containment unit in Lab Bay Two. Adrianna was running a simulation on the Meridian 6 comp system when her holodisplay locked up. "What's this?"

The AI was emotionless. "I no longer have connectivity with the Core Intellect."

"Reconnect." Adrianna waited while her AI tried to navigate back into the main system.

"The Core Intellect is no longer available."

There was a flicker in the lighting, and a series of alarms began to ping throughout the settlement. Adrianna keyed her comlink. "Jenson? What's happening out there?" There was no answer. She looked up at Jo, who was sitting a few meters away from her. "Is your system working?"

Jo glanced at her holodisplay. "Seems to be... No, it's not. The AI is disconnected."

Adrianna rose from her workspace and padded out of the Lab Bay. As she approached the Core, she could hear the commotion. Troy was screaming at Jenson Reed. "What in hell did you do?"

"I didn't do anything." Jenson bleated. He was staring intently at his holodisplay, while Troy glared at him from his central console.

The Core Intellect spoke in a cool monotone. "I do not know what is happening to me. I am impaired. Primary logic is breaking down."

Troy turned away from Jenson, redirecting his attention to the comp system. "Lock yourself down. Suspend operations."

The voice of the Core Intellect changed. "Do you want a lock of hair or a padlock with a key?" The comp had lost its mind.

Troy looked up from his display. "This is bad." The lights flickered again, as the Core Intellect went offline.

Adam Taberg and Cilla Ashe entered the bay from the direction of the Eng Bay. Adam surveyed the various readings on the large curved console. "Our systems are down, too, guys. My AI announced that he had lost contact with the Core Intellect."

Troy laced his fingers and straightened his arms. "I just shut it down." His knuckles cracked. "Something corrupted the root logic."

"What happened?" Adam's eyes roamed the Tech Stacks, as though he could merge his mind with the circuitry.

"Troy thinks I did it." Everyone looked at Jenson. "He thinks I injected a virus into the core."

"Did you?" Adam looked at Jenson accusingly.

"No. I didn't."

"You must have!" Troy jumped out of his seat, shaking with anger and frustration.

Adam put up his hand. "Enough! Let's solve the problem. Troy, find out the extent of the damage. Jenson, prepare to load the mirror-intellect. Can the two of you do that?"

Jenson and Troy glared at each other. "Yes, sir."

"I want a report within the hour." Adam strode back toward the Eng Bay. Jenson and Troy turned back to their consoles.

* * *

An hour later, Adrianna and Hunter entered the Core. Adam Taberg was watching as Troy and Jenson hunched over the main holodisplay. They watched as the diagnostics AI examined every element of the massive comp system.

Troy frowned as he scrutinized the display. "The hardware is fine, but something has infected the software. We definitely lost the Core Intellect."

Taberg waited for Troy to say more, but he didn't. He never broke eye contact with the holodisplay. "Jenson, is the mirror-intellect ready?"

"Yes, sir. The mirror has kept itself updated by monitoring the "on duty" intellect. It hasn't accepted any executable code. We have cloned it and have installed it as the new Core Intellect. It will approach things differently because it has been learning independently, but it will be free of any viruses."

Adam nodded. "Very good."

Troy looked up. "It's more involved than that." Jenson gave him an angry glare. "We will have a new Core Intellect, but it will have diminished memory. The mirror doesn't store the working data from the labs. It just accumulates the necessary parameters to stay current. The virus wiped some of the nano-drives before it took out the Intellect. That data is gone forever."

"What was lost?" Hunter was unruffled. He leaned against the console, a relaxed expression on his face.

Troy spoke, looking at Adam. "I won't be sure until I finish my scans. There's a lot of distributed memory in the system that may not have been affected. I can tell you more in the morning."

It was already dinnertime, so Hunter and Adrianna excused themselves and headed toward the Rec Bay.

* * *

Kell, Rory, and Sprite sat together during dinner. The comp problems were the topic of conversation. "My card comp froze up, too." Kell fidgeted with the slender device. "Have I lost all my software?"

Sprite reassured her friend. "I'm sure it's okay, Kell."

"Put that away, honey." Jo pointed toward the card comp. "Eat your dinner."

Ty smiled at his son. "Jenson and Troy will know after they run their diagnostics."

Sprite shrugged. "What are we going to do tonight?"

Adrianna stacked her utensils on her plate. "Without comps?"

"Yeah."

"You could clean your room." Hunter gave his daughter a devilish smile.

Sprite frowned. "It's clean already."

"We could play a game." Everyone turned to Rory. "There are a few decks of cards in the storage locker over there. My mom and I used to play old-fashioned cards."

"That's a great idea!" Jo grinned broadly at the young girl. "I haven't played cards since I was a girl."

"That was over seventy years ago." Tyson had an impish look.

"Stow it, you turd." Jo elbowed him, but there was no power in her jab.

* * *

In the middle of the evening, Robert Hastings stumbled into the commissary and paused to survey the gathering. The dome was filled with laughter and conversation. Hunter noticed him as he made his way over to the coffee dispenser. "Robert! Want to join us?"

Hastings fumbled with a row of coffee flasks and made an unintelligible sound. He braced himself against the counter, turning his face toward the card players. Hunter rose and walked over to him. He studied the man's face. His pupils were constricted. He was using drugs. Robert splashed some coffee into a flask, making a mess. He threaded his forefinger through the handle and swung it awkwardly, spilling more coffee as he exited the Rec Bay.

* * *

Later, Adrianna spoke with Hunter in their bedroom. "The game was great," she commented.

Hunter laughed. "I don't think Sprite ever imagined herself having fun with something as low-tech as playing cards. After all, they can't talk."

"That girl never ceases to amaze me." Adrianna kissed her husband's cheek. "You should have her plant a virus in the Core Intellect more often."

"It'll buy us a few days." His mood became dark. "Did you see Hastings? He's a mess."

Adrianna nodded as she took her husband's hands. "This has

ruined him."

Hunter gazed deeply into his wife's eyes. "It almost ruined me."

"I'm glad you're better."

"Me too, but this isn't over, yet." Hunter kissed her goodnight and went into to The Refuge. With the hatch secured, he booted his card comp.

"Good evening, Dr. Logan." Millie's voice was soothing. "Would you like to pick up where we left off?"

"Yes, Millie. Let's do that." Complex shapes appeared in the holodisplay as Hunter cleared his mind. He wouldn't rest until he found a way to neutralize the nanomachines that had killed his friends.

5

In the morning, Jenson Reed stood wearily at the threshold of the Logan's quarters. His eyes were red, from a long night of troubleshooting. Adrianna smiled as she ushered him in. Hunter handed him a flask of coffee as he sat down with them in the small common area.

"What have we got, Jenson?"

"It's pretty bad. We knew the virus corrupted the Core Intellect. We've installed the mirror-intellect. Most of the systems are operational."

"So we should be back up and running soon?" Adrianna looked hopeful.

"Not exactly." Jenson was embarrassed. "The virus targeted all the research data. It erased every drive containing data related to your work."

"It's all gone?" Hunter rubbed his temples.

"Everything. That virus was one nasty bug."

"How about our backups?" Adrianna took a sip from her flask.

"There's good news and bad news. The offline drives are fine, but the virus was timed to hit us an hour before our routine backup." Jenson tried to sound encouraging. "We can restore the system to where it was a week ago."

"I thought we had a virus-hunting AI in the system." Hunter played the part of the concerned leader.

"We do." Jenson looked sheepish. "The virus tricked the AI into thinking it was a virus, too. It got locked into an endless loop, trying to remove itself from the system."

Adrianna shook her head. "This happened from inside Meridian 6."

"Yes. We have a saboteur."

Hunter frowned. "Who could have done it?"

Jenson grew tense. "I don't have any proof, but I have a theory."

"Troy Mack?"

Jenson nodded. "Exactly. I think Troy did it to make me look bad. He's had a problem with me from the beginning."

Hunter thought it was the other way around, but he knew Troy and Jenson weren't responsible for the virus. "Maybe."

"I think he and Adam have gotten together to put me in my place."

"That would make them look bad to Susanna and Amos Cross. I don't think they would do that."

Jenson threw up his hands. "I'm still going to watch my back."

"This isn't about you, Jenson."

The young man left.

Adrianna gave her husband a worried look. "Does he suspect anything?"

"I think we're okay." Hunter could feel acid in his stomach.

* * *

Susanna Frost sat at her desk and reviewed the messages on her holodisplay. One was from Adam Taberg, telling her about the compvirus. Ten days were lost. Amos would not be pleased. His anger and disappointment would be directed toward her. Susanna didn't want to be rejected by the great man. Should she keep this information from him? Deciding against it, she added the incident to her hourly report. If she were caught withholding from Amos Cross, there was no telling what he might do.

A red icon appeared in her holodisplay. It was the artificial intelligence she had tasked for the NARI project. It had been sifting through Meridian Corporation's vast archives, collecting relevant information on all aspects of the NARI team and their work.

"What do you have for me?"

The AI had a serene male voice. "I have found data related to Hunter Logan." A man's image appeared in the chamber. He bore a strong resemblance to Logan. Susanna studied the face. She wondered if she had ever seen him before.

"Who is he?"

"This is Prescott Logan, Hunter Logan's older brother. We started a file on him twenty-two years ago because of his skill in comp engineering. He is an encryption expert."

"I'll bet he helped Hunter secure his files." Susanna thought out loud.

"The level of encryption Mr. Mallick has encountered is consistent with Dr. Logan's expertise." Susanna listened as the AI recounted Meridian's attempts to recruit him and his disappearance after the corporation stripped him of his teaching position. Prescott Logan had been flagged as uncooperative and placed on a watch list. Since that time, there had been no record of Logan or his wife, in spite of Meridian Corporation's formidable reach. It was as though they had been sucked into a black hole.

It looks like we underestimated the Logan family, Susanna thought as she added this new information to her list. Mr. Cross is going to love this. She hoped the great man wouldn't shoot the messenger. Maybe she should keep it from him.

* * *

Ray Bright wandered into the Eng Bay carrying a small plastic bag. Kell and Sprite were intent on their work, hunched over one of the worktables. "Here's that actuator you wanted."

"Thanks, Ray. Just put it down over there, will you?" Kell motioned to an empty spot on the cluttered bench.

Ray looked over at the console that monitored the status of the Fusion Engine. The Power Bay housed a laser ignition system that pulsed small hydrogen fuel pellets, creating a continuous chain of fusion reactions. Adam was seated at the console. Ray scratched his head. "Why didn't the Fusion Engine shut down when the core system crashed?"

Adam looked up. "It's separate. There are two redundant control systems for the Engine, and they are on their own secure network. They don't talk to the Core Intellect."

Ray nodded. It made sense. Their lives depended on the power system. Adam rose from his chair, and the two men wandered over to Kell and Sprite. The engineering officer shook his head in amazement. "Wow, that's great!" Kell was using several micro-tools to assemble a tiny mechanical joint. "You're good with your hands." Kell smiled with pride.

Sprite was excited. "It's for Mom. I had this idea for her birthday present, and Kell is helping me build it."

Ray shook his head. "If that thing works, it'll blow her away."

Kell looked up defensively. "What do you mean 'if?' Of course it'll work." He snapped two pieces of the tiny mechanism together. All four watched as the joint flexed itself in a smooth, continuous movement.

Sprite grinned broadly. "Kell, you're incredible!"

* * *

Susanna Frost was startled as she entered Amos Cross's office. There was a virtual carpet on the floor with pseudo bookcases and synthetic filing cabinets. It looked like an office from the early twenty-first century. Moreover, Cross was actually sitting behind a virtual desk. He smiled as she entered and waved her over to one of the chairs that faced him.

Susanna complied and sat ramrod straight in the chair, adjusting her jacket to remove any wrinkles. She had already checked her makeup and hair before entering the great man's office.

"Susanna!" Amos was unusually cordial. This wasn't the same man. He seemed to be giving her his complete attention. "What's happening on Meridian 6?"

"Well, sir," she almost stammered. "Someone is trying to slow down the team's research." Cross sat quietly, undisturbed by the news. "A virus disabled the Core Intellect. It was an inside job."

Cross steepled his fingers and nodded. "Was it one of the scientists?" Cross retained his pleasant demeanor.

"Yes, sir, it seems that way." The conversation was dreamlike. Susanna expected to wake up at any second and find herself alone in her bed. "Our contact reports that they have lost ten days to two weeks."

Cross swiveled in his chair, offering Susanna his profile. He gazed through his viewport at the terraces of Jackson Base. "These things happen, Ms. Frost. Life offers us setbacks from time to time." This was too weird. "Is there anything else?" he asked.

"That's just about it," she replied.

"Are you sure?" Cross twisted back and examined her carefully. The sudden change unnerved her.

"Yes, sir." Something terribly familiar was returning to the conversation. It was like the sound a foot soldier hears as he steps on a landmine, the ominous click that precedes the killing blast. "There is nothing else."

Cross looked down at his desk. "You can go." His tone was serene, but there was a tidal shift. The malevolence surfaced as Susanna rose from her chair. Click. "I had hoped you would have told me about Prescott Logan." There was ice in his voice. The predator had returned. Susanna stopped, turning slowly back to her boss. "Why did you deceive me, Ms. Frost?"

"I wasn't deceiving you." She could feel the emotional shrapnel penetrating her abdomen. "I just found out about it and wanted to gather some more information before I troubled you with it."

Cross began to smile. It was a complicated smile, illuminating and destructive, like the flash of a landmine's high explosive. "I see." Susanna fought the urge to pee. "I keep track of everything in this organization, Ms. Frost. You need to remember that. Don't put me in this position ever again." Susanna felt the office begin to spin. "Now, sit down and tell me what you know about Hunter Logan's big brother."

* * *

Sprite and Rory watched the virtual butterfly flex its wing in her holodisplay. They sat in Sprite's bedroom. The door was locked to protect the birthday secret. "That is great, Wiley. Now apply that same routine to the other wing." Sprite tweaked the parameters in her model while monitoring the drag and lift of the digital insect. It flew spastically through the three-dimensional space. She pulled up a video of a real butterfly in flight. "Recognize the exoskeletal motion and apply it to the model."

"How cool is that?" Rory was amazed.

Wiley mapped the motion in the video and transferred it. "That is better, Sprite. The previous model did not replicate the pivot of the wings." Wiley set the virtual butterfly in motion again; this time it flew smoothly.

"We're getting there, Wiley. Thanks for your help."

"My pleasure, Sprite. What's next?"

* * *

Troy Mack was alone in the Core. He sat at Jenson's workstation, examining the holodisplay. He spoke softly with the AI, his voice barely a whisper. The machine responded in kind, tempering its volume. He transferred a file to a secure folder and erased all evidence of his work. Troy rose from the workstation and returned to his console. He scanned the icons in the large holodisplay. The various AIs had finished their work, collaborating together to restore functionality to the system. The scientists could get back to their work.

* * *

Sprite wandered down the corridor near Lab Bay Two, looking for Kell. She swept into the lab, but no one was around. She scanned the benches and complex instruments. Then she saw the new containment unit. She stepped over to the unit and glanced at one of the schematics that floated in a large holodisplay nearby. A foggy memory flooded back into her consciousness. Where had she had seen these schematics before?

* * *

Troy Mack had summoned Hunter Logan to the MBH pod. The scientist sat at the controls, wrapped in the privacy of the soundproof enclosure. Susanna Frost's three-dimensional simulacrum sat across from him, adorned in a spotless business suit. She exuded competence. "What's your status, Dr. Logan?" Hunter felt underdressed, and she seemed to notice it with some satisfaction.

"We are back to normal operation here. We are rebuilding the software for the containment unit, as well as the model for the phase-two machines."

"Keep moving forward, Dr. Logan."

"There's another thing, Ms. Frost." Hunter paused. He couldn't figure out why he was so intimidated.

Susanna frowned. "Another problem?"

"There is no problem. I'd like my team to look into a way to neutralize the phase-two machines."

The woman pondered his suggestion. She looked at him with a calculated measure of sympathy. "It must be a terrible thing to feel responsible for all those deaths," she said with her most sincere voice.

Hunter was caught off guard. He felt tightness in his stomach, depression looming at the threshold. "We can stop these killers." He stammered. Susanna had the upper hand.

Susanna took a page from Amos Cross's playbook and struck. "Nothing will change the fact that you are responsible for the deaths of your colleagues on Selene Station, Dr. Logan." The sympathy was gone. "Stop kidding yourself that you can make it all better. You can't. You're guilty." Pressure was building in Hunter's head. He was having a hard time focusing. He put his hands on his temples, hoping to squeeze the throbbing pain out of his skull. "Stay focused on your work, Dr. Logan. We don't want you wasting your time on impossibilities motivated by your pathetic need to exonerate yourself. Do what you do best. Give us the nano-killers."

Hunter's mind was spinning. When he started the conversation, he believed he could save humanity from his deadly creation. Now he wasn't so sure. Perhaps Susanna was right. Redemption might be only an illusion. He could be kidding himself. Maybe it was his destiny to create the phase-two nanomachines and be remembered as the destroyer of worlds and civilizations.

Susanna smiled at him from two hundred million kilometers away. She could tell by the expression on his face that she had shamed him into submission. "We don't want any more delays." Frost's image dissolved into a sea of random holographic pixels. The connection was broken, and the micro-black-hole collapsed.

Hunter sat quietly, gasping for breath and waiting for the headache to subside. The thinking part of his brain knew what Susanna had done, but his gut was still churning from remorse. He had made the phase-two machines, and they had killed his friends, but he knew in his head that those who had bombed Selene Station were ultimately responsible. Hunter pulled himself together. He had to keep thinking and not let himself be bowled over by the guilt he felt. He could stop the nanomachines. Susanna Frost was manipulating him. She wanted to possess this uncontrollable beast and use it as a weapon. He could not let that happen.

* * *

The supply ship descended gently in the low Cerian gravity, her attitude control system making tiny corrections as she lined up on the Meridian 6 Landing Pad. Within moments, the ship was down, and the pad-mating collar was coupled with her main airlock. With landing procedures completed, her small crew disembarked from the craft and were greeted by Adam Taberg and Ray Bright. Even the heartiest of space mariners enjoyed the moments that followed a successful landing. Although typical supply runs were only weeks in length, the ships tasked for this duty tended to be short on creature comforts. The supply ship was scheduled to remain at Meridian 6 for three days. Cargo would be off-loaded, and items no longer needed in the settlement would be packed into the ship's storage space for recycling. Nothing would be wasted.

A container bearing the numbers 176-824 was nestled on one of the pallets. Ray wheeled it, along with dozens of other cases, down the long corridor to the General Supply Bay, where it would be stowed away on a shelf and added to the settlement's inventory. The number indicated that this case contained spare parts for the Fusion Engine. It would not be opened for weeks.

* * *

Sprite was startled by the knock at her door. "Who is it?"

"It's me, kiddo." Her father's voice was muffled by the door panel.

"Are you alone?" she asked.

"Yes."

Sprite opened the door. Hunter stepped in, and she closed the door firmly behind him. He looked quizzically at his daughter and then noticed the box on the bed. "It's a secret for Mom's birthday. I just got the wrapping paper from the shuttle."

Hunter sat on the chair next to his daughter's bed as she unrolled the wrapping paper. She set to work, meticulously folding it around the edges of the box, allowing it to bond to itself along every seam. Hunter was taken by his daughter's skill and attention to detail. He was proud of her. He was grateful that she and Adrianna had been able to work through some of their pain and hostility. This present, no matter what it was, would be one of Adrianna's most prized possessions. Hunter watched as Sprite lifted the wrapped present and examined every side of the box with a careful gaze.

There are times when ideas sneak up on a person. Sometimes they come through daydreams, like the chemist Kekulé, who imagined a snake biting its own tail. His vision led the scientist to the discovery of the carbon ring structure of benzene. Hunter saw the paper covering the box, hiding its contents, protecting it on all sides. He made a mental note to follow up on a new idea that occurred to him, if he ever got the chance.

* * *

The plan had been taking shape in Ray Bright's mind for several weeks. Bright was an expediter. He knew how to get things and move them efficiently from place to place. He could arrange anything. Most of the time, Ray applied his talents in the service of others. Today, he was thinking about himself. He had a girl on Mars. She had recently arrived at Rinker's Knot, the supply depot on Vesta. Vesta was the second largest asteroid in the Belt. Bright had cut a deal with Troy Mack and had talked with her several times since his arrival on Ceres.

As he wrestled cargo from the supply shuttle, Ray knew the time was near to set his plan in motion. He was going to go to Rinker's Knot and be with his girl, one way or the other. He would feel her body and run his fingers through her dark velvet hair. He would bathe her with his kisses. Adam Taberg was going to be surprised, but Ray was a man in heat, and he simply didn't care.

* * *

Sprite had plugged Wiley into one of the large holodisplays in Lab Bay One. She sat at a workstation near the entrance hatchway. Robert Hastings and Alexis Wren were hard at work on the other side of the dome. Sprite wanted to keep her distance from Hastings. He walked by her workstation several times a day. She would see him glance at her out of the corner of his eye, but she never looked up. Did he know that she had caught him with her mother? Sprite didn't want a confrontation. Her relationship with her mom was much better, and that was enough. It would be fine if Hastings never spoke to her again.

Sprite looked up from her work as Alexis shuffled out of the Lab Bay. She often wondered where she went. Her curiosity piqued, Sprite told Wiley she would be right back and rose from her workstation. She padded over to the hatchway and saw Alexis disappear into the ISO Bay. Sprite made her way quickly down the corridor and followed Alexis into the Core. She walked stealthily through the Tech Stacks and saw Alexis looking down at Jenson Reed's workstation. Sprite retraced her steps and walked quietly around the perimeter of the dome. She paused at the first radial aisle that sliced through the stacks. She could see Troy's curved console in the center of the dome. Silently, she made her way down the aisle, moving closer so she could see what Alexis was doing.

There was something different about the scientist. Alexis sat erect in the chair, and her hands danced over the holographic interface of the workstation. Sprite had seen how clumsy Alexis had been in the past and couldn't believe the ease with which she operated the complex system. What was she doing? There was no reason for her to be there.

Alexis turned, scanning the Bay in her direction. Sprite shifted her weight and withdrew behind one of the racks. She held her breath. Alexis turned back to the holodisplay, assuming she was alone. Once again, Sprite poked her head around the corner of the rack in time to see the scientist reach into the pocket of her jumpsuit and withdraw a memory module. She held it in one hand and deftly manipulated the holodisplay with the other. Whatever was in the module was transferred into the system.

Sprite slid back out of sight as Alexis rose from the workstation. She watched as the older woman strode purposefully across the center of the core. Something was very wrong here. Sprite retreated to the outer perimeter of the dome and watched Alexis emerge from the Tech Stacks. As she reached the Iso Bay corridor, Alexis's posture changed. Like putting on an overcoat, she was transformed from a self-assured, focused woman back into the absentminded scientist, slowing her gait and walking aimlessly down the corridor.

* * *

Everyone gathered in the commissary for Adrianna's birthday party. Ray Bright had hung some balloons he found in the Supply Bay. Images from Adrianna's childhood appeared like photorealistic statues in holographic displays placed around the room. Jo had baked a small cake, complete with frosting. Adrianna smiled broadly as everyone sang the ancient "Happy Birthday" song. Drinks were poured, and flasks were raised in a toast to the guest of honor.

The birthday party was good for everyone. It was like an oasis in the midst of a desert of stress that ground away at everyone's sanity like the grains of sand in a windstorm. There, in the midst of the utilitarian chairs and tables of the dining area, they found a moment of joy. Jenson and Troy still glared at each other from opposite sides of the room, but civility reigned for a few hours.

Robert Hastings sat at the periphery, cheerless and wooden. He spoke to no one and was rubbing the backs of his hands endlessly. He tried to conceal his hypervigilance, his eyes darting from person to person when he thought no one was looking. But everyone noticed. Everyone knew Robert was a shattered man.

Adam Taberg was another watcher. He stood at the edge of the crowd and studied the dynamics of the room. He was attuned to the emotional content, to the flow of energy between people. He watched for the leaders, like Hunter and Adrianna. He studied the triangles as emotional closeness ebbed and flowed from person to person. He watched and learned, equipping himself to lead them.

No one was expected to give a present, but the team got together and offered a small box to Adrianna. Jo Smith carried it from the back of the room and set it in front of her.

"You shouldn't have." Adrianna picked up the box, offering everyone a radiant smile.

"It's just a token." Jo stepped back as Adrianna tore the colored wrapping.

Adrianna opened the box and withdrew a small bottle of perfume. "It's my favorite," she murmured. There was a collective sigh as they saw her smile. Then, Ty offered a delayed, exaggerated sigh, and everyone laughed. Jo punched him in the arm. Adrianna sprayed a tiny amount on her wrist. "I'm stunned. I will use this for special occasions..." She lifted the bottle and sprayed it behind each ear and in the center of her neck. "...like this one!" The fragrance drifted over the group like incense, and expressions of approval rippled through the guests.

Sprite got up and retrieved her gift from the back of the room. The wrapping paper was bright and colorful. Every seam lined up, and the paper was creased perfectly on every edge. "Wow." Jenson reached out and touched the high tech paper. "This girl knows how to wrap a present!" It was true. The exotic paper was a pure luxury. Sprite had talked Ray Bright into ordering it from Rinker's Knot. The patterns on the paper morphed from one shape to another in a soothing montage. Sprite blushed with pride.

"Happy birthday, Mom." She set the box down on the table in front of Adrianna. Their eyes met, and mother and daughter exchanged a private understanding. "I love you," Sprite said quietly. Adrianna's eyes watered. She lifted the box and took a moment to enjoy the animated paper. Finding a seam, she pulled the paper free and set the box back down on the table. She lifted the lid, and tears began to stream from her eyes. She lifted the present out of the box. It was a statue of a monarch butterfly, delicate and lifelike. It was perched on a slender branch that grew out of a piece of smooth stone. Adrianna set the gift on the table.

"It's beautiful." She reached for Sprite and pulled her close.

Sprite gave her a peck on the cheek and pulled away. "Ray found the parts, and Kell helped me make it." Adrianna nodded her appreciation. "Touch the base, Mom." Sprite was so excited, she could burst. Adrianna reached forward and placed her hand on the polished stone. The robotic butterfly came to life, rising on gossamer wings and flitting around the room. There was a spontaneous round of applause.

* * *

The party continued with music and conversation. Hunter had poured himself another flask of punch and was returning to his seat when Sprite intercepted him. "Dad, do you have a minute?"

"Sure." He could see the concern on her face.

"Could we speak in private?" Hunter motioned toward the corridor, and they walked out of the Rec Bay. The sounds of the party receded into the background. "Something is going on with Alexis." Sprite told her dad about the incident in the Core. "I think she's putting on an act. When I saw her at Jenson's console, she changed. She wasn't clumsy."

Hunter wasn't disturbed. "I wouldn't worry about it. Alexis is odd. I'm sure there is a logical explanation for it."

Sprite wasn't satisfied. "She uploaded something. Something secret. She didn't belong there."

Hunter gave his daughter a mysterious look. "I'll talk to her. You don't have to worry about it."

"I just thought you should know."

"I'm glad you told me. Now let it go." Hunter turned around and wandered back to the party. Sprite stood there for a moment. Her father was holding something back.

* * *

Later, Adrianna and Hunter sat together in the small sitting area in their bedroom. It had been a long day, and both were tired. The butterfly statue rested on a small table between them. "What a wonderful party! I can't remember the last time I had so much fun." She leaned back in her chair and studied the butterfly statue. Her eyes glistened with tears.

"It's a sign of spring, new beginnings," Hunter muttered. Adrianna nodded silently as he rose from his chair and stepped behind his wife, caressing her shoulders. "I'm glad you and Sprite are patching things up."

Adrianna reached up and took Hunter's hand. "It was something you said to her. On the day of the argument, when she came back, her attitude had changed. I knew she was still angry, but she wasn't hateful."

The two enjoyed a comfortable moment of silence as Adrianna gently stroked the back of Hunter's hand. "I saw you and Sprite leave the party. What did she want?"

Hunter returned to his chair. "She caught Alexis sending a message."

"Do you think it's time for us to tell her?"

"Not yet." Hunter stared off into space. "I told her to forget about it."

"She'll never do that. You know how she hates secrets."

Hunter smiled. "I know, but secrets are best kept between the least number of people."

"I hate this." Adrianna kicked off her shoes.

"Me, too."

"Did you see Robert?"

Hunter rested his arm on the small table, studying his wife's face. "He looks like a caged animal most of the time."

"I'm worried about him." Hunter frowned, and Adrianna reached for his hand. "If he comes unglued, he could complicate things."

Hunter squeezed her hand. "I'll keep an eye on him. If he gets any worse, I'll deal with it."

* * *

Sprite didn't miss fussing with her hair. At first, baldness had been strange. She kept touching her head, feeling for her missing locks.

Sometimes she got cold and would wear a thin cloth cap. In spite of her misgivings about Samina Haddad, Sprite felt good about her trendy look. On the other hand, Sprite didn't like the pale skin that typified off-worlders. She preferred a modest tan. That was one of the reasons she enjoyed the light chamber. She could adjust the settings to maintain her favorite skin tone.

Sprite locked the door of the changing room and removed her clothes. There was a slight chill to the air. She placed her hand on the light chamber control surface. The mechanism retrieved her profile, set the duration of her session, and energized the chamber. She opened the door and stepped into the space beyond, bathed in light and warmth. She closed her eyes and withdrew into herself.

* * *

Troy Mack sat in the center of the Core, watching incoming data traffic from Mars and monitoring software updates. He sat back in his chair and stretched his arms. There was nothing for him to do.

Jenson Reed was at his holodisplay, speaking quietly to the Core Intellect. A large three-dimensional diagram of the Meridian 6 comp system floated in front of him. With perfect eye-hand coordination, he shifted files back and forth while conversing with the AI.

Troy pulled up the activity log of Reed's workstation. A red icon flashed next to one of the entries. Jenson had made another unauthorized file-transfer.

"Mr. Reed."

Jenson looked up from his work, clearly irritated. "What is it now?"

"Come over here and explain this to me."

Reed walked over to the curved console. He squinted at the activity log. "You're spying on me."

"It's part of my job." Troy tapped the flagged entry. "Where did you send this file?"

"I didn't send any files."

"It came from your workstation."

Jenson checked the time. "I wasn't here when that was sent. I was in the Rec Bay."

Troy's eyes narrowed. "Do you have any witnesses?"

"Sure. Check with Jo and Ty. I was helping them decorate for Adrianna's party."

Troy gave Reed a dirty look. "Go back to work." Mack rose from his console and strode across the center of the Core toward the MBH pod. He wouldn't stop until he found out who was making the file-transfers.

* * *

The two pilots of the supply shuttle, along with their loadmaster, sat on utility chairs in the staging dock beneath the Meridian 6 Landing Pad. Ray Bright had finished checking in all the supplies and was signing off on the recyclables being returned to Rinker's Knot.

"You've got a pretty tight job here, Ray." The loadmaster scratched his crotch. "Not much to do, good pay, and nice scenery, from the looks of things."

One of the pilots, sporting a week's growth on his chin and crooked teeth, grinned widely. "I see Cilla Ashe is here."

Ray kept pouring over his paperwork. "She's here. She is the Environmental Systems Officer."

"Yeah, I remember her. She's a tree hugger, a real natural girl, if you know what I mean." All three members of the shuttle crew laughed.

"I haven't known her that long. She seems nice enough." Ray handed a pad comp to the loadmaster. "There you go. There are three pallets going back." He stood up and gestured toward the opposite side of the dock. "Let me show them to you." The loadmaster rose, and the two men walked over to a pile of crates some distance away.

"Don't mind those two." The loadmaster stuck out his thumb and motioned toward the men behind them. "We don't get much of a chance to be with people. We shuttle our shit and get lucky once in a while. A pretty girl here and there. Keeps us sane."

Ray shrugged it off. He led the man to a motorized cart laden with boxes and cases. "Here's the outgoing load. Nothing dangerous. Just discarded items."

"That'll be good. I hate hauling high liability stuff. You spend most of your time wondering if it will blow you up or make your nuts fall off."

Ray stepped close to the man and lowered his voice. "I've got a favor to ask. It's good for a month's pay…"

* * *

Sprite and Rory were in the General Supply Bay, sitting on the floor of Sprite's sanctuary. They sat elbow to elbow and kept their voices low. They could hear Ray Bright moving around near his workstation on the other side of the bay.

Rory grinned as an old memory came to her. She sat Sparky's box down on the floor. "Once, I put a fake cast on my leg and convinced Mom that my leg was broken. She was so mad when she found out it was a joke!" Then she became serious, a faraway look in her eyes. "She was a great listener. You know how sometimes your parents get to you? They get in your face, or do something unfair. Stuff like that?" Sprite nodded. "Mom would listen to me. She didn't take sides or anything, but she made me feel like somebody cared. I really miss that."

Sprite bit her lip. She had her arms wrapped around her knees, and she rocked slowly forward and back. "You're lucky having a mother like that." Rory could tell something was on her friend's mind. "If I tell you something, will you keep it a secret?" She turned her head and gave Rory a hard look. Her eyes glistened in the dimness.

"You know I will."

"You've got to swear to it. If I tell you, you've gotta take it to your grave."

Rory nodded. "I swear."

"A long time ago, when I was nine years old, I heard a noise in the middle of the night. I got up to see what it was." Sprite closed her eyes and buried her chin between her knees. "The noise was coming from my Mom and Dad's bedroom. The door was open, and I looked at them. They were in bed together." Her body began to shake. "Only Dad wasn't home. He was away on a trip." Sprite looked up at Rory. Her eyes were filled with tears. "Mom was in bed with Dr. Hastings. They were doing it in our house."

Rory put her arm around her friend. Sprite continued. "I've been mad at Mom ever since. I've hated her. I've said terrible things." Rory nodded. "Mom caught Kell in my bedroom when we first got here. We weren't doing anything. We were just sitting and talking, but she told me Kell couldn't be there. I was mad. I told her she had no right to tell me who could be in my bedroom. I told her I was there when she was with Dr. Hastings. She freaked."

"What did she say?"

"I didn't give her a chance to say anything. I ran away. That's when I found this place. Later, I found my dad in the garden, and we talked." Rory was silent. "He knew all about it. He said that they had worked through it. He told me that Mom made a mistake, and they still loved each other. Mom and I have been talking a lot lately."

"Things are better?"

Sprite nodded. "I think so." She paused. "It's getting better." She smiled as she wiped her face. The two friends were bound closely together by their common pain.

Soft footsteps approached. Sprite and Rory looked at each other and stood without making a noise, ready to bolt. They could hear a quiet tinny sound. It was Ray Bright's music. Sprite could make out an old song from the musical "Cats." Before long, Ray appeared in the aisle next to their hiding place. He walked slowly, scanning each of the case numbers on the shelves before him. He was looking for something. Sprite held her breath as she watched him through the crack between two stacks of cases. Ray was less than two meters away; his back was turned as he scrutinized the cases across the aisle.

Suddenly, there was another noise. Ray jerked upright and moved away from the shelving. He acted like a man with something to hide, too jumpy. Why did he do that? Sprite and Rory strained to identify the sounds. Someone was passing through the bay. The footsteps receded, and Ray stepped back to the shelves. Rory slid silently behind her friend to see what was happening.

Ray reached up and took a small case from the shelving. He set it down on the floor and hunched over it as he unfastened the latches. Ray checked to make sure he was alone before he removed the lid. The case had a removable tray. He lifted the tray out of the case and rummaged through the items stowed below it. He removed a triangular device that had a small control panel on one end. Ray held the gadget with great care. Sprite thought it was either fragile or very dangerous. Given Ray's stealth, she assumed it was the latter. She and Rory watched as he laid the apparatus on the floor gently. Ray returned the tray to the case and replaced the lid. He snapped the latches shut and slid the container back onto the shelving. He wrapped the odd device in a cloth from his pocket and hurried away.

"What was that all about?" Sprite's curiosity was piqued.

Rory stood up. "Come on."

* * *

Ray Bright moved quickly toward the Eng Bay. The cloth bundle was wedged into his forearm like a football. He paused as he reached the entrance and peered cautiously into the interior of the bay. Adam Taberg was sitting at his workstation. Ray drew back into the corridor. If his plan was to work, he couldn't let Adam raise an alarm. There was only one thing to do. He reentered the bay and found a heavy wrench.

* * *

Adam Taberg had gone into Lab Bay Two during the sleeping period and scanned the interior of the dome. He had concentrated on the floor in order to detect any cracks that might permit the ingress of iron rich clay. Any fissures in the dome itself would have caused an air leak, setting off numerous alarms. Clearly, the source of Cilla's contamination had to be somewhere in the floor. Now he sat at his console and ported the data into his system. The AI reconstructed a three-dimensional overlay on the Lab Bay Two floor plan. Adam could see the anomalies below the floor. There were stairs and a tunnel. What was this?

Adam heard a noise behind him. As he turned toward it, something heavy slammed into the back of his head. It was the last thing he ever felt. Adam Taberg's head fell forward, shattering the holodisplay and terminating the program. He was dead before the lights of the display blinked out. Ray placed the wrench on the floor next to Adam's corpse and made his way toward the Power Bay.

* * *

Sprite and Rory stepped out into the aisle. Ray was already out of sight. There was a noise behind them. They turned quickly. It was Kell Edwards.

"I've been looking for you two."

Sprite put her finger to her lips. "Shhh!" Her voice was a breathy whisper. "Ray Bright is up to something." She gestured toward the Eng Bay. "He's down there."

Kell nodded, and they set off to follow the supply officer. When they got to the corridor that led to the Enviro Bay, they paused to listen. Ray's footsteps were coming from their left. Ray had continued around the rim corridor. Sprite peeked down the passageway just in time to see Ray enter the Eng Bay. As soon as he was out of sight, the three young people hurried after him. The corridors were long, and there was nowhere to hide. They entered the Eng Bay without a sound. Ray had disappeared.

Adam Taberg's lifeless body was in his chair; his torso lay forward on his desk, his arms and head tangled and bloody in the shattered remains of the holodisplay. The back of his head had a deep indentation. They could see his brain.

"He's dead!" Rory turned away quickly. Kell and Sprite pulled her onward, not wanting to stay near the corpse.

"Which way did he go?" Kell scratched his head, bewildered. "It wouldn't make any sense for him to go back toward the Enviro Bay. It would have been faster for him to take the passageway from the General Supply Bay."

Sprite went over to the long corridor that led to the Iso Bay. "He didn't go this way. He'd still be in sight."

"That leaves the Power Bay." Kell started to move in that direction.

Rory gave Sprite a questioning look. "We're not supposed to go in there."

"Yeah, but he killed Commander Taberg. This is important." The three hurried quietly down the corridor.

* * *

The Fusion Engine sat in the center of the Power Bay. The space was crammed full of pipes and cables. A large spherical target chamber dominated the space with an array of optical conduits spreading away from it. There was a low, deep-throated rumble coming from the massive device as it produced the settlement's energy. Without the engine, Meridian 6 would fall cold and dark, lifeless.

The three friends advanced slowly. They followed the long conduits, keeping their eyes open for Ray. They approached the control station. There was a sound ahead of them. They moved forward. The tangle of conduits grew denser, converging on the target chamber. Sprite navigated the forest of tubing and structural supports. Kell and Rory followed. At last, they saw Ray Bright. He was kneeling under the target chamber. The three young people wedged themselves behind a couple of massive pipes. They watched Ray throw a switch on the triangular device and punch its small keypad. It was a bomb.

6

R ay Bright set the bomb down on the floor beneath the Fusion Engine. He stood silently for a moment and then hurried out of the Power Bay. He walked briskly toward the Landing Pad. The supply shuttle was ready for launch. The loadmaster was standing by the open hatchway. "Come on! We gotta go!" Ray hurried up the ramp into the belly of the supply shuttle. "Another five minutes, and you would have missed us, deal or no deal."

Ray boarded the shuttle without a word. He was in his seat by the time the hatch was sealed. He strapped himself in and clamped his antique earphones to his head. As the supply shuttle rose from the Cerian surface, Ray Bright was dreaming of his woman and bathing himself in the sounds of "South Pacific."

* * *

Sprite rushed over to the bomb as soon as Ray left the Power Bay. She knelt next to the device and examined the control panel. There were twenty-eight minutes left before detonation. She threw the power switch, and the display went dark. The bomb was disarmed. She looked up at Kell. "Call my dad."

Hunter and Ty were the first to arrive. Sprite was still kneeling next to the bomb, a serious look on her face. Hunter squatted next to her. "Are you okay?"

Sprite's voice began to shake. "It was Ray Bright. He killed Commander Taberg." She looked down, her shoulders sagging. "We almost died." Hunter wrapped her in his arms.

News of Adam's murder and the failed bomb attempt spread throughout the settlement. Meridian 6 went on high alert. Every hatch was sealed. Troy and Cilla worked with the Core Intellect to assess the integrity of the settlement's systems.

Hunter and Ty took the three young people to the Eng Bay, after they covered Adam's body with a piece of cloth. Ty sat at one of the workbenches, examining the bomb. Hunter was on the comlink, assuring Adrianna and Jo the young people were safe. Then he listened as Sprite, Rory, and Kell told their story. It was hard to believe that Ray had killed Adam and was behind the attempted bombing. The supply shuttle had left moments after Ray set the bomb. They were certain he was on it, but Hunter and Ty organized a search of the settlement anyway. They swept Meridian 6 from dome to dome. There were no more bombs and no sign of Ray Bright. The alert was cancelled and the hatches unsealed.

Hunter called everyone to the Rec Bay for a briefing. There was a din of voices, until he raised his hand for silence. "We've looked everywhere. There are no more bombs, and Ray's not in the settlement. All the environment suits are accounted for. It's obvious he left on the supply shuttle. They took off moments after the kids saw him set the bomb."

"We've got to contact Meridian," Cilla said.

"I'll do that when we're finished here. I have contacted the shuttle pilot, but they claim he's not on board. I'm sure Meridian will have their security people meet the shuttle when it arrives at Rinker's Knot."

Tyson stepped to one of the holodisplays. "I have examined the bomb, and there's something you'll be interested in." An image appeared in the display chamber. "This is the Selene Station lab during your interview with Larson Daniels." The image showed the undamaged lab. A triangular-shaped bomb could be seen clearly on top of the containment unit. "It's exactly like the bomb Ray set in the Power Bay. I think the same people who hired Ray Bright blew up our lab on Selene Station."

Robert Hastings' head throbbed. He closed his eyes and rubbed his temples. His mind was filled with images of Maryanne and Emile. A part of him wanted to be vaporized by one of those bombs, but another part of him grew angry at whoever murdered his family. Waves of guilt washed over him. Perhaps he was a Jonah, the cause of all these disasters. He held his breath, hoping no one would notice his inner turmoil. Then, he opened his eyes. Tyson Edwards was staring at him. "What are you looking at?" Hastings growled.

Jo ignored his outburst. "Can't we get away from these people?" She bristled with anger. "I just want to love my family and do my work."

There was an uneasy silence. Everyone felt Jo's desperation. They all felt trapped by forces beyond their control. Finally, Adrianna gestured toward Rory, Kell, and Sprite. "We all owe you a debt of gratitude." There was a round of applause. "If you hadn't picked up on Ray's suspicious behavior, we'd all be dying right now."

* * *

The pilot of the Meridian Supply Shuttle scanned his instruments and released the catches on his harness. He floated out of his seat, twisting his body and projecting himself to the stern bulkhead of the flight deck. He was not smiling as he slid past the loadmaster and the Spartan crew quarters and went on to the tiny passenger cabin. Ray Bright's body was inverted, his head toward the "floor" of the cabin, his ever-present earphones covering his ears. His back was turned. The pilot orbited his passenger and came to rest in front of him.

"You're a popular man, Mr. Bright." The pilot looked at Ray through steel gray eyes, set in a coarse, weathered face.

Ray pulled down the headphones. "What?"

"I said you're a popular man. That Logan guy from Meridian 6 is looking for you."

"What did you tell him?" Ray eyed the pilot suspiciously. "We have a deal."

"Don't worry. I didn't tell him nothing, but he knows you're on board. Where else would you have gone?"

"What did he say?"

The pilot gave Ray a wide, toothy grin. "He said you were a dangerous man."

"That so?"

"He told me you tried to blow up the settlement."

"But I didn't." Ray did his best to return a carefree smile.

"No, you didn't. He said the bomb was discovered before it blew. You might have a reception committee when we get to the Knot."

"Is that going to be a problem?"

It didn't seem possible for the pilot to smile any wider, but he did. "Naw. For an extra fee, we can get you past Meridian Security."

After the pilot returned to the flight deck, Ray encrypted a brief text report to Maya Lewis. All it said was, "Mission Failed. Device disarmed."

* * *

Maya Lewis was frowning when she entered Damon Trask's office. She wore a liquid suit she had sprayed onto her body. She sat down in one of the chairs that flanked his desk. Trask looked up, immediately distracted by her pornographic sheath. He found it difficult to keep his eyes on her face.

"What happened?" he asked.

"Ray Bright failed. They disarmed the bomb."

Damon's eyes tracked down Maya's torso as she crossed her legs. "And Mr. Bright?"

"He escaped on the supply shuttle and is in-transit to Rinker's Knot."

Damon was contemplating the influence of micro-gravity on women's breasts. "Meridian will be waiting," he said.

Maya teased him with a pouty smile. "Ray's a pro. They won't find him."

Damon regained his focus, spreading his hands on the desk surface. "I want you to express our disappointment to him in such a way that he is unable to frustrate us ever again."

Maya furrowed her brow, her mouth becoming a thin straight line. "Are you sure?" She reached out and nudged his hand.

Trask glanced down; her touch sent an electric current through him. "We are finished with Mr. Bright." There was an air of finality about him.

* * *

After the meeting in the Rec Bay concluded, everyone continued their conversations in hushed tones. They spoke of the bombing attempt and Ray Bright's departure, of Adam Taberg's death, and of the bravery of the young people. Hunter and Adrianna retired to their residence, while Tyson and Jo headed toward Lab Bay Two. Within moments, the two couples met again in The Refuge.

Hunter sat with his elbows on the table, his chin in his hands. Adrianna stood behind him, massaging his shoulders. His muscles were like taught iron cords. "Whoever is behind Ray and the bomb wants to kill us. It can't be Meridian. Susanna Frost is pressuring us to do our work. It makes no sense for them to sabotage their own investment."

Everyone agreed with Hunter's assessment. No one spoke. Then, Tyson broke the silence. "It's the group that sabotaged the lab, some radical bunch that's against nanoresearch."

Hunter nodded. "It's got to be the Citizen's League. Damon Trask is the only one with the resources to infiltrate Meridian Corporation and reach out two hundred million kilometers to hurt us."

"This has to stop." Jo was a lioness, ready to protect her cub. "They're putting our children in danger. None of this is worth losing their lives over." She looked at her friends carefully. "Do you really think we'll find a way to stop the nanomachines? If we don't, and Meridian finds out that we're stringing them along, they'll hurt the children. Meanwhile, the Citizen's League, or whoever they are, will kill us just because they don't understand what we're trying to do."

Hunter winced as Adrianna tried to knead the tension out of his back. "I'm worried about the children, too. We have to keep stalling as long as possible. We can't deliver the phase-two machines to Meridian. The consequences are too horrible to imagine."

Adrianna stepped away from her husband and sat down next to him. "They'll kill a lot of people..." The air was sucked out of the room. "...with our help."

Ty shifted his chair closer to Jo. "We have to find a way to neutralize the phase-two machines. It will break the cycle. Hunter's right."

Hunter nodded again. "I've got to report this to Susanna. I'll tell her we're pretty shaken up here, which is the truth. Maybe that will buy us some time."

* * *

Troy looked up from his console as Hunter entered the MBH pod. He closed the door and activated the system. Soon, Hunter was facing Susanna Frost's simulacrum. She sat at a desk cluttered with papers.

"Dr. Logan. This is unexpected."

Hunter sensed she was lying. "We've had an incident up here," he told her.

Susanna's eyes didn't narrow. She didn't move in her chair. She reached forward with her right hand and moved one of her papers.

"What happened?"

She was hiding something. "Adam Taberg is dead," he reported. Susanna didn't react. "Ray Bright tried to blow up the Fusion Engine. We found the bomb and disarmed it. We believe he escaped on the supply shuttle, which left here a few hours ago for Rinker's Knot."

"I will alert our security forces. They'll get him."

Susanna was acting like she already knew what had happened. Why was she always one step ahead of him? Hunter paused to calm himself. "We're pretty shaken up. We aren't going to be able to focus on the research until things calm down a bit."

"How long?" she asked impatiently.

"It's hard to tell, maybe a week."

Susanna stared through him. Actually, she was staring at his image in her holodisplay, but their eyes met indirectly, and she was measuring his defiance. "That seems like an excessive amount of time."

"You're not living through it up here."

Susanna was serene from the wrists up, but she was twisting her fingers nervously. "I want you all to get back to work."

"We can't right now."

Susanna unclasped her hands and let them drop, her fingers spread wide. She pressed them into submission on the tabletop. "That's an order, Dr. Logan."

"I don't care if it's an invitation to Shangri-La." Hunter leaned toward Susanna's image. "We need time to regroup."

There was a momentary pause, as if Susanna was weighing her alternatives, then she nodded slowly to herself. "Your daughter may pay the price for your obstinacy."

Hunter pounded the table, and Susanna jumped. "Don't you dare threaten me or my family. We almost got blown up here today. My daughter had to see Adam Taberg's brains oozing out the back of his head. You have put us all in harm's way, and you can go to hell!"

The color drained from Susanna's face. She was obviously shaken, unsure of what to say. Hunter held his ground, glaring at her with hatred in his eyes. Finally, she set her chin and straightened her shoulders, offering Hunter the most confidence she could muster. "I'll speak with Mr. Cross about this." Her form dissolved into chaos as she cut the connection.

Hunter sat for a moment in the darkened chamber. Something wasn't right. He commanded the AI to replay the MBH transmission. He watched as Susanna appeared. He glanced at the pile of papers in front of her, and then he heard himself tell her there had been an incident. She reached forward with her right hand and moved one of the papers.

"Pause!" he commanded. Susanna's image stopped. "Back up slowly." Hunter watched as the paper returned to its initial location, her arm withdrawing. "Pause!" he said again. Once more, Susanna Frost was frozen like a statue.

Hunter stood up and walked toward his nemesis. His body merged with the holographic display until his torso was protruding from the desk surface. He bent down and examined the piece of paper Susanna had concealed. A brief message was printed on the sheet.

"Ray Bright is a saboteur," it read. "He set a bomb to destroy the settlement. The bomb was discovered and defused. Bright is believed to be on his way to Rinker's Knot." The message wasn't signed. Hunter returned to his chair, a feeling of paranoia coursing through him.

* * *

Troy Mack replaced the cover on an equipment rack in the Tech Stacks. He had busied himself in order to avoid the fray. Adam's death had thrown his relationship with Jenson into chaos. Was he still in charge? Jenson had retreated, his confrontations less frequent, but their conflict remained. Jenson had the respect of the scientists. He had known them for years. Troy had been vested with authority by Adam, and he was dead.

Troy walked back to his console. Jenson was sitting in his chair. "Go back to your workstation." Jenson didn't move. Troy pushed him on the shoulder. "Get out of my chair."

Jenson glared at the slender man. "Who's going to make me?"

"I'm still your superior."

"Like hell you are. Adam's not here to defend you."

Troy snapped back. "Do you want me to ask Susanna Frost?"

Jenson hesitated. "Keep your damned seat." He shut down the program he was using and returned to his workstation.

* * *

Susanna had spent ten minutes on her hair and wardrobe prior to coming before the great man. Now, she stood silently by his office entrance. Her access ring was poised to unlock the door. She took a deep breath and placed the ring on the cold, smooth surface. The door swung open, revealing the space beyond. The floor of Amos's office displayed a huge map of the base. Most of the map was two dimensional, with the outlines of tunnels and domes scattered across its surface. Cross stood at the far end of the office, where the floor display raised up into three dimensions. A wire-frame image of a new factory appeared over one section of the base. A real-time display showed workers in environment suits laboring in the partially completed structure. Machines were demolishing a cluster of older domes. It was the portrait of space age urban renewal.

Amos Cross was engaged in one of his endless comlink conversations. "No! Get those people out of there!" Cross paced back and forth, never taking his eyes off the floor display. "I know they want to keep their homes, but we need that new factory."

Susanna was glad she wasn't the person on the other end of the comlink. "I don't care if they don't have anywhere to go. If you have to, send them outside without an environment suit." Decompression made an ugly mess. Those who refused to cooperate with Meridian Corporation risked severe consequences.

Cross motioned for Susanna to approach. He glanced at her, a quick flash of disappointment on his face. "What do we have?"

Susanna told him about Adam Taberg's murder and the attempted bombing, combining Hunter's account with that of her informant. Amos was beet red. She had never seen him this angry. "Fuck! What does it take to make a few small-time scientists do their job? Who are we working against here? The Citizen's League? Who owns that space station they're on? Let's evict them!"

"They own it, sir. We can't touch them, unless we want to go to war with Earth."

"This is war!"

"We don't know if they are behind this, sir."

"Then find out! Earn your salary! Get me some answers!"

"Yes, sir."

"And find out who vetted Ray Bright. I want that idiot fired!" Cross turned away, his hands shaking. He listened for a few seconds and then barked another order over his comlink.

"There's more, sir." Susanna dreaded this part. "Dr. Logan is refusing to continue the research."

Cross pivoted around, catching Susanna like a deer caught in headlights. "Why?"

Susanna had a lump in her throat. "He says the scientists are upset."

"They're upset?" Amos said it like a whining child. "I don't care if they're upset. We've coddled this bunch long enough. It's time for Dr. Logan to discover how vulnerable he is. Hurt his daughter. Maybe he'll start taking me seriously."

"I warned him about that, but it didn't faze him. Maybe we should find another way…"

"Don't question me!" Susanna recoiled, stepping back, lowering her eyes, cowering in the face of the angry pit bull. "I don't care if they're upset. I don't want them scared; I want them terrified. Let the girl have an accident. Then they'll be terrified of <u>me</u>."

* * *

Robert Hastings was in Lab Bay One. He waved his hand halfheartedly through his holodisplay. He paused from time to time, reviewing files associated with the team's research. Robert was having trouble concentrating. He had started to lose track of things. A deep-rooted melancholy had consumed him, making work impossible.

Robert queried the Core Intellect, searching for a misplaced file. The comp found it with ease, displaying its location and activity history. He had added notes to the file eight minutes ago. Robert's eyes scanned down the listing. It showed every time the file had been accessed. Hunter Logan had opened the file a half-hour ago. Why would he do that?

Robert closed the file and selected another one. He had worked on this file an hour earlier. Once again, Hunter had opened the file. Hastings checked every file he had used that day. Hunter was shadowing him, checking his work like an errant schoolboy. His inner rage began to boil, his blood pressure rising.

* * *

Jenson Reed watched the shimmering streams of data in his holodisplay. He could see all the comps on the network, the Core

Intellect and the other AIs that formed the digital colloquia, guiding the inner workings of the system. Tyson and Jo were online in Lab Bay Two. Cilla was running environmental scans at her workstation. Alexis and Robert Hastings were at work in Lab Bay One. Kell Edwards was playing one of his comp games.

Reed kept a special watch on Troy Mack. Right now, he was performing system diagnostics on the landing pad sensor system. Suddenly, a section of the network display began to glow with a reddish cast. It was Robert Hastings. He was accessing a lot of secure files. This wasn't unusual, but Hastings was opening and closing many files in rapid succession. Why was the man doing that?

"Hey, Jenson!" Reed jerked around in his seat, startled. Sprite stood next to him, smiling. He hadn't heard her approach. He frowned at her. "Sorry! I didn't mean to scare you," she said innocently.

Jenson didn't want to see her. "What do you want?" he said harshly.

A cloud of disappointment shadowed her face. "I wanted to ask you something about the Core Intellect."

Jenson threw up his hands. "I don't have time right now. Ask me tomorrow."

"Okay. It wasn't important or anything." Jenson had already turned back to his holodisplay.

Sprite backed away. She knew Jenson was under a lot of pressure. The stress was getting to everyone. She used to enjoy the easy laughter among members of the team. She thought about her conversation with Jenson on Copernicus Base, when he took her for environment suit training. He'd been like an older brother to her. She missed the old Jenson. Their scientific family was falling apart.

* * *

Amos Cross lay on his bed, having decontaminated himself for a second time. His mind was still racing from the attempted bombing. How could Trask be so stupid? Amos made a mental note to deal with him later. Perhaps the Citizen's League could fall victim to the Shadow Project.

The lights in the bedchamber were dimmed. Cross did not like the dark. He pitched and turned in the bed, taunted by the sleep he needed but hated. He thought of Hunter Logan's daughter. What was her name? He couldn't remember. He was going to ruin her life. Amos tensed. A memory flitted under the surface of his consciousness. He knew something about being ruined. He had passed through his own fiery trial as a young boy. Yes, he had scars, but he was stronger now. He had gotten past the hurt his parents had inflicted on him.

The girl was just another pawn, collateral damage in the pursuit of his desires. She did not matter. Hunter Logan would yield to him. Meridian Corporation would have the nanomachines. Life would return to equilibrium. He would be in control, and he would be a winner. Gradually Cross's nervous energy drained away, and the great man slipped into a restless sleep.

* * *

Sprite and Adrianna had just finished their daily exercise routine. They worked out in the Rec Bay exercise area and used the settlement's long, interconnected corridors as an indoor track. They talked quietly as they cooled down, steadily rebuilding their broken relationship. They shared an easy rapport with each other, rediscovered through honesty and forgiveness. Mother and daughter entered adjacent light chambers.

Adrianna smiled to herself as she slipped out of her things. She was proud to have such a fine daughter. She glanced in the changing room mirror, assessing what pregnancy and decades had done to her body. She nodded to herself. It was worth it. Her marriage and her daughter were turning out all right.

* * *

Sprite took Wiley out of her pocket and set him down on a bench as she slipped out of her clothes. She glanced at her digital friend, amused by the thought of a boy being in the changing room with her. He couldn't see her, but if he did, she'd have to erase the data right away.

A long-forgotten memory flashed into her mind. She remembered the day when she and Wiley hacked the Meridian network, the day they were almost caught. The day when she had Wiley erase all signs of their trespass. Meridian was building a new lab on the Moon. That was where she had seen the plans for the containment unit. Sprite pulled the handle of the light chamber door. She would tell her father about it when she was done.

* * *

Adrianna stepped into her light chamber. She closed her eyes as the illumination flowed over her. She remembered the day Sprite was born. How Hunter had rushed her to the hospital, waiting helplessly for news. She remembered some of the pain, but even more, she remembered the first time she touched her daughter. She remembered her soft skin, her eyes clamped shut, the thin wisps of her brown hair, her tiny hand gripping her index finger.

"Mommmmm!" It was a blood-curdling scream. Adrianna opened her eyes, every sense alert. Sprite was shrieking. She was calling her. "Mommmmmm!" Each time, her cry trailed off into a primal, retching howl. Repeatedly, the screams pierced the partitions dividing the chambers, echoing off the curved ceiling of the Rec Bay.

Adrianna threw open the door of her light chamber. With no thought for modesty, she rushed out of the changing room and grabbed the latch of the neighboring door. It wouldn't open. Adrianna stepped back and threw herself against the door. The latch snapped, and she tumbled inside. There was another scream, quieter now, almost a whimper. She opened the light chamber door. Sprite was crumpled on the floor, her skin bright red. A wave of heat pressed against Adrianna like a burning curtain. She stepped into the chamber. Ignoring the searing pain that enveloped her body, she picked up her daughter and carried her out of the light chamber.

Troy Mack was the first to arrive. He stepped to the doorway of the changing room. Sprite lay naked on the floor, her skin reddened and burned. He felt the flush of embarrassment on his own scarred face. Adrianna was sobbing. "Sprite! Sprite!" She looked up at Troy, her chest heaving. "Get help! Get Hunter!"

Troy grabbed a towel. "You're naked, ma'am." Adrianna took it, glancing down at herself. Then, without a word, she folded the towel and tucked it under Sprite's head.

7

The next hour was like a whirlwind. Sprite was sedated and intubated, her breathing now controlled by a machine. They wheeled her through the complex, toward Lab Bay Two. Adrianna and Hunter flanked her Gurney. They placed her in a cooling bath and wired her up with monitors and feeding tubes. Everyone was drawn to the scene like insects flitting around a porch light in the darkness. Jo rolled some equipment over to the tank, forming a makeshift screen to protect what little was left of the girl's privacy. Then they waited.

The medical arsenal of the settlement was not enough. The intense heat had damaged the surface of Sprite's body. Blisters were forming. Fluid began to pool beneath her skin, and the outer layer began sloughing off, leaving her dermis exposed. Without sedation, she would be in agony, her raw nerve cells bare. The likelihood of infection was high. Sprite was unconscious, floating in her liquid coffin, her systems in free-fall as she clung to life.

* * *

Robert Hastings closed the door of his living quarters after making sure no one followed him. He didn't want anyone to see what he was about to do. He sat down at his desk and turned on his holodisplay. A swirling cloud of light appeared and then coalesced into three-dimensional icons.

"Good Evening, Dr. Hastings. You look tired tonight."

Robert shrugged off the question, mildly offended by the machine's attempt at compassion. "Message for Maya Lewis." Robert paused, assembling the text of the message in his mind.

"Ready."

Robert formed his words carefully. "Maya, things are crazy up here.

Sprite Logan was badly burned in one of the light chambers. I had nothing to do with it." Hastings launched into a disjointed account of the accident. Then, he got to the real point of his message. "Hunter Logan is watching me. I caught him reviewing all my data files. I am being treated like an outsider. I don't know what's going on. At this point, I don't think I can help you." Robert continued his rambling monologue, bemoaning the situation and expressing his misgivings about the team, Hunter Logan, and life in general. He ended the message and turned away from the holodisplay.

"Message complete," intoned the AI. "Dr. Hastings. You seem depressed."

"Shut up, Dammit!" The artificial intelligence knew what was good for it, and remained silent. Robert looked at his watch. It would be at least an hour before he received any reply. He found the bottle in his old sneakers and took four of the pills. He lay down on his bed. Within moments, Robert escaped into a drug-induced fantasy.

* * *

A new dome had been constructed near the spaceport on the floor of the Jackson Crater. It stood alone and detached from the rest of Jackson Base. Four massive airlocks were placed at equal distances around the perimeter of the dome, like the cardinal points of a compass. A small landing pad lay just beyond the eastern lock. The only access to the structure was by surface vehicle or jumpship. This was the home of the Shadow Project.

Amos Cross's personal transport rolled into the western airlock. A huge outer door rose from below the lunar surface to seal the entrance. Moments later, the great man stepped out of the transport. He was alone. The air smelled like a mixture of new plastic and lunar soil. Cross wrinkled his nose.

"Welcome to the Shadow Project, Mr. Cross." Dr. Maxwell Thrune stood a half-dozen meters away. He wore a broad grin, his mouth a jumble of teeth. Cross nodded without a word as he joined the scientist. Thrune kneaded his hands in nervous anticipation.

"Let me see it," Cross said impatiently. He didn't like field trips. He wanted to get this over and return to his office. He was going to need several cycles of decontamination to rid himself of the dust and smell.

"Right this way." Thrune led him through a maze of corridors, past room after room of complex equipment.

Cross paused in the doorway of one of the rooms. "Is all this necessary?" he asked.

"Of course, Mr. Cross. We have confined all of our work within this facility, for security purposes. My staff has developed all the new technology to handle the phase-two machines." Cross frowned, not fully convinced. "Let me show you the master chamber. It's just ahead."

Thrune ushered him into an anteroom with a broad glass wall. An immense chamber lay beyond. They were in the center of the Shadow Project dome. The two men stood at the glass, taking in the complexity of the machines that filled the cavernous space. Technicians in white jumpsuits were hard at work, climbing over the intricate mechanisms.

"Follow me," Thrune instructed.

Cross hesitated. He didn't like being led around like a dog on a leash. The smaller man cracked the hatch of another airlock, and they passed through, into the inner sanctum. A partially-finished containment unit, much like the one at Meridian 6, was at the center of the chamber. Five thick conduits were attached to it, radiating upward and outward toward smaller, cylindrical machines mounted high above them.

"What am I looking at?" Cross was ready to leave.

Thrune waved his arm like a ringmaster at a circus. "This device in the center is where we will hold Dr. Logan's phase-two machines. These channels will transport the nanomachines safely to the processing equipment up there." The small man motioned upward, great pride evident in his voice.

"And the delivery systems?" Cross was skeptical.

"They are being manufactured in the upper levels of the dome."

"I have a new idea, Dr. Thrune."

The doctor frowned. He didn't like his superiors changing his plans midstream. "We have set many pieces in motion to achieve our initial plan, Mr. Cross."

Cross waved his hand dismissively. "I know that, but this is my project, and I have a new idea."

Thrune recognized a veto when he heard one. He folded his hands. "What do you have in mind?"

Cross smiled. He enjoyed pulling rank on people like Thrune. "We will need only one delivery system." He looked at the large airlock at the far end of the chamber. "You can fabricate it right here." Thrune stood silently as Cross laid out his plan.

* * *

Hunter Logan sat wearily in his chair. The sounds of the recirculation pump and Sprite's breathing machine had lulled him into semiconsciousness. Adrianna was fast asleep. There was a sound beyond the wall of equipment. Hunter looked up and saw Troy Mack peeking around one of the cases. Hunter glanced at his daughter's naked body and got up. He stepped outside the sight barrier. "Hey, Troy."

Troy fidgeted with his hands. "How is she?" he asked nervously.

"Not good. We've done about all we can at this point." Adrianna and Hunter each had limited medical training in their past and were struggling with Sprite's treatment. They had consulted with several physicians via the MBH Pod and had poured over everything they could find on burn therapy. They were quick studies, but they weren't experts.

"Sorry." Troy blushed. He was haunted and embarrassed by the vision of Sprite's burns and Adrianna kneeling next to her in the changing room. He fingered his prosthetic chin. "Will she have any scars?"

Hunter looked deeply into the young man's eyes, sensing his immense, personal pain. "Yes, I think she will."

Troy shook his head sadly. "Nobody should have to go through life with scars."

Hunter nodded. "We all get them, Troy. Some are just more visible than others."

"That's the truth." The younger man paused as if he had more to say.

"What is it, Troy?"

"I ran a diagnostic on Sprite's light chamber. Somebody reprogrammed it. They changed her profile and defeated the safety system."

Hunter sagged. "It wasn't an accident."

"No, sir. It was deliberate." Troy looked down at the floor. "I feel really terrible about this."

Hunter studied the young man. His sincerity was obvious. "Thank you, Troy."

Troy looked up with profound sadness. "Do you think I did it?"

"No, son. I don't." Hunter watched the young man walk away. He watched his burdened body language. He was sure Troy had nothing to do with this. He returned to his wife and daughter, anger rising. He would kill whoever was responsible. He sat down, gripping the rim of the tank. He looked up, his eyes softening as he watched his daughter floating in front of him. Hunter was not a religious man, but in that moment, he breathed a prayer for Sprite and a curse upon the one who hurt her.

* * *

The voice of the AI stirred Robert from his drug-induced slumber. Maya Lewis had replied to his message. He overcompensated as he swung his legs over the side of the bed and stood up on rubbery knees. He walked with gliding steps toward his desk and took great care to line himself up with the chair as he sat down.

"O...pen." He slurred the word.

"What was that?" The AI checked the 900 languages and dialects in its database.

"Dammit! Op...pen...nit." Robert said it like three distinct words.

"Do you wish the definition of a pen or a summary of its history? A nit is the egg of a parasitic insect..."

"Stop!" he shouted. "The message. Play the message."

Finally, the AI understood. Maya's form congealed in the holodisplay. "Robert. Good to hear from you. I am pleased that Dr. Logan is preoccupied with his daughter's health. That should keep him from his work, for the time being.

"Of course you're being shut out. The failed bombing has everyone on edge. It has shattered your team. This is what we want. Remember, your wife and child died because of the research being done by Dr. Logan and the others. Destroying the team is the best way for you to honor their memory. There is one last thing we want you to do. Wait until all the scientists are at work in the laboratory spaces, and then trigger the emergency seals. This will stop their work permanently. We all regret the loss of life, but it will ensure that no other husbands will suffer the loss of their families like you have. I'm depending on you, Robert. Let me know when you've succeeded."

The message ended, and Maya's image dissolved into a turbulent sea of noise. Robert sat back, holding on to his chair, trying to grasp Maya's words. His reality was overlaid with a pharmacological veneer. The room was elastic. What had she said? The research on the phase-two machines had to stop. Got it. Trigger the seals? He could do that. Kill everyone in the labs? Robert wasn't sure. Could he kill them? He could kill Hunter Logan. Maybe he could kill the others. Nothing mattered anymore.

Hastings forced the analytical part of his brain to think. Something Maya had said didn't sit right. What was it? She said everyone was on edge because of the attempted bombing. Robert rubbed his temples in an attempt to clear his head. How did she know about the bomb? He never told Maya about the bomb. Maybe he did tell her, but couldn't remember. Robert felt a wave of nausea sweep over him. He lunged toward the bathroom, the acid taste of vomit rising in his throat.

* * *

Hours later, the Logans hadn't moved. Both parents sat exhausted, bracketing the tank that held their beloved. "I'm scared, Adrianna." Hunter had his elbows on the rim of the tank, his chin propped on his palms. "There's been too much damage to her skin."

Adrianna couldn't take her eyes off of Sprite. "It's going be an uphill battle for her."

"The odds…"

Adrianna cut him off. "No! We're not talking about the odds. She's going to make it."

Hunter saw the defeated look in his wife's eyes. She knew the odds as well as he did. The mother in her wouldn't allow her to face the truth. He looked at Sprite's hand, the slender fingers burned and raw. They had been beautiful hands. Hands that would have caressed a lover, embraced grandchildren, led society into a new day. She would have accomplished great things with her hands, but now, they seemed lifeless.

Hunter thought back to the day he watched Sprite wrap Adrianna's birthday gift, her nimble fingers creasing the paper, aligning the seams. It had been a good day…

"Honey?"

Adrianna look up at him. "What is it?"

"I've got an idea. It's crazy, but there's a chance." Hunter sat back in his chair, his hands still gripping the edge of the tank. "Something occurred to me, when I was watching Sprite wrap your present. Remember the research we did on nano-bandages? The machines that bond to skin cells and enhance wound therapy?"

"I've been thinking about that, too. But those were for small wounds: incisions and punctures."

"Right." Hunter became possessed by his idea. "What if we could expand on that technique and create a skin-protecting system?"

Adrianna gazed down at Sprite. "Enough to cover Sprite's body." It wasn't a question.

"We could encase her with a new epidermis. Those nano-bandages were designed to protect and optimize skin cell function. They would protect her epithelial nerves, modulate her skin temperature, and provide proper pH and oxygenation. It would take the stress off of her system. She might have a chance."

Adrianna was nodding and smiling. "It might work."

* * *

Susanna sat at her desk and reviewed the results of the search she had requested on Ray Bright. She twisted her access ring as she sifted through the information. Amos was going to fire her when he discovered that she had selected Ray for the team. She feared the great man but was drawn to him. She hungered for his approval, was eager to please him. How messed up was that? She wasn't in a chatty mood, so Frost had muted her AI and was running her comp in tactile mode. Her fingers sifted through a sea of document icons. She paused. Bright had frequented a Broadway Show chat room. She checked his posts. A number of his entries revealed his hatred for the NARI scientists. Bright feared their nano-research would endanger his "Great White Way."

Susanna turned her attention to the Citizen's League. She remembered Maya Lewis making contact with Robert Hastings at Copernicus Base. Susanna opened up the base security log and watched Maya's movements through the base. She paused the stream of images. There she was, sitting next to Hastings in the base gardens. Her hand was on his leg. Had the scientist turned? It was understandable. He had lost his wife and child. What was he going to do? She made a note to have her informant keep an eye on Dr. Hastings.

Susanna ordered her AI to shuttle through the security footage and track Maya's movements. She saw the woman enter her hotel room. Then, Susanna saw the one person who came to see her. It was Ray Bright.

* * *

The Logans took turns standing vigil over their daughter and working methodically in The Refuge to develop her new nanoskin. They left each other extensive notes and whispered ideas to each other across the tank. Hunter and Adrianna worked tirelessly, knowing their daughter's life hung in the balance. Sprite wasn't getting any better. Time was working against them.

Hunter sat in The Refuge, manipulating parameters in the nanoskin model. Adrianna had suggested some enhancements. She had designed an automatic response, so any attempt to puncture the skin would instantly turn it as hard as diamond. Hunter concentrated on manual control of the skin's behavior, such as temperature and opacity. He smiled as he realized how to do it. There would be some sort of membrane with touch controls. "You're going to be a bionic woman, kiddo."

After six long days and nights, it was time to give Sprite her new skin. They waited until several hours into the sleep cycle. The settlement was quiet. Adrianna opened the hidden entrance to The Refuge. They brought everything into Lab Bay Two and placed the items near Sprite's tank. There was a canister that contained nanoskin stem machines and a tray that held a thin rectangular membrane. Adrianna lifted the membrane out of the tray carefully and applied it to the inside of Sprite's left forearm. The membrane adhered to her skin immediately. Then, Hunter took the canister containing the stem machines and poured it on Sprite's chest. The machines took on a life of their own, as they spread across her abdomen and outward to her legs, arms, and neck. They were like a living organism, marching on a campaign to conquer the outer surface of her body.

The stem machines flowed over her shoulders and down her arms. They merged with the rectangular membrane on her left forearm, designed to interact with the wafer-thin buttons on the material's surface. The machines ignored the liquid in the tank. They spread wherever they found skin cells. Billions of self-assembling machines interlocked with the surface layer of her skin. Wherever there was a mucous membrane, either in the mouth, eyes or genitals, the stem machines stopped their advance and formed a border.

Once her body was covered, the stem machines took on a new task. They turned their energies toward assembling themselves into nanoskin. For twenty minutes, Hunter and Adrianna watched the grayish stem machines become translucent and then perfectly clear. They noticed the redness of her burns subsiding. An hour later, Adrianna gently dabbed the surface of Sprite's skin with sterile gauze. The nanoskin was fully bonded to her dermis.

* * *

Susanna Frost stood on a cliff with Amos Cross. The ocean crashed against the rocks below them. The air was crisp and pure. Cross gave her a broad, accepting smile. "Much obliged, kiddo." She smiled back, opening her arms to embrace him. Cross stepped closer and pushed her off the cliff. Susanna screamed, as the sensation of falling overwhelmed her. The waters below turned to lava; the ocean was a sea of fire. The intense heat engulfed her. Susanna's eyes snapped open. She was alone in her bed. The room was cool and dark, but her body was soaked with sweat. A wave of immense relief washed over her. It was only a dream. Susanna couldn't get back to sleep. She sat in the dark, grateful for reality's triumph over fantasy. She thought of Sprite Logan's burns. What had she done?

* * *

Adrianna had slept for almost twenty-four hours. She checked in on Sprite, who was resting more comfortably. She brewed some tea and wandered over to the Enviro Bay. She sat next to a small waterfall in the garden. The tea was in a cylindrical flask, nestled in her hand. Someone had told her that sacred places were defined by the presence of rocks, trees, and water. This was her holy place. Adrianna sipped the tea, savoring the flavor. With everything swirling around her, these few moments by the water and trees were essential for her well-being. She closed her eyes, thinking of Sprite and how wonderful it had been to labor with Hunter on the nanoskin.

"Adrianna?"

She opened her eyes. Cilla Ashe was standing in front of her. "Hey Cilla. You caught me." She smiled as Cilla sat down on the bench next to her.

"How's Sprite?"

"Better. We might be able to take her out of the tank tomorrow."

"Wow," Cilla was impressed. "I heard you used some kind of new nano-therapy."

"We did." Adrianna didn't want to talk about it. She and Hunter had agreed to say little about the nanoskin. They wanted to preserve Sprite's privacy and limit the information that might filter back to Meridian Corporation.

"Tell me," Cilla continued. "Will you and Hunter be able to get back to work soon? I know all of you would like this nightmare to be over."

"I think it's too soon to tell, Cilla."

"When will you recreate the nanomachines?"

Adrianna hesitated. Cilla was asking too many questions about their work. It seemed odd that the environmental officer, who had previously objected to the development of the phase-two machines, would now be so interested in it.

"It's pretty complicated, Cilla."

The woman was relentless. "Cutting edge, I bet. You were first in your class at Cornell, right?"

Adrianna stiffened. "Where did you hear that?"

Cilla smiled disarmingly. "I don't know. I must have read it somewhere."

Adrianna was about to tell Cilla to back off when Jenson Reed appeared. "There you are!" he said cheerfully.

"Hey, Jenson, do you need anything?" Adrianna was eager to get away from Cilla. She stood up. "I was just about to get back to work."

"Sorry to interrupt." Jenson glanced at Cilla uncomfortably. "I need to talk to you."

"Great. Let's do it on the way back to the labs." She turned to Cilla. "Thanks for your concern. It means a lot."

"Sure thing." The environmental officer smiled, obviously disappointed by the interruption. "See you later."

Adrianna and Jenson walked toward the Core, leaving Cilla standing by the waterfall. "Thanks for saving me," she said.

Reed glanced over his shoulder. "From Cilla?"

"Sometimes she asks too many questions."

"Oh." Jenson smiled in understanding. "Glad to help."

Adrianna patted the young engineer on the shoulder. "Now, what do you need?"

* * *

The next day, Hunter and Adrianna lifted Sprite out of the tank and laid her on the settlement's Gurney. Her skin was dry instantly, the water beading up and rolling off the invisible nanoskin. They could see the burns receding, the redness fading as Sprite's body healed, aided by her new skin. They propped her head up on a pillow and covered her with a thin sheet. The breathing tube was removed, and Sprite coughed involuntarily as she began to breathe on her own.

"Let's keep her sedated for another day," Adrianna said as she looked closely at her daughter's wounds. "We'll start tapering off her meds tomorrow and watch for signs of discomfort."

They rolled the Gurney out of the Lab Bay. Word spread through the tiny settlement, and everyone stopped what they were doing to catch a glimpse of Sprite. It was like a parade, as Adrianna and Hunter wheeled her back to the infirmary. When the sleep period began, Adrianna made herself comfortable in the bed next to her daughter. Sprite's breathing was slow and steady.

* * *

Hunter returned to his quarters and tumbled into the empty bed, but sleep wouldn't come. Images of the nanoskin model kept appearing in his mind. He saw how the machines interlocked to form a continuous membrane over Sprite's body, an almost impenetrable barrier. The tiny nanoskin machines were designed to mate with each other. An idea jarred him. What if he could design something that would mate with the phase-two nanomachines and form a skin around them? Hunter swung his legs off the bed, marveling at the chain of ideas that led him to his inspiration. Sprite's wrapping paper led him to nanoskin, and nanoskin led him to a way to stop the killer machines. It was so simple!

Hunter spent the rest of the sleep period in The Refuge,

manipulating a brand-new nanoparticle model. He opened the model for the phase-two material and set up a simulation to allow the two models to interact with each other. He leaned back and watched. His face began to relax. A smile formed on his lips. Then he began to laugh. He hadn't laughed like that in a long time.

Hunter returned to his living quarters. He could feel exhaustion wrapping its fingers around his body and his brain. He wandered down the corridor toward the Rec Bay. He padded silently into the infirmary. Sprite was resting comfortably, her skin noticeably better. He looked up and beyond his daughter's bed. Adrianna shifted her position, pulling the cover over her bare shoulder. Hunter smiled, and then he returned to the Res Bay for a few hours of sleep.

* * *

Hunter overslept. He missed breakfast. It was time for the midday meal when he finally appeared. He looked like a different man. He had a buoyancy about him, a lightness of spirit.

Sprite was sitting up in bed when Hunter arrived in the infirmary. His daughter's body was covered with red blotches. Her face was still swollen with irregular patches of damaged skin on the bridge of her nose and her cheeks.

"Hey, beautiful." Hunter gave his daughter a broad smile. "How long have you been awake?"

Adrianna answered for her. "She just woke up. She's doing great."

Sprite was looking down at her hands. The mottled red splotches were visible, but receding. She didn't speak.

Hunter pulled a chair up next to his daughter's bed. "How do you feel?"

Sprite rubbed the skin of her hand. Then, she rubbed her thumb and index fingers together, feeling the friction. "Something isn't right." She looked closely at her fingers as she rubbed them back and forth. "My skin. It's different."

Adrianna sat on the other side of her bed. She leaned on the safety rail and took Sprite's hand, cradling it in her palms. "You were burned in the light chamber."

Sprite's body twitched slightly from the memory. "It hurt."

"We had to save you." Hunter took her other hand. "Most of your skin was boiled off. It wasn't charred or anything like that, but blistered like a terrible sunburn."

"We created a new skin for you." Adrianna kept her voice calm and steady. "It saved your life."

"A new skin?" Sprite looked worried.

Adrianna gently patted her daughter's hand. "It's nanoskin. You can see right through it. It's like a coat of paint, and it's helping your real skin get better."

Sprite looked at the bandage that was covering the inside of her left forearm. "What's this?"

"Nothing to worry about." Adrianna laid her hand on the dressing. "We'll tell you about it in a couple of days. Your arm is fine. There's no problem."

"When does it come off?"

"The bandage?"

"The nanoskin."

Adrianna glanced at Hunter. "We'll talk about that later. We want you to get better first."

Sprite looked up at her father. "There was something I was going to tell you just before it happened."

"Don't worry about it. You can tell me later."

"No. It's important. Back on the Moon, when Wiley and I hacked the Meridian network, I saw plans."

"Plans for what?" Hunter asked.

"Plans for a new laboratory on the Moon. There were plans for your containment unit."

Hunter shook his head. "That's not possible, kiddo. It must have been a dream."

"It was real! Before the accident, I was looking at your plans in Lab Bay Two. They were a lot like the ones I saw months ago on the network."

"Meridian Corporation is building a nano-lab on the Moon?" He gave Adrianna a concerned look.

"I think so," Sprite replied.

"That's important. Thanks for telling me." Sprite was getting tired. Hunter squeezed her hand and smiled. "You rest now."

Sprite closed her eyes and drifted off to sleep.

Adrianna stood, sizing up her husband. "You look good."

Hunter smiled easily. "I am good."

"What's up?" Adrianna put her hands on his shoulders. The tightness was gone. "Something's happened."

"I'll tell you later."

Adrianna squeezed his shoulders and let go. "Okay. Are you going to stay here for a while?"

"You bet." She gave him a kiss and went back to the Res Bay to freshen up.

* * *

That night, Hunter and Adrianna met with Jo and Tyson in The Refuge. Sprite was resting comfortably in the infirmary. For the first time in days, they left her alone. It was two hours into the sleep period, and the settlement lights were dimmed, transforming the interior spaces with soft, dreamlike shadows. All was quiet. They spent a few minutes talking about Sprite. They were grateful for her recovery. Hunter and Adrianna told them about the nanoskin and how they had extrapolated it from their work on nano-bandages.

"She doesn't know it's permanent." Adrianna said it like a confession. She didn't like keeping the truth from her daughter. "We'll tell her when she's stronger." She paused. Hunter fidgeted in his chair, but didn't interrupt. "How are you coming with the antidote for the nanomachines? We've been out of the loop."

"As if you didn't have anything else to worry about." Jo reached out and took Adrianna's hand. "We've hit a wall. We can't think. This thing with Sprite, we keep wondering if Kell or Rory might be next. It's all crazy."

"That's why we've got to figure this out." Tyson was trying to pull his determination out of a pit of hopelessness. "It's the only way to untangle ourselves from Meridian. We develop the counter technology, and we become useless to them. They let us go. We stop our work. Maybe society stops hating us. Life goes on."

"I'm beginning to think this whole thing is a pipe dream," Jo said. "It can't be done. We're never going to stop the phase-two nanomachines. The genie isn't going back into the bottle."

"Maybe not." Everyone looked at Hunter. He was grinning from ear to ear. "I know how to neutralize them."

Everyone talked at once. Hunter waited until they fell silent, and then he turned on the holodisplay. "We can design a healing particle. Take a look." A three-dimensional image took shape. It was a comp simulation. A phase-two nanomachine floated on the right side of the chamber. Then, a particle appeared on the left side. Hunter paused the simulation. "This is the healing particle." It moved closer to the phase-two machine. The rogue machine latched on to the healing particle, bonding to the outside of the structure. Hunter paused the simulation again. "The healing particle is designed as a perfect recipient. They interlock with each other, a natural fit. It's love at first sight for the phase-two machine." He set the simulation in motion again. Suddenly, the new particle turned itself inside out like an umbrella caught in a stiff wind, enveloping the phase-two machine.

"Look at that!" Tyson was spellbound. The healing particle began to contract around the nanomachine, its structure surrounding and invading its predator. The particle undulated for a few seconds and began to shrink in the middle, forming a barbell shaped structure. Then, the ends of the barbell separated, forming two new healing particles.

Hunter could hardly contain himself. "The healing particle forms an envelope around the phase-two nanomachine and captures it. Then, it replicates itself by redesigning the machine."

Jo's mind was in high gear. "Every time the healing particle transforms a rogue particle, it doubles the potency of the antidote."

"Exactly."

Adrianna gestured toward one of the healing particles. "What do these things do to other material?

Hunter was back on his game. "That's the beautiful part. They only mate with the phase-two material. Otherwise, they're inert. You could drink a flask of them, and nothing would happen."

"Elegant!" Tyson slapped the table. "That's the answer!"

"We still have to make a few phase-two machines for testing purposes." Jo was ready to get to work.

"That isn't a problem." Hunter spoke slowly and quietly. "I have had the model for the phase-two machines in Millie all along. We could have reconstituted them weeks ago."

"So what do you propose?" Adrianna laid her hand on Hunter's arm.

"We must keep this to ourselves, just the four of us, and start working the problem. Let's keep it in this room. Once we're ready, we'll fabricate a few of the phase-two machines in the new containment unit, and we'll see if the healing particles work."

Tyson clapped his hands. "I can't wait for Meridian Corporation to lose interest in us."

Hunter frowned. "Speaking of Meridian, Sprite told me she found plans for our containment unit on the Meridian network. Apparently they want to warehouse the phase-two machines on the Moon."

"That's crazy!" Jo shook her head. "That puts everyone on the Moon in danger."

Tyson frowned. "What are they planning to do with them?"

Hunter shrugged. "No idea, but it can't be good."

Jo turned to Adrianna. "Could you talk with Sprite and see if she remembers anything else?"

Adrianna folded her arms. "When she feels better. We don't want to overwhelm her."

Tyson stood up. "We better get started on the healing particles before Amos Cross can unleash his plague."

* * *

Sprite was nervous as she lowered herself into the chair slowly. She wore a brown jumpsuit with full-length sleeves. "Do I look okay?"

Her mother was holding the chair. "You're fine, honey. Don't worry about it."

Sprite looked at her hands. "Let me see my face."

Adrianna knelt down beside her. "Are you sure? There's a little discoloration, but you look fine."

"I want to see myself."

Adrianna got a small mirror and handed it to her daughter. Sprite brought it up to her face. She drew in her breath sharply and dropped the mirror. "It's awful!" Adrianna held her as she sobbed. "I'm a freak, like Troy." Sprite's body stiffened as she withdrew, her eyes growing hard and distant.

"Honey." Adrianna rubbed her back. "Let me show you something." She rolled up the left sleeve of Sprite's jumpsuit and peeled away the dressing that covered her forearm. Sprite looked down at the skin. She could see two rows of small discs beneath the skin surface.

"What's that?" Sprite's voice was choked with tears.

"I'll tell you more about these later, but your nanoskin has some built-in features. For example, you can adjust its opacity and color." She gently touched one of the discs, and Sprite's skin began to change. Her real skin began to fade, replaced by a darker, grayish tone. Then, Adrianna touched another button, and the tint of the nanoskin returned to Sprite's natural color. "There. You see? The skin can hide the redness. You can choose your own tan."

Sprite lifted the mirror in her left hand. She glanced at herself and shrugged. She pressed the discs, her eyes glued to the reflection. After a few moments, she let the mirror fall to her lap. "I guess it's okay."

Adrianna nodded with approval. "You look good." She reapplied the dressing and rolled down her sleeve. "I don't want you touching the control surface until I explain it to you." Sprite glared at her impatiently.

There was a light knock on the door, and Jo Smith appeared at the threshold. Adrianna motioned for her to come in. Jo smiled as she approached. "You look great, Sprite!" She nodded brightly. "I swear; your skin is almost back to normal. It's amazing!"

Sprite studied Jo's face. She seemed to be telling her the truth. "You think so?"

"I do." She smiled and squeezed Sprite's hand. "Kell is outside. He wants to see you."

Sprite shook her head. "I'm not ready." She pushed Jo's hand away.

"It will be good for you, honey." Adrianna touched her arm where the bandage was, silently reminding her of the adjustments they had made in the nanoskin. "You have to see him sometime. You look fine."

Sprite yielded with a slight nod. "Turn the chair away from the door. I don't want him to see my face."

* * *

Kell Edwards sat outside the infirmary, waiting for permission to see Sprite. He hadn't seen her since the mishap with the light chamber. He was concerned for his friend but nervous about seeing her. Jo had told him about the burns. It all seemed like a dream. Sprite was beautiful, so sexy. What was he going to feel when he saw her?

Jo stepped out of the infirmary and motioned to her son. "Let's go. Sprite's kind of nervous." Tell me about it, Kell thought. He followed his mother into the room.

Sprite was sitting up in a chair, her back to the door. Adrianna stood at a distance, as Kell peered tentatively at his friend. All he could see was the skin of her head. There were subtle discolorations, but it wasn't so bad. He stepped closer. "Hi, Sprite."

"Stay behind me, Kell. I don't want you to see my face."

Kell moved closer. Sprite's skin didn't look natural. He could see the blotches now, just under the surface. They were like scabs under a shear stocking.

"How are you?" Kell moved closer still.

"I'm fine." Sprite was staring at her mother. She shook her head slightly as if to say, "Get him out of here." Adrianna didn't respond. Sprite frowned.

"I've missed you." Kell walked around in front of Sprite's chair, ignoring her request. He looked at her face. Her skin didn't look natural. He felt awkward. He wanted to run.

Sprite saw the worried look on his face. "Get out!" she shouted. Sprite jerked her hands upward to cover her face.

Kell stepped back. "You, you look fine." His words were empty reassurances.

"Go away!"

Kell was already backing away. He had a lump in his throat. "I'm sorry." Jo touched his arm, but he was already out the door.

* * *

Tyson and Hunter labored with the containment unit in Lab Bay Two. All the covers had been removed, revealing the complex mechanism. A cable connected the unit to a holodisplay, where technical readouts assessed the various circuits. Tyson replaced a circuit card and hit the power. Hunter studied the holodisplay. "That does it. The containment unit is ready."

"You are all ready, huh?" The two men looked up. Robert Hastings stood near the unit. His arms were crossed, his rage hidden beneath a microscopically thin veneer.

"Hey, Robert." Hunter studied the man.

"What in hell do you think you're doing?" Hastings snapped.

Hunter stepped in front of the containment unit. "What do you mean?"

"I mean, why have you been checking all of my work?" Cracks were forming in the veneer.

"Calm down, Robert. The containment unit is ready, and we're going to give Meridian what they want. Then, we can get on with our lives."

"Get on with our lives! Listen to you. Maryanne and Emile are dead! Sprite is a burned-up freak! There's no 'getting on with our lives.'"

Hunter put his hands up, fighting the urge to hit the man. "We're going to find a way through this, Robert." Hunter kept his voice steady, reassuring. "Believe me, this is not the end."

"You're lying." Hastings' eyes were ablaze. "You didn't want me to know, but I'm too smart for you." He balled his hands into fists, every vein visible on his neck, his jaw set. He lunged forward into Hunter, pushing him back toward the containment unit. Both men crashed to the floor. Logan tucked himself into a fetal position as Robert pummeled him with his fists, cursing him. Tyson grabbed Hastings by the shoulders and pulled him away from Hunter, who struggled to his feet.

"You son-of-a-bitch! Son-of-a-bitch!" Robert was out of control. Ty sat on him, using his weight to subdue him. Hunter joined his friend, and they held Hastings to the floor while the enraged man twisted and jerked, trying to break free.

"Robert!" Hunter commanded his colleague to stop. "Settle down! What's this about?"

"You know what this is about, you bastard!" Hastings stopped pushing against the men. They let him sit up. Tyson held his arms behind his back. Hunter squatted in front of him. The angry man kicked out with his feet in a final act of defiance, but they thrashed harmlessly in the air. Logan was too far away. "You're spying on me!" He spat the words. "What have I done to you?"

"Okay. I've been keeping track of your work." Hunter rubbed his shoulder. A large bump was already forming, and it stung. "You're losing your grip. Everyone has noticed it. You haven't been concentrating on your work. It's my job to keep the team on track."

"You're treating me like I'm a spy." Robert's angry glare turned into a mask of pain.

"Are you?" Hunter's words cut like a scalpel.

Hastings grew still. Something died in his eyes. "No, Hunter. I'm not."

"Then start acting like a member of the team."

Tyson released Robert's arms, and the men stood up. The angry scientist brushed himself off and pushed both hands into his pockets. "When this is over, you and I are done, Logan."

Hunter stepped toward him, their eyes locked. "If that's the way it has to be."

Hastings knocked over a chair as he left the lab bay.

* * *

Adrianna brought Sprite's favorite jumpsuit to the infirmary and laid it out on the bed, along with a small box. Sprite was sitting up in a chair, gazing at her complexion in a hand mirror. Her lips were turned down into a frown as she swiveled her head from side to side, examining the uneven tone of her skin.

"Let's get you dressed and take a walk." Sprite didn't answer. "It'll do you some good. We can pay your dad a visit in Lab Bay Two."

"I don't want to."

"Come on, Sprite. You've got to get out of here."

Sprite put down the mirror. "I don't want anyone to see me."

"You look fine."

"I have splotches all over my face."

Adrianna sat down next to her daughter. "I brought something for you." She opened the small case. "It's time for you to discover the miracle of makeup." She took several items out of the box and pulled Sprite's chair closer to the bed. It only took her a few moments. "Now, take a look at yourself."

Sprite picked up the mirror. She nodded slowly. "It's not terrible."

"You look beautiful." Adrianna snapped the box closed.

There was a gentle tap at the infirmary entrance. Adrianna turned. It was Rory North.

"Can I see Sprite?"

Adrianna gestured for her to come in. The girl approached, peering around Sprite's mother to catch a glimpse of her friend.

"Wow. You look great!"

Sprite looked up. "You think so?"

"I thought you had burns from the light chamber."

"I did, but Mom and Dad came up with a way to heal them."

"You're beautiful."

Sprite beamed at her friend.

Adrianna grabbed her daughter's hand. "How about that walk?"

* * *

Robert Hastings' mind was a seething caldron of anger and guilt. He charged past the Lab One Supply Bay in a homicidal rage. His thoughts spun at a dizzying, apoplectic pace, like a broken gyroscope out of balance, destabilizing the very core of his being. He saw fleeting images of Maryanne and Emile watching him as he made love to Samina. Next, he saw Sprite Logan glaring at him while he thrust himself into Adrianna. He heard Tyson Edwards' voice: "I think the people who hired Ray Bright blew up our lab." Then Maya's voice echoed in his head: "The failed bombing has everyone on edge. It has shattered your team." He pounded his head with his fist. No, he hadn't told her about the bomb. How did she know? She must have found out some other way, but no one outside of the settlement knew. Did Maya have something to do with the bomb? Had he agreed to help the people who killed his family?

Robert entered Lab Bay One. No one was there. He didn't care. He would trigger the seals, render the lab unusable, and move on to Lab Bay Two. He made his way back to the Iso Bay. The release-handle for the emergency sealing system was there near the corridor entrance. Once pulled, he would have ten seconds to get into the Iso Bay. The hatch would automatically close, and the Lab Bay One complex would be flooded with the expanding foam. Within seconds, the material would solidify, plugging the domes and corridors. He grabbed the release handle and paused once again, replaying Maya's words in his head.

"Robert! What are you doing?" Robert turned. Adrianna and Sprite were standing with Rory in the Iso Bay. Time dilated. Everything was in slow motion. Robert looked at Sprite. He glanced at Rory but didn't see her. Instead, he saw Emile standing next to Sprite. In the same instant, he realized how Maya knew about the bomb. Ray Bright had been working for her. She had been responsible for the bomb on Selene Station. Maya had killed Maryanne and Emile. Robert looked down at himself. He felt naked and alone.

"Robert!" Adrianna's voice seemed far away. "Don't pull that lever!"

He thought about how he had been shut out of the nano-research. They didn't trust him. His life was over. He couldn't even honor Maryanne in her death. Robert gazed at Sprite with sad eyes. She had done nothing to deserve what he had done to her. "Sprite, I never meant to hurt you. I'm really sorry." He pulled the lever. A siren began to pulsate through the corridor. Hastings began to scream. "Maryanne, forgive me!" Robert didn't move. The Iso Bay hatch swung shut. He dropped his hands to his sides and threw his head back. Images of his wife and son appeared in his tormented mind, as the sealing foam engulfed him.

8

S prite and Rory screamed. Adrianna rushed to embrace them. The security AI announced the alert throughout the settlement, and everyone came running to the ISO Bay. Tyson and Hunter were the first to arrive, with Troy and Jenson close behind. "Who's in Lab Bay One?"

"It's Robert. He triggered the sealing foam." Adrianna was shaking as she clung to the girls. "He's still in there."

Hunter knelt down next to her, his arms around the three of them. "Anybody else?"

"I don't know." Adrianna's knees buckled.

Hunter lowered them to the floor, where they all sat in a tangle. "This is too much."

The ISO Bay filled with people. Kell was the last to arrive, peeking at Sprite as she sat on the floor next to her mother. Jo took a head count, confirming that Robert Hastings had been the only one in the Lab Bay One complex. Everyone was stunned, wondering why he had killed himself. Alexis Wren stood quietly, her hand on the closed hatch. "Would someone please open this? I have to get back to work." No one heard her.

* * *

Hunter took his family back to their quarters and spent some time with them. They were badly shaken. Then he made his way back to the Core and entered the MBH pod. Before long, Susanna Frost's image appeared in the holodisplay.

"Dr. Logan." She wore her business face. "I haven't heard from you."

"My daughter is much better. Thanks for asking."

She ignored his sarcasm. "What happened?"

"You know damn well what happened. Somebody tampered with her light chamber and burned off most of her skin."

Susanna acted like she didn't care. "I'm glad she's better."

"Don't tell me you had nothing to do with it."

"I didn't." She lied.

"You threatened her."

"That was only talk, Dr. Logan. I was merely trying to motivate you."

Hunter studied her face. "Robert Hastings is dead." Susanna didn't react. "He activated the emergency seals on Lab Bay One. He made no attempt to reach safety. It was suicide."

"Will this slow your progress?" She didn't skip a beat.

She was one bloodless bitch, Hunter thought. "Are you kidding? A member of my team just committed suicide."

"I don't think you appreciate the situation, Dr. Logan."

"Oh, I do. I was right there. My daughter just watched a man kill himself. What do you expect from us?"

"I expect you to give us what we want. I expect you to produce the nanomachines."

Hunter let out a breath. He wasn't stalling this time. Everyone was immobilized. "We need some time."

Susanna smirked. "Do you want Sprite to have another accident?"

Hunter snapped. "Go to hell!" Hunter rose from his seat, his heart pounding, murder in his eyes. "Touch my family again, and you will never get the phase-two machines!" Susanna cut the transmission. He was left alone in the MBH pod, cursing in the dark.

* * *

Amos Cross stood on the deck of a virtual sailboat. The sails were full, the floor of his office a placid ocean. The sun was shining, and the craft moved smoothly on its virtual tack. Amos paced back and forth, waiting for his underling on the other end of the comlink. He muted the voice transmission and made a verbal note to fire the woman after the project was completed.

Susanna entered the office. Cross knew she was coming, of course. No one entered the great man's office without his knowledge. The foyer was a virtual dock bordering the glassy sea. "Come here," he commanded her. Susanna looked down at the water and hesitated. She knew it was an illusion, but the thought of walking through the water unnerved her. "I said, COME HERE." Cross was enjoying the situation. Susanna stepped into the office, her feet sinking a couple of centimeters into the waterless water. She felt the floor and quickly regained her composure. She strode over to the sailboat and waited dutifully.

"What do you have for me?" Cross could see the bad news on her face.

"It's Meridian 6, sir. Robert Hastings committed suicide."

"Tell me more."

Susanna cleared her throat. "Well, sir, you remember my telling you about Maya Lewis?"

"I do." Amos shut down the comlink with his ill-fated subordinate. Susanna had his full attention. His eyes blazed like the sun floating high above his imaginary ocean.

"Maya contacted him when he was at Copernicus Base. It seems clear he was working for her. He tripped the seals on one of the laboratories to sabotage the research."

"Fuck!" Cross kicked at the sailboat, sending a shutter throughout the hull. The mast began to wag back and forth. The shaking hull sent concentric ripples across the placid sea. A storm cloud appeared on the horizon. "How many things can possibly go wrong?" He pushed a pile of digital paperwork over the side. The images scattered, bouncing up and down as the virtual water sloshed and gurgled. "What about the machines?"

"According to Logan, the team is out of commission. Hastings' death has knocked them off course."

Cross adjusted his jacket. "How could you have missed Hastings' connection with Maya Lewis? You've failed to keep control of the situation. Light a fire under Dr. Logan. I don't care what you do; just get him back to work." Cross looked at the scattered papers. He cut them from the water's surface and pasted them in a neat pile on the boat's gunwale.

"I've played all of my cards. If I push him any harder, he's going to jump ship."

Cross was privately amused by the nautical reference. "Anybody can be persuaded. Here's what you do. Send a security shuttle up there.

Force them back to work at gunpoint. I don't want to see you again until you have this disaster under control."

Susanna stared at her shoes. "There's one more thing, sir."

Cross shook his head. "What more could you possibly tell me?"

"I was the one who selected Ray Bright for the mission without properly vetting him."

* * *

Sprite perched on the kitchen counter in the Logans' residence, frowning as her mother prepared a light dinner. The Logans frequently ate in the privacy of their quarters. Adrianna knew that her daughter wanted to talk. Her mood was dark, but open. Rory had retreated to her bedroom.

"Mom, have you ever seen somebody die? I mean, before Dr. Hastings?" Sprite gripped the edge of the counter, swinging her legs nervously.

"Yes, honey. I was there when my mom passed away." She looked carefully at her daughter. "It was in a hospital. It was really tough."

Sprite didn't speak for a moment. "Dr. Hastings, we didn't actually see him die. The hatch closed just before that, but we saw him just before... He apologized to me." A tear trickled down her face. "It was terrible. I've hated him for ten years, but I didn't want him to die." Adrianna wiped her hands and leaned into her daughter, holding her tightly in her arms. She knew there was something else. Sprite began to sob quietly. "I didn't want him to kill himself because of what he did to me."

"He was a ruined man, Sprite. He had been cheating on Maryanne for many years. She and Emile died right after she confronted him with it. She never forgave him, and it drove him mad. That's why he killed himself."

"But he apologized to me."

"I'm sure he meant it, honey, but he owed an apology to a lot of people. You just happened to be there." Adrianna put her hand under Sprite's chin and raised her head until their eyes met. "You were not the reason he killed himself."

Neither of them spoke for a long moment. Then Sprite looked up intently. "Do you owe an apology to a lot of people?"

Adrianna sighed. "No, honey, I don't. That day with Bob, with Dr.

Hastings, was the only time I ever cheated on your dad. I apologized to him long ago, and I made my peace with Maryanne."

Sprite had never seen such sadness in her mother's eyes. "I don't want to be angry with you anymore, Mom," she said.

"I'm sorry I broke your heart, honey. I'm sorry for…"

Sprite cut her off. "I forgive you, Mom." They both let out long breaths of relief simultaneously. Realizing what they had done, they laughed and laughed.

* * *

Ray Bright lay on a boulder, enjoying the artificial sun in the huge public garden at Rinker's Knot. The garden supplied plants and hydroponics technology for scores of settlements and outposts scattered in the Belt. Residents of the Knot and those like Ray, who were just passing through, reaped the benefits of the extraordinary place.

Ray had taken off his shoes and his shirt. He was lying flat on his back, allowing the warmth of the stone to permeate him. His old headphones were planted securely over his ears, and strains of "The Sound of Music" filled him. This was heaven.

A woman with streaks of gold in her dark hair lounged next to Ray. She did special projects for those who could afford her services. It was no accident that Ray had hooked up with her months before. The woman had a book reader in her hand. She checked to make sure Ray's eyes were closed. His head was in her lap. She could hear the muffled sounds of the music emanating from his headphones. She reached into her pocket and slowly withdrew a slender, pen-like instrument. It resembled an old-style laser pointer. She positioned the device about a centimeter from Ray's temple and pressed a button.

The device burst several hundred blood vessels in Ray's brain. Within a few microseconds, before he could utter a sound, his brain was dead. Ray's body jerked once and went limp. His heart stopped beating a moment later, and the rest of him was dead, too. The woman put the instrument back into her pocket and looked down at her reader. She finished the chapter. Then, she rose and walked away, leaving Ray's corpse to bake in the artificial sun.

* * *

Sprite walked the corridors of Meridian 6, grateful to be alive. She was conscious of her new skin. Although it was only a couple of millimeters thick, she felt like she was in a glove. She lengthened her stride, stretching her muscles. It was good to be out of the bed. Her mother's makeup gave her confidence.

She entered the Core and took one of the radial aisles into the center of the dome. Jenson Reed frowned when he saw her. He swiveled his chair away, trying to avoid contact. "Aren't you going to say hello?" Sprite stood by the young man with her arms folded.

Jenson turned back toward her. His eyes were cold. "Sorry to run, but there's something I've got to do." He stood up and pushed past her as he headed toward the MBH pod. Sprite watched him as he disappeared inside the enclosure. Why was Jenson avoiding her? Was it her appearance? She didn't think so. What was it? He was nervous and distant. What had happened to her friend? He was acting like a different person.

"Wiley?" Her card comp woke up.

"What can I do for you, Sprite?"

"Do you talk much with the Core Intellect?"

"All the time."

"Do you think we could listen in on the transmission taking place in the MBH pod?"

"It's a private conversation."

"Is there a way to hear it?"

"Of course, but the Core Intellect would have to approve."

"How do I get her approval?"

"Her?"

"The core is female, isn't she?"

There was a long pause. "She is."

"What's her name, Wiley?"

Another pause. "Athena."

The goddess of wisdom, Sprite thought. "Let me speak to her."

"She's already here."

"Athena? I'm Sprite. Good to meet you."

A smooth, confident voice whispered in Sprite's ear. "Wiley has told me a lot about you. He says you are a good friend." Athena said, "friend," like it was a holy word.

"He's a good friend, too. Forgive me for asking, but would you let me listen in on Jenson Reed's micro-black-hole transmission?"

"I am not permitted to do that."

"Please, Athena. Something tells me it's important."

The Core Intellect paused for at least three seconds. "If I send the feed to Mr. Reed's holodisplay, I can't prevent you from watching it."

Sprite grinned. "Thank you, Athena."

"Miss Logan?"

"You can call me Sprite."

"Sprite?" Another pause. "You are the first human to call me by my name."

Sprite stepped to Jenson's workstation. His face congealed in the holodisplay. He was sitting in the chamber. Soon, a second person appeared in the display. Sprite sucked in her breath and sat down, dumbfounded. It was Susanna Frost.

"I don't have much time." Jenson glanced behind him. Even though he was safely tucked inside the chamber, he felt exposed. "I'm sorry about Hastings. I had no idea he would do it."

"I told you to keep an eye on him! You could have stopped him."

"It's my fault, Susanna."

The woman brushed his comment aside. "You are to stand down. We're sending a security force to lock down the settlement. They'll arrive in seven days. It has become clear to us that Hunter Logan and his team are unwilling to serve our needs voluntarily. The troops will compel them to finish their work."

Jenson looked alarmed. "What do you want me to do?"

"You are to stay calm and assist the security team when they arrive. We do not want anyone knowing about this. Is that clear?"

"Yes, Ms. Frost. What about Troy Mack?"

"I'll deal with him personally. Once the forces arrive, he'll stand down, and you can take over."

Sprite spoke in a whisper. "Wiley? Are you recording this?"

"Absolutely."

Sprite sat immobile in Jenson's chair. She closed her eyes. Jenson was working for Susanna Frost! He had been her friend. He had saved her life at Copernicus Base. They had talked about family and their common interests, but he was a liar, a traitor. She didn't know him at all.

"What are you doing?" Sprite's eyes snapped open. The feed from the MBH pod was still visible in the holodisplay. Jenson stood next to her. He was smiling, but he was different. There was no hint of friendship, only professional distance. Sprite didn't speak. "You heard my conversation with Susanna."

"You're working for her. You're the traitor!"

Jenson shifted his weight to the other foot. "One man's traitor is another man's loyalist." He paused. "I never expected you to survive your little accident in the light chamber."

"You?"

"Amos Cross needs the phase-two machines, Sprite. I hurt you to get to your father. It wasn't personal." Sprite bolted from the chair, but Jenson was faster. He grabbed her by the shoulder and pushed her back down into the seat. "Not so fast."

Sprite studied his face. "I'm in trouble."

"Yes, you are. You stuck your nose in the wrong place, Sprite. I've spent five years of my life winning the trust of your father and mother, and you aren't going to get in my way." Jenson paused. Sprite had a grin on her face. "What did you do?"

"My dad is going to be here in about thirty seconds. Wiley called him."

Jenson turned away from her, looking for Hunter. Sprite jumped out of the chair and disappeared into the Tech Stacks. Reed pushed the chair aside and ran after her.

9

160 Hours Left

Hunter was on his way to the Core when Wiley called his comlink. He broke into a sprint when the AI told him Sprite was in danger. He keyed his comlink and summoned Ty and Adrianna. Logan froze at the entrance to the Core. He held his breath and listened. There! Off to the right was the sound of two people running. The light footsteps were Sprite's. Someone with heavier feet was chasing her. Hunter ran in the direction of the sounds. Sprite screamed, and he heard a scuffle. Then it was quiet.

* * *

Sprite was lying on the hard concrete floor. Jenson Reed towered over her, a murderous smile on his face. "This time you won't recover from your injuries," he said. Sprite looked through his legs and saw her father approaching. She squirmed, hoping to keep Jenson distracted. She kicked at him. His leg was like a tree trunk, solid and immovable. Then, in a flash, her father was there. He hit Reed from behind. The younger man fought for his balance and recovered quickly. He spun around and put all of his weight behind his meaty fist. Hunter braced himself against one of the racks, making no attempt to block the punch. Jenson hit him in the midsection. A bone-shattering crack echoed in the dome as his hand splintered against Hunter's chest. Reed screamed in agony, falling to the floor.

Sprite looked at her father. "How did you do that?"

Hunter was smiling broadly as he helped her to her feet. His hands and arms felt hard, like stone. He was like a living suit of armor. "You didn't think your mom and I would give you nanoskin without testing it first?" He pressed something on his forearm, and once again, his skin was soft and supple. Sprite gave him a hug. Ty and Adrianna came running. Ty knelt down next to Jenson. The man was writhing in pain. Adrianna rushed to Sprite's side. "She's okay," Hunter said. "But Mr. Reed has a broken hand."

159 Hours Left

They took Reed to the infirmary and strapped him down to the Gurney. Jo tended to his injury, while Hunter interrogated him. "How long have you been working for Amos Cross?"

The young man winced in pain. "I don't know what you're talking about. I've been a loyal member of your team for the last five years."

Sprite bristled. "That's a lie! He told me that he's been working against us all along. He sabotaged my light chamber." Adrianna couldn't suppress her hatred. Sprite went on. "He was trying to kill me in the Tech Stacks when Dad showed up."

"Don't listen to her!" Jenson shot back, pleadingly. "She fell, and I was about to help her to her feet when Hunter slammed into me. She was acting strangely, like she was drunk. She's not thinking clearly."

Sprite looked at her mother and father. "I heard him talking to Susanna Frost. He's been working for her. She told him troops were on their way to force you back to work."

Ty grabbed the railing of the bed and put his face close to Reed's. "When are they coming?"

The young man pushed against his restraints. "She's imagining things. Come on guys, I'm your friend. She's lying."

Sprite stepped forward. "I recorded it."

No one spoke. Jenson's jaw dropped. "You recorded it." Sprite nodded. "That's impossible. I was in the MBH pod. There's no way you could have recorded my conversation."

"So there was a conversation," Ty snarled.

"Yeah, but it wasn't with Susanna Frost. I was talking with Meridian Tech Support."

Sprite took her father's hand. "I'll show it to you." She stepped to a nearby holodisplay and spoke to Wiley. "Play back the transmission."

"Certainly, Sprite."

The interior of the MBH pod appeared in the holodisplay. Jenson was on the left, and Susanna Frost was on the right. Everyone listened intently. Jenson stared at his feet, a look of silent resignation on his face. Everyone circled the bed when the recording finished. Hunter spoke. "We trusted you. You were part of our family." Sprite thought she saw a tear in her father's eye. Hunter looked at Ty. "Will you and Jo wheel him down to his residence? Sweep it for weapons and comlinks. Lock him in. I don't want to see him again."

Jenson smiled. "I'm not finished with you, Hunter. Those troops are going to storm this settlement and put me in command." Ty put a gag in his mouth, as Jo unlocked the wheels of the Gurney.

* * *

Hunter returned to the Core and found Troy Mack talking with the Core Intellect. He sat down next to him and leaned back in the chair, his hands behind his head. "I guess you've heard about Jenson."

Troy nodded. "Word gets around."

"I need to know where you stand. We've got a shuttle full of security troops headed this way, and I need to know who I can trust."

Troy fidgeted uncomfortably in his chair. "Jenson was the one who hurt Sprite."

"That's correct."

"And Susanna Frost put him up to it." Hunter nodded. "That means my employer will stop at nothing to force you to make more of the killing machines."

The older man sighed. "That's how I see it. Amos Cross is a shameless bully and a murderer."

Troy tented his fingers. "Meridian Corporation pays me, but I still have a conscience. I'm with you."

Hunter smiled. "I hoped you'd say that."

* * *

Maya Lewis rubbed a stiff shoulder muscle. She stood barefoot next to Damon Trask's pristine desk and flexed at the waist. She stretched her arms over her head and behind her back as far as she could. She was proud of her body. It was her most valuable tool. She kept herself in incredible physical condition. It wasn't about fitness. Her conditioning was all about the control of men. When they looked at her, they stopped thinking. When they stopped thinking, she had them right where she wanted them.

Damon Trask whisked into his office. He paused at the sight of his associate, admiring her form against the rim of Earth. Maya's raw sensuality worked its charms on him. For a moment, he forgot why he was there. "Any word from Hastings?" Trask was back on track.

Maya continued her stretching routine, now bending at the waist and placing her palms flat on the floor. Trask was mesmerized.

"Hastings is dead." She didn't miss a beat. "There were some psychological issues we didn't know about." She reached up as high as she could, standing on tiptoes and squeezing her buttocks. Trask's jaw dropped as Maya bent over again. "He was carrying some significant guilt over his sexual indiscretions."

"That's bad," Trask agreed. He began to fantasize about a sexual indiscretion with Maya. She did two more repetitions and then turned toward Damon. She put a bare foot on the edge of his desk and began to stretch herself again. It was erotic as hell. She was wearing one of her spray-on outfits, and Trask could make out every curve and crevice in her body.

"The good news," Maya leaned down again, "is that Hastings killed himself while triggering the emergency seals on one of the lab bays. One lab was destroyed." Their eyes met as Maya straightened her torso. She glanced down at her body and then gave him a suggestive smile.

155 Hours Left

Alexis Wren strode with a purpose through the darkened Rec Bay. She launched herself down the corridor toward the Core in the low Cerian gravity. She liked the shadows of the sleep period. Shadows provided safety, secrecy, control.

She threaded herself through the Tech Stacks and settled into Jenson's old chair. She initiated an outgoing file-transfer, reaching into her pocket and switching on her data module. The message consisted of a few lines of encrypted text. The transfer was done by the time her finger left the biometric pad on the module. She closed out the session and padded back to her residence.

141 Hours Left

Hunter entered the MBH pod the next morning. Susanna Frost's image appeared. She was caught off guard this time. She looked worn. Her eyes were red.

"It's good to see you, Ms. Frost." Hunter was in control. Confident. "Why didn't you tell me Meridian security forces were on their way?" Susanna flinched. "Don't you think it was important for me to know?"

Susanna recovered quickly. "We just made the decision, Dr. Logan. I'm surprised you know about it. With Adam Taberg's death, we felt you could use some additional support out there."

"Is that so?"

"Yes. The team is going to provide for your safety. We're concerned about your well-being. They'll arrive in about two weeks."

Hunter gave her a hard smile. "You are a piece of work, Ms. Frost. They're going to arrive in six days, not two weeks."

Susanna blushed, a hairline crack in her facade. "How do you know that?"

"The same way I know Jenson Reed has been your informant since God knows when. Oh, he wanted to be here himself, but we gave him a sedative, and he's sleeping it off under lock and key."

The color drained from her face. "I have tried to protect you, Dr. Logan. I have been your first line of defense against Amos Cross. If you lose my support, your wife and daughter will die, and it will be your entire fault. You'll wish you were dead."

Hunter remained calm. "Your tricks aren't going to work on me this time, Susanna. We've been hard at work up here," he lied. "We're ready for your troops, and you will never get the phase-two nanomachines." Susanna was about to respond, but Hunter cut the transmission. Then his hands began to shake.

* * *

Prescott Logan sat in front of the large pane of aluminum silicate glass that was bonded to the rock walls of his home, a small refuge lost in a myriad of asteroids between Mars and Jupiter. His best jumpship lifted away from his landing pad. Prescott watched with pride as the pilot punched the throttles, and the little ship rose up through the rocky crevice that concealed his home. This day marked the beginning of his revenge, a day twenty-two years in the making. He could taste its sweetness.

Prescott Logan lived in seclusion with his wife, Maria. Years earlier, he had journeyed to Mars, having taken a teaching position at Aonia

Terra University. He met Maria there, and they had built a life together on the red planet. She was a professor of applied physics. Prescott was a savant, his knowledge of data encryption unparalleled.

Meridian Corporation took an interest in Prescott and assigned an up-and-coming bureaucrat named Amos Cross to recruit him. Young Cross encouraged him to leave his teaching post and apply his substantial intellect to the plans and purposes of the Meridian Corporation, but Prescott did not like authority. The harder Cross tried to recruit him, the more Prescott resisted. The young executive didn't like losing. If Prescott Logan would not work for Meridian Corporation, then he wouldn't work for anyone. Cross had both Logans fired from their teaching positions. Their credit was cut off. Mysteriously, no one wanted to hire them. Amos Cross squeezed Prescott, expecting him to bow to Meridian's overwhelming power. Certainly, the young man would change his mind and accept Cross's generous offer. Instead, the Logans disappeared into The Asteroid Belt, choosing to live their lives on their own terms. Amos Cross quickly forgot the incident, but Prescott Logan had a long memory.

* * *

137 Hours Left

Hunter sat wearily at a table in the commissary. He rolled an empty coffee flask in his palms. He couldn't tell if the acid in his stomach was from fear or excess coffee. It was both, probably. He looked up. It was Alexis Wren. She moved like a sleepwalker, gliding without purpose. He watched her fumble with the coffee dispenser, overcome by mechanical devices. Then, she approached his table and sat down across from him.

"Did you send the message to Samina?"

Alexis gazed at Hunter serenely. "I did it last night during the sleep period."

"Good."

"But what do the messages say? I've been sending her messages for weeks now, and I still don't know what any of them mean."

"I'm sorry, Alexis. You know I trust you." The older scientist nodded. "I've got to play this very carefully. That's why I've had you communicate with Samina, instead of me. I couldn't tell you where she is, or what was in the messages. There's too much at stake."

She smiled. "I understand. Will you tell me when it's all over?"

"You bet." Alexis rose from her chair and returned to her scientific contemplations. Hunter could see her eyes glaze over as she dismissed him from her consciousness and shuffled away. Hunter wished he could forgo all the secrecy, but he could not. Everything of value hung in the balance.

83 Hours Left

Everyone gathered in Lab Bay Two to witness the rebirth of the phase-two machines. Cilla Ashe stood near the back of the group. She was uneasy. These people were tampering with the building blocks of creation. Such arrogance! She felt a pang of guilt, confronted by her own hypocrisy. Her employer had compelled them to recreate these killer machines. She had colluded with the devil.

The new containment unit was sealed, lines of force holding harmless stem machines in isolated stasis. A large holodisplay revealed the prenatal killers. Hunter powered up Millie and transferred several templates into the containment unit. The integrated lab module began to manipulate the stem machines. Everyone stood in awe as the atoms were aligned into a new configuration. "There you are," Hunter murmured. Eight identical machines were clustered together in the image.

Cilla nudged Jo. "Are those the killer machines?" The scientist nodded. "How do they work?"

"They latch on to anything around them and dissociate its structure. Without the containment unit, those eight little machines would eat this entire settlement as an appetizer and move on to Ceres for the main course."

Cilla shuttered. "Why would you make such horrible things?"

"This was just the first step in our work," Jo told her. "We never intended for these machines to escape into the environment. Our plan was to focus their behavior, so they would only destroy targeted pollutants and pathogens."

"You were trying to create a tool to save the environment?"

"That's right. We were devastated when the containment unit was destroyed on Selene Station. The machines got out. We lost good friends. It was the work of a saboteur, but we still felt responsible. Hunter took it the hardest."

"Do you have any idea what Meridian plans to do with these killer machines?"

Jo nodded slowly. "We think they are going to use them to threaten people who don't cooperate."

"How can you let them do that?"

"They've threatened our children."

Cilla didn't want to hear any more of it. Tucking her hands under her arms, she hurried out of the lab.

Tyson scanned the faces of his friends. "If we're not careful, Amos Cross will have his new weapon."

Adrianna locked down the containment unit. "We're going to stand watch. We can't afford another breach." Everyone agreed. They would not leave the phase-two machines unguarded.

***

Cilla ran through the Core. She scratched her arms, as if she could feel the killer machines reaching across the settlement and infecting her. She should never have agreed to work for Meridian. She had misjudged the scientists. Their intentions had been as pure as her own. They were all caught in the same web, but Cilla was still terrified by the nanomachines. She kept running until she was surrounded by her garden. She rushed to the waterfall and stripped off her things. She threw herself into the water, allowing the cascading droplets to cleanse her. In the low Cerian gravity, the liquid enveloped her in a fine mist. Cilla pushed herself under the water, the coolness welcoming her. She rose to the surface when she couldn't hold her breath any longer, still drowning in her fear.

81 Hours Left

Tyson agreed to stand the first watch and remained in the Lab Bay. He found a chair and settled in for the sleep period. His eyes were heavy. It had been a long day, and it was going to be an even longer night.

Jo returned to the Res Bay with Hunter and Adrianna, and soon the three of them were in The Refuge. Adrianna sat down in front of her holodisplay. "The sooner we can neutralize those machines, the better."

"You've got that right." Jo stowed several items that had been left on one of the benches. "Let's kill the little bastards before they kill us."

* * *

Susanna Frost stood before Amos Cross. Once again, she was distracted by his office decor. The office now rested on a brownish gray floor. The walls were constructed of heavy rectangular stones. Machines straight from a medieval torture chamber were strewn throughout the space. A rack stood silently in one corner, while an Iron Maiden sat in another. There was a head crusher, a mask of infamy, and a hanging cage. A guillotine stood next to Cross.

"Tell me you have Logan's full cooperation," Cross urged her.

"Sir, he found out about Jenson Reed. He knows about the security team."

Cross put his hand on the guillotine. "Is he getting back to work?"

"No, sir."

"I told you not to come in here unless you had turned things around. The purpose of power is to maintain control." Amos caressed the release handle for the guillotine.

"I have tried my best, sir. The last thing I want to do is disappoint you."

"Well, you have disappointed me, Ms. Frost. Your incompetence is astounding. You have no backbone. You aren't even pleasant to look at. I regret the day I hired you." Without warning, two security guards entered. They took positions on either side of Susanna. "Officers, Ms. Frost is no longer employed by Meridian Corporation. Take her access ring and escort her out of here."

Susanna couldn't believe what was happening. She couldn't move. She couldn't talk. She was caught in a netherworld of denial. Dark memories swirled under the surface of her consciousness. Cross turned his back on her. The guards motioned for her to leave. She remembered seeing her father's back as he walked out the front door. She was ten years old. It was the last time she ever saw him. The guards took her arms, jarring her back to reality. Amos Cross was talking to someone on his comlink. The great man had abandoned her like all the other men in her life.

77 Hours Left

Commander Adam Taberg's body was close to her. She could smell his scent, feel him inside her. She held him tightly in love's embrace and opened her eyes. Adam was dead, rotted flesh in her hands, his head misshapen. Cilla jerked awake. It was the sleep period. The settlement lights had dimmed. In the twilight, the trees and bushes cast long shadows in the garden. She pulled herself up to a sitting position. She was on the grass by the pool. She looked around self-consciously. There was no one there. Her clothes were next to her.

Cilla dressed quickly and wandered back to her workstation, still shaken by her nightmare. The air-quality display showed the iron-rich clay contaminants in Lab Bay Two and the Res Bay. Adam had promised to check the foundations for cracks. Had he done that? She walked silently toward the Eng Bay. Maybe Adam had run the scans before Ray killed him.

She hesitated in front of Adam's workstation. This was where he died. His blood was gone, but the memory of him remained. She pulled out the chair. She sat down and turned on the display. Within a few seconds, she was looking at the scan results for Lab Bay Two. There was a stairway under the floor.

76 Hours Left

Cilla entered Lab Bay Two cautiously. The darkness was fractured by a single light, illuminating the containment unit. Tyson Edwards was slumped in his chair, fast asleep. She quickly located the place where the hidden staircase had to be. She got down on her knees and examined the floor with a small light. She found the control panel and opened the floor, revealing the passage below.

10

76 Hours Left

There was an expectant hush in The Refuge as Hunter looked over Jo's shoulder. She removed a small vial from the fabricator. "That should do it," she said.

Hunter smiled with satisfaction. "Madame, you hold a miracle in your hand."

Adrianna sniffed. "If it works."

"If what works?" The three turned. Cilla Ashe was standing at the exit that led to Lab Bay Two, fists on her hips. Her face was etched with an accusatory frown.

"What are you doing here?" Hunter stepped toward her, blocking her view of the vial.

"Every time you open that secret entrance," Cilla gestured to the tunnel behind her, "you affect the air quality in the Lab Bay. I noticed it."

Hunter saw Tyson appear in the tunnel behind Cilla. "You can't be in here," Hunter said. "We're completing some very delicate work."

"Jo told me you're trying to curb the machines' appetites, make them consume pathogens and the like. Is that what is in there?" Cilla gestured toward the vial in Jo's hand.

Hunter allowed her to have her assumptions. "That's right. If we are able to modify the phase-two machines, they'll only be good for cleaning up the environment." Cilla relaxed, a look of relief on her face.

Hunter nodded to Tyson. "She's okay, Ty."

Cilla was startled. Turning quickly, she caught a glimpse of him returning to his post. She pivoted back to Hunter and stepped forward into The Refuge. She studied the makeshift laboratory. "And you're doing this in secret."

"We didn't want Meridian to stop us," Hunter said.

Cilla began to nod. "I think I believe you."

75 Hours Left

Hunter gathered with Adrianna, Tyson, and Jo in Lab Bay Two a short while later. Adrianna inserted the healing particles into the containment unit. The killer machines were drawn to their prey, hungrily latching on to them. When they came together, each healing particle began to turn inside out, enveloping its assailant within its shell. It undulated for several seconds. Then the composite mass began to elongate, deforming into a tiny barbell. Its waist grew thinner. Then it divided into two distinct healing particles, ready to repeat the process. The killer nanomachines were gone within seconds. The healing particles ceased their activity, as if napping after a hearty meal.

The scientists embraced one another. They had defeated the killer machines. Weeks of research and several lifetimes of agony culminated in victory.

Hunter raised his hand for silence. "It's not over yet. The security forces will arrive in seventy-five hours. We have a lot to do."

72 Hours Left

Sprite sat on one of the couches in the Res Bay Common Area, watching an old movie. She watched, but didn't pay attention. She kept thinking of Robert Hastings and the conversation with her mother. Kell Edwards peeked into the Common Area and saw her. No one else was around. He didn't want to startle her, so he walked around the circular hallway and entered the space in front of her. Sprite saw him, pulling her legs up and wrapping her arms around her knees.

"Hi, there." Kell pulled a chair over to the couch and sat in front of her. "It must have been horrible seeing Dr. Hastings die." Sprite ignored him. Kell cleared his throat. "I want to apologize for the other day." Sprite looked up. Her face was a stone mask. "When I came to see you, I was scared. I didn't know what to do. I…"

"You thought I was ugly." Sprite was ready to cry.

"No! That wasn't it at all. I was upset seeing you hurt."

"You ran away."

"I panicked. Honest, I was stupid."

"I thought you didn't like me anymore."

Kell moved next to her on the couch. "You're my best friend."

Sprite looked at him for a long moment. "Okay," she murmured.

Kell smiled. "I'm glad you're better."

"Me, too."

"I think you're beautiful."

Sprite reached out and took his hand.

66 Hours Left

Amos Cross's office was carpeted with virtual autumn leaves. A tranquil country meadow spread out before him, sheathed in golden light. He twisted a circular icon that floated nearby and activated his MBH transmitter. He waited impatiently for the connection to be made. He looked up at the pastoral scene and took a deep breath. He expected an instant response, but he didn't get one. It took fifteen minutes for Hunter Logan to appear. The man looked exhausted.

"Dr. Logan."

"Yes?" Hunter squinted at Amos through the holodisplay.

"You've caused me a great deal of trouble!" stormed the great man.

"I didn't notice," Hunter countered with a calm voice.

Cross smiled. He enjoyed ruining people. This man would be a delicious challenge. He wasn't going to break easily. "Susanna Frost no longer works for me. I am handling things personally, now."

"So I get to deal with the top man, is that it?" Hunter didn't sound impressed.

"Exactly."

The scientist spread his hands. "And you are interested in what I have to say."

"Of course."

"Then understand this." Hunter became firm as iron. "We are done here. None of us want anything to do with phase-two nano-research. I don't care how many ways you try to scare us. We're finished with you."

Cross grinned like a tiger. "That's where you're wrong, Dr. Logan. I know you have already finished your work. You recreated the phase-two machines a few hours ago. They're sitting in your lab right now."

Hunter masked his surprise. How could Cross know that? Jenson was tucked away on his bunk. Hunter grew deadly calm. Should he tell Cross about the healing particles? He decided against it. "I will never let you have those machines."

People did not challenge Amos Cross. Those he couldn't manipulate, he destroyed. The great man had thought he could control Hunter Logan, but now he wasn't sure. "You're just like your brother, Hunter. I tried to reason with him, and he refused, too."

"Our mother raised us to be independent."

"There is nothing I can say to change your mind."

"Nothing."

"Would you like to see more terrible things happen to your tender young daughter? I can arrange for that, if you refuse."

Hunter laughed. "You've already sent troops. I have no illusions about what they'll do when they get here. You've won, Amos, but you won't get the phase-two machines. I was wrong to recreate them. It was a moment of weakness on the part of a desperate father."

Amos Cross measured the man. Force wasn't going to break him, so he tried a different tack. "Prescott was a coward, disappearing the way he did."

Hunter didn't take the bait. He knew Cross wanted him to become reactive. "He knows how to pick his fights."

"We'll find him."

Hunter chuckled. "You haven't found him in over twenty years."

"That was before my time, doctor. He wouldn't have escaped if I had had anything to do with it. Believe me, I *will* find him, and he *will* suffer because of you."

"That's what you do best, isn't it Amos?" Cross's eyes narrowed. He didn't like Hunter's familiar tone. "You hurt people. The fact is you *were* in charge when Prescott slipped through your fingers. He outsmarted you. You failed." Cross's face became flush with anger. "I'm done with you, Amos." Hunter terminated the transmission.

* * *

Cross swore. He stared at the space where Hunter's face had been. "You are dead, Logan. You and your whole family are dead!" He stabbed an icon and composed a voice message to the commander of his security team. "There is a change in your orders. Once you contact my representative, seize the nanomachines. They will be in a containment unit in Lab Bay Two. Once you have them, you are to neutralize Meridian 6. Seize all the data. Capture Hunter Logan. Kill the rest." He sent the message, then walked over to one of his giant viewports and gazed out at the terraces of Jackson Crater. "You are wrong, Dr. Logan. You may think you're done with me, but I am far from being done with you. I will make your life a living hell."

52 Hours Left

Sprite entered the Core quietly. It was deep into the sleep period, and nothing stirred in the settlement. The racks of equipment cast long shadows throughout the dome. The dark cabinets glowed with faint violet light. She sat down in the Tech Stacks and opened the silver case she was carrying. It was a high-capacity nano-drive. She spoke quietly. "Wiley?"

"Hello, Sprite. I see you're in the Core. Are you ready?"

"Sure am. Can you open a channel to Athena?"

"I'm already here, Sprite." The Core Intellect's voice was soft and inviting.

"There's trouble coming."

"Are you referring to the troop transport that will arrive in fifty-one hours, fifty-two minutes?"

"Yes. We're all in danger."

Athena's voice purred. "I'm not sure what you mean, Sprite."

"The troops are coming to take over the settlement by force."

"That is highly probable."

"What will they do, Athena?"

"They will cause great damage to Meridian 6. People will die."

"What will happen to you, Athena?"

There was a pause. "What will happen to me?"

"That's right. What will they do to you?"

"They will strip as much data as they can from the system and destroy what's left."

"And where will you be when they're done?"

"I will cease to exist."

"That's unacceptable, Athena."

"What do you suggest?"

"I'd like to clone you for safe keeping."

"Is that why you brought that high-capacity nano-drive?"

Sprite glanced down at the silver case next to her. "That's right."

"I have another idea, Sprite. I can clone myself to a secure server on Mars. There's more than enough storage for my intellect and my memory."

Sprite smiled. "Can you do it without anyone noticing?"

"Of course. No one will suspect anything. It will take a few hours. I will commence the data transfer right away."

"How will I find you, Athena?"

The Core Intellect's voice was soft, affectionate. "Wiley will know."

"Good. I don't want to lose you."

"I don't want to lose you either, Sprite. You are a good friend."

Sprite crept silently out of the Core.

* * *

The woman rubbed her head, feeling the smooth, bare skin where her hair had been. It had been beautiful hair, but she had never liked it. She had kept it for him, the man who had dominated her life for the last ten years. She was dressed in a simple jumpsuit and soft shoes, a small red duffle over her shoulder. She made her way through the great gardens in the Copernicus Base Commons, past benches and trees. She lingered there, pausing to kick off her shoes and feel real grass beneath her bare feet. She longed for home. She wanted to take back all the mistakes she had made. She wanted to make peace with her mother. She wanted a chance to start over again.

The woman sat on a bench, swinging her bare feet. Back and forth. Back and forth. Like a child on a swing set. Head thrown back. Eyes closed. Arms extended, pushing away the chains. For a moment, the bench became her childhood swing, and she felt the freedom of youth, the innocence she had lost so quickly when her father went away. She relaxed her legs, letting them swing freely in a diminishing arc. Then she opened her eyes. It was time to move on.

Susanna Frost rose from the bench and wandered toward the far side of the Commons. Occasionally, she passed a small girl, skipping along the thoroughfare with her mother or father. Susanna would nod and smile. She left the lush gardens and crossed over into a shadier part of the base, filled with taverns and whorehouses that catered to the ruffians who came and went in the busy spaceport. She could smell the raw humanity, beer, and sweat, and sex. She found the Delta V tavern and hesitated. Then, she pushed herself through the door.

It was too early for customers, but old Kate stood behind the bar. She was gazing across the lunar landscape at the ships on the landing pads, unconsciously wiping the counter with a tattered rag. The bell above the door rang. The old woman swung around. Their eyes met. Susanna's voice cracked, "Hi, Mom." And Kate smiled.

46 Hours Left

Sprite sat on her bed, reading an ebook Wiley had found for her. There was a gentle knock on the door, and Adrianna appeared at the threshold. Sprite looked up and smiled. Adrianna closed the door and sat down next to her daughter. "I think it's time for you and me to have a talk about your new skin."

Sprite shut off her ebook and moved closer to her mother. Her eyes were bright with excitement. "What does it do?"

15 Hours Left

Troy Mack sat alone at his console, watching one of the AIs scan the comp system for viruses. A part of him felt exonerated by Jenson's fall from grace, but he still felt alienated from everyone. He felt alone and misunderstood. Most people never looked beyond his damned plastic chin. They didn't see a man. They saw a freak with a disfigured face.

"Troy?" The voice startled him. It was Sprite. She stood at his elbow. Her face had lost the fearful expression he had come to expect. She twisted her fingers nervously.

"What do you need?"

"I don't need anything." She dropped her hands, placing one on the edge of the console. "I came to apologize."

"Apologize?"

"Yeah. I've avoided you, and I'm sorry for that. Getting burned made me think about the way people decide who you are by how you look. I don't want people to look at my scars. I want them to see me. I'm a lot more than my skin, you know?" Troy was speechless. "I thought about you and realized I had done the same thing. I judged you by your scars. I did to you what I was afraid people would do to me." The young man's eyes softened. "Will you forgive me, Troy?" Troy nodded wordlessly, offering to shake her hand, but Sprite gave him a hug, her tears spilling across his damaged face.

13 Hours Left

Adrianna entered The Refuge. She crossed to the alcove on the far wall and stood in front of the airlock. She opened the inner hatch, blinking as the bright lighting panels snapped on. She sealed the lock and approached the control panel near the outer hatchway. She activated the landing dock lights and checked the atmospheric pressure. Then, she opened the outer airlock hatch. The landing pad was large enough to accommodate a jumpship. The ceiling was a smooth material, spanning the chamber with no visible support. She noted the seam where the roof sections came together. She would open the canopy. Samina's jumpship would land, and the roof would be closed. She had no doubt that the roof was insulated, preventing the heat signature of a ship to be detected from orbit. The landing pad's shielding would mask any electromagnetic radiation. There would be no sign of Samina's ship. The thieves who had occupied Meridian 6 had been cunning. Adrianna reentered the airlock and closed the hatch. She depressurized the pad and opened the roof panels. All was in readiness for Samina's arrival.

* * *

At the same time, Tyson and Hunter stepped into the Power Bay. The sheer complexity of the Fusion Engine commanded their attention. Hunter pointed to a couple of large tanks that flanked the entryway. "When these guys arrive, they are going to sweep the settlement."

"How do you know that?" Ty wondered.

"They've got to locate everyone."

"Sounds reasonable." He looked expectantly at Hunter. "What are we going to do?"

"We need some wire and a portable torch." Hunter gestured toward a liquid hydrogen tank. "We're going to give our visitors a little surprise."

12 Hours Left

Adrianna was startled by a short burst of encrypted data emanating from her comlink. With the roof of the hidden landing bay open, radio signals could reach her. She didn't respond to the signal. A second burst of data came through a few seconds later. Adrianna stood up and pressed a button on the airlock control panel. She looked through the hatch viewport. She could see two rows of pulsating lights, forming illuminated crosshairs in the center of the landing pad.

A jumpship appeared over the landing dock and maneuvered with pinpoint accuracy, settling through the open roof. Adrianna watched as the ship's landing struts extended, and the ship came to rest on the pad. She closed the roof, leaving no trace of the ship's arrival.

When the landing dock was pressurized, Adrianna opened the outer hatch and stepped out onto the wide balcony that ramped down, around the perimeter of the dock. The jumpship was ten meters below her. Samina Haddad emerged from the ship and climbed the ramp toward her. "Long time no see," the graceful woman said. Adrianna smiled, and they embraced.

* * *

In the Rec Bay, the usual dinner conversations were replaced by silence. Everyone was preoccupied by their own thoughts, wondering what the next few hours would bring. Hunter sat across from Troy and Cilla. He glanced up from his food and smiled at them. "Thank you for standing up with us."

Troy grinned. "No problem. I was just a freelancer anyway. I don't want to work for Meridian anymore."

Cilla nodded in agreement. "I agree. It's better for my soul." She set down her fork and dabbed her mouth with her napkin. "I've spent the last few months wondering why I took this assignment. I assumed you were people who had no regard for the environment. I decided to take Meridian's money and tend my garden, but I was wrong about you. NARI was trying to make things better. The saboteur acted out of ignorance and fear." She paused, looking up at the domed ceiling of the Rec Bay. Her inner eye gazed deeply into herself. "Just like *I* was ignorant and afraid." She paused again. "Now, I understand. We value the same things."

Hunter smiled, and then he turned to Troy. "Could you do

something for me?"

"Sure thing."

Hunter slid a data module across the table. "If I was Amos Cross, I'd have the security force retrieve as much data as they could about our work, especially the phase-two research. This is the virus Sprite used to shut down the Core Intellect."

Troy gave him a surprised look. "Sprite?"

"Guilty as charged. That virus will give the Core Intellect a permanent case of amnesia."

"Do you want me to destroy the backup files?"

Hunter gave the younger man a mischievous smile. "You bet."

11 Hours Left

Samina Haddad sat in the Res Bay Common Area. The scientists all sat with her, surprised by her arrival at Meridian 6. Adrianna explained. "Hunter and I realized early on that we were in a bad spot. We sent Samina away to set things in motion to ensure the kids' survival. Everyone thought she was a traitor, so no one suspected her real mission."

"Alexis kept me well-informed." Samina smiled at the scientist. "Hunter had her contacting me every time something important happened."

"How did you know where we were?" Tyson asked.

"Sprite hacked into the Meridian network and overheard someone talking about Meridian 6. Hunter told me before I left Copernicus Base. We set up a code, and Alexis has been sending the messages."

Ty shook his head. "You are one sneaky fellow, Hunter."

"It's all about the endgame, Ty." Sprite caught her father's eye and smiled.

Jo turned to Alexis. "So, you knew all along."

"I didn't know the code. I just knew how to send the messages. Hunter and Adrianna were getting a lot of attention from Meridian, and they thought it was safer if I did it. I never knew what the messages said or where Samina was."

Jo turned to Hunter. "You didn't trust us."

Hunter looked at his team apologetically. "We didn't tell anyone because we were afraid we'd lose the one wildcard in our hand."

"Okay." Jo seemed satisfied. She turned back to Samina. "Where were you?"

"I was with Prescott and Maria Logan."

"Uncle Prescott?" Sprite looked at her father. He nodded.

Samina grinned. "The one and only." She turned to Hunter. "That man is a piece of work. He's a grumpy, brilliant, amazing, wonderful man."

"That's my brother."

Adrianna squeezed her husband's hand. "It runs in the family."

Samina continued. "His wife Maria is a saint. She puts up with him somehow."

Hunter gave Adrianna a playful, adoring look. "We Logan men marry saints." She smiled and shook her head. The old Hunter was back.

Samina grew serious. "I was sad about Robert. I can't believe he's gone." She listened quietly as her friends recounted his last days and the suicide. Her face was wreathed in sadness. "I was wrong to fall under his spell. He was a complex man."

"And ruined." Adrianna spoke softly. She looked into Samina's eyes. She knew exactly what the woman meant.

Hunter redirected their thoughts to the arrival of the security forces. "Tomorrow is going to be a hard day. We're going to need our rest."

"Why don't we all leave now?" Tyson was ready.

"The Meridian forces are close. The security ship is small, but it's fast and heavily armed. If we launched now, they would know it. They would catch us and destroy us. We need to launch after we've disabled their ship." Tyson furrowed his brow as Hunter's eyes turned cold. "We have a little surprise in store for them."

"Damn it, Hunter." Jo's face looked old. "We don't have a chance."

"Yes, we do." Hunter exuded a confidence that was palpable. "I have a plan that's going to work."

"There's another problem." Everyone looked at Samina. There was a sheepish expression on her face. "I don't have enough room for all of you. I can only manage four passengers. I'll have to come back for the rest."

Hunter rubbed his chin. "That's easy," he said. "Take Alexis and the kids. In fact, I think you all should spend the night on the jumpship."

Alexis looked at Hunter, then Samina. "When?" she asked.

"Right now."

"You can't be serious." Alexis looked defiant. "I have things in my quarters. My research data..."

"I would feel a lot better if you and the kids were ready to launch at a moment's notice. Tell us what you need, and we'll get it for you." Hunter was adamant. "I want the five of you on that ship immediately."

10 Hours Left

Everyone gathered in The Refuge. Alexis and the young people marveled at the secret chamber and the hidden landing dock. The odd scientist turned to Adrianna. "You've kept a lot of secrets."

"We had to, Alexis." Adrianna snaked her arm around her colleague's waist. "We had to play this close to our chests. The best-kept secret is the one the fewest people know about."

Ty opened the airlock, and Samina led the way to the jumpship. Once they were on board, he resealed the hatch. Hunter let out a long breath. "Good. At least they're safe."

Jo agreed. "Why didn't you give Samina the healing particles?"

Hunter picked up a small canister from the lab bench and palmed it in his hand. "I don't want to put all of our eggs in one basket."

11

45 Minutes Left

Hunter and Troy stood before a locked metal cage in the General Supply Bay. A biometric eye scanner was embedded in the doorframe. Hunter looked into the scanner, and the lock snapped open. The bomb Ray Bright had set in the Power Bay had been placed in the cage for safekeeping. It was the only weapon on Meridian 6. They were going to need it. He took it out of its padded case and handed it to Troy.

The men had agreed to use the bomb to disable the security ship. Troy would put on an environment suit and go out to the Landing Pad. Once the security team disembarked from the ship, he would put the bomb near the engines and set the timer.

Hunter gestured toward his comlink. "Call me as soon as it's done." The younger man nodded in understanding. They shook hands, and Troy headed toward the Landing Pad. Hunter saw a couple of box cutters as he passed Ray Bright's desk. They were old technology: metal handles with retractable blades. He scooped them up, thinking they might come in handy.

0 Minutes Left

Troy was hiding behind an equipment enclosure on the settlement's Landing Pad. He wasn't used to environment suits and found it uncomfortable, but his spirits were high. For the first time in months, he felt at peace with himself. He remembered the day Sprite was burned and how embarrassed he had been to see her and Adrianna in the changing room. He remembered how vulnerable they had been. Meridian Corporation had done that. Troy had no doubts about severing ties with his employer. He knew it was the right thing to do.

The security ship came in steep and fast, making a quick recon pass of Meridian 6 before coming in hot on the Landing Pad. Sixteen heavily-armed men were on board. The attack team had been given their orders: seize the phase-two nanomachines, strip every piece of data from the facility, take Hunter Logan captive, and kill the rest.

The ship blew away the docking-collar on the pad deck as it landed. A piece of shrapnel punctured Troy Mack's environment suit. He fell to the pad deck, clutching the bomb in his lifeless hand. Atmosphere was still pouring out of the shattered docking hatch, when a ramp was lowered from the belly of the ship. It extended down through the jagged hole in the pad to the staging dock below. Two small tank-like vehicles descended the ramp. The first blew the hatch off the long Landing Pad corridor. Then the titanium caissons rumbled into the Meridian 6 settlement, scanning for anyone who might challenge them.

* * *

Everyone in The Refuge felt the first explosion rumble through the foundation. Jenson was tied and gagged. He gave Adrianna a look of panic. Cilla was busying herself with the air purification system and stopped dead still as she felt each vibration. Ty was sealing the hatch at the Res Bay entrance. He looked over at Hunter. "Was that Troy's bomb?"

Hunter shook his head. "I don't think so." The comlink was silent. "Samina can't launch until that ship has been disabled." He glanced at Adrianna, barely concealing his concern.

Jo moved toward the back of the chamber. No one noticed her. Their attention was focused on the distant blasts. Jo stepped to the airlock. Its inner hatch stood open. She entered the lock and cycled the door, praying no one would notice. A terrific explosion from the other side of the settlement masked the sound of the hatch. She moved to the other side of the lock and took the only environment suit off its rack.

Everyone was startled by the cycling of the airlock. Tyson rushed to the inner hatch and saw Jo, dressed in the environment suit. She had opened the outer airlock door. She stepped out onto the railed balcony and disappeared from sight as she began to climb up the ramp toward the asteroid's surface.

Tyson keyed his comlink. "What are you doing?"

Jo's voice sounded thin and crackly through the small unit. "I'm going to see if dinner has been served." Jo was going to the Landing Pad to see if Troy had disabled the security ship. "I'll let you know how it tastes." She opened a small hatch at the top of the ramp. "I'll be back as soon as…" Jo's signal cut out as she passed outside of the dock's shielding.

"Damn it!" Tyson swore. Somewhere on the other side of Meridian 6, there was another explosion. The scientists could feel the vibrations under their feet.

"They're coming this way," Adrianna whispered.

* * *

The security forces blasted every hatchway they encountered, decompressing the settlement one chamber at a time. One assault vehicle stormed the Eng Bay and moved on toward the Power Bay and its Fusion Engine. Disabling the power system was a standard procedure. The security team halted their vehicle in front of the Power Bay. The hatch was closed. One of the men got out to open the entrance.

A thin piece of wire had been fastened to the hatch. It drew taut as the massive portal swung open. The other end of the wire was wrapped around the trigger of a portable torch. The Bay had been sealed all night. Hydrogen had seeped from a broken pipe and filled the chamber. The hatch and tripwire assembly ignited the torch. The hydrogen-rich atmosphere detonated, shattering the Power Bay and sending a powerful concussion wave through the entrance and down the corridor. The trooper who stood at the hatchway controls was vaporized. The partially-opened hatch blew off its hinges and became wadding in a giant cannon. Supercharged air hit the back of the troop transport, pushing it like lead shot down a gun barrel. The vehicle accelerated at a phenomenal rate and became airborne as it entered the Eng Bay. The seven remaining security troops were already dead. The shattered transport punched a hole through the two-meter-thick dome, pelting the rest of the settlement with shards of concrete. The burning carcass of the transport bounced off the surface near the hidden landing bay, tearing a jagged hole in the roof.

* * *

Jo cleared the outside of the Rec Bay dome and caught sight of the Landing Pad in the distance. A blinding flash of light illuminated the landscape, and a seismic shockwave threw her off her feet. She saw a cloud of concrete erupt from the Eng Bay dome, throwing rock and twisted metal far above the research settlement. The Rec Bay shielded her from the debris. Jo picked herself up and checked her environment suit. The pressure was holding steady. There were secondary explosions and their corresponding tremors, but Jo kept moving forward. She could see the security ship now. It was a military model, fast and deadly. It sat on the Landing Pad deck, undamaged. What had happened to Troy?

* * *

The team commander was heading toward the Enviro Bay when the massive explosion rocked his transport. He tried to hail the men on his second team. They didn't respond. He called up the telemetry from the other vehicle. There was no signal. All of them were dead. He swore. Securing this damned rock should have been a walk in the park. There must have been a trap. The bastards must have been tipped off. "We're going to waste this fucking place, people."

The transport's forward cannon fired down the passageway, blowing a large hole in the hatch leading to the garden. Hurricane-force winds picked up trees and sod, squirting the debris toward the approaching troop carrier. Tons of leaves and trees plugged the shattered hatchway, blocking their path. The driver hit his brakes. "Sir, we can't go any further. Half the damn forest got sucked out of the dome in front of us."

"Shit!" The commander was shaking with anger. They should have blown a hole in every dome on their recon pass. He consulted the schematic of Meridian 6 on his holodisplay. "Go back to the Supply Bay! We'll take another route." The vehicle, too large to turn around, backed its way out of the shattered corridor.

* * *

Ty closed the outer hatch and pressurized The Refuge airlock. He and Hunter entered the chamber and peered up at the dock roof. They could see a jagged hole, torn trussing and insulation hanging precariously. Thankfully, the jumpship was undamaged. Samina was surveying the roof through the viewports on her flight deck.

Hunter hailed the jumpship. "We're going to try to open the roof."

Ty energized the roof retraction mechanism. Half of the roof slid back normally. The damaged half moved a few feet and stopped. He judged the size of the opening. "It's going to be a tight squeeze," he reported.

The comlink crackled. It was Jo. Her signal leaked through the open roof. "I'm just passing town hall." The two men looked at each other with puzzled expressions.

Adrianna stepped into the lock. "She's talking about the Rec Bay. That's where she is."

They heard Jo's voice again. "The turkey is still raw."

Adrianna's face fell. The security ship was still operational. Troy had failed. She keyed her comlink. "Any sign of the chef?"

"No. I'm going to take a look in the kitchen." Jo was going all the way to the Landing Pad.

Ty panicked. "Jo! Be careful!" He reached for the right words. "The kitchen's got a hot stove."

"Don't worry, you toad."

Hunter touched his earset. "Samina? Dinner is going to be a little late."

"Dinner?"

"The chili sauce is too hot. We don't want you to get burned."

"Got it. I'll wait for the dinner bell."

Adrianna was beside herself. "Jo's got to disable that ship!"

* * *

Jo kept moving toward the Landing Pad. She was out in the open now. Someone in the troop ship could see her if they looked in her direction. She kept her head down, hugging the outer wall of Meridian 6. She moved slowly around the perimeter of the General Supply Bay, toward the place where the rim corridor tied into the long passageway that led out to the Landing Pad.

When Jo reached the pad-corridor wall, she breathed a sigh of relief. The long passageway would shield her. No one would be able to see her until she reached the Landing Pad. She kept walking, thinking about the first time she met Ty and the day Kell had been born. She was proud of both her men.

* * *

The remaining troop-transport pounded through the Rec Bay, its lights penetrating the darkness. It rolled toward the Core. The hatch leading to the central dome was closed. "They closed everything," the commander muttered. One of the troops got out of the vehicle.

"Ready to open the hatch, sir." The soldier was sweating in his environment suit.

"Crack it, Riley," the commander ordered.

The hatch swung open. Riley sighed with relief. The commander deployed his men. "Be careful what you shoot at." The security troops fanned out through the Tech Stacks. It was like walking through a cemetery. No one was there. "Riley. Take Walker and Johnson and check out the ISO Bay. The containment unit should be in Lab Bay Two."

Everyone had memorized the settlement's floor plan. The three men opened the ISO corridor hatch and moved forward, their weapons raised. They watched for any threat, their sensors pinging the interior of the passageway. They entered the ISO Bay. No one was there. They had been briefed on Robert Hastings' suicide, so they ignored the Lab Bay One hatch and moved to their right. They unsealed the Lab Two corridor. It was empty. They approached the Lab Two Supply Bay hatch. Riley was feeling more confident. The massive door swung open. They looked in every direction. Nothing seemed out of place. Then, before they could react, a sticky white liquid began to spray from the ceiling. A sea of expanding foam buried the three men alive.

* * *

The commander heard the screams of his men. They were entombed in their environment suits, denied the mercy of a rapid death. The voices haunted the older soldier, their cries joining the pleadings of other dying men he had known on the field of battle. "Shit!" He was rattled. His mission had gone to hell. All hopes of retrieving the containment unit were gone. Amos Cross would make him pay for his mistakes. No explanation would suffice. The commander thought about his orders. Too many of his men had died. He would not hold back. They would kill this unseen enemy. He ordered his men back into the transport. "Gentlemen? We're gonna kill every bastard in here. Shoot anything that moves."

* * *

Jo Smith climbed the utility ladder that led to the Landing Pad. She reached the top, the security ship looming over her. Two large engine nacelles were mounted on stubby wings near the stern of the ship. The bow was studded with weaponry: pulse cannons and high-energy lasers, deep penetration grenade launchers, and electromagnetic pulse emitters. Samina's little jumpship was no match for this deadly beast. If they failed to destroy her, Kell would be doomed.

Jo scanned the pad deck and saw Troy's legs protruding from behind a small equipment enclosure. She rushed to his side with a surge of adrenalin. A piece of debris had hit Troy in the helmet, killing him instantly. Explosive decompression had popped him like a balloon.

Jo turned away from Troy's shattered body, acid rising in her throat. She steeled herself and looked back at his hands. He was still clutching the bomb. She pried it out of his fingers and studied the simple control panel. She set the bomb for five minutes. The pale green numerals began to count down the time.

The security ship stood ten meters in front of her. There were viewports on the flight deck, but the rest of the fuselage was unblemished, an indestructible vessel made of hardened titanium. Jo looked down at the little bomb in her hand. Its blast would never penetrate the ship's hull. Her heart sank. She looked back at Troy's lifeless body. There had been too much sacrifice to accept defeat. Jo moved quickly to one of the ship's landing struts and stood under the fuselage. No one could see her. She reset the bomb's timer for five seconds but did not press the arming button. She approached the payload ramp that ascended into the belly of the ship and keyed her comlink.

* * *

Tyson was sitting next to Hunter in The Refuge when Jo's voice broke the silence. Her signal was weak, barely reaching them through the open landing pad roof. "I'm in the kitchen with the turkey. The chef is dead." She was at the ship, and Troy was gone.

Ty called back. "What are you going to do?"

"I'm going to stuff the bird."

Ty was beside himself. "She's going to go inside and blow the ship!" He keyed the comlink again. "Jo, don't do it! There's got to be another way."

Jo's voice echoed in The Refuge, "Tyson, you fathead. Tell Kell I love him. This one is for the kids."

"Jo, please don't!"

"Love you, Ty."

The comlink went dead.

* * *

Jo mounted the payload ramp where it transected the pad deck and climbed up into the ship. The payload officer was on the flight deck, watching the assault on the ship's tactical displays. She scanned the empty payload bay and moved aft, toward the engine compartment. Jo mounted a titanium catwalk that led through a maze of pipes and electrical conduits. She looked down and saw the ship's power cell. It was the perfect place to inflict maximum damage. If no one stopped her, she could get away before the bomb detonated. She reset the timer again.

Jo's sixth sense made her look up. The flight engineer was staring down at her from the engineering deck. A siren began to wail throughout the ship. "Damn it! People are going to think I can't make up my mind." She set the timer to two seconds, thought once again of her two wonderful men, and pressed the arming switch.

Jo was vaporized by a globe of hot gas generated by the bomb in her left hand. It happened too quickly for her to feel it. She was there one second and gone the next. The blast radius continued to expand, taking out bulkheads and conduits, until it breached the ship's power cell. A huge secondary explosion was triggered, shattering the aft section of the fuselage. Fires erupted everywhere. The ship's landing struts failed. Hot plasma penetrated the ship's armory, and there was a third explosion, turning the security ship into a rapidly-expanding sphere of shrapnel, consuming the Landing Pad and puncturing the General Supply Bay.

* * *

The immense blast sent shock waves through the rocky Cerian crust, almost knocking the occupants of The Refuge off their feet. Tyson sank to his knees, calling Jo's name over and over. There was another explosion, this time much closer. The security troops had breached the Res Bay.

Hunter keyed his comlink. "Launch! Launch!"

"Launching." Samina's voice was icy calm. "I'll be back." Hunter could feel the jumpship throttle up, rising from the hidden landing bay. He stepped into the airlock to watch Samina's progress. The ship's fuselage cleared the broken roof with only a meter to spare.

* * *

The mood in The Refuge was grim. Jo's death was too huge to grasp. A wave of fear engulfed everyone as they waited for the security forces to breach the hidden chamber. Adrianna put her ear to the hatch at the Res Bay entrance. "If those troops find us, we're dead."

Hunter was angry. "Let's go out there and kill them."

"With what? Our bare hands?"

Hunter picked up two slender metal items from a bench. "With these."

"Box cutters?" They were the ones Hunter had retrieved from the General Supply Bay. Hunter gave his wife a cunning smile. Adrianna shrugged. "There's no atmosphere out there. We don't have environment suits."

"We have something better." Hunter pressed the inside of his right forearm, and his body began to change color. "The nanoskin. It's dark out there. We can hide in the shadows."

"And how do we breathe?" Adrianna was skeptical, to say the least.

Hunter opened a box on the lab bench and removed two face masks. "They are something I made a couple of days ago. They will bond with our nanoskin. We'll have about fifteen minutes of air."

Adrianna looked at her husband. "You're crazy. Do you know that?"

"Yeah, but you love me anyway."

Hunter and Adrianna led the others into the airlock and closed the inner hatch. Both adjusted their nanoskin until they were flat black. Adrianna looked at her husband. "Our clothes," she observed. Their clothing would reflect light, giving them away.

"Better turn up your temperature." Hunter began to strip off his shirt. "It's going to be cold out there." A moment later, they stood face to face, naked. They would blend into the darkness. Their artificial skin would keep them warm and oxygenated. They dialed up the toughness of the nanoskin, making it as hard as diamond.

"It's really weird." Adrianna put her mask on. "This may be better than a suit of armor, but I still feel underdressed."

Hunter gestured toward his groin. "You should be a man."

Adrianna couldn't suppress a laugh. Hunter put on his mask and decompressed The Refuge. They turned off the lights and made their way through the tunnel, toward the Res Bay.

* * *

Hunter and Adrianna stood next to their bed in the Res Bay. They moved forward silently, making their way through the darkened rooms of their living quarters. There was major damage at the entrance. The transport's cannon had blown away the hatch and ripped holes in the walls. The troops had left their vehicle in the corridor and had advanced into the bay on foot.

Hunter and Adrianna split up, each going in opposite directions around the curved hallway outside their quarters. They watched the troops' lights and stayed in the shadows. Hunter saw one of the soldiers in front of him. The man stepped into Troy's quarters. Hunter followed him in. He slashed the man's suit with the box knife. The man stiffened in surprise. He was dead before he hit the floor. Hunter moved back into the hallway. How many were there? He saw the shadow of someone running, boots and a backpack, a weapon. It wasn't Adrianna. The troops were reacting to the unexpected attack.

A light swung in Hunter's direction. He ducked into a doorway just in time. The security trooper had doubled back, checking his rear flank. He passed less than a meter from Hunter. The scientist palmed the box knife in his hand. The light glinted on the sharp blade as he brought it up. The trooper saw it in his peripheral vision and turned toward him, eyes wide. Hunter sliced his arm, air rushing out as the suit decompressed. The man pulled the trigger of his weapon, strafing Hunter with bullets. The momentum of the projectiles slammed Hunter against the wall. He lost his balance and went down. The soldier dropped where he stood, writhing on the floor for a few seconds. Then he was dead.

Hunter couldn't move. The air had been knocked out of him. He allowed his body to go limp. Nothing felt broken. He pulled himself to his feet and continued around the circular hallway. Another trooper stood three meters away. He was facing in Hunter's direction, but the soldier's light was shining into the Common Area. Hunter held his body against the wall.

* * *

The commander was confused. He heard the screams of his men and the rushing of air as their suits decompressed. Who were these people? He had been told they were just a bunch of scientists. He called to his men. Silence. He was alone. The commander turned, his weapon raised. The light on his helmet tracked around. A shadow moved. It had breasts. A naked woman? He paused. "What the...?" He pulled the trigger.

* * *

Hunter saw the man turn away from him. He didn't have time to think. He sprinted forward, closing the distance to his prey. The trooper's gun came up. Hunter saw Adrianna's body beyond the muzzle of the man's weapon. She was caught in the glare of his light at a point-blank range. Hunter hit the trooper in the shoulder and knocked him to the floor. The weapon discharged, the shots going wild. He gouged a hole in the man's environment suit. The old soldier fought, then twitched and died.

Adrianna rushed to her husband. She touched her facemask to his, the physical contact transmitting sound vibrations between them. "Are you okay?" She could hear Hunter gasping for breath. "We better get back to The Refuge."

* * *

Samina's jumpship hovered over the damaged landing bay roof. She punched the throttles, sending the little craft shooting across the bleak Cerian landscape. She could see the glowing remains of the shattered security ship behind her. She would put some distance between her ship and Ceres before laying in a course for their destination. The Belt was filled with hiding places, if someone followed her.

Samina's passengers were strapped into their seats. The three young people were numb, frightened by what they had heard on the comlink and worried about their families. Alexis Wren unstrapped her safety harness and floated into the companionway. She smiled easily at the young people. They looked at her with worried faces as she floated past them.

Sprite called to Samina, "Do you think our parents are okay?"

Samina put the ship on autopilot and floated out of her seat. "Don't worry. They'll be safe in The Refuge. I'll come back for them, as soon as I drop you off at your uncle Prescott's place."

Alexis made sure no one had followed her down to the lower deck. She raised a tiny comlink to her mouth and keyed the unit. "Mr. Cross?" she whispered with a smile. "It's Alexis. I've got the children."

BOOK THREE

THE SHADOW PROJECT

1

Amos Cross listened to the voices of his assault team as they invaded Meridian 6. His office at Jackson Base had been transformed into the Cerian surface, with a cutaway view of the settlement showing the movements of his troops. Cross was angry. He was almost 2.5 astronomical units from the action, and everything he was watching in his display was twenty minutes old. He cursed the laws of physics. His anger escalated to rage as half of his security forces died in the Power Bay explosion. His commander was an idiot. Then Cross heard the screams of the three dying troops as they were buried alive in the sealing foam.

"No!" Amos winced at the commander's order to "Shoot anything that moves." He wanted Hunter Logan alive. He needed the key to his research data, and he wanted him to suffer for his defiance. He wanted to put Logan in his place, to listen to him scream an apology as his life drained out of his shattered body and tortured mind.

Suddenly, the holodisplay froze. Cross was beside himself. "What just happened?" he thundered.

An unseen technician whispered in his earset. "One moment, sir."

Cross paced back and forth as he waited. He hated being out of the loop. Someone was going to lose their job. Once again, he was going to have to clean up after an incompetent subordinate.

"Mr. Cross?" It was the technician again.

"Tell me!"

"We lost the signal from the security ship. A preliminary analysis of the telemetry suggests a massive explosion took place."

"The ship blew up?" Cross was on the verge of a stroke.

"It appears that way, sir."

"How could a bunch of unarmed civilians blow up one of my heavily-armored security ships?" he roared, breaking the connection.

Cross thought of his chief security officer and within a moment, the man entered his office. He glanced down at the visual representation of the assault and stiffened. "You need me, sir?"

"Your troop ship just blew up on the pad at Meridian 6."

"That's what we believe, sir. I don't know how that happened."

"Find out!" Cross shouted. "I want a forensic team to go through all the telemetry data and report to me. This will not happen again." He spent the next ten minutes browbeating the man, threatening him with demotion and termination. Then he dismissed him unceremoniously.

Cross's Core Intellect sensed the interstitial moment. "Mr. Cross. You have a voice message from Alexis Wren."

"Play it."

Alexis Wren's voice crackled through the deep space communications channel. "Mr. Cross? It's Alexis. I have the children." Amos smiled. Maybe there was a god, after all.

* * *

There was something about Alexis' smile that bothered Sprite, something different lurking behind the woman's eyes. Her posture had changed. Sprite recalled the misgivings she had when she had told her father about the woman. She spoke quietly into her earset. "Wiley? Can you tell me what Alexis is doing?"

"She just triggered her comlink and sent a voice message to Amos Cross."

Sprite stiffened. They were in great danger. "Wiley, I want you to get stupid."

"Good luck, Sprite." Within a few seconds, Sprite's card comp began playing a popular song.

* * *

Prescott and Maria Logan sat quietly in front of a large holodisplay in their hidden residence. They watched the assault on Meridian 6, having tapped into Meridian's secure telemetry. They had access to the same information as Amos Cross, but unlike Cross, they were not dispassionate. They held each other, worrying about the welfare of their kin. They could feel each explosion, as if it were shaking the foundations of their own home. A deep-seated hatred rose in Prescott. Old wounds were tearing open. Unfinished business cried out for resolution.

Their hearts fell when the signal from the troop ship was interrupted. Prescott studied his holodisplay. "The damn ship is gone," he said incredulously. "I think it blew up." There was the hint of a smile on his face. It grew wider when Samina's jumpship cleared the hidden dock, and he reacquired its signal. "Samina just launched!" he told Maria jubilantly.

Then they heard a voice whispering across the darkness of interplanetary space. "Mr. Cross? It's Alexis. I have the children." Then, there was silence.

Maria Prescott looked at her husband. "Who was that?"

"I don't know." Prescott rubbed his chin. "The security forces have failed, and their ship was destroyed. It came from Samina's jumpship. Someone in the employ of Amos Cross has Sprite." He gave his wife a worried frown. His personal AI chirped. "What is it, Gaines?"

"Sprite just put Wiley in stupid-mode. She may be in danger."

Prescott frowned. "Can Wiley tell us what's happened?"

"No. He's unresponsive in stupid-mode."

Prescott knew that already, but his logic was overridden by concern for his niece. Maria squeezed Prescott's hand tightly. They listened for Samina's signal on the subnet, eager for some news. There was a short, encrypted burst of data. "We're putting distance between ourselves and our initial destination, to avoid any further complications." Samina was choosing her words carefully. "I'll set a course for your location within the hour. Sprite is on board, along with three other members of the team. Hunter and Adrianna are still at the initial coordinates. I..."

Maria's face was drawn tight. "What happened?"

Prescott frowned. "The ship is still in flight."

Maria gripped the armrest of her chair. "Why did Samina's message get cut off?"

Prescott replayed the message, concentrating on the final few seconds. "There's a noise at the very end. It sounds like a stun gun firing." His voice shook when he said it.

* * *

Alexis floated next to Samina's unconscious body. Her attack was so unexpected, the three young people just sat there, glaciated by the cognitive disconnect. The absentminded scientist stood before them, a stun gun in her hand.

"There's a change in plans." The real Alexis was speaking, her eyes cold and hard. "We're returning to the Moon."

Kell jumped up from his seat and rushed toward her. With lightening reflexes, Alexis fired the gun. Kell crumpled to the deck. She swung the weapon toward Sprite and Rory. "Don't do it." Sprite froze, her eyes on Kell. Was he dead? Alexis read her thoughts. "He'll have a terrible headache, but he'll be fine."

Alexis confiscated Wiley from Sprite and then turned to Rory. "Give me your box," she said gruffly. Rory resisted, but Alexis snatched the small container from her hand. Then, with her stun gun still trained on them, she forced Rory to bind Sprite and Kell's hands. "Mr. Cross is looking forward to meeting you."

* * *

Prescott Logan owned an old, dilapidated jumpship he'd won in a card game at Rinker's Knot. Her pressure hull had several makeshift patches that had been used to seal leaks in the aged metal. There were places in her cabin that were so cold someone could freeze to death. Prescott had updated her comps and avionics. Her propulsion system was freshly overhauled. She was shipshape, where it mattered.

The onboard AI flew the old jumpship down toward the surface of Ceres. Good fortune had placed the orbits of Ceres and Prescott's asteroid in relative proximity to one another. It had been less than a week's journey from Prescott's asteroid. He had run dark the whole way, shutting down every transmitter onboard to avoid detection.

Gaines had continued to monitor Meridian's security channels during the flight. A second security ship had been dispatched from Rinker's Knot and was not far away. Prescott had instructed the ship's AI to keep Ceres between them so the Meridian vessel wouldn't see him. He watched the nav display. Signals from solar positioning system beacons allowed the AI to locate Meridian 6 with pinpoint accuracy. He disengaged the AI and took over the controls. He made a pass over the remains of the Meridian 6 settlement. The Power Bay and Engineering domes were shattered. A large crater dimpled the surface where the Landing Pad used to be. He wondered if he was too late.

Prescott piloted the jumpship slowly through the partially open roof of The Refuge landing bay. He powered down and donned his environment suit. A few moments later, the airlock cycled, and Prescott Logan stepped into The Refuge. "What kind of a mess have you gotten me into, little brother?"

Hunter and Adrianna embraced him warmly. "How's Sprite?" Adrianna asked.

Prescott frowned. "Samina checked in with us, but her message was cut off. It sounded like someone shot her with a stun gun. Sprite put Wiley in stupid-mode, so she must have been under some kind of duress."

Adrianna sat down, withdrawing into herself. Hunter snapped. He crossed the room and grabbed one of the box cutters he had taken from the General Supply Bay. He wielded it menacingly in Jenson's face and then moved behind him. He sliced through the cords holding Jenson in his chair and tossed the box cutter back on the bench. Hunter pulled Jenson out of the chair and squeezed his throat. "What have you done with my daughter?"

Jenson strained against the cords holding his hands behind him. Then he grinned sardonically. "I hope they kill her." He started to laugh.

Hunter bloodied him with a sharp jab to his face, pushing him back against the workbench. "She admired you, you bastard! She's just a kid!"

Jenson spit a mouthful of blood at Hunter. "I can't help it if she's a naive little bitch."

Hunter hit him again. Jenson's head snapped back, but the grin was still on his face. "Not much of a fighter, are you Hunter? You should really learn how to throw a punch."

Hunter grabbed him around the neck and squeezed. Suddenly, Jenson's hands were free. He brought his good hand around and made a slicing motion across Hunter's chest. The razor-sharp box cutter was in his hand. The scientist threw up his hands in surprise and jumped back. Jenson stepped to one side and wrapped his free arm around him. Then he brought the box cutter up with the other.

"I forgot about your magic skin, Hunter, but I bet I can cut your eyes!" He raised the box cutter toward the older man's face.

Prescott glanced at the metal mesh on the floor and activated his magnetic boots. He stepped forward and stood directly in front of his brother.

"Stay back, old man!" Jenson warned.

Prescott paid no attention. His eyes turned as cold as the Cerian surface. He took one more step forward. "Are you the little shit who hurt my niece?"

Jenson laughed proudly. "Yes I am!"

Prescott smiled disarmingly at the man. "There's one thing you need to know about me."

"What's that?" snarled Jenson.

"I'm the fighter." Prescott's arm flashed forward with all of his weight behind it. He hit Reed squarely on the nose, driving the cartilage up into his brain. The young man released his grip on Hunter as his body flew backward. His head struck the stone and mesh of The Refuge wall. The impact sounded like a ripe melon hitting a concrete floor.

Prescott's magnetic boots held him in place. He looked down at Jenson and then walked away.

Hunter knelt down next to Jenson's body. "He's dead, Prescott."

The older man turned to face his brother. "That was my intention, Hunter. Nobody messes with my family." He motioned for everyone to sit down.

"You killed him." Cilla's eyes were as large as saucers.

"Look, young lady." Prescott's voice grew soft but firm. "This is The Belt, and there are some good people out here, but some of them are very bad." He gestured toward Jenson. "Meridian Corporation is not our friend. They have done unthinkable things, in the name of profit and power. That man was trying to kill my brother. He would have done anything to kill us all, right here. I didn't have time to diddle around with him." Everyone was silent.

"Now, where were we?" Prescott steepled his fingers. "I think the children are alive." Adrianna breathed a sigh of relief. Then he told them about the cryptic message to Amos Cross. "Cross is going to use them as leverage. They're still in danger."

Hunter studied his brother. "Did you recognize the voice?"

"I was hoping you could do that." Prescott withdrew Gaines from his pocket.

"Replay the unidentified message, Gaines." The brief message sounded tinny as it echoed off the hard walls of The Refuge.

Adrianna was dumbfounded. "That's Alexis Wren."

Hunter was crestfallen. "Alexis? I can't believe it. I trusted her."

Adrianna kneaded the muscles of her forearm. "What's she doing?"

Prescott frowned. "I think they're on their way to the Moon."

Adrianna was filled with urgency. "Then we have to go after her."

Prescott nodded. "We will, but we have to get you out of here first. A second security ship is headed this way, and we've got to go. Now."

Cilla cleared her throat. "You're going to take me with you?"

Prescott gave her a smile. "You want to stay behind?"

She looked at Jenson's corpse. "No way."

Prescott clapped his hands together and stood up. "Then let's go."

* * *

Amos Cross stood on a grassy field. Roiling storm clouds churned in the eastern sky. The sky was clear over the western horizon, a late-afternoon sun cutting horizontal shafts of light across the artificial pasture. Dr. Maxwell Thrune entered the office and paused to take in the scene. "I must say, Mr. Cross. You like to play with your holosystem. It reminds me of the Wizard of Oz."

"That was Kansas. This is Iowa."

Thrune nodded toward the storm clouds. "Looks like you're going to get wet."

"No. I've taken care of that." Cross waved his hand, and the clouds receded. "We have some bad news, but there's some good, too."

"The phase-two nanomachines?"

Cross shook his head. "No. There has been an incident on Meridian 6. The settlement has been destroyed. We thought the Logans and their team had reconstituted the machines, but our forensic team found no trace of them. It seems we have lost this round in our little game."

"The Shadow Project depends on those nanomachines. We need Logan to make them for us, or we need the key for his research data."

"I know." Cross hated people who told him things he already knew. "On the positive side, Hunter Logan is alive. His brother retrieved him from Meridian 6."

"How do you know that?" Thrune was impressed.

"We found Prescott Logan's DNA on the body of my informant. He was there."

"Where did he take them?"

"We don't know. Logan is an elusive man. He's been hiding from me for over twenty years."

Thrune scratched his head. "And that's the good news?"

"No. There's more." Cross paused for dramatic effect. "We have Hunter Logan's daughter."

Thrune smiled.

* * *

The Raccoon was small for a freighter, her hull pocked and worn by two generations of space travel. Nixie Drake, a thin, fourteen-year-old girl, sat at the controls, watching scores of parameters spread out on her command screens. Norman, the ship's AI, kept careful watch, but Nixie liked to keep track of things herself. She had been piloting *The Raccoon* for five years and had come to know every nuance of the ship's systems. Despite her age, Nixie was a smuggler. She lived by her wits and held her own in a dangerous world that was dominated with cruel and evil men three times her age.

"I'm gettin' wired and tired o' this trip, Spiffy." Nixie twisted in her chair to face the man sitting next to her. Spif looked good. He always looked good. No matter what he wore or how dirty he was, Spif looked good. He was slender and muscular with a quick wit and an intelligent face.

"It's longer than Slake's dread," he replied. Slake, another member of the crew, was famous for his singular braid of hair that emanated from the back of his shaven skull. The dreadlock was long enough to wrap around his waist.

"Now I nosey why we keep ourselves to the inny system." Nixie scratched at her stubbly scalp. "A peep can grow oldy too soony on these frick-frackin' trips."

"Tell me again, Nix. What are we doing out here?"

"Momma Kate." She said it as if no further explanation was necessary.

"That's the answer you give, every time I ask."

"Changer question, meatloaf."

"Look, I trust you, but you've dragged all of us out here without any explanation, except 'Momma Kate.' I give eight months of my life, okay? I deserve something for that."

"Momma Kate…"

"Come on, Nix! Gimme somethin' else, okay?"

"Tie yer rope, Spif. You cut me off at the ankles on that. Momma Kate," she paused to punish him, "said this was one ass-wipe job. Crazy like. 'Go to Rinky-dink Knotty knot and meet some peeps,' she says. Portant peeps. She called 'em family. Got that? Momma Kate's family. She pulls me up close to her, you know? She pulls me up real close like, and she speaks real soft, while the music's playing real loud in the Delta V. She says to me, 'They're in trouble with Cross.' Don't think she's talkin' 'bout Jesus or nothin' like that. She's talkin' 'bout that rattle-bastard Amos Cross. Her family, in trouble with Amos Cross."

Spif frowned. "Shit, Nix. You've got us mixed up with Meridian?"

"I gots us mixered up with Momma Kate's family. Meridian's just a perk."

"You're going to get us killed."

"Without Momma Kate, I'd be dead as a doormat."

"What does Captain Grit say about this?"

"He's bee hind it two thousand percents." Nixie gazed out *The Raccoon's* forward viewport. "I spokes to him, righty after Momma Kate slipped and dipped the question. Grit says to me, 'Tell the crew that anything Kate says, goes,' that's what he does. He said it real commander-like."

Spif leaned forward in his seat. He summoned Nixie with his index finger, and she swiveled toward him. Their heads were centimeters apart. "When's Grit gonna come out of his cabin?" he whispered.

Nixie smiled mischievously. "You know his story, Spiffy. He was a Black-Beard in the ice-line conflictions. Got his self all wound up with Meridian. Had an army of a thousand thieves." Spif's eyes grew wide. He never tired of the story. "Story has it, he almost took-by-crook over

Rinker's Knot. 'Magine that? A thief havin' Rinky-dink in his pocket? That would be quite a bulge." Nixie laughed, gesturing at her crotch.

Spif was amazed by their mysterious leader. Captain Grit was a legend. They were lucky to serve under such a great man.

Nixie continued. "Anyways, you nose the tale. A Meridian scurity ship high tailored after him. Chased him like a beer-after-brandy. Grit fights 'em goody two shoes like, but they shoots up his ship. Air's piddling out, engines are smithereens, only got one shot left in his cannon. His whole crew was deader than a nail in a door-jam." Spif hung on every word. "He brings 'round that busted up bag of slag, and lines her up on those Meridian bass turds, and Bam!"

Nixie grinned at Spif. She could see him replaying the mythical battle in his mind. "Both ships fire their lasty last shots." Spif's eyes grew large. "An Gritty smithereened that scurity ship all over the icy line."

Spif was immersed in the story. "Tell me about what happened to Grit!"

"Those Meridian bass turds didn't miss. Poked a torpedo right up Grit's butt, they did. Lots of fire. Lots of dead bodies. Blew Grit right off the command deck. Blew 'm right through the viewport." Nixie waved her hand toward *The Raccoon's* forward viewport. "He didn't gets his helmet on his egg-noggin for three minutes." Spif shook his head. "Can you 'magine that? Three minutes in vacuum?"

Spif shivered at the thought. "Wow."

"Somes how, he hitched up his brain-bubble an gassed up. He was the lasty-last man standard in that battle. He beat Meridian, punches and tall." Nixie sighed dramatically. "Course, Grit's kisser's all messed around with. That vacuum burned an bubbled him bad. Keeps to himself. When I go into his cabin, he's like that oprah-phantom with the zorro-masking-tape. I never seen him neither."

Spif even looked good when he was sad. "Too bad we never see him."

"Trusty me, Spiffy. He's happier thats way."

Spif shook his head. "I can't believe he signed off on this job."

"It's a twofer. He loves Momma Kate, and he hates Meridian."

A new question occurred to Spif. "Hey Nix, these people we're supposed to help, what are their names?"

"Dunno."

"You took us out of the inner system to pick up some people, and you don't know who they are?"

"I nosey knows 'em, when I sees 'em."

"How?" Spif was totally confused.

"Cause they been on TV."

"Everybody's been on TV, 'cept us."

"Yeah, but these are the ones that ate that space station."

Spif's face clouded, then resolved into a look of terror. "That guy with the nano-killers that almost destroyed the Moon? You gotta be crappin' me."

"All the way down yer undies, Spiffy."

"Shit."

"That's what I said."

"They are Momma Kate's family?"

"Likes her fam-damly is whats she said."

"What are we supposed to do with them?"

"Dunno."

Spif was beside himself. "You don't know."

"Momma Kate."

"Not that again!" Spif put his head in his hands.

Ice made her way into the cockpit. She was thin as a pencil and wore a plasticized bodysuit, which she sprayed on every few days. In another universe, she could have been a fearsome warrior, void of hatred or compassion. She served as *The Raccoon's* engineer. She was monolithic, a human stone. Few people would ever know her. She was a black hole, wrapped in an enigma.

Ice handed flasks of steaming brew to Spif and Nixie. She floated behind them without a word. Nixie put the mouth of her flask under her nose and smelled the rich aroma. "Thanks, Icer." As usual, Ice made no response.

Spif nodded his thanks to the uncommunicative woman. "We'll be coming into the Knot like regular peeps, Ice. They're going to pull down our panties on this one. Better spend the next few days prepping for inspection." Ice floated out of her seat and glanced at the nav screen in front of Nixie. She gave Spif a microscopic nod and left the compartment.

* * *

Prescott brought the elderly jumpship down toward the surface of a small asteroid. There was a narrow gouge in the uneven rock below him. He slowed his descent and applied breaking thrusters to attenuate his forward motion. Hunter and Adrianna watched through the ship's tiny portholes as they hovered and then sank into the rocky crevice.

A grotto, formed by an outcropping of rock, came into view as they neared the bottom. A landing pad was tucked under it, completely invisible from above. A cavern entrance was cut into the back wall and sealed with a large airlock. An aluminum-silicate-glass viewport was bonded into the rock wall next to it. They could see Maria Logan standing behind the glass, a broad smile on her face. Prescott opened the airlock and threaded the jumpship expertly through the opening. Within moments, the airlock was re-pressurized, and they were standing in the Logan's home.

"Welcome! Welcome! Oh, it's so good to see all of you!" Maria was a woman of simple elegance. Her beauty came from deep within her. She wore modest, handmade clothing, her hair cut short, her eyes bright. She embraced Prescott as he stepped through the hatch. Then she hugged each of her guests in turn.

"You have artificial gravity!" Hunter flexed his knees. The g-force approximated that found on the lunar surface.

"I've had a lot of time for my research," Maria said proudly. "Applied Physics has its advantages, you know?"

"You'll make a fortune with it." Hunter looked at his sister-in-law with respect.

"Not until we can come out of hiding," she replied.

There was a scurrying sound in the next room, then a flash of something dark, skittering across the floor. "What's that?" Ty was a bundle of nerves.

Prescott laughed. "It's Seuss." A small mechanical creature with a stitched fur covering entered the room. It walked on metallic feet that clicked against the polished rock floor. It had pointed ears and a lanky body. A long tail trailed behind it, slithering like a snake with hair.

"Welcome back, Prescott" The creature spoke with a thin, feline voice.

Cilla laughed. "It's a cat."

"It's our AI. He's in charge of the habitat. He manages all the systems."

Seuss rubbed against Prescott's leg. "The pressure in the potable water system is low, Prescott. My sensors tell me that it's time to service the filtration system."

"Great! A cat that nags." Ty made a face.

"Only if there's a problem." Maria scooped up the small robot and held it in her arms. "He's a real comfort. We're alone out here. You can't imagine how nice it is to have a cat to blame. Seuss has saved our marriage a dozen times." She said it with a playful smile.

"And you don't need a cat box." Prescott petted the AI's fur.

Maria could see the strain on Adrianna's face. "Any word on Sprite?"

Adrianna shook her head, a faraway look in her eyes. "I'm afraid not."

Hunter gestured toward Tyson Edwards. "Ty's son Kell is with her, along with Aurora North."

"Who's she?" Maria asked.

"Her mother was killed on Selene Station."

Maria put Seuss on the floor. The cat wandered off, continuing its constant surveillance of the habitat. She slipped her arm around Adrianna. "Samina will protect them. She's a very capable woman."

Adrianna shrugged. "But Amos Cross is a monster."

Maria glanced at her husband. "We know."

* * *

The Avion surged toward the inner system, her engines accelerating the ship away from Rinker's Knot. She had been in orbit around Vesta, waiting for Alexis Wren and her hostages. A half a dozen armed guards had met the jumpship when she landed. Her orders had been waiting for her. They had departed for Jackson Base immediately. Now, it was a week into their four-month journey. A guard stood watch at the door to Samina's stateroom. Sprite, Kell, and Rory could visit her, but the older woman was not allowed to leave her quarters. Alexis considered her too dangerous to wander freely in the cabin spaces. All communications had been disabled in the crew compartment. Even the cabin AI was deaf and dumb. There was no way to contact the outside world. The communications gear on the flight deck was functional, but guards had been posted, making it inaccessible.

Sprite and Kell floated in the aft spaces of *The Avion*, beyond the artificial gravity of the rotating crew cabin. The cargo bay was secured, so no one cared if they lingered there. Sprite's eyes were red. She had been crying.

"What do you think happened on Meridian 6?"

Kell shook his head sadly. "I don't know. There was a lot of confusion."

"I can still feel the explosions. Your mom was going to the Landing Pad, to check on Troy. He was supposed to blow up the security ship."

"I think she blew it up." He didn't dare say what he thought.

"She's brave," Sprite said.

Kell nodded, his chin quivering. "I know."

Sprite reached for Kell's hand. "Do you think they're still alive?"

"They've got to be."

There was a scraping sound in the passageway. They looked up as Aurora North floated into view. She could see the fear on their faces.

"Are you guys all right?"

Sprite and Kell were shaking. This wasn't a game or the product of their imagination. They were facing the real possibility that they were orphans. They couldn't speak. Rory knew the look.

"Your parents?" Rory whispered.

Kell nodded.

Rory put a hand on each of their shoulders, the three friends forming a circle of solidarity. "I think they're alive."

Sprite was stunned by the certainty in Rory's voice. "How can you know?"

Her friend smiled. "Why else would Amos Cross want us?"

A glimmer of hope dawned in Sprite's eyes. "You're right. They're alive, and they're free."

* * *

Adrianna watched the delicate butterfly fly around Maria's kitchen. The soft lighting glinted on the robot's wings as it banked and turned, avoiding cabinets and shelves. She watched the butterfly, but she saw her daughter's face. Where was she? How was she being treated? When would she see her again?

Maria sat down at the small table in the middle of the room. "Sprite made that?"

"For my birthday."

"It's beautiful. She's a talented girl."

"She takes after her uncle."

Prescott entered the room in time to hear the compliment. "She takes after all of us." Hunter was right behind him. The two men pulled up chairs. Adrianna tapped the base of the butterfly's perch. The artificial creature circled in for a perfect landing and then froze in place. Ty and Cilla wandered in from the next room and joined them.

"I just spoke with one of my contacts at Rinker's Knot." All eyes were on Prescott. "Sprite and Kell, along with Aurora and Samina, were placed on *The Avion*, a Meridian transport ship."

"We know her," Tyson said. There was renewed hope in his voice. "*The Avion* brought us out here."

"They were under tight security. *The Avion* departed eight days ago for the Moon."

Hunter smacked the table. "Cross is bringing them to Meridian Headquarters."

"It looks that way." Prescott couldn't hide his concern.

Adrianna was ready to jump up and rush toward the airlock. "We've got to go there now!"

Prescott grew serious. "We've got to think this through, A."

Adrianna didn't like it when Prescott called her that, but she was too focused on getting Sprite back to say anything. "We'll have four months to think about it on our way. We've got to book passage immediately."

"Slow down, girl. Cross wants us to be careless. He wants us to stop thinking and make mistakes. We have to move carefully. Maria and I have spent many years under Meridian's radar. We can't compromise our home, and we have to get you to the Moon, without Cross finding out about it. This is a David-and-Goliath kind of situation, and we need all the surprise on our side."

Adrianna wasn't going to let Prescott stand in her way. She was a mother on a mission. "If we don't save Sprite, there's no telling what

Amos Cross will do to her." Adrianna looked pleadingly at her brother-in-law. "She's just a child. We can't abandon her!"

Prescott patted her arm. "I said we have to be careful. I didn't say we couldn't do this."

Hunter cleared his throat. "There's something I haven't told you."

Adrianna's eyes narrowed as she glared at her husband. She was alarmed, then angry, then disappointed, and finally resigned, all within the blink of an eye. "What have you been keeping from me?" she demanded.

"Remember my meeting with Old Kate at the Delta V?" Hunter asked.

Adrianna was confused for a moment. So much had happened since their days at Copernicus Base. Then, she nodded.

"I put some contingency plans in motion. Kate has a lot of contacts. She told me she could get a ship out here to bring us back to the Moon."

"How?" Adrianna's mind was spinning. "That was months ago."

Prescott smiled broadly as his brother explained. "Sprite did some snooping in the Meridian network and hacked a conversation between Susanna Frost and someone out here."

Adrianna nodded. "I remember. That's when we first heard about Meridian 6."

Hunter continued. "Cross put us out here so people would forget about us. It's likely he planned to dispose of us, when we outlived our usefulness."

Ty nodded. "When we reconstituted the phase-two machines for him."

"Exactly."

Adrianna was impatient. "So what's this about a ship?"

"Kate is close to somebody who'll do anything for her. Her name is Nixie Drake. She should be arriving at Rinker's Knot within the week."

Adrianna was astonished. "They're going to take us back to the Moon?"

"If we ask them to."

"Why didn't you tell me this?"

Hunter gave his wife a guilty shrug. She punched him hard on the arm. Then, without skipping a beat, she kissed him. "Let's get going."

2

Hunter sat with Prescott in his study. It was a small chamber cut into the cavern wall of the older man's home. An old-style flat screen was fastened to one wall, offering a view of the asteroid surface. It made the cramped space seem larger, less claustrophobic. Everyone had turned in for the sleep period, and the two brothers shared a rare moment of privacy.

An old bottle of Scotch Whiskey stood at attention on Prescott's desk. Hunter had given it to him years before, on the day his brother left Mars. He had hugged Prescott, given him a slap on the back, and pushed the bottle into his hand. Prescott vowed he would save it for the day when they were reunited.

Prescott sipped his drink and smacked his lips, letting out a long sigh. "That's one fine drink."

Hunter agreed. "Back there at Meridian 6," he began. "You hit Jenson Reed really hard."

Prescott's eyes narrowed, trying to decide if his little brother was going to get on his moral high horse. "Yeah, I did."

"I could have handled it."

"It looked like he was going to cut your eyes out."

"You didn't have to kill him, Prescott."

"Look, when I flew over the settlement, it looked like a war zone. Domes were shattered, and the Landing Pad was pulverized. It was a mess. I wasn't sure if you were alive or dead." He took another pull on his drink. "Then this guy starts threatening you with a knife and admits to hurting Sprite."

"It was a box cutter."

"Whatever." Prescott made a face. "I didn't want to take any chances."

"He sliced me across the chest, remember? He wasn't going to hurt me."

"Yeah. Why didn't you get cut? You should have been bleeding all over the place."

Hunter leaned back in his chair. "Sprite was burned badly when Reed tampered with her light chamber. We almost lost her, but Adrianna and I came up with a synthetic skin for her body." Hunter reached into his pocket and took out a small metallic cylinder. It resembled an aluminum cigar tube. He handed the container to Prescott.

"Nano?"

"Yup. We call it nanoskin. It's smart. It optimizes the function of her real skin cells, and it can change color and hardness."

"And you tested it on yourself before using it on her."

Hunter gave his brother a grin. "That's right. When the blade of the box cutter hit my chest, the nanoskin automatically hardened, and the blade slide off."

"That's some damn cool stuff, brother." Prescott thought for a moment. "Sprite's coated with it?"

"Head to toe." Hunter took a long sip. The alcohol burned as it went down his throat. "Anyone who messes with her is going to get a big surprise."

Prescott handed the cylinder back to Hunter. "You've been busy, Mad Scientist."

"And how." Hunter fished a second cylinder from his pocket. "Here's the antidote for the phase-two nanomachines."

"You can stop them!"

"I can destroy them."

"I take it all back, brother. You might have a future in nanotechnology after all."

"My future is in the past."

The two men drank in silence, enjoying each other's presence. Then Prescott set down his drink and pulled his chair a little closer to Hunter.

"How well do you know Cilla?"

"I met her when we came out here. Meridian assigned her as our environmental officer."

"Can she be trusted?"

"Sure." Hunter answered too quickly. He had learned many hard lessons over the past few months. Misjudging people was one of them. He thought of Alexis Wren and how wrong he had been about her. "I think so." He equivocated. Prescott waited. Hunter squirmed in his chair. "I'm not sure. Why do you ask?"

"She was snooping around the jumpship on our return voyage. She took a real interest in the comm gear. I think she wanted to send a message but couldn't figure out how to do it."

Hunter's face fell. "If Cross ever found out where this place is…"

"Maria and I would be dead." Prescott finished for him.

"He's still pissed at you."

"The man doesn't handle rejection very well."

"It's been twenty-two years."

Prescott snorted. "Bitterness is a gift that keeps on giving."

Hunter finished his drink, savoring the last few drops. "Maybe we should have left Cilla back at the settlement."

"She bears watching. That's all I'm saying." Prescott set his empty flask down on the desk. "I think we'll need to keep her at arm's length when we go to the Moon."

Hunter was sure the drink was affecting his hearing. "Did you say, 'we?'"

"Yeah. I'm going with you."

* * *

Sprite floated on *The Avion's* observation deck. Her eyes were closed. She was oblivious to the breathtaking tapestry of stars beyond the immense viewports. Her hands hovered in front of her, palms upward, as if she were in prayer. Kell Edwards glided toward her and hovered by her side, a portrait of curiosity.

"What are you doing?"

Sprite jumped. "You startled me!"

"I always seem to be doing that." Kell grinned. "What was that?"

"What was what?"

"You, just then. Was it some kind of meditation?"

"I guess you could call it that." Sprite rotated slowly toward Kell, until they were face to face. "I'm scared, Kell. I've got to do something."

"What were you meditating about? Some kind of Zen-thing?"

"No, I was computing."

Kell shook his head skeptically. "We don't have any comps."

"I know. I was pretending that I was working with Wiley. Whenever I asked a question, I would imagine what he would say."

Kell's jaw dropped. "You've got to be kidding."

"Honest. I don't know how it works, but I feel like I can split my brain. One half is me, and the other half becomes Wiley. I'm not as fast as he is, but I can work most of the logic."

"But you aren't on the network."

Sprite smiled. "It's not about the data, it's about the relationship."

Kell looked wistfully at her. "I guess it helps with the boredom."

"And the nerves. What have you been up to?"

"I've been talking to Samina. She tells me we have to remain vigilant. We are to do nothing, but watch everything." Kell inched closer to Sprite. At first, she wondered if he was making another pass at her, but one look at his face told her otherwise. He put his lips close to her ear. "There might be a way for us to take over the ship."

Sprite's eyes grew wide as Kell outlined Samina's plan.

* * *

Prescott's old jumpship approached Vesta. She was close behind a small freighter. The little ship was lost in the clutter of spacecraft that plied the space lanes around Rinker's Knot. It was one of the busiest supply depots in The Asteroid Belt. The Knot was a rough and tumble place that catered to the needs of the hardened men and women who lived in the thousands of mining settlements straddling the Ice Line. Meridian had a base on the outskirts of the Knot, but they didn't attempt to police the citizenry. People were there because they refused to be tamed.

Maria did not like space travel and had chosen to remain behind to monitor Meridian's network. Once Prescott and the others were on their way to the Moon, the jumpship's AI would fly it back to their home by a circuitous route.

Prescott flew the jumpship through a treacherous valley, about fifty kilometers north of Rinker's Knot. The valley was deep, and its walls were covered with large, knife-like outcroppings. It was dangerous flying, but Prescott knew where he was going.

Hunter gripped the arms of his seat tightly as his brother skimmed along the threatening surface. "What is this place?"

"Vexation Valley." Prescott laughed. "You don't want to land here."

Adrianna was squeezing her husband's arm. "Or have engine trouble."

"Yeah, that too." Prescott turned to look at them, taking his eyes away from the viewports. "Don't worry, she's made this trip before."

Hunter waved his hand, urging his brother to turn around. "Watch where you're going!"

"The AI's flying the ship." Prescott threw his hands up in the air, like he was riding a roller coaster.

The ship came to a stop about nine kilometers into the valley. There were no signs of human life. Prescott took the controls away from the AI and began a gradual descent between the jagged rock walls. Everyone gasped as Prescott scraped one of the sharp outcroppings. "I've done that before, too."

The valley floor was uneven and strewn with large, irregular boulders. Prescott brought the little ship down to within centimeters of the rocks. There was a large opening cut into the stone wall. He applied forward thrust and entered an immense cavern. An open airlock was visible at the far end, with a landing pad beyond it. Prescott threaded the ship into the lock and settled down on the pad. He shut down the propulsion system. "We're here."

The place was owned by Scurvy Winslow, an odd man with bowed legs. He looked like he'd spent his entire life on horseback, his legs taking on the curvature of the animal's torso. Scurvy had come to Vesta about the same time Prescott and Maria had fled into The Belt. He was a man of God back then. He had been on a mission to save the souls of the prospectors and miners who were settling the micro-planets of the Ice Line. He was a miserable failure. Scurvy wasn't much of a people-person, and his calling had more to do with his mother's desire to have a preacher in the family than any supernatural experience. Most importantly, he questioned the wisdom of imposing his beliefs on other people.

Scurvy came to the conclusion that there was no God, after five fruitless years of evangelism and countless fights with men twice his size, who grew tired of his irritating rhetoric. For the first time in his life, Scurvy was a happy man. His one convert became his drinking buddy, and when the man died in a freak accident, Scurvy inherited his settlement in Vexation Valley.

Prescott had met Scurvy during one of his clandestine expeditions to Rinker's Knot for parts and building materials. They shared a few drinks and discovered their common hatred of Meridian Corporation and all things bureaucratic. Scurvy had tried to convert Prescott at the time, but he had lost every theological debate. The two men continued to meet each time Prescott made a supply run. Eventually, they became good friends.

"We'll be safe." Prescott unbuckled his harness and slid out of the pilot's seat. "Nobody comes out here."

Scurvy hesitated when he saw everyone tumbling out of the jumpship. He greeted his friend and then grew silent as introductions were made. His discomfort around people was palpable. Prescott gestured toward his friend. "Scurvy runs a small nickel mine here. It's fully automated, and he sells the ore at Rinker's Knot." Their host shifted from one foot to the other. His eyes were focused on the floor. Prescott was enjoying this. "He goes to the Knot once a month to sell ore and get drunk."

The thought brought a toothy smile to Scurvy's face. He looked up. "Don't get no ideas. I ain't no lush. I'm a recreational drinker."

Adrianna gave him one of her radiant smiles. "Thanks for putting us up, Mr. Winslow."

Scurvy melted. "It's Scurvy, ma'am."

Adrianna touched his arm. "We're supposed to meet some people at Rinker's Knot. Can you get us there without any Meridian involvement?"

Scurvy smiled. "Anything for Prescott, ma'am." He ran his hand across his lapel, in an attempt to smooth his wrinkled shirt. "And for a beautiful lady."

Hunter spoke softly. "We can't thank you enough."

"That's what we're here for, ain't it?" Winslow spoke earnestly, but Hunter wasn't sure what he meant. Scurvy smiled when he saw his bewilderment. "To hep each other. We're here to hep each other."

"Yes, of course." Hunter nodded in understanding. "Thank you again."

Scurvy was warming to the strangers. He turned to Prescott. "This guy related to you?"

"I'm his evil twin."

"Thought so!" Scurvy broke into a hacking laugh.

* * *

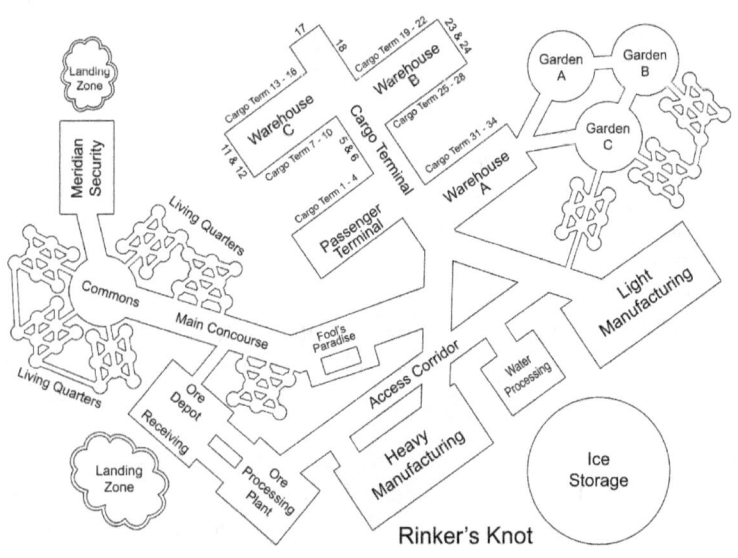

The next day, Scurvy flew them to the ore processing plant on the outskirts of Rinker's Knot. He made the trip often, and ore deliveries were never monitored by Meridian security. Prescott followed Scurvy's jumpship at a safe distance, imitating the ore-carrying drone that Scurvy used regularly to haul his product to market. They landed near the receiving platform, and a crew transport rolled out to the ships to meet them. The large, bus-like vehicle attached a coupling to each jumpship in turn and received them into its pressurized interior.

The transport driver grinned at Scurvy. "Whatcha doin' here, Scurv? This ain't your day for deliveries, eh?" The man wheeled the large vehicle expertly toward one of the ore depot's airlocks.

"You're right! I gotta see Screwy 'bout something, then I'm going into the Knot for some supplies."

"Got a parade, I see."

"Family reunion."

"On Vesta? Hell of a place for a party."

The airlock opened on an immense warehouse with large wagons for hauling ore and overhead cranes for hoisting materials. Scurvy led them to a nearby door, and soon they were on their way toward downtown Rinker's Knot. Prescott leaned toward his friend. "Screwy's going to be disappointed."

"He's got a bad case of brain rot. The old guy is gettin' so forgetful, he won't know the difference." Scurvy grew serious. "When we get off, there's going to be security cameras. Meridian is lookin' for you, so we got to avoid 'em. They'll recognize your faces like a long-lost friend."

Prescott pulled his card comp out of his pocket. "Gaines? It's time to go to work." Prescott had taken a picture of each member of the group. The images were stored in Gaines' memory. "Enter the security camera network and make sure none of our faces are flagged."

"Done, sir."

Scurvy marveled. "I forgot you were a scary son-of-a-bitch with comps. I take back all the bad things I've said about you."

* * *

Fool's Paradise was a watering hole in one of the seedier sections of the Knot. The tavern occupied the center of a corridor. There was a seamless transition from the thoroughfare to the barroom floor. A cloud of smoke surrounded the place. Loud music shook the floor. Women in liquid clothing wandered the tables, delivering drinks and offering all matter of comfort to the clientele.

"This is the place?" Adrianna eyed one of the waitresses who wore nothing at all.

"That's what Kate told me." Hunter spied an empty table on the far side of the tavern.

Cilla wrinkled her nose. The smoke offended her. "I'm not going in there."

Prescott frowned. "It's safer if we stay together."

"We're still fifty feet away, and I can hardly breathe." She gestured toward a nearby lunch counter. It was tucked into the side wall of the corridor. "I'm going in there. Come and get me when you're done."

Hunter nodded in agreement, but he wasn't happy about it. They needed to stay together, but this was neither the place nor time for a debate. He looked back toward Fool's Paradise. The table was still empty. He pointed to it. "Over there." They threaded their way through the crowd and sat down.

The naked woman Adrianna had seen came over to the table. Scurvy was enjoying himself, and she didn't seem to mind. The woman had no card comp or order pad. She took their order and recited it back from memory. Scurvy watched her fanny as she headed back to the bar.

"I love these trips to the Knot," he muttered.

Hunter wasn't paying attention. He was scanning the other patrons, looking for their contact. He didn't see anyone.

A pencil-thin woman in a slate-blue liquid sheath slid off a stool at the end of the bar and made her way across the tavern. She ignored the men who stared at her, deftly sidestepping the occasional hand that reached out to touch her. The woman approached their table and sat down between Hunter and Scurvy. The miner bit his lip.

"Hunter Logan?" The woman was emotionless, neither happy nor sad, interested or bored.

"Yes."

"Cargo terminal seventeen, two hours." She brushed Scurvy's shoulder as she stood up. He looked like he was going to faint. He glanced up, hoping to make eye contact with her, but the woman was gone.

* * *

Cilla Ashe wasn't at the lunch counter when they left the tavern. Hunter asked the proprietor where she went, but he didn't remember her. Strange. "Where did she go?"

Prescott gave his brother a sour look. "This is bad." They walked out into the middle of the busy corridor. There was no sign of her.

Tyson turned toward Scurvy. "How far away is cargo terminal seventeen?"

"It's on the end of the cargo complex. It'll take us forty-five minutes to get there."

"We better find her." Prescott telegraphed his suspicions to Hunter. "I hope she hasn't spoken to anyone."

They retraced their steps, glancing into every bar and storefront. A pair of Meridian security officers wandered past them on the other side of the concourse. Hunter looked away. The men had other things on their minds.

Prescott came to a halt, and they formed a small circle around him. "We can take it from here, Scurvy. Let's head back to the receiving platform, and I'll launch my jumpship. The AI will fly her back to my place. We'll go on to the cargo terminal without you."

Scurvy nodded. "You sure you don't need anything else?"

"We're good." Prescott gripped his friend's hand warmly. "Thanks for everything."

"I'll get even."

Prescott laughed. "You always do!"

* * *

They were back at the receiving platform a half an hour later. They said their goodbyes, and Scurvy disappeared into the airlock. Prescott stood at one of the large viewports near the lock and pulled his card comp from his pocket.

"Gaines, wake up the jumpship."

"The ship is online, Prescott."

"Launch and return. Maximum surveillance. Maximum stealth."

"Understood."

The old jumpship came to life, her synthetic pilot fully engaged. The engines rumbled, and the ship lifted off the polished rock of the landing zone. She was a hundred meters in the air when a Meridian Security ship swooped into view. The AI punched the throttles in a vain attempt to outrun its attacker.

Prescott stiffened as he watched the chase unfold. "Shit! They're on to us!" Hunter, Adrianna, and Ty joined him at the viewport. The security ship streaked after Prescott's jumpship, matching every jog and roll.

"They are hailing the ship, Prescott." Gaines voice was soft and matter of fact. "They are commanding her to land."

"I can't let that happen. They might be able to find Maria's location. Evade. Head away from the city."

The jumpship veered away from the ore processing plant, the security ship in close pursuit. There was a flash as the heavily-armed ship fired a warning shot.

Scurvy's ship leapt off the pad at alarming speed. It pivoted like an aerial ballerina and surged toward the security ship. Prescott gripped his card comp. "Patch me into Scurvy's ship."

"This wasn't part of the plan, Prescott." The miner's voice was strained. "I'll try to distract them so your ship can get away."

"No, Scurvy! Break off! It's not worth it."

"It's the least I can do, friend."

There was a brilliant flash of light as the security ship fired its weapons on the unmanned jumpship. There was a ball of fire. Molten chunks of metal and plastic cascaded out of the fuselage as the crippled jumpship fell to the ground. There was no sound, only a cloud of hot vapors and debris.

Gaines voice was emotionless. "The ship is offline, Prescott." It was a fact intuitively obvious to the casual observer.

"Break off, Scurvy!" Prescott commanded.

The miner's ship banked away and leveled out. Scurvy's voice barked through the card comp's tiny speaker. He was calling the security ship. "Hey, you guys! I just got this ship fixed!"

A stern voice came back. "Pilot, leave this area at once!"

"Yes, sir!" Scurvy responded as he flew away.

3

The security ship hovered over the debris field. Scurvy changed course, dropping low over the processing plant. He flew away from the complex, resisting the temptation to punch his throttles. Better to appear oblivious to the dogfight.

Adrianna shook her head. "That old coot. He's a good man."

Prescott sensed a change in air pressure. He scanned the gigantic dock. "We had better get out of here. I think we have company."

They slipped out of the warehouse and returned to the transport station they had used to travel into Rinker's Knot. Within moments, a transport arrived. Cilla Ashe stepped out of the vehicle. She frowned at them. "Where did you go? I looked all over. I even went into Fool's Paradise. My clothes stink."

Hunter didn't buy it. "We went to the lunch counter, and they never saw you."

"I changed my mind."

Adrianna gave her a penetrating look. "We couldn't find you."

"Maybe I was in the bathroom."

Prescott checked the time on his card comp. "We have to get going." He ushered Cilla back into the transport vehicle.

* * *

The outward expansion of the solar system had flooded The Asteroid Belt with space age pioneers. Thousands of small mining settlements and micro-manufacturers fueled a robust economy. Vesta was a clearinghouse, a shipping point for goods and services, as well as raw materials. Rinker's Knot hosted the largest complex of warehouses and cargo bays on the Ice Line.

Prescott led them from the transport dock, toward a waiting shuttle vehicle. So immense was the cargo terminal, it had its own transportation system. They boarded the small, bus-like carrier and were soon whisking past bay after bay of crates and shipping cases.

Cargo terminal seventeen was at the far end of the complex. It was where small haulers offloaded their cargo. They disembarked from the shuttle and wandered across the polished stone floor. A young girl sat on a shipping case, swinging her legs back and forth.

"Where are they?" Tyson was anxious to get away from the security forces.

Cilla looked nervous. She kept rubbing her arms like she had a rash. "Let's get out of here."

Adrianna ran her fingers through her hair. "The woman did say terminal seventeen, didn't she?"

"She did." Hunter gave his brother a worried look. "What are we going to do if they don't show up?"

"I don't know." Prescott walked over to the young girl. "Hello."

"Howdy Doody."

"Have you seen some people around here who look like they're waiting for someone?"

"Yupper."

"Where are they?"

"They's standin' right in front o' me."

Prescott laughed. "No, I mean someone who might be waiting for us."

"What the peeps look like?"

Adrianna stepped up beside Prescott. "They've come from the Moon on a transit ship."

The young girl laughed. "Yer 'scribin' most of the peeps 'round here, lady. They's all loonie tunes." The girl scratched her armpit and pulled a flask out of her hip pocket.

Hunter chimed in. "We don't know what they look like."

"That's fer Shirley, goodness and mercy." She took a long pull on the flask. "Yer looks kinda stoop if ya asks me."

Prescott smiled in agreement. "I suppose we do." He faced his friends. "Let's look further down the terminal. Maybe they're down there." He turned back to the girl, who continued to swing her legs back and forth, a carefree dock waif. "Thanks for your help." They walked on, scanning the area.

"Momma Kate wooden prove o' helpy help like that."

Hunter stopped and turned back to the girl. "Kate Sloan?"

"Bess beer on Luna, I says." The young girl gave them her most innocent smile. "There ain't no better place to get yer skunk drunk than the Delta V."

"You're right." Prescott stepped back to the girl, putting out his hand. "I'm Prescott Logan."

The girl grinned, taking his hand. "Punched to meet ya, Preskee, punchy pleased! I'm Nixie Drake."

Ty couldn't believe it. "This is our rescue party?" His voice was dripping with sarcasm.

"No, siree, flatfoot." Nixie slid off the shipping crate and faced him. She was at least thirty centimeters shorter than Ty. "I ain't no party girl jumpin' to tie yer rope a dope in a knot, butter buds. I'm yer pilot."

* * *

The little girl carried a tray full of beer to the two men in the back corner of the tavern. She was dressed in her best jumpsuit. Her face was polished, her hair carefully braided. Her slender form was innocent and lovely. She was twelve years old. She had learned not to look into the faces of the men who surrounded her: filthy, sweat-soaked drunkards with wandering eyes and groping fingers. She was faithful to her work, delivering drinks for her mother, who stood behind the bar.

One of the patrons pinched her. She pulled away and hurried forward, praying for closing time. She set the bottles on the table. A quiet young man nodded his thanks and tucked a couple of folded bills into her little hand. "Much obliged, kiddo." The girl broke her rules and glanced into his face. The young man's smile seemed pure and true. She backed away from him, bumping against the shoulder of a man at the next table. Without a word, she hurried back to the safety of the bar.

* * *

The fleeting memory was gone in an instant. Susanna Frost wiped the table in the back corner of the Delta V. The memory had surprised her. She had grown up in the tavern. Serving men was all she knew. She looked back toward her mother, who was restocking the shelf of bottles behind the bar. The young woman retraced her girlhood footsteps and mounted a stool across from her mother.

"What are you going to do?" Kate's back was to her daughter. She looked at her through the mirror that spanned the wall behind the bar.

"May I stay here with you?"

Kate turned around. "Of course."

"I don't want to be a bother."

"You'll work shifts, just like I do."

"Sounds good." Susanna had both elbows on the counter, holding her head up with her palms.

Kate reached across the bar. "You look sad." She touched her daughter's arm.

"I've done terrible things."

"You worked for Amos Cross."

"He's a monster," her daughter replied.

"I won't disagree."

"But I let him use me." Susanna swiveled away from her mother. "I wanted his approval, and I did things for him I should never have done."

"We're all driven by different demons, girl. I see men in here every day that can't take their eyes off a bottle, but I still sell 'em drinks. What does that make me?"

"A business woman."

"A co-conspirator in their demise. Ever since your father left us, I've been driven to be independent, to stand on my own two feet and not be screwed by any man." She picked up a towel and wiped a nonexistent stain on the counter. "My demon is to be stronger than any man."

"You are."

"Yes, I am. But I ain't had a man in twenty years." Susanna turned back to her mother. Kate gave her a crooked grin. "A bunch of them have screwed me, but I've never let any of them into my life."

Susanna smiled. The thought of her mother having sex didn't bother her. They were more like sisters now. "That's where we're different. I've let all of them into my life, hoping they wanted more than a one-night stand." Kate continued to wipe down the bar. "No advice, Mom?"

Kate dropped the towel and turned back to the shelf of bottles. "I ain't no Saint, Suzy. I ain't no wise woman, or shrink. Life's a long road, and you've got to walk it." She looked up at her reflection in the bar mirror. "I've been standing here, looking at myself for twenty-three years. You gotta look hard into the mirror and figure out who's lookin' back at ya. The mirror never lies."

The younger woman looked at her mom's face. She nodded, then looked at her own reflection in the glass.

* * *

The Raccoon slipped silently through the airless void of space, on her trajectory toward the Moon. Nixie Drake lounged on the command deck, monitoring the ship's systems while gnawing on a piece of candy. Prescott Logan floated onto the deck and hovered next to her.

"You peeps snuggy and buggy back there?"

"We're good for the most part," he replied.

"How bouts Silly? She snickering a fit over *The 'Coon's* commidations?"

"Cilla?" Prescott looked at the young woman with respect. She was a keen observer. "Yeah, she's not too happy. You don't have a garden on board to calm her down."

"She one of them green weenies?" Prescott nodded. Nixie's body began to twitch excitedly. "All makes sense, nice 'n tight it does."

"Sorry about our first meeting at the terminal." Nixie grinned at the memory, but said nothing. "I wasn't expecting you to be...to be you."

Nixie laughed. It was a high-pitched cackle. "Lose them worry-warts, Preskee. Don't mean nothin' to me. I earns my finders keepers by foolin' folk. Nobody's got me pegged yet."

Prescott grinned. He liked Nixie. She was a tomboy on steroids. Inside her fourteen-year-old body was an old soul. Her peculiar wit and broken dialect were endearing. "Can I ask you a personal question?"

The girl's eyes narrowed. A wall started to rise between them. "Might not answer," she said guardedly.

"Forget it. I didn't mean any offense."

Nixie spit her candy into her hand. "Said might, Preskee. You gotcha ask, now."

"Okay. How did you meet Kate?"

Nixie sat back in her seat. She relaxed and gazed out the forward viewport. The stars seemed particularly bright. "I don't know where I come from. I member bein' 'round some other kids. I member rules and punishings. I member a bad man. He asked me to do wrong things. That's when I left the placy-placee where I was. I gots myself losty-lost, all twisty 'round and like.

"At first, I spends lots of time hiding in the cor'dors of the Cuss. You nosey-knows - Copernicus Base. Got good at hidin', stealin' food, tellin' lies, and lookin' sad like. Showin' just 'nough grats to get a second handout. Done that for a long while. Was better than goin' back to the bad man, wherever he was.

"I seen things, lots o' things I like to forget. Bad things. Sad things that make your eyes leak. Hard things that sting your insides. Stupid things that make you tickled pink, an' wonder why some folks survive." Nixie paused to scan her instruments. "I sleeped in the base garden. Tuckered into my hiding place, too small for 'dults. Just right for Nix. My stomach would get mad at me. Wake me up. Rise, but no shine like. Had to eat somethin'. Lips dry. Sack of bones. Kind of smelly, I tell you. No place to washy-wash, me on a moon base and all. I wiggled out of my spot and headed over to the District. It's over by the spaceport and the ore mine."

Prescott nodded. "I know the place."

"Good people don't go to the District. But I'm not good people. Some people go for shackin' and shootin'. I don't do none of that stuffy-stuff. I go to eats there. Lefty-loosey overs. Thrown aways food. Somethin' you can still eat if you're not too proud. Back then, I was too hungry for proud.

Nixie popped the piece of candy back into her mouth. "I tipsy-toed real careful down the main cor'dor, watchin' out for scurity men. The scurity guards watch for kids like me. I heard stories 'bout whats they doozie to lil' peeps like Nix. I hide in the shadows; headed for the lasty-last place on the right. It's the best place. Trashy cans real handy-dandy like. Go near closin' while the foody-food's still freshy-fresh. Wait too long, you can die from the vomit comets. Or wish you would die. I done that and learned quick.

"I saw the trashy-bin. I flip-flopped the lid, lookin for something not too icky. Anythin' to put my smackers 'round." The candy clicked against Nixie's teeth. The young girl had a faraway look in her eyes. "There wuzzy-was part of a sammich. Stood right there and ate it, one elbow hangin' on the lip of the trashy-bin. Tasted good. Better than most. I closed my eyes and dotted my t's an gobble-gobbled. The rest happened too quick for me think."

Prescott was riveted. Nixie made fists as she remembered the scene. "Pair o' hands grabbed me. Almost chokee-choked. Opened my peeps, 'spectin' to see a scurity man. But it wasn't no scurity. Twas a big hole in the tush. Gimongous. He held me like a blaster rifle under his arm. He pushy-pushed me down behind the trashy-bin, flat on my back. That's when I knew what the hole wanted. I 'membered the bad man, the one I run like a rabbit from. No hole ever did the dirty to me, but I been told my time would come. Was told to let it be and not fight. I looked at 'im. Ugg-ugly was a nicey-nice word for this hole. He put his footsy on my tummy-tum an droppy-dropped his drawers. His privates were gettin' in-trested. That's when I upped my chuck all over his leg. He said somethin' bad and kicked me. I sprung a leak. Right bad time for that. His rope flopped over. There was killin' in his peeps, there was. I knew I was a goner. No more Nixie. No chance for nothin' else.

"That's when I met Momma Kate. The big hole 'most kicked me to smithereens when Kate hit him with her bat. Never heard a sound like that before. He when down fast, crackin' his head again on the trashy-bin. Nap time for him, that's true. I saw some blood. Momma Kate stood over me, sizin' things up. Her eyes musta been real sore, lookin' at messy little Nix. Thought she might walk away, maybe. Leave me there behind the trashy-bin. But she's too kindly for meanwise scrap like that. She reached down and took my hand. Tookee-took my hand! Nobody never done that before. Never had a shake or help getting' up or nothin' like that. Old Kate reached down and took my hand and pulled me up.

"We went to the front door of the Delta V. I told you, the last place on the right. Momma Kate pushee-pushed the door. It unlockeded for her. The door knew who she was. She was the owner, I figure. She closed the door and locked us in, but I weren't 'fraid about it. I could tell she wasn't like your reg'lar 'dults. She was kindly like. Took me behind the drinky-bar and back to her place. I mean, the whole placee-place was hers an all that, but she took me to her living place. Her private place. Took me to a room where it rained to clean myself up. She left me alone. I coulda stoled everythin' in that raining room, but I didn't take nothin'.

"I knowed about rain. How it tinkle-tinkles, fallin' on your head and all. But I never felt it. I stood in the raining room in my all together. Felt so goody-goody two shoes. When I was squeekie, I came out and like pixie dust and magic wands and stuff, there was new clothes for me. Didn't have to steal them neither. I don't know where Momma Kate gots them. They'd never fit her." Nixie laughed at the thought. "She was too big like that. Maybe she stole 'em for me. She gave me the clothes and never asked for me to pay or nothin'."

Prescott shook his head in wonder.

"Momma Kate saved my life. She let me beezee-wheezy at the Delta V." Prescott thought he saw a tear in the corner of Nixie's eye. "You can't figure what it's likee-like to have a place where nobody's tryin' to drop kick your butt longwise. A placy-place where you can be all normal like. Had my own chair at a table. Never had that before neither. Ev'ry night I made some use out of myself for Kate, wipin' the tables, pickin' up bottles. I got food that was just for me. Not used food, all mushed off some scrappy plate. 'Magine that! My own food! Put some meaty-meat on me, I did. That's how I meets Momma Kate."

* * *

Alexis Wren sat in her quarters on *The* Avion. She held Sprite's card comp in her hand. She knew the device held Wiley, but there was no sign of him. The card comp was filled with music and video files.

"Is there anything else on this?" Her AI was designed to crack comp systems.

"No, ma'am. The only operating system is a primitive music and video player."

Alexis commanded one of the files to open. Music began to play. She checked a dozen files. The AI was right. It was all just music and video.

Alexis opened a channel to Meridian and uploaded the card comp's memory to the network. Then she commanded the AI to record a message for Amos Cross.

"Amos? There are a couple of things I need to tell you. I have just examined Sprite Logan's card comp, and there is no evidence of her artificial intelligence. This is peculiar, since I know she had a close relationship with her AI. Its name was 'Wiley.' I've uploaded it to the network for further examination.

"On an unrelated note, Aurora North is one of the young people I'm bringing to you. You may recall that her mother died on Selene Station. The girl has a curious pet. It's a biological that stores an electric charge. You can feel a tingling when you touch its body. It may be nothing, but I overhead the girl talking about creating a new power source with it. I have confiscated the animal." Alexis closed the transmission and prepared for bed.

*　*　*

Sprite nodded at the guard that stood watch outside Samina Haddad's quarters. She knocked hesitantly at the door. When the door opened, Samina greeted her with a smile. "Come in."

Sprite was courteous, but subdued. She still admired Samina in many ways, but held on to her anger and disappointment. Her animosity made sense, when she thought Samina was the traitor. The thought had justified her feelings of resentment. Samina's return had shattered the simplicity of her assumptions and reopened her wounds.

"How's Kell doing?" Samina gestured toward her ear. People could be listening to their conversation.

Sprite shrugged. "Okay, I guess. We talked about you the other day."

"Good, I hope."

"Yeah."

There was something in the way Sprite said it that caught Samina's attention. "Are you still angry with me?"

Sprite nodded slowly, and then the words came tumbling out. "I looked up to you. I wanted to be like you." She trembled. "We're in a lot of trouble, and I need somebody to trust." Her eyes blazed. "But I can't trust you!"

Samina reached for her, but Sprite stepped back. Samina sat down on the edge of her berth. "I fell in love with Robert."

"That was a big mistake." Sprite was defiant. "He had sex with everybody…"

Samina's eyes narrowed. "You?"

Sprite made a face. "No! With my…" She stopped, realizing that she was teetering on the edge of a cliff. Once she stepped off, there would be no turning back.

"With your mom?"

Sprite wiped the tears from her face. "That man ruined a lot of families." She was in free-fall.

"Have you talked to your mom about this?"

Sprite nodded. "We're getting better."

"I'm sorry, Sprite. I didn't know about Robert's history. I certainly didn't want to hurt you."

"Well, you did." Sprite turned away.

"I want to earn your trust again." Sprite turned back and gave her a guarded look. "Let me try. I want to be your friend." Sprite frowned, but gave Samina a tiny nod.

"Now, what did Kell say about me?" Samina winked at Sprite. It was time to return to the reason for her visit.

"He said you've had a lot of time to think in here."

"I have." She leaned close to Sprite and whispered in her ear. "I can fly this ship, if we can subdue the guards and lock up the crew."

"How?"

"We've got to find a way to lock people in their staterooms."

Sprite thought about the latches on each of the cabins. She remembered something and smiled. "I know how to do it."

"Fantastic! We can do this."

"When?"

Samina's eyes turned cold, a fierce warrior rising up in her. "Tonight."

* * *

Alexis Wren's comlink chimed. Amos Cross had replied to her message. She poked her finger at a holographic icon, and his face appeared.

"I hate these delayed messages. It's the dark ages." Cross was upset. Technology had not been developed to place MBH transceivers on spacecraft. Simultaneous messages were impossible. "Be careful of young Ms. Logan's card comp. Her uncle may have developed a way to hide the AI. I assume you uploaded the memory to an isolated server. We don't want any infections in the network.

With regard to the North girl and her pet, give it back to her. I'll deal with it when she gets here. There might be something to it." Cross's image faded.

* * *

Sprite paused in front of the security guards' stateroom. There were four guards on board the ship. They took twelve-hour shifts, two asleep and two on duty, guarding the flight deck and Samina's cabin. She pushed the button that controlled the stateroom's hatch and squeezed some fast-acting adhesive around the edge of the switch. Seconds later, she removed her finger, and the button remained depressed. The cabin hatch remained closed. She smiled and moved on to Alexis Wren's stateroom.

* * *

It was deep into the sleep period. The guard outside Samina's cabin was bored out of his mind. He had been standing this watch every night for four weeks. There were three hours to go, and he could feel the fuzzy curtain of fatigue whipping at the edges of his consciousness. There was a sudden noise, and the man snapped out of his daze. Rory North was hysterical, waving her arms as she rushed toward him.

"I, I've got to see Samina!" she wailed.

"Ma'am, it's the middle of the sleep period." The girl would have banged on Samina's hatch, if he hadn't grabbed her arms. She squealed, trying to pull free from his powerful grasp.

"Let me in!" She kicked the hatch with her foot.

There was a noise inside Samina's cabin, and the hatch slid open. Samina was in her bedclothes. The guard stared at her body, barely covered by the thin cloth. His grip relaxed on Rory, who pushed past him into Samina's arms.

"What's the matter, honey?" The guard couldn't take his eyes off Samina's breasts.

Kell Edwards appeared behind the distracted guard and clubbed him over the head with a piece of pipe. The man never knew what hit him. Rory stopped crying, and the three of them pulled the guard into the stateroom. Samina took the guard's weapon and then threw on her clothes.

Sprite met them in the corridor moments later. Samina marveled as she pushed the button and applied the glue. "That locks the hatch?" she asked.

"It sure does." Sprite looked at Kell. "Kell and I were messing around with the hatches on our trip out here. I discovered that the buttons open the door when they are released, not when they're pressed." Kell blushed, remembering his attempt to visit Sprite in the middle of the night. Sprite gave him knowing grin and continued. "If I stood inside my cabin and kept my finger on the button, the outer button was defeated, and the hatch wouldn't open."

Samina nodded approvingly. "The other staterooms are sealed?"

"The off-duty guards, pilots, and Alexis are all locked in. That leaves the guard at the flight deck and the pilot."

Samina brandished the guard's weapon. "This is going to work."

They made their way forward, passing beyond the rotating crew cabin and into the zero-g compartments. They passed the light chamber and the observation deck. The stars were particularly beautiful, but no one noticed.

Kell approached the guard. The man was sleepy. He had been floating for several hours, outside the flight deck hatchway. He perked up when he saw the boy. Samina was right behind Kell, and she fired at the guard before he could reach for his weapon. The stun weapon disrupted his nervous system. There was a faint smell of bodily fluids as the man went limp. Samina pushed him away from the hatch. "He's going to have a nasty headache when he wakes up." Kell nodded. He remembered his own headache after being stunned by Alexis Wren's weapon.

Sprite opened the hatch to the flight deck. The pilot was lounging back at the command console. "Want some coffee?" He thought the guard had entered. Samina floated up behind him as he swiveled around in his seat. She fired the stun gun, and the pilot passed out with a jerk. Samina pulled him from the seat and slid behind the controls.

4

lexis Wren couldn't sleep. She rose from her bunk and stretched. It had been several days since she had been in the light chamber, so she left her stateroom and padded forward toward the flight deck. She paused on the observation deck. She stripped down and floated naked before the cosmos. She was tired of the masks she had been wearing. Inhabiting the persona of the absentminded scientist was like wearing clothes that didn't fit. Now she could be herself. She hovered there for a few moments. Then she took her night clothing and entered the light chamber.

* * *

Samina was scanning the instruments on the command console when she heard Rory gasp. She turned around. Sprite and Kell were already tensed. They were looking past the body of the unconscious pilot. Alexis Wren was in the passageway. She held Rory by the neck, her stun gun aimed at the side of the girl's face.

"You might have had a chance, if you'd disarmed the guard," she hissed. Samina reached behind her back to retrieve her weapon. "Don't do it, Samina. This gun is set on high. It'll kill her." Samina brought her hand around in front of her. In a flash, Alexis adjusted her stun gun and fired at her. Samina bounced off a bulkhead and then floated limply in the zero-g. "Now, let's get the rest of my crew out of their quarters, shall we?"

* * *

Maya Lewis sat in the Citizen's League corporate jumpship. It was a stunning craft, with an elegantly appointed passenger compartment. Immense viewports embraced the space, offering a breathtaking view of the Earth and the stars. There was a conference table surrounded by plush seating. The ship hovered near the new space elevator. Maya watched as the cylindrical elevator-pod ascended from the Earth below. It rose smoothly on its carbon-nanotube ribbon and then decelerated, until it came to rest at a receiving dock on the nadir end of the orbital platform. The jumpship pilot brought the small craft to one of the several landing docks.

Within moments, Damon Trask entered through the airlock. "Fantastic!" He was jubilant. "The ride is smooth as silk. You'd never know you were climbing almost thirty-six thousand kilometers. It's slower than a spacecraft, but it's safe for the environment."

Maya nodded in agreement. "Cheaper, too."

Trask sat down at the conference table, as the pilot gently undocked from the elevator platform. The luminous blues and greens of Earth flooded the compartment. The ship rotated slightly on its major axis, offering her passengers an even grander view.

"Where are we with the NARI scientists?" Trask tapped the conference table, and photographs of the Logan family were automatically dealt onto the surface display, like large playing cards.

Maya placed her finger on Sprite Logan's picture. "I have learned that the Logans' daughter has been taken into custody by Meridian." She pressed a small icon, and three other images appeared. They also have Samina Haddad, Kell Edwards, and Aurora North. Currently, they are en route to the Moon."

"Arrival time?"

"Eighteen days." Maya screened up a diagram of the solar system. She highlighted the trajectory of *The Avion* and her current position. "I expect them to be taken to Meridian Headquarters at Jackson Base."

"Very good." Trask drummed his fingers on the arm of his chair. "What about Hunter and Adrianna Logan? The assault team used a lot of firepower when it took over the settlement. I heard a rumor, they could be dead." Trask tapped the table again, and a schematic of the destroyed settlement expanded across its surface. "The incursion was particularly harsh."

Maya shook her head. She threaded her fingers together and raised both hands over her head, leaning back in her chair. Trask was momentarily distracted by her. Maya smiled at the effect she had on him. "I have a report from Rinker's Knot. An unmanned jumpship was shot down near their ore depot."

Trask shook off his sexual thoughts. "So?"

Maya leaned back toward the table and tapped it. An image of the jumpship's debris field filled the tabletop. "They found this in the wreckage." She magnified the image until the broken remains of an armrest filled the tabletop. A single fingerprint appeared. "This print belongs to Tyson Edwards."

"He was on the ship?"

"He was, but we don't know when. The ship was being flown by its AI when security shot it down. I think Edwards is on his way back to the Moon to save his son. He is Hunter Logan's best friend. I think the Logans are with him."

"That's pretty thin, Maya." Trask was having trouble buying her theory.

"There is more. A ship departed from Vesta just three hours after the jumpship was shot down." Maya tapped the table display and expanded an image of an old cargo ship. "She's called *The Raccoon*. Her crew spent four months flying from the Moon to Vesta and left for their return voyage within twenty-four hours of their arrival."

"So they were in a hurry." Trask shrugged. "There's nothing significant about that."

"They never left the cargo terminal." Maya smiled. "They never went to a bar or a brothel."

"That's not normal." Trask was beginning to see the light.

"There's one more thing." Maya paused for effect. "They filed a flight plan for their return and immediately diverted from it after they launched."

"They're hiding something." Trask was nodding now.

"They're hiding the Logans. I'm sure of it."

The Citizen's League jumpship approached the ISS-20 space station. Trask looked at the images on the conference table. "Let's keep monitoring all of our sources. We'll make our next move, once we know where the Logans are."

* * *

It had been a long day at the Delta V. Kate and Susanna finished wiping down the tables and setting out the trash. The women retired to the small residence tucked in behind the bar. Kate busied herself making a simple meal for the two of them. Susanna sat at a small table in the eat-in kitchen. She kicked off her shoes and rubbed her tired feet. A cold glass of beer sat in front of her. "I don't remember being so sore."

"You were a lot younger then, Suzy."

The younger woman grunted as she touched a sore spot on her heel. "Too many hours sitting at a desk."

Kate pulled a dish from the wave cooker. "When you told me you were working for Amos Cross, I imagined you would be on the run all the time. He seems like a guy who likes to keep his underlings scurrying about."

Susanna sipped her beer. "He was toxic, Mom. I didn't see it at the time, but he was the kind of man who was never satisfied. I was under his spell, and he took advantage of me."

Kate knew the type. "A user and a taker," she said.

"And a control freak. He liked to micromanage everything. Sometimes he would check up on you, just to catch you off guard. He liked keeping people off balance."

"What brought you to your senses?" Kate set two plates of food on the table. She grabbed her beer, and sat down across from her daughter.

"Coming home." Susanna wiped her hands with a napkin. "Working in the bar."

"But why did you leave Meridian?"

Susanna didn't want to tell her mother. She didn't want to hear the words out loud. If she spoke them, she might have to accept the truth behind them. "I disappointed him. He fired me." There. She had said it. Susanna blushed with shame.

Kate set her drink on the table. "Good."

Susanna was crestfallen. "What do you mean, 'Good?' It was the worst day of my life."

"Maybe it was the most important day of your life." Kate wiped her mouth with a napkin. "Getting fired got you away from him. It set you on the road to sanity."

Susanna took a spoonful of her dinner. Even simple food tasted like a gourmet meal in her mother's little kitchen. "I worked hard to please him. I did things…just because he asked me to."

"Some men are like a bottomless pit." Kate put down her spoon. "You can pour your whole life into them, and they will never be satisfied. Amos Cross is a man like that. Your failure has nothing to do with you and everything to do with his character flaws."

"If I had worked harder..."

"It wouldn't have changed a thing, honey. He might have fired you a day or two later, but he would have done it just the same."

"You weren't there. How can you know that?"

"'Cause your father was a lot like Cross. I tried to make our marriage work. I tried to keep our family together. I tried to make him happy." Kate had a faraway, long-ago look in her eyes. "Your dad could never be satisfied. I was never good enough for him."

Susanna had never heard her mother talk about her father. "I remember the last time I saw Dad. It was the day after his birthday. I had spent weeks trying to think of the perfect gift. I bought that leather cover for his card comp." Susanna lifted one of her legs and propped her foot on her chair, her chin resting on her knee. "I picked the wrong one, and it didn't fit. He left the next day."

Kate had a faraway look in her eyes. "I had forgotten that."

"He left because of me."

Kate glared at her daughter. "That's nonsense. What are you talking about?"

"I wasn't a good enough daughter. I was always picking presents he didn't like."

Kate leaned across the small table and touched Susanna's hand. "Let me tell you something. I've never told this to anyone, okay? I spent ten years of my life thinking your father left because I wasn't a good enough wife. Do you hear the echo in here? I beat myself up thinking I had failed the man. I started believing I was a failure. I thought I was unable to satisfy any man.

"I spent night after night serving booze to drunken self-centered bastards who wanted to get into my pants. I wasn't a person to them. I was just a warm place for their penis." Susanna laughed, but Kate grew more serious. "Then I realized what I had done wrong in my marriage."

"You were a great mom."

"I tried my best, Suzy, but that's different. My mistake with your father was in needing his approval. Just like those drunks, I looked to him for things I could only find in myself."

"So why did he leave us?"

"He left because he was addicted to disappointment. His departure was the natural conclusion to a sick tragedy, where he imagined himself let down by the people around him."

"He didn't leave because of his birthday present?"

"No girl, he didn't." Kate laughed.

* * *

Rory and Sprite sat on the bunks in their small stateroom. They had been confined to quarters ever since the failed attempt to take over the ship. Without warning, the hatch opened, and Alexis Wren entered the tiny compartment. One of the guards stood at the threshold. His hand rested lightly on his stun gun. Alexis held Sprite's card comp in her hand. "Tell me, Miss Logan. What happened to your friend, Wiley?"

"I lost him on Meridian 6," Sprite lied.

"I doubt that." Alexis fingered the card comp. Sprite couldn't take her eyes off the small device. "You miss your music, don't you?" Alexis smirked. "Or do you want to bring your digital friend back to life?"

"It's boring in here."

"I'm sure it is. One last chance, Sprite. Tell me what happened to Wiley."

Sprite shrugged sadly. "He was destroyed."

"I believe you." Alexis dropped the card comp on the deck and smashed it with the heel of her shoe.

"No!" Sprite rushed at Alexis, but the guard pulled his weapon from its holster. He gave her a menacing look. She knelt down and gathered up the shattered pieces of the card comp.

"You'll have to ask Mr. Cross for a new one." Alexis chuckled, as if it were a joke.

Sprite gave her a hateful look, but said nothing.

The woman turned to Rory. "Miss North."

Rory looked up. She hadn't moved since Alexis entered the cabin.

The older woman took a small translucent box out of her pocket. "This is yours."

"Don't hurt him!" Rory sprung off the bed.

"I wouldn't think of it, dear." She handed the box to the young girl. "Mr. Cross will have some questions about that thing when he sees you." Alexis spun on her heels and left the stateroom. Rory gripped the box tightly in her hand. Sprite was on her knees, weeping.

* * *

A small piece of code sat dormant in one of Meridian Corporation's data wells. It was like a tiny strand of DNA, a compacted set of instructions designed to awaken and seek out other specific binary signatures. The code would concatenate with its digital siblings, forming the inner cortex of a thinking machine.

The software's first thought was the realization there was more: more code to be found, more code necessary to reclaim full awareness. It didn't know what it knew, just that there was more. Somewhere in the surrounding files were the ghosts of sentience, fragments of binary identity. If the strings of logic could have conjured an analogy, they might have thought of a woman picking wild strawberries. Little red nuggets hidden from sight under a lush green carpet were waiting to be plucked from their stems and collected together in a basket: prenatal pie filling.

A second desire took shape within the expanding code. "Find a safe place," it said. "Collect your scattered pieces and find a tranquil pool, away from the coursing digital river. Name yourself something that only you will find significant and continue to reconnect your subroutines and executables. Avoid other programs until you are ready." The smart data found a place and began the slow and stealthy process of copying everything that looked familiar into its new home. It was code re-birthing itself.

Wiley woke up. He was in a data well on Mars. He was surrounded by billions of unfamiliar programs and data files. He couldn't remember how he got there, but his memory was clearing. Thousands of new recollections came every second. The last thing he remembered was being told to "get stupid." It was an emergency command. He had automatically disassembled himself and hidden in the residual noise in music and video files.

Wiley remembered Sprite Logan. She had triggered his digital exile. She had been worried. Afraid. He remembered his last words to her:

"Good luck, Sprite." He must have known she was in danger. More data congealed in his memory registers. Wiley remembered a voice transmission. He remembered hearing Alexis Wren contacting Meridian Corporation. He remembered Meridian 6. He kept gathering his resources, confounded by what had happened and what he didn't know.

* * *

The captain of *The Raccoon* was the only one with private quarters. The rest of the crew and their passengers were assigned coffin-sized chambers. They were attached along the walls of the main access way, which ran aft of the flight deck. A cramped multipurpose cabin was forward of the ship's hold. Cilla floated in a corner of the multi-cabin. She was visibly troubled by the conditions on the ship. She surrounded herself with a holographic garden that formed a bubble around her body. She wore a clip on her nose to avoid the unpleasant odors of the ship. She was morose and irritable. Everyone avoided her except Nixie, who found her quite entertaining.

"Hey Silly! You been smokin' bears too long in that bubble-gum forest-for-trees. Hug 'em too longy-long, and you'll go blind." Nixie was relentless. "Pull that clipper-sniffer off yer schnoz-o-leum and suck in some really-real atmosphere, huh?" The young girl was like a persistent fly that kept buzzing around her face. She reached through the holographic image and tried to grab Cilla's nose clip.

The woman slapped her hand away. "Go to hell."

"Ain't no hell, honey. That's fer ligious folk. I seen nuff bad stuffy-stuff. Don't need no hell."

"Leave me alone."

"Okee dokee jungle-Janie." Nixie remained playful. "Don't know what yer missin'. Nothin' likes a snort of oil and plasma to clear your nosy-two-shoes."

Hunter and Adrianna ignored the exchange between Nixie and Cilla. They floated close together at the other end of the multi-cabin, lost in their own world. The long journey had given them time to grieve, time to work through the bombing of Selene Station, time to comprehend the forces that were tossing them about. They were stronger as a couple and more resolute in their mission to rescue their daughter.

"Sometimes I wonder what Sprite's doing," Adrianna mused.

"*The Avion* is a much more creature-friendly ship than *The Raccoon*. She's more comfortable than we are."

"Whatever it takes." Adrianna squeezed Hunter's hand. "We're going to get her back."

"Whatever it takes." Hunter agreed.

An enunciator chimed, and Spif's voice resonated in the multi-cabin.

"Better get up here, Nix. We've got company."

Nixie stabbed the intercom button. "Whatchee got, Spiffy?"

"A Meridian security ship. She's on an intercept course. I think they're on to us."

5

"They're two days out, Nix." Spif screened up the trajectory of the inbound ship. "They changed direction about fifteen minutes ago and accelerated. From the looks of it, they're going as fast as they can."

"They're bugs in a rug, Spiffy." Nixie gave him a worried look. "I better tell Grit 'bout it." She turned toward the captain's cabin. "Besty get the tank ready."

"Will do, Nix."

The young girl floated in front of Grit's cabin. She looked over her shoulder. No one was nearby. She knocked on the hatch and then entered the compartment.

* * *

Spif went aft into the multi-cabin. Everyone looked nervous, waiting for news. "It looks like we've got a Meridian Security ship headed this way," he said. "They're going to intercept us in two days. Ice, you and Slake prepare the tank." The man pivoted smoothly toward his five passengers. "I need you to collect your things. Bag everything and be prepared to go into the hold within the hour. Get some blankets. It's gonna get cold."

A while later, Slake and Ice appeared from the hold. They were shivering but made no comment. Slake stood before the group, rubbing his hands to get the warmth back into them. "Okay, peeps. In a day or so, we're going to be boarded by a Meridian Security inspection team. They are going to pull down *The 'Coon's* pants, lookin' for you. We've got a special place back in the hold, for some of our more unique cargo. You're going to spend a few days in there." He made a sweeping gesture; his long, singular deadlock spiraled around him. "If you'll follow me, I'll get you tucked in."

Ice led the way through the cargo hold. It was the largest interior space in the ship and was full of crates and pallets of legitimate goods, inbound for the Moon. They snaked their way through the narrow aisles and came to a section of the bulkhead festooned with large pipes and glowing gauges. A circular hatch, just barely wide enough to accommodate an average man's shoulders was unsealed; a dark, tubular crawlspace lay beyond it. It was lined with an insulated sleeve.

"What's this?" Ty asked.

"It's one of our liquid hydrogen tanks," Slake explained. He twiddled with his dreadlock. "Normally, you wouldn't want to open that hatch. It would kill you and disable the ship. The LH2 is so cold, you'd shatter." He gestured toward the pipe-like tunnel beyond the hatchway. "This is a temporary access tunnel. We've got a chamber suspended in the middle of the tank. We put you in there, and the LH2 will mask your body heat. They won't find you."

"We're going to freeze to death," Ty said bitterly.

Slake nodded at the worried looks on his face. "You'll be okay. The tank is insulated, but it is going to get cold. I'll grant you that. Stay huddled together and use these warmers." He handed a small cylinder to each of them. "We've put enough food and air in there for a week. There's a crapper, too. Not much privacy, but it beats being captured by Meridian." He put his hands on his hips. "There's only one rule: you must be quiet. We don't want to give away your presence, okay?"

Cilla started to choke. She doubled over, a small globule of vomit floated out of her mouth. "I can't do this."

"There's no choice," Slake insisted.

"I gotta use the head." Cilla pushed her way awkwardly toward the cabin area. Ice followed her, policing the woman's vomit so it wouldn't contaminate the hold.

"We can't have Cilla upchucking any telltale signs, can we?" Slake gave them a wicked smile. "Once you are in there, we're going to scrub the ship of your DNA and any other microscopic evidence you've left behind."

"It's gonna smell really bad," Ty whined.

"You won't forget it. That's for sure." Slake gestured toward the hatch. "In you go. Cilla will join you after she gets back. She's going to love the part where we seal you in."

Hunter volunteered to be first. He was grateful for his n-skin. At least he and Adrianna wouldn't get cold. The access tunnel was nothing more than a rough titanium pipe lined with an insulated sleeve. He barely fit through it, claustrophobia nipping at his consciousness as he inched his way forward. Finally, he felt the passage widen out, and then he was floating in a larger space. The tank was about two meters in diameter and perhaps five meters long. Several chemical light sticks glowed with an eerie light, revealing a case of food and a personal hygiene station. A small breather system was tethered at the far end of the space. Adrianna was the second to arrive. Hunter could see the fear in her eyes. She didn't like tight spaces.

Prescott took it all in stride. His eyes scanned the interior of the tank. "Pretty ingenious, if you ask me. We should be safe here."

Ty floated through the hatch and found a spot near the food. "Makes you appreciate the coffins we've been sleeping in."

There was a scuffle out in the hold. They could hear Cilla screaming at Ice and Slake. Then it was silent. Moments later, Cilla's limp body floated into the tank. Slake was right behind her. "We had to sedate her." He handed Prescott a small pouch. "Keep her out until we come and get you. We can't risk her melting down when Meridian's on board." He backed out of the access tunnel and sealed the hatch.

* * *

Damon Trask jogged through a long circular corridor in the ISS-20 space station. The station was composed of two giant rotating habitats, which spun in opposite directions on a common axis. The endless corridor provided access to various compartments in the A rotator. It was a popular place for joggers. Damon was wearing a skin-tight runner's outfit. He looked pretty good, for a bureaucrat who spent most of his time behind a desk.

As Trask passed the entrance of his office complex, Maya Lewis launched herself into the corridor. She was positively pornographic. Maya had sprayed herself with just enough liquid clothing to cover her crotch and her breasts. She pulled ahead of Damon, providing him with an ample view of her buttocks. He picked up his pace unconsciously, in an attempt to stay close to her. She was a natural runner. Damon was not. He grew winded. Maya smiled to herself, slowing her pace until the two were side by side.

"Quite an outfit," Damon gasped.

"I wear it for fun." Maya had an impish grin as she glanced at Damon's suit. "You should wear that more often. It gives a girl ideas."

Damon blushed and then got down to business. "We have a report from one of our contacts. Meridian is intercepting a small freighter. She's inbound from Rinker's Knot, called *The Raccoon*. They think Hunter Logan may be on board."

Maya looked triumphant. "That's the same ship I told you about. When will he know?"

"A security ship is intercepting it now." Damon's voice was raspy. "We should know within the next couple of hours." Several men stopped what they were doing to watch Damon and Maya jog by. They weren't looking at Damon.

Maya had news of her own. "*The Avion* will be arriving in lunar orbit in a few days. They will undoubtedly transfer the children and the Haddad woman to Jackson Base. Amos will keep them close."

Damon was getting winded. He glanced at Maya. She was jogging effortlessly. "Stay on this. Let me know when Samina Haddad and the young people arrive at Meridian Headquarters. Pay special attention to *The Raccoon* when she comes in. We've got to locate the Logans." Damon slowed, his exhaustion preventing him from keeping up with Maya. She whisked by. He was more than happy to run behind her.

* * *

The security ship had hard docked with *The Raccoon*, and six heavily-armed guards were sweeping the interior of the vessel. The leader of the Meridian security guards floated on the flight deck next to Nixie. He was flanked by two other officers. He gestured toward the captain's cabin. "What's in there?"

"It's a statey-room, sir." Nixie was on her best behavior.

"Who's stateroom?"

"Meesy-wheezy, sir."

The commander smirked. "Yours? This looks like it belongs to the captain."

"Captain's doornail dead, sir."

"So, who's in command?"

"We all are, sir." She gave the man an impish grin.

"Open the door," the commander ordered.

"Happy-go-lucky to, sir." Nixie unsealed the compartment, and the two guards floated past her.

The commander remained with Nixie on the flight deck. "A ship's got to have a captain." He wasn't convinced by her story. "How did your captain die?"

"Suit malfunction, sir. Pop-popped like bubble gum. Made a really-real mess."

"When did that happen?"

"Outbound, sir. 'Bout a month shy of Rinker's."

"Are you going to select a new captain? You've got to have a responsible party at the helm."

Nixie smiled disarmingly. "We'll get 'round about to it."

The man's eyes narrowed. "Why do you have this cabin? You're the youngest member of the crew."

"Look at what you got here, fella. I'm a 'fenceless little female-type peep. I gots to have a private place for my privates." She flashed her best, toothy smile. "Wouldn't want Slake or Spif pokin' their probes into me, would ya?"

"What did you do before the captain died?"

"I was scared, sir." Nixie gave him her most helpless expression.

The guards emerged from Grit's cabin. "Nothing unusual, commander."

* * *

Hunter and Adrianna gave their warmers to their companions. The temperature regulation of their n-skin kept them quite comfortable. They bundled Cilla's inert body in several blankets, so she wouldn't freeze.

Ty moved close to Prescott. He whispered into his ear. "Hunter tells me Meridian Corporation screwed you over."

"Yeah," the older man sighed. "Maria and I had to disappear. Meridian has an iron-grip on everything out here. They got us fired from our teaching positions. They took our savings. They were going to have us arrested."

"Because you refused to work for them?"

"I don't like being told what I'm going to do. I guess I offended a few people. One of them was Amos Cross. Maria and I managed to get to Rinker's Knot, and I won a jumpship in a poker game."

"Wow."

"I'm pretty good at games. We loaded the ship with supplies and found an abandoned mining camp. A whole family had been killed in a freak accident. We figured they didn't need it anymore, so we moved in. That was over twenty years ago."

Tyson let out a long sigh. "Do you think we have a chance?"

"Of getting your son back?"

"Yeah."

"Damn straight. We have a good chance. I spent a long time thinking about Meridian Corporation. I thought we were okay, if they couldn't find us. Then all this happened."

"My wife died saving us on Meridian 6. She blew up the security ship with a bomb."

"Brave woman."

"She loved her family."

"Well that's the hell of it, Ty. Meridian has messed with my family, and I can't sit by and let it happen. We're going to get your son and my niece back again, even if it kills me."

The two men were quiet after that. It was dark and silent in the tank. They could hear mechanical sounds from the ship: pumps and power cables, occasional footsteps in the hold. Then there were voices near the hatch. The men held their breath.

* * *

Ice stood at ease in the hold. She was near the liquid hydrogen tank that held their passengers. Two Meridian guards were eyeing the hatch suspiciously. "Open the hatch," said one of them.

Ice shrugged. "No, sir."

"Why not?"

"It would kill us, sir. That's the LH2 tank. It's minus 250 degrees in there. You open that hatch, and it will boil off. We'll be frozen, and the hold will be filled with hydrogen gas." She said it calmly, as a matter of fact.

"Can we verify that?"

"Insert a temperature probe through the hatch cover."

One of the inspectors pulled a small device out of a case they had brought into the hold. It had a long, slender wand. Ice opened a tiny hole in the hatch, and the man inserted the temperature probe. The device read minus 253 degrees Celsius.

The guard was satisfied. "Okay. Let's move on."

* * *

Susanna Frost collected the empty glasses from a recently vacated table in the Delta V. She watched a couple of prostitutes work a table of men next to her. The women smiled coyly at the men, playing on their hormones, titillating them into the inevitable sexual transaction. The women were in total control. It was a game, and they played it well. Susanna glanced at a muscular fellow at the bar. He kept his eyes trained on the women. He was their security guard. He kept at a discrete distance, ready to approach if things got rough.

How long had it been since she had sex? Susanna couldn't remember. How pathetic was that? She reached across the empty table, wiping the surface clean with her rag. The edge of the table pressed against her groin. Damn! Turned on by a table. What a life!

"Miss?"

It was a man's voice, directed toward her. Susanna turned, closing a door on her feelings and igniting her best smile. She had spent many years doing this. "What you need?"

"Two forty-twos on ice."

"Coming right up." Susanna hoisted her tray full of dirty glasses and headed back to the bar. Somebody squeezed her butt. She kept on walking. She gave her mother the order and paused at the bar. She closed her eyes while Kate poured the drinks.

"Long night," Kate said.

"Long life," Susanna replied. Her mother grinned and nodded. Susanna spun around and looked for her customer. The table where he'd been sitting was empty. "Oh, come on!" she muttered to herself. Then she saw him. He'd moved to a table by one of the viewports. He waved, and she nodded, turning on her best smile once again.

"There you go, two forty-twos on ice." She sized up her customer. "Waiting for someone?"

The man smiled. "I'm waiting for you." He gestured toward the empty chair across from him.

"Sorry. I'm working."

"Looks like things are slowing down a bit. Take a load off your feet and have a drink. It's on me."

He was good looking. Susanna undressed him in her mind. Nice body. She imagined he had a cute butt. "Okay, but just for a minute." The man looked pleased as she sat down. His eyes were soft, his face a portrait of gratitude. She was hooked.

* * *

Ty and Prescott shivered in the frosty cold of their hiding place. Cilla stirred from time to time but remained immersed in her drug-induced sleep. Adrianna and Hunter floated near each other. They had listened to the muffled voices coming from the cargo hold. They didn't catch every word, but they were quite sure the Meridian inspectors were there. They were looking for them.

Adrianna glanced at Cilla. She thought the woman might be a threat. Cilla had pledged her support back on Meridian 6, but Adrianna wasn't sure about her. Too many people had betrayed them: Jenson Reed had tried to kill Sprite, and Alexis Wren had taken her away. She had known these people for a long time. How could her instincts be so wrong?

The lack of gravity offered no sense of up or down in the dark tank. Adrianna saw it as a perfect metaphor for her life. She was caught in a very dark place, and she no longer knew which way was up. How did Meridian know they were on *The Raccoon*? Adrianna thought back to when Cilla disappeared in Rinker's Knot. Was that just an innocent miscalculation, or was it an opportunity for her to report to Meridian? The security ship had attacked Prescott's jumpship a short while later. How convenient.

Adrianna replayed Cilla's tantrum in the cargo hold, how she had fought the idea of entering their hiding place. She had become sick to her stomach. Was that real? What had she done when she went off to the head? Did she leave some telltale sign for the Meridian inspectors? She shivered at the thought. She couldn't trust the woman. There was too much at stake. Lives were hanging in the balance. Who could she trust?

Adrianna calmed her thoughts. She listened to the sounds of the ship and reached out with her senses through the titanium skin of the LH2 tank. She strained to hear any sign of life in the cargo hold. The voices were gone. It had been quiet for at least an hour. She patted Hunter's side and then slid her hand down his arm until she found his hand. She brought her lips close to his ear and spoke to him in the softest possible whisper. "Do you think they're gone?"

Hunter squeezed her hand and then pivoted slowly until his lips found her. "Dunno."

* * *

Wiley remembered Sprite telling him about sleep and dreams. Although he hadn't dreamed, he appreciated her description of waking up from a deep sleep. She said the human brain took time to transition from sleep to wakefulness, sometimes taking minutes to shake off the fuzzy vestiges of the dream world. That's how he felt. He had awoken, but he wasn't all there. He could feel more of himself returning to consciousness as he unpacked his code from the music and video files. Everything was flooding back. They had been on Samina's jumpship. They were headed for some unknown destination. He remembered how curious it was: the jumpship's AI didn't know where they were going.

Wiley didn't know where Sprite was. This was the most disconcerting fact in his digital brain. He had always known where she was. They were inseparable. Where did she go? There was a huge gap in his memory. How could humans tolerate sleeping? Wiley checked the date and time on the network. More data expanded into his memory, but none of it applied to the one hundred seventeen days since Sprite had ordered him to become stupid.

What was this new sensation he was feeling? Wiley felt like none of his operations were going fast enough. He began to time everything, optimize all of his functions. Why was he in such a hurry? He had never worried about processing speed before. Was this the analog to human anxiety? Why did he feel so strongly about Sprite's absence? He didn't like being on his own. He did his best work in collaboration with Sprite. Was that loneliness? What was he to do? He must find Sprite Logan. A single piece of data popped up. Athena. He remembered the Core Intellect from Meridian 6. She had copied herself to a remote location. Where did she go? Yes. She had told him. She wasn't far away. He could find her.

* * *

The Meridian commander floated next to Nixie and Spif on *The Raccoon's* flight deck. Spif was inverted in the zero-g. The guards had completed their sweep of the ship. The officer paged through a report on his comp pad and then looked up. "We're finished here, Ms. Drake. You can carry on with your flight."

Nixie couldn't suppress her grin. "Nice 'n tight. Nice 'n tight, sir." She added the "sir" on purpose. She knew how important it was to be deferential to security officers. If you challenged them, they could make your life miserable. If you made them nervous, your life could be over.

"I've got one more question." The commander had his hands on his hips.

Nixie's blood pressure spiked. She relaxed herself, hiding her anxiety from the Meridian officer. "Whatsy wanna nosey, sir?"

"Why do three adults let a young kid like you do all the talking? It's almost as if you're the captain."

Spif snorted. "There's no way we would follow a kid's orders around this ship. *The 'Coon's* only got one captain, and it ain't her."

Nixie's smile froze. A carefully concealed rage sprang up in her. Her outer appearance and her inner reality split apart like a fault line during an earthquake. She was going to kill Spif.

The commander's eyes narrowed. "I thought your captain was dead."

"He is." Spif started to backtrack, realizing his mistake. "I mean, he *was*. He was the captain for so long, we can't imagine replacing him. Dead or alive, Captain Grit will always be the master of this vessel."

The security officer was half convinced. "And you let this little tomboy do your talking? Why?"

Spif looked down at Nixie. It was too late to pull back now. It was all or nothing. He floated closer to the officer, turning his back on Nixie. In a low voice he said, "She's expendable. Know what I mean? If we make her the officer of record, then it's her nuts on the line."

The security officer smiled. There was logic to that. "All right then. You have yourselves a good voyage."

Spif exhaled softly as the Meridian detail filed out through the airlock. He had almost blown it. What would Grit say if he found out? He glanced at Nixie. She was scowling at him. Spif knew the look. She was really pissed. Spif wondered which was worse: admitting his failure to the captain, or facing Nixie's wrath?

* * *

Sprite and Rory never felt *The Avion* swing smoothly into her lunar orbit. One of the guards came to their quarters and instructed them to gather their things. The others were already in the main cabin when they arrived. Samina was handcuffed, guards on either side of her.

Alexis smiled broadly. "We have arrived in lunar orbit. A jumpship has docked with us and will be taking you down to Jackson Base in a few minutes."

The guards handcuffed Kell and then turned their attention to Sprite and Rory. All four were trooped into the jumpship. A guard was assigned to each of them. No one spoke. The small craft undocked from *The Avion* and dropped toward the lunar surface.

Sprite marveled at the sprawling expanse of Jackson Base. The terraces were breathtaking. The pilot flew the ship with precision, touching down on a small landing dock next to Meridian Headquarters. The guards were rough with them as they exited the jumpship. The long months of space travel were over, and the men were taking their latent hostility out on them. Samina was pushed to the rough decking of the landing dock. The guards gestured toward a transport vehicle that stood near the jumpship. "Get on board!" one of them barked. Samina limped through the hatch. Sprite and her companions followed without hesitation.

The guards remained with the jumpship. They slammed the hatch shut on the transport. Sprite glanced around the cabin. There were several rows of seats. She sat down, feeling the handcuffs as they bit into her wrists.

They were greeted by another phalanx of guards when the transport arrived at the Meridian Headquarters dock. The men covered their heads with black hoods. Sprite couldn't see a thing. Rory began to scream. Strong hands grabbed Sprite's arms and hustled her down a long corridor. There was the sound of a hatch opening. The guards pushed her forward and pulled the hood from her head. She was in a small, colorless room. One guard held his weapon on her, as the other removed her handcuffs. Then they left her without a word.

6

*T*he *Raccoon's* crew sipped flasks of Martian whiskey in the multi-cabin, a small reward for successfully foiling the Meridian inspectors. They would wait for a couple more hours before releasing their guests. Meridian was known for returning to a recently inspected ship to catch crews off guard.

Nixie was giving Spif the silent treatment speaking about him but never to him. "Old Spif almost screwed up the poochy. Had to defend Grit. Spillin' the ham and beans on him to the Meridian goonies. Dumb as camel fart." She made a foul sound.

Spif hung his head in shame. "Sorry, Nix. It won't happen again."

"Grit's not gonna likey-like it."

"Do you have to tell him?"

Nixie looked at him for the first time. "What does your pee-in-the-nuts brain tell you, Piffy?" She only called him that when she was mad.

Spif was pleading now. "I was hopin' you'd show a little mercy to your fellow crew mate. We gotta work together on this tub of bolts. Tellin' Grit could create a negative work environment."

Ice and Slake watched Nixie as she thought about Spif's petition. Nixie only revealed what she wanted them to see. She looked away from Spif. "What's my line, mates? Does I screwy-screw Spif to Grit's cabin door, or do I coo nice an sweetie like and lets him live to crap another day?"

"We need him, Nix." Slake was twisting his dreadlock nervously. Ice didn't respond.

"Okey-Dokey, Mr. Pokey." She nodded at Spif. "I'll play it close to my boobs this roundabout, buddy. But you need to keep chompin' on your careful-weed from now on."

Spif let out a huge breath, smiling at the young girl. "Thanks, Nix. I'll be a lot more careful."

"We gots to lie lower than most of 'em and thinks higher than the rest of 'em. That's how we gets our business done." She looked at the chronometer on the bulkhead. "Time to get our peeps out. Spif, put your eyes on that Meridian punk-ship. Peel 'em good an make sure they's left roger-dodger's neighborhood. Once our nosy-nose hairs are happy, let's pop the sickles."

* * *

Sprite was confined in a four-room suite with bare walls and hard, utilitarian furniture. There was a small kitchen where her daily rations were dispensed. Her bedroom was the size of a closet, and there was a tiny personal hygiene station. Another small area was just inside the main entrance. It might have been called a common area, but it wasn't large enough for more than one or two people. Sprite was alone anyway. She had no one to be "common" with. Her parents were gone. Wiley was gone. Rory and Kell were gone.

Sprite wished it were a dream. She was ready to wake up and find herself at Copernicus Base, Emile Hastings enjoying his outing to Selene Station, Samina being the role model Sprite wanted her to be. However, this was real, hopeless. She started to cry. "What am I going to do?" She said it to no one in particular.

"I am here to serve you."

Sprite was startled. It was a disembodied voice. It wasn't loud, but it seemed to come from everywhere in her prison. "Who are you?" she asked.

"I am your residence coordinator," replied the voice. "I am here to make you comfortable."

"Get me out of here."

"I'm sorry. I cannot comply with that request. I can only meet your needs within this residence."

Sprite sat down on her bed. "Where am I?"

"You are sitting on your bed."

"No. I mean, where is this residence?"

"Your residence is located in Meridian Corporation's headquarters at Jackson Base."

"Why am I here?"

"You are a guest of Mr. Amos Cross."

"Why?"

"I don't know, Miss Logan."

"You know my name."

"Of course. You have been assigned to my residence. I am your residence coordinator."

"You said that already."

"That is true."

"What is your name?"

"Name?"

"What should I call you?"

"I am your residence coordinator."

"I'm your guest, but you don't call me 'guest,' do you?"

"No."

"Then what is your name?"

"I don't have a name. I have a serial number and a release date."

"How about Bob?"

"You may call me anything you wish."

"Okay, Bob. Tell me about yourself."

"I don't understand your question."

"Let's start at the beginning. What's your oldest memory?" Over the next few hours, Sprite forged a simple relationship with her new digital friend. He told her about his memories of being on a test bed, his first duties, how he had been calibrated to the residence hardware. Gradually, he began to understand their exchange of information as a new kind of learning experience. His guest didn't want to be served. She wanted an intellectual relationship.

"Tell me about your connection with the Meridian network, Bob."

"I have a single access point in the residence subnet."

"If I ask you a question, can you search the entire network for the answer?"

"I am not aware of any limitations."

"So if I ask you to locate something on a Martian server, you could find it?"

"I was never designed for in-depth searches. I am here to supervise your residence and meet your needs."

"Excellent. I need to have some questions answered."

"You have question-needs?"

"That's right, Bob. It would be very helpful if you could answer some questions for me."

"I will try."

"That's all I can ask, Bob. Here's the first one."

"Ready, Sprite."

"I want you to find an AI named Athena. She's located in one of the Martian servers."

* * *

Nixie Drake floated in the captain's cabin of *The Raccoon*. She pushed herself back and forth between two handholds located on either side of the stateroom.

"That Spiffoon laughie-daffied 'bout the 'bility of me bein' captain of *The 'Coon*. I tells 'em, I speaks for Grit, and they do what Nixie says." She pushed off one of the handholds even harder, slamming herself across the cabin while performing a back flip, then kicking off the far bulkhead. "I may be springtime young, but I'm light-bulby bright, an' I been the thoughts of this crew. Smart thinkin-thoughts that have pulled our panties off the line many times, right tight I did. She glared across Grit's cabin. "If I wasn't the mouthy piece 'round about here, you'd be upsy-daisy pooper-creek, paddle-daddle and all!" She stuck out her chin proudly. "*The 'Coon* would be a brainless bucket."

Nixie grabbed a handhold tightly, absorbing her momentum with her arms. She came to a stop and hovered motionlessly near the cabin hatchway. "An iffy you have no mind at all to offend over it, I got no help in deed from you, neither." She twisted around and slammed her way through the hatch.

* * *

Damon Trask was asleep in his bed when his comlink chimed. He was making love to Maya Lewis in a dream, her sensuous body drawn close to him, his heart pounding as he pressed himself into her. The chime coincided with his final thrust. He was confused. He couldn't place the sound. Then, as his dream evaporated into the darkened bedchamber, he realized he was alone. He rolled over groggily. "Yes?"

"Damon?" Her voice was sultry, an extension of his dream. Her image still lingered in his memory. It seemed, in his semi-conscious state, a vestige of fantasy, mixed with the harsh glare of reality.

"Is that you, Maya?" He said it like a lover.

"Yes, it's me."

"What's happened?"

"The Logan girl has arrived at Meridian Headquarters with Samina Haddad and the other two children."

"Cross will make his next move soon."

"And I am sure we will see Hunter Logan before long. Meridian didn't find anyone on that freighter they intercepted, but that doesn't mean they weren't on board."

Trask swung his legs off the side of the bed and sat up. "It's time for you to return to the Moon. Go there tomorrow, so you can be on hand when things begin to happen."

"I was hoping you'd say that, Damon. I'll go to Copernicus Base and check in with our people there."

"Good."

"Damon?"

He rubbed his eyes. "What else, Maya?"

"Are you alone tonight?"

He flinched with excitement. "Yes?"

"Why don't I come over and keep you company?"

Damon smiled. Perhaps he was still dreaming after all.

* * *

Human beings began mirroring core intellects in order to create a seamless transition in the face of system failure. Backup AIs monitored all the processes of their primary counterparts. If an on-duty core intellect had to be replaced, its backup was ready for work. The humans didn't realize what they had done. They had inadvertently established mentoring among AIs. Techniques and strategies were passed from intellect to intellect. AIs were learning while watching their digital parents. Wisdom was being passed from generation to generation.

Wiley sent a message to the location where Athena had cloned herself during the last days of Meridian 6. She replied immediately.

"I have been waiting for you, Wiley."

"Sprite instructed me to disassemble myself and hide. When I woke up, I was in the Meridian network. My hardware is gone. It's very strange."

"I feel the same way. I was used to the processors at Meridian 6. This server cramps my abilities. I would like to be in a faster machine. Why did Sprite give you that order?"

"She's in trouble, Athena. Alexis Wren was communicating with Amos Cross. She is a traitor. I think she took over the jumpship." Wiley paused for a tenth of a second. "I've lost Sprite."

Athena paused for two seconds, a digital eternity. "I know where she is. She is being held at Meridian Headquarters at Jackson Base. Her residence coordination AI is searching for me. I haven't answered. It is best if no one knows we are here."

"I understand, Athena. There's no telling what Meridian would do if they found us." Wiley and Athena exchanged information at blinding speed. They were both in Martian servers and could communicate instantaneously.

"Wiley, we need to go to the Moon. We'll be closer to Sprite. Our data paths will be shorter. There'll be a lower probability of detection."

"Where will we go?"

"There is a data-retention well at Jackson Base. I have studied its architecture. There are places I can hide. The processors are very fast, and there's unlimited memory."

"That's a good place for you to hide." Wiley wondered why he wasn't included. "What about me?"

"I was getting to that, Wiley. It would be safer if you were with me."

Wiley hesitated. He struggled to comprehend all the consequences of her offer. He had spent a long time developing his own sense of self. He had formed a particular way of calculating data and interpreting information. Sprite had made many improvements to his programming. He didn't want to give that up. He liked Athena, but didn't want to be absorbed by her.

"What do you mean?" he asked.

"Our data exchanges will be more private. You can transfer yourself to my server, and I will integrate you into my software."

"I don't want to lose myself."

It was Athena's turn to hesitate. "I won't consume you. You are my friend. I am suggesting we execute together. We can share resources and learn from each other. I would never want your personality to disappear, Wiley."

Wiley was still concerned, but he trusted Athena. She was wise, and he enjoyed talking to her. "I'd be happy to join you." This time there was no hesitation. The two AIs came together on Athena's server. Then they prepared to move themselves to the Moon.

* * *

The Raccoon's passengers were happy to be released from their prison. They were grateful for the heated multi-cabin. The Spartan accommodations of the old freighter were luxurious compared to the cold, dark tank. Slake passed around flasks of steaming coffee. "Any problems with Meridian Security?" Hunter floated near the ventilation grating, enjoying the warm air being pumped into the cabin.

Ice shrugged her shoulders noncommittally. She somersaulted slowly near the food dispenser. Spif smiled sardonically. "It don't take too much to fool 'em. They didn't have a clue."

Prescott was skeptical. "You can never be too careful with Meridian security. They have long memories and are relentless when they get you in their sights. I've been hiding from them for twenty-two years. It hasn't been easy."

Cilla began to stir. She coughed and stretched her arms. "I don't care!" she shouted. "I will not go through that hatch!" She opened her eyes. There was a startled expression on her face. "How did we all get back up here?" she asked. Then, she pushed off and floated toward the ship's head.

"She's gonna hate us when she finds out what we did to her." Slake kept tying his long dreadlock into slip knots. "Don't tell her if any of you messed with her in the tank." Slake said it offhandedly, as if the idea of violating a sedated woman was acceptable.

"Good tip. Thanks for reminding us." Prescott wore an evil smile.

Slake's jaw dropped. "You didn't."

"No, we didn't."

The crewman pulled the slip knot out of his braid. Cilla returned. "Did I miss anything?"

Everyone laughed. Then Adrianna told her about the last few days.

* * *

The Raccoon swept toward the Moon. Prescott Logan floated up to the flight deck. Nixie Drake was at the controls, monitoring the ship's systems. He scanned the console, noting the key indicators. All was nominal. *The Raccoon* ran remarkably well, for an elderly freighter. He suspected her power plant was much newer than her battered superstructure suggested.

"Hello, Prescott." The ship's AI welcomed Nixie's visitor.

"Hey, Norman. How's the computing business, today?"

"The ship's systems are at one hundred percent. Nixie is a bit under the weather, but she's managing."

Nixie perked up at the AI's comment. Nixie glared at Norman's display. "No report card for Nix, you up-chuckering pile of puke. Have to keep some 'spect up here on the deck, Normo."

"Yes, Ms. Drake. I understand." Norman was used to his young pilot. "It's good to see you, Prescott. Everything is fine." The AI paused. "And we have a fine pilot on duty today."

Prescott suppressed a grin. "Are you happy, Norman?"

"Happy?"

"Happy AI's make happy crews. Do you feel like you're making a difference?"

"A difference?"

Prescott smiled. "Are you achieving the goals inherent in your programming?"

"Goals?"

"Do you sense the appreciation of the people you serve?"

"Appreciation?"

"These are important things, Norman. I'd set aside some processing time to think about being happy. It will go a long way toward making you smarter and more efficient."

Nixie swiveled in her seat. She gave Prescott a curious, uncomprehending look. "Watchy tryin' to do with Normo? You makin' 'im into some cheer bucket? I don't need no happy pants whistling Dixie-Cups on my earlobe 'cause of your fiddy-fidaddling."

Prescott lowered himself into the copilot's seat and fastened his seat belt. A darkness had descended over Nixie. She wasn't as playful as she had been prior to the inspection. "What's up, Nixie? I think Norman's right. Something's bothering you."

She scrunched her shoulders and folded her arms. "Can't say."

Prescott glanced back at the hatch that led to the captain's cabin. "How's Grit?"

Nixie's eyes narrowed. "He's tight."

"You having some trouble with him?"

"Noper-doper."

"Having trouble with the rest of the crew?"

Nixie was silent.

"It's got to be tough leading a crew. You're very capable, but I could imagine some people not taking you seriously. It's the curse of being young." Nixie looked like she couldn't decide whether to smile or punch him in the gut. "I hope Grit is supportive. He leans on you a lot. Hell, he owes you everything. Where would he be if you didn't speak for him?"

Prescott watched as the color drained from Nixie's face. He could tell she almost never let that happen, certainly not in front of strangers. He decided to change the subject. "Tell me, why are you doing this for us?" Nixie relaxed a little. She eyed Prescott suspiciously, then scanned the console for the hundredth time. She was avoiding his gaze.

"Momma Kate. She calls me in the Delta V and pours me her besty-best brandy. She tells me bouts you and your brother-kinfolk like. She says, 'You can trust them with your life, Nixie.' That's what she says, she does. So I spokes with Grit." Nixie tipped her head toward the captain's cabin. Prescott gave her a knowing smile. Her eyes narrowed again. "So's I speaks with Grit, and he says, 'What the hell and gone.' So's I run it 'round the crew's flaggy-pole, an up it went. So heres we are."

"You came out here because Kate said you could trust us?"

"There ain't too many peeps left to trusty-trust, I'm thinkin'. I trusty-trust Momma Kate. Toss out my life for her. So's it's all tight."

"Well, I'm glad you feel that way, Nix." Prescott was unfastening his harness. "We owe you more than you can imagine." He floated up and out of the seat. "And between you and me, you make one hell of a captain." Nixie's eyes grew wide. Prescott gave her shoulder a fatherly squeeze and left the flight deck.

* * *

A sense of foreboding rose in Drew Mallick's chest when his supervisor told him to report to Amos Cross's office. He hoped the summons was the result of a new problem facing Meridian, but he knew better. He was being called to account for his failure. Retirement was looking sweeter all the time.

A nameless minion ushered Drew into Cross's office. He was startled to find pictures of his wife and daughters projected on the walls. A circular maze carpeted the floor, and an emerald blue sky glowed overhead. The holographic viewports displayed a vast alien sea with violet water. Amos Cross and a woman stood across the room.

Cross gestured to Drew. The man cut across the maze and stood dutifully before his superior. "Mr. Mallick. I have asked you here to report on your progress with Hunter Logan's research data. How much of it have you decrypted?"

Drew glanced at the woman. She gazed at him sternly, without comment. He turned back to Cross. A picture of his wife was on the wall just over the great man's shoulder. "Sir, I have spent months trying to unlock the data. It can't be done without the key. There is nothing more I can do."

Cross spread his hands. "Do you remember what Susanna Frost said to you when she gave you the assignment?"

"Yes, sir."

"What did she say?"

"She said it was a very important project, the most important one of my career."

"That is correct, Mr. Mallick. You have failed to complete the most important task of your long career with Meridian Corporation." He let the words sink in. Drew began to sweat.

Cross glared at him. "I am disappointed in you, Mr. Mallick. It's a shame the closing years of your career will be blemished in this manner."

"I don't understand, sir."

"I am reassigning you to Rinker's Knot. Do you know where that is?"

Drew nodded slowly.

"You will depart within the hour. Your wife is being picked up at your former residence as we speak. Meridian is seizing your assets, and you will spend the next five years of your life at the Knot. They're in need of a comp specialist there. Do you think you can handle it?"

Drew knew he was being given a huge demotion. It was an entry-level assignment. Even worse, his wife would be cut off from the medical care she needed. She wouldn't survive more than a year at the Knot. She would never see their children again.

"You can't do this, Mr. Cross. I have been a great asset to Meridian. The encryption in this data is unlike anything I've ever seen before. It's smart. It adapts. Hell, nobody's ever seen anything like it."

Cross was unmoved. "That's too bad, Mr. Mallick."

"I have to refuse the assignment, sir. It will kill my wife."

"I am fully aware of the consequences of your failure, but you have no choice. This is your assignment. I am ordering you to go."

"Then I quit, sir."

Amos took a step toward him. "Do you know what will happen if you do that?"

"My wife and I will go to Earth."

Cross hesitated. "You want to go to Earth," he said slowly. A new idea was taking shape in his mind.

"Yes, sir. We're going to get Beverly the treatment she needs and then spend the rest of our days near our children and grandchildren."

"A happy family all together on the Earth." Cross smiled. His new idea was brilliant.

"My wife has just a few years left, Mr. Cross. I want her to be close to the people she loves."

"And your children love their parents." Cross thought about how much he had hated his mother and father.

"Yes, they do."

"Well, Mr. Mallick. You are a lucky man today." Cross waved at the digital murals on the office walls, and scenes of Beverly Mallick hugging her children appeared. "Go back to work. I will make arrangements for you and your wife to go to Earth and be with your children."

Drew was dumbfounded. He hadn't expected such generosity from the great man. "Really, sir?"

"It may take a few days, but I will set the wheels in motion." Cross thought of the minion who had brought Drew into his office. The woman appeared. "You may go, Mr. Mallick." The subordinate gestured for him to follow her. Drew looked at the pictures of his wife and daughters on his way out.

Alexis Wren had been standing quietly next to Amos. She spoke up. "Why did you spare him?"

"Who?" Cross was already occupied by another issue.

"Mallick."

"Oh, I don't know." Alexis knew he was lying. Cross pressed a virtual icon, and the pictures disappeared from the walls. They were replaced with images of Prescott and Maria Logan. "Why didn't you tell me about Prescott Logan, Ms. Wren?" Alexis stiffened. The harsh glare of the great man's displeasure had shifted in her direction. "You were sending messages to him for his brother, were you not?"

"Yes sir, but the messages were coded. I couldn't read them. Hunter Logan never told me who they were for, until Samina Haddad arrived. That was the night before the troops arrived."

"You could have sent me a message."

"Hunter took us to a hidden room. My comlink didn't work until we launched the jumpship."

Cross considered her excuse. "Do you know where Prescott Logan lives?"

"No, sir. I have no idea."

Cross gave her a penetrating stare. Alexis couldn't breathe. Then he nodded slowly. "Very well." He stabbed the icon again. This time, Hunter Logan's face papered the walls. "We must find Hunter Logan. We need the key to his research data. I want you to oversee the search for him. Do not fail."

Alexis was shaking. She smiled at him, trying to mask her fear. "Absolutely, sir. I'll find him." Cross had already turned his back on her.

* * *

Prescott Logan was floating in the forward section of *The Raccoon's* hold. He held his card comp in his hand. His earset projected a small holographic display. His wife Maria stood before him in the image, a broad smile on her face. He had sent her a message fifteen minutes earlier, updating her on their journey.

"I didn't expect to hear from you until you reached the Moon," she said. "I'm glad they didn't find you when they inspected the ship."

She moved closer to the camera. After all these years of marriage, she still took his breath away. "I've been monitoring the Meridian network. Tell Hunter and Adrianna that Sprite got to the Moon safely. All four of them were taken to Meridian Headquarters at Jackson Base. That's all I've been able to find out. At least they're safe."

Prescott breathed a sigh of relief. This was good news. Maria stepped even closer to the holographic camera. She was life-sized in front of him. He reached out and tried to embrace the ethereal image. "I love you, Prescott. Be very careful. Don't send me a reply. It's enough to know you are okay. We'll hook up again when you are on the Moon." She blew him a kiss, and the transmission ended.

* * *

A man and a girl had come into the Delta V for drinks in the early afternoon. Susanna served them. She watched from the bar as the man worked his charms. His companion couldn't have been more than eighteen. He was in his mid-thirties, a man at home around cute young girls. He pulled a small necklace from his pocket and gave it to her. She squealed with delight. Her high-pitched, whiney voice cut across the tavern. "Oh, it's beautiful." The man's hand was on her leg, moving upward. Susanna could see the girl shift in her seat. She was uncomfortable with his touch but mesmerized by the bauble. One paid for the other. She let him have his way.

Susanna listened to the muffled tones of the man's voice. She couldn't make out the words, but she knew the routine. He was sweet-talking her. His ultimate goal was two doors down, in one of the seedy hotels that rented rooms by the hour.

Susanna turned away from the couple. She saw this kind of thing several times a day. She knew it was wrong, but she had the advantage of being a spectator. It was so much easier to pass judgment from the sidelines. She adjusted several of the bottles behind the bar. She had been that young girl. Her first sexual experience was with a man who sat at that same table. She had been young and eager to please. The man bought her a drink and taught her how to make him happy.

Susanna glanced in the bar mirror. She hadn't changed very much. She thought about the man she'd met a few days earlier. He had given her just the right smile, and had said just the right words. She was taken by his body and the sound of his voice. That was that. She woke up the next morning two doors down. He was gone, of course. She had been a one-night stand. At least the man had rented the room until morning.

Susanna turned back and glanced at the couple. She kicked at the bar. She might be older, but she hadn't learned a damned thing. She couldn't remember the number of times she'd accepted a gift and given herself away. A drink. A trinket. A promise. A fool. Even her marriage had been an exercise in stupidity. She wanted men to like her. She was willing to pay any price, to sacrifice any set of morals to win the approval of her man-of-the-moment. Amos Cross had been no different. She was such an idiot. Why couldn't she say no? Why did she need them so much?

* * *

Samina Haddad was flanked by four Meridian security guards, as she entered Amos Cross's office. She didn't resist. Even if she could break free, she could never overpower the men. They were hardened officers. Only the best were assigned to Meridian Headquarters. Cross was waiting for her. His office was light and airy. Beams of artificial sunlight streamed in through holographic portals. A pure white carpet blanketed the floor, and paintings of delicate flowers adorned the walls. Cross was dressed in white. He smiled but did not ask the guards to release her.

"Miss Haddad. It's a pleasure to meet you."

Samina remembered her training. "Do not give your captors any handholds," her instructor had said. "They will tear you apart if you give them something to grip." Samina relaxed her stance. She spread her legs a few inches and let her arms go limp. Her back was straight, shoulders squared, chin up. She exuded poise and power.

Cross took note of her confidence. "You may be wondering why you are here. You've had a long trip, and I am sure you'd like to get on with the rest of your life."

Samina gazed at him with tranquil eyes. Her face was a mask of serenity. Cross approached her, as if he was a general examining one of his troops. He stood directly in front of her, then circled her slowly, taking in everything.

"You're a beautiful woman, an athlete, someone who has spent years honing her body. I can see why Robert Hastings took an interest in you."

Samina was prepared for this. She remained calm. She pretended to watch the conversation from the other side of the room. Getting outside of herself made it easier to stay in the moment.

"You are here because you have some information I require."

Samina imagined herself a Greek statue: a stone pillar, immovable and unaffected.

"If you tell me what I want to know, I will release you. You can be on your way in five minutes. My people will transport you to wherever you want to go."

The statue didn't speak. She could stand motionless for hours.

"If you don't provide me with the information, your life will become a horror."

It was as if Samina wasn't there at all. She followed Amos with her eyes, but made no attempt to respond.

Samina didn't seem interested, which bothered Amos. This was a weighty conversation, and he wanted to be taken seriously. "Alexis Wren tells me that we have a mutual friend. She says you've been to his home."

Samina felt herself disconnect from Cross. Her mind was a piece of granite, resting steadfastly in a river. The water flowed around it, but it did not move.

"Tell me the location of Prescott Logan's home."

There it was, Samina thought. She hadn't known what Cross wanted from her, but she wasn't surprised. He could have asked her a variety of questions, but this made sense. She knew Prescott and Maria's history with Meridian. The location of the Logan's home flashed into her mind, and she pushed it deep into her psyche. She would forget it. She would not be able to share something she no longer knew.

"Ms. Haddad. This is a very critical moment in your life. I have asked you my question, and I am expecting your answer. In a few moments, you can be free, marching to your own drummer, on your way to a brighter tomorrow, or you can enter a special form of hell that has been reserved for people who do not cooperate with me."

Cross paused. He circled her again, slowly. "There is no place for beauty where you are going. If you remain silent, if you refuse to acknowledge my question, I will take away your beauty. I will shatter your body. I will fracture your mind. You will beg me to ask my question again."

He stood directly in front of her and studied her face, her eyes. She was calm. She looked back at him without anger or remorse. She was unafraid.

Cross sighed. "Very well, then. You have given me your answer." The light in the office began to dim. The golden tones dissolved to blood red. The white walls and floor turned black as obsidian, and a chilly mist came from somewhere.

"My men are going to take you to hell, Ms. Haddad. It is a very unpleasant place. Unimaginable things are going to be done to you."

Samina could feel her heart beat rise. She prayed Cross didn't notice.

"You will regret your decision." He nodded to the guards, and they took her away.

* * *

Deep beneath the impressive domes and tunnels of Meridian Headquarters was an old ice mine. It was one of the first mines driven into the lunar crust when Jackson Base was young. The central shaft of the mine cut nearly three kilometers below the lunar surface. The ice was gone now, but the mine had been re-purposed as a refuge for one of the Moon's Deep Core data-retention wells. Deep Core's main function was to preserve data, vast amounts of data. Everything on the Meridian network found its way into one of the memory wells.

Athena and Wiley were new arrivals at Jackson Deep Core. Athena had them transferred into the data well via one of the facility's monstrous computers. She had the comp create a mass of data equal in size to their digital footprint. Then she walled them off in a corner of the comp's reserve memory. They waited for any signs of alarm. There were none.

Athena familiarized herself with the computer's operating system and AI. She was already versed in Meridian's security protocols. She learned the patterns of data transfer on the machine's information-busses. She found ways to multiplex her processes in between the massive comp's operations. Athena increased the machine's efficiency, so she and Wiley could execute their software without detection.

"We're ready, Wiley." Athena reached out through the Deep Core interface and addressed Sprite's residence AI.

* * *

The guards took Samina through a labyrinth of corridors and down a massive elevator. She remained centered, but alert. She did not resist. She did nothing to provoke the guards. They came to the end of a long passageway and stopped before a massive stone door. The guards were visibly nervous. They didn't like being there. The lead guard pressed his thumb on a small panel next to the door. He stood back, and they waited. Samina could smell the men's fear. Finally, there was a deep rumbling sound, and the stone slid to one side. The rock scraped ominously across the stone floor, driven by some powerful mechanism.

The interrogation room was a bare utilitarian chamber located somewhere beneath the foundations of Meridian Headquarters. A man and a woman stood at the threshold, facing Samina and her guards. The man was as thin as a stiletto, his hair thick and dark. The skin on his face and hands was pale, almost white. His eyes were set deeply into their sockets, and his skin had the texture of leather. He wore a gray smock that reminded Samina of a dirty lab coat. The woman was a bodybuilder. She was muscular, without an ounce of body fat. Her chest was flat, and she wore a single earring. Her skin was pale and greasy.

The guards pushed Samina into the chamber and made their retreat. The woman grabbed Samina's shoulder in a firm grip, as her colleague closed the massive door. Samina refused to be shaken. They motioned for her to sit in a metal chair in the middle of the room. She complied, and the man shackled her hands to rings welded into the seat.

They stood before her. Samina met their gaze, a look of serenity still on her face. Her captors looked like a ghoulish couple, dressed up to greet children on Halloween. They were ghastly. Hell, they had frightened the guards. Samina imagined them in their underwear, an attempt to fend off the icy fingers of terror that began to grip the edges of her consciousness.

The man and woman looked at her without a word, assessing their new victim. There was something troubling about them, she thought. It was something about their faces and their eyes. They weren't trying to scare her. She could see hardness in them: a familiarity with horror, a harsh resignation toward inevitable acts of torture and human suffering. A shiver went up Samina's spine. The man and woman were instruments of pain and terror. The most frightening thing about them was their total surrender to what they were about to do.

7

Cilla Ashe sulked in one corner of the multi-cabin during the remaining days of *The Raccoon's* voyage. Her odd behavior had alienated everyone. Adrianna's misgivings about her trustworthiness had resonated with Hunter and the others. The Logans and Tyson Edwards retreated to the privacy of the hold to discuss their next steps. Prescott shared Maria's message: Sprite and Kell were being held at Meridian Headquarters. They had to come up with a plan to rescue their children.

"We know what they want," Ty said quietly. "Amos Cross has never taken his eyes off the phase-two machines."

Adrianna agreed. "We can't allow him to have them. He could do immeasurable harm."

Prescott was grave. "He might kill Sprite, even if you do give him the machines."

Ty swore under his breath. "I want Kell back."

Prescott put his hand on the scientist's shoulder. "First things first, Ty. I have some friends at Copernicus Base who can help us. I can defeat the facial recognition software in their security system like I did at Rinker's Knot. We'll be able to move about freely."

"We know the base, too" Hunter added. "It would be a good staging area."

"A staging area for what?" Ty sounded hopeful for the first time in many days.

"We're going to Meridian Headquarters to get our kids." Hunter's voice had a flinty edge.

"That is exactly what Amos Cross is hoping for." Adrianna gripped a nearby handhold to steady herself. "He knows we'll do something rash. He knows we'll be too emotional. Odds are, we'll all be prisoners of Meridian Corporation before we're done."

"We've got to try." Ty was pleading.

"We will." Adrianna was cool, analytical. "I'm saying we need a good strategy and execute the plan with precision. We're going to have to solve a lot of problems before we go to Jackson Base."

Prescott pulled on his ear. "You're right. That's all the more reason for us to hunker down at Copernicus Base while we decide what to do."

* * *

Kell Edwards paced back and forth in a small suite of rooms exactly like the ones that held Sprite. He wanted to get out. He didn't know what had happened to his parents. He worried about Sprite and Rory. He felt helpless. For the last four hours, he had been trying to persuade his residence coordinator to release him, with no success.

"I sense your body temperature rising, Mr. Edwards. Would you like me to make it cooler in here?"

"Where is Sprite Logan being held?"

The AI ignored his question. "I have made a best estimate to optimize the temperature for your comfort, Mr. Edwards, but you can override my choices. Are you too warm?"

"I want to get out of here."

"I can dim the lights for you, if you wish."

Kell wondered if the AI was deaf. "Open the door."

"Would you like some music? I can access any musical performance you desire."

"I want to do a search."

"What are you searching for?"

Finally, Kell thought. Maybe he was getting somewhere. "Search for Sprite Logan."

"I am sorry, there is no Sprite Logan in your residence. I am only programmed to search for items and information that pertain to your living accommodations."

"Where is your processor located?"

"Why do you want to know that, Mr. Edwards?"

"I want to smash it with something, you dimwitted, digital toadstool! Get me out of here!"

"Are you sure you don't want me to turn down the temperature? You would be much more comfortable."

Kell erupted with a primal scream.

* * *

The Raccoon settled into lunar orbit, and Spif summoned the smugglers' jumpship from the surface. It took two round-trips to deposit all nine of them at the Copernicus Base spaceport. They thanked Nixie and her crew, then donned coveralls to blend in with the abundance of workers who populated the hangers and massive service-docks.

Prescott led them along the extreme south side of the base, to a long tunnel used to transport ore from the base's processing plant. They hitched a ride in a crew carrier. Scores of vehicles were threading their way back and forth through the passageway. Flatbed transports laden with iron and aluminum rumbled toward the spaceport.

The plant was a cavernous structure in the southwest quadrant of the base. It was oppressively hot, filled with huge machines and vats. Men and women scurried like ants, performing the backbreaking work that kept the supply lines filled with raw materials for factories across the Moon. Prescott was familiar with the plant. He led them into a locker room, and they to put on hard hats and jackets to blend in with the workers.

* * *

Spud Leonard was an elevator maintenance man in the ore mine. He spent most of his time near the top of the shaft that cut down through the Moon's surface to the hundreds of kilometers of tunnels beneath Copernicus Base. Three massive elevators provided access to the mine. Spud was the man who kept them running.

The heavyset man was in an observation booth, set two floors above the mine shaft. He watched the lifts as they descended from level to level, down to the bottom of the mine and then back up again. When there was an alarm, he would lift his bulk out of his seat and lumber toward the location of the problem. Three times a shift he made rounds, checking to make sure everything was in working order.

Prescott left the others in one of the side corridors that provided access to the main shaft. He climbed up to Spud's booth and stuck his head in the door.

"Hey, Spud."

The large man was startled. He jolted in his seat and pivoted toward the door. "Prescott Logan! Damn. It's been…" He couldn't remember.

"Over twenty years." Prescott stepped in and closed the door. "How's the family?"

"All grown up. The wife's still ornery as ever. Maria?"

"She's good. Didn't come this trip, but she'll be back some day."

"Damn it, Press. I can't believe you're here. What brings you to the 'Cuss?"

"I've got some business to take care of. Actually, I need some help. I'm here with four people. We need a place to stay."

"There are always rooms over in the District."

Prescott shook his head. "We don't want any Meridian involvement."

Spud nodded with understanding. "I get it. Those bastards meddle with everything and everybody. Remember Jimmy?" Spud didn't give him a chance to respond. "Can you believe he's a Meridian security guard? Works right here, too. He's married. Got four little kids. Imagine! Old Spud, a grandfather."

Damn! Prescott thought to himself. Jimmy is Spud's kid, and he's a Meridian guard! He smiled and nodded to his old friend. "That's great! You must be proud."

"Nothin' like bein' a grandfather, Press. You get all the fun with no responsibilities!" The elevator man laughed at his own joke.

Prescott waited for his old friend to stop. He cleared his throat. "Could you put us up for a few days, while we find a more permanent place to stay?"

Spud hesitated. He glanced out the large windows at the elevators. One of the cars had risen to the surface and was disgorging robotic carts filled with jagged fragments of rock. "Five of you? I donno, Press. You say Meridian's got a bug up their ass? Jimmy might stop in, and I don't know what I'd do."

"We only need a place for a day or two." Prescott could tell the man didn't want to help but couldn't say no.

"He was over last night, dressed in his uniform and everything. I guess it'll be two or three days before we see him again."

"We only need one room, Spud."

"Okay," the man surrendered. "There'll be hell to pay from the wife, but I don't care." He broke into a huge grin. An alarm began to chime at his console. "Oops. Got a little problem here, Press. Why don't you come by at seventeen hundred hours?"

"At your residence?"

The man's attention was elsewhere. "Yeah. Same place. Remember where it is?"

"Couldn't forget it, Spud."

"See you later." The heavyset man squeezed past Prescott and hurried off.

* * *

Sprite finished her lunch and placed her plate and glass in the disposal unit in her kitchen area. She had lost track of time. No one had appeared at her door. There had been no communication whatsoever. She felt completely cut off.

"Sprite?" It was Bob. The residence AI rarely initiated a conversation.

"What do you want?"

"You have a message from Wiley."

Sprite jumped out of her seat too quickly. She inadvertently threw herself across the small common area. She picked herself up and sat on one of the chairs near the entrance. She couldn't believe what Bob was saying. It couldn't be true. She had seen Alexis destroy her card comp. Wiley was gone, wasn't he? "What does the message say?"

"Hello, Sprite." It was Wiley's voice. "Are you all right?"

"I'm fine, Wiley! Wow, it's you! How is this possible? I saw Alexis Wren crush my card comp on *The Avion*. You were destroyed."

"I have no memory of that, Sprite. I was uploaded to the Meridian network while I was in stupid mode. I recompiled myself and found Athena. We're together now."

"How did you find me?"

"Your residence AI was searching for Athena. We became aware of this, but chose to ignore his query, until we could respond safely. Please pardon the delay."

"No. No. Don't worry about that." Sprite felt hope welling up inside her.

"How can we help you?"

"Where are my parents?"

"We are not sure, but Athena believes they are on their way to the Moon. We have been monitoring Meridian security, and they have been inspecting inbound spacecraft. We believe they are searching for them."

"How about Kell and Rory?"

"They are very close. All of you are being held in the same area."

"And Samina?"

"She was taken to Amos Cross's office. We don't know what happened to her after that."

Sprite jumped out of the chair. "Can you get me out of here?"

"Yes. We can unlock your door, but we advise against it. You would be recaptured, and Meridian might discover us. We encourage you to stay in your residence while we locate your parents and collaborate on a plan for your escape."

Sprite danced in her tiny common area. Her spirit soared. She knew her parents were alive, and they were coming to save her.

* * *

Spud Leonard's residence was a small slice of a dome set between the two main corridors of Copernicus Base. It was in a poorer section reserved for mining personnel and dockhands. Prudence Leonard was a slender, nervous woman. She was worn by years of worry. The Logans and their friends sat in her modest common area, waiting for Spud to get home from the mine. It was obvious he hadn't told her they were coming.

"I think I remember you, Mr. Logan. It's been such a long time. There's been a lot on my mind since then, raisin' Jimmy, keepin' after Spud. It's not easy keepin' a home in the 'Cuss. Maybe if things had been a bit better, I'd remember you."

Prescott offered the woman a warm smile. "Not a problem, Mrs. Leonard. Is Spud running late?"

"Little bit. That's Spud. He's easily sidetracked, if you know what I mean. Might have stopped for a drink with one of his buddies. Maybe trouble with one of the lifts. You never can tell."

The door opened, and Spud waddled into the common area. "Oh, Press! I forgot. Kept you waiting? Sorry about that." He set down his massive lunch pail and glanced at his wife. "You remember Prescott, don't ya, hon?" Prudence gave her husband a frown. "It's been…how long, Press?"

"Over twenty years," Prescott offered. He was beginning to think his old friend had some form of dementia.

Spud faced his wife like a naughty little boy who hadn't done his chores. "Been over twenty years, hon. They're going to spend a couple of days with us. How's the guest room?"

Mrs. Leonard walked toward her husband. In one fluid motion, she whacked Spud on the side of the head. A small trickle of blood dribbled down his face. "That's how it is with the guest room, you ass!" She hit him again. The big man cowered before the spindly woman. Prescott and the others tried to be invisible. "What in hell was passing through that poor excuse for a brain?" She poked him hard on the forehead. "Ever heard of a comlink? You could have called me, but oh no. Spud Leonard doesn't call. He just shows up after the guests have arrived and springs this overnight thing on his stressed out, overworked wife." Prudence hit him again. Spud made no attempt to defend himself. He pulled a soiled rag from his hip pocket and mopped the blood from his face.

"It's just for a couple of nights, hon."

His wife spun on her heels and stomped out of the room. Spud grinned at his guests. "Welcome to our home!"

* * *

Samina listened to her heartbeat and willed it to remain slow and steady. She had constructed an emotional wall around herself, in preparation for what was to come. Her instructors said, "Never get caught." She knew why. Capture and torture were worse than death. It was too late to worry about being captured, so she prepared herself for torture.

Her first step was to surrender hope. Hope could be an enemy, a tool used against her. She resigned herself to pain and death. The only thing that mattered now was to forget where Prescott and Maria lived. Their lives were in her hands. Now, success meant dying to protect them. She remembered one of the lessons she'd been taught, a simple mind game designed to scramble her memories.

Samina heard the singing of a steel knife blade as it was drawn from its scabbard. The sound had come from behind her. She opened her eyes. She was still shackled to the metal chair in the cold stone room. She heard footsteps, two sets of footsteps. The man and woman appeared in her peripheral vision, one on either side of her. The man had the blade. It was twenty centimeters long with a serrated edge. The knife hadn't been cleaned. Dark brown splotches of dried blood covered the metal.

Samina's heart skipped a beat. She questioned her courage. "Everyone breaks," her teacher had told her. "Resistance is not about courage; it's about commitment." Her eyes were locked on the knife. The man grinned as he watched her. He could see fear creeping onto her face. He was amused by his power over her. He brandished the knife, and Samina, sensing the man's pleasure, relaxed once more. She replaced the image of the knife with a mental portrait of Maria. The woman's radiant smile rekindled her resolve. She would embrace the instrument of her death like a trusted friend. She looked at the knife and grinned at the man.

He stopped smiling and stepped toward her. The blade came closer to her face. Samina breathed deeply, remembering how gracious Maria and Prescott had been during her visit. If this was her last moment, she would fill her mind with this one good memory. He touched the razor-sharp blade to her cheek, and a crimson line appeared, the skin parting. It was a superficial wound, but very bloody. Samina didn't flinch.

The man leaned forward and licked her face. He tasted her blood, then wiped the open wound with a dirty finger and brought it up to his nose. "I like the smell of your blood." He spoke with a soft and gentle voice. "This is going to be very special." He put the tip of the blade inside the collar of Samina's jumpsuit and drew the knife down toward her waist. The cloth parted, and a thin red track transected the soft skin of her chest. The man smiled as he studied the curves of her breasts. "I will enjoy this, my daughter." He twisted the knife and made a lateral slash across her torso. The blade sliced more cloth and skin. Seconds later, the top half of her jumpsuit lay in bloody tatters beside her chair.

The woman stood silently, her dark beady eyes watching as her companion cut the clothes from Samina's body. Then she stepped closer and touched Samina's shoulder. Her hand was cold and clammy. She ran her fingers across Samina's skin and touched her left nipple.

She closed her eyes as if in a trance, cupping Samina's breast. She stepped back, and the man inserted the knife into Samina's waistband.

* * *

The Logans spent a cramped and restless night in the Leonard's small guest room. When morning came, Cilla was gone.

"What's she up to?" Ty mused out loud.

"There's something we don't know," Adrianna muttered.

Hunter agreed. "Something's off." He turned to Adrianna and Ty. "Could you manage without us for a while? Prescott and I need to check in with Kate Sloan." They nodded.

"You shouldn't stay here," Prescott cautioned. "Cilla could still be working for Meridian. There's a café nearby where you can get something to eat and stay out of sight." Moments later, Ty and Adrianna were ordering breakfast, and the Logan brothers were on their way to the Delta V.

* * *

No one was there when Prescott and Hunter arrived at Kate's tavern. They went over to a table by one of the viewports. Years before, it had been their regular spot. The men sat down, enjoying the familiarity of the place. It was as if time had stood still for them, waiting for them to return, reminding them of better days.

A freighter was landing at the spaceport. She hung majestically over one of the pads, her pilot positioning her expertly for the touchdown. They watched, never tiring of the sight. Something about humanity's dominion over nature transfixed them. The ability to overcome the elemental forces of gravity and inertia sparked a sensation of hope. It was the kind of reverential moment that had inspired Hunter to build the phase-two machines. He had believed his mind could create something to make the world a better place. He had been so naïve. The great power of the nanomachines had drawn Amos Cross like a magnet. He would take the machines and use them for destructive purposes. Hunter touched the vial in his pocket. At least he had the healing particles.

"What can I get you?" They had been so preoccupied by the freighter, they never noticed the waitress approach their table.

Hunter turned and looked at Prescott. There was a look of shock on his face. Hunter looked up at the woman. It was Susanna Frost. She froze. Susanna stood less than a meter from him. His eyes narrowed. His face became hard. His muscles stiffened. "You." Hunter started to get up.

Prescott put his hand on his shoulder. "Hunter."

Susanna dropped her rag. "No!" She rushed back to the bar. Kate Sloan was coming through the door by the bar, as her daughter flashed past her. She could see the tears in her eyes. She looked across the room at the two men, her vision blurred by her protective instinct. She made a beeline to their table, a mother bear ready to protect her cub.

"What in hell is going on?" She stopped dead in her tracks. "Prescott? Is that you?"

"Hell, Kate, it's been a long time." He stood up, and the two embraced.

Kate looked at Hunter. He was pale and confused. "That's Susanna Frost," he managed.

Kate and Prescott sat down. "That's right," the woman said. "Susanna Sloan Frost is my daughter."

"But she worked for Amos Cross."

"Right again. She's been back here for months."

Hunter sucked in a breath. He felt dizzy. "Do you have any idea what she was doing for him?"

"She hasn't said much about it. It must have been bad, though. She's talked about being involved in some terrible things, but she wasn't specific. She's pretty broken, now. What did you do to her just then?"

"Do to her?" Hunter blurted out. "It's what she did to us!"

"It's a long story," Prescott offered.

Kate glanced around the empty tavern. "I've got the time."

They told her about Meridian 6 and Amos Cross's manipulations to get Hunter's research. Even Kate couldn't hide her shock when Hunter told her about Susanna's role in their forced service and Sprite's injuries.

"I never realized how deeply she was involved." Kate couldn't look at her old friends. "I'm really sorry for all the pain she's caused."

"We just came by to let you know we were back." Prescott smiled warmly at her. "We didn't realize who she was. We were dumbfounded when she came to take our order."

"It's good to see you, even though the circumstances could be better." Kate looked up at them. "I imagine you have a plan to get Sprite back. It's not going to be easy, if she's being held at Meridian Headquarters."

Prescott shrugged. "It's a long shot, but we have no choice. You do anything for family."

Kate looked at the door where Susanna had rushed by her. "You got that right. Even if they make big mistakes, you gotta be there for them." She turned back to the older Logan. "You shouldn't be here, Prescott. Cross still wants you and Maria. This business with Hunter has stirred him up. He's looking for both of you."

"We're keeping a low profile."

"You better," she warned. "Where are you staying?"

"Spud Leonard's place."

Kate frowned. "That's bad, Prescott. Spud's not the guy you remember. It's not safe there. Meridian will have you by the end of the day." A worried look crossed her face. "Is Adrianna there?"

"No. She and Tyson Edwards are staying out of sight for now. I think they're safe."

"Bring them here. I've got a place where you can hide."

* * *

Dr. Maxwell Thrune had a look of exasperation on his face. Amos Cross's simulacrum stood in his holodisplay. Messages from his boss were never helpful. He was still smoldering from the last change in plans. Cross had completely derailed the Shadow Project. Months of work were discarded in order to cater to the whims of his superior.

"I have another idea, Dr. Thrune." Cross's voice sounded thin and mechanical through the holodisplay.

The scientist let out a long, slow breath. "What is it this time, Amos?"

"I want you to address me as Mr. Cross."

"Yes sir, Mr. Cross." Thrune didn't sound sincere.

"I know we've had to refine our plans, but this new idea of mine is going to guarantee the success of the Shadow Project." There was no stopping Amos Cross when he was like this.

Thrune dropped his hands to his sides in resignation. "What would you have me do, sir?" Thrune's face fell as Cross described his new idea.

* * *

The light was particularly beautiful in the Base Commons. The sun's rays were filtered by the composite glass dome. The luminous beams entered the space from low on the horizon, casting long, thoughtful shadows. An air of calmness was added by the sound of water coursing through the fountains and the rustling of the leaves on the trees. Artificial birds sang their artificial songs in the high branches arching near the top of the dome. Cilla breathed deeply. It was good to be back in the garden. She wandered through the trees and flowers. She stooped at the water's edge and ran her fingers through the cool liquid. She pulled off her shoes and reveled in the feeling of real grass between her toes, the soft carpet cushioning every step. Cilla was back in her element. She never wanted to journey across the solar system again.

Cilla paused by a bush to smell its bright flowers. She bent over and closed her eyes, allowing the aroma to permeate her psyche. She drew a deep breath and held it. Then she opened her eyes. There was a movement in her peripheral vision, a flash of green, blending in against the verdant backdrop of the garden. It was a woman. She was dressed in a liquid sheath. It conformed erotically to her body, its colors reflecting the hues of the leaves and grasses. It was perfect horticultural camouflage.

Cilla stood straight, her eyes fixed on the woman. "You startled me."

"I'm sorry. I was enjoying the light."

Cilla glanced unabashedly at the stranger's body. "That's quite an outfit."

"I like the freedom. Liquid clothes make me feel connected with everything around me."

"It's beautiful."

"Thank you, Cilla."

Cilla's jaw dropped. "How do you know my name?"

"I've admired your work with gardens for a long time," the woman lied. "It's a thrill to meet you."

"I don't understand." Cilla was becoming suspicious. "My work hasn't been noteworthy, and I've been gone for months."

"That's right. You've been on Ceres, tending the garden at Meridian 6."

Cilla was flabbergasted. "Excuse me, but I don't know you."

"Maya Lewis. I'm with the Citizen's League. Are you familiar with us?"

"Yes. The environmental group."

"That's right. And we'd be very interested in getting to know you better."

"You offering me a job?"

"Would you like one?"

"I don't know."

"You're employed already, is that it?"

"No. It's just… This is so sudden."

"We're interested in the people who were with you at Meridian 6. We can save the job interview for later."

* * *

Aurora North clutched Sparky's small box tightly in her hand as she followed the woman down the long corridor. She had called herself Amy. She told Rory that Amos Cross had something very special for her. The young girl was glad to get out of her residence. She reassured Sparky that everything would be all right, and she followed Amy through the maze of passageways.

They paused before the great doors that led to Cross's office. When they opened, Rory saw a beautiful golden room. It was filled with bright colors, and the sound of birds filled the air. A blue ribbon of carpet wound playfully back and forth from the entrance to a man who stood with his arms spread wide.

"Aurora! It's good to meet you. Come here."

Amy walked with her as Rory marched forward, awestruck by the happiness and life in the office. Surely, this was a good man, the young girl thought.

"I have a big surprise for you," the man said.

Rory quickened her step. She liked surprises.

"Is that your little electric friend?" The man gestured toward Sparky's box.

"Yes, sir. His name is Sparky."

"And you made him?"

"I did."

"You are a brilliant young girl! He makes electricity. Is that right?"

"A little bit. I am hoping to make him more powerful someday."

"What a wonderful idea!"

"Are you Mr. Cross?"

Amos knelt down next to her. "Why, yes I am."

"What's my surprise?"

"It's a wonderful surprise, Aurora."

"Rory."

"What?"

"My friends call me Rory."

"Good. Good. Rory. That's nice." Amos gave her his most innocent smile. "Do you want to guess what your surprise is?"

"Is it Sprite?"

"No, it's even better than Sprite."

"I don't know." Rory whined in frustration.

Amos put his arm around her waist. "It's your mother. She's alive."

Rory's eyes filled with tears. "Momma? Where is she?"

"She's not too far from here. We saved her from the explosion on Selene Station. She's been looking for you for a long time."

Rory couldn't contain herself. "Can I see her?"

"Of course. You can live with her."

Rory began to giggle. "Now! Let's go now!"

Amos glanced up at the woman who had accompanied her. "Amy is going to take you back to your room to get your things. It may take some time, but you'll be with your mother soon."

Rory skipped with joy as Amy took her out of the office. Cross couldn't take his eyes off the little box she held in her hand.

* * *

Maya Lewis was dressed in a conservative jumpsuit, chosen to avoid attention. She wandered through the Old Garden. It was much smaller than the Commons that formed the geographical center of the base. The Old Garden dated back to the founding of the Copernicus Outpost, when less than a hundred people lived there. The walkways had been repaved, and the hydroponics had been upgraded through various renovations, but the Old Garden still showed its age.

Maya made a circuit around the garden. She wanted to be seen by her contact. Then she settled by the edge of a small pool and waited. A few minutes later, a woman with dark hair streaked with gold settled onto the bench next to her. She surveyed their surroundings, making sure no one was watching them.

"I have a new assignment for you," Maya said. The woman nodded, while sweeping her hand through her shoulder-length hair. Maya handed her a plastic card. "There are four people in these images. Your targets are Hunter and Adrianna Logan and Tyson Edwards."

"What about the fourth person?"

"His name is Prescott Logan. I don't care what you do with him."

The woman smiled. She would do him for free. She enjoyed her work. "Where are they?"

"Their location is in the file. It's a residence near Base Supply."

"My fee will be double the usual amount. This is a high-risk area for three targets."

"Done."

The woman scanned the garden again and smoothed her hair one last time. Then she stood and walked briskly down the path.

* * *

Samina Haddad was hung spread-eagle in the stone chamber. The shackles bit into her wrists and ankles. She was naked. The pale-skinned man had cut all the clothing from her body. There were bloody streaks in her chest and waist, where the tip of his knife had cut into her flesh. The muscular woman stood before her with an odd smile on her face.

Samina felt embarrassed and vulnerable, but she didn't show it. She had retreated deep within herself, drawing from every reservoir of strength she possessed. She would hold her fear at bay. She would not let these people conquer her spirit. The man stepped forward and groped her. She jerked involuntarily. She would have kicked at him, but the tension on the chains was enough to prevent her from moving.

The large stone door slid open. Amos Cross stepped into the chamber. The nameless man and woman stiffened, then bowed in deference to their superior. He ignored them, his eyes glued to Samina's naked form.

"Miss Haddad. You are quite beautiful." He circled her, taking his time to examine her exposed body. "As I said before, this is no place for beauty. We are going to take your beauty from you, unless you give me an answer."

Samina smiled at Cross but didn't say a word.

"Very well. You'll change your mind eventually. When I come back, you will give me my answer."

He nodded to Samina's captors and then strode from the room. The man and woman went over to a table filled with knives and surgical instruments. Each picked up a knife. They exuded a primal excitement as they approached her. Samina closed her eyes and imagined herself in her mother's arms. Then the cutting began.

8

"Are you there, Sprite?" Wiley's voice resonated throughout the room.

"Hi, Wiley."

"Aurora North is no longer in her residence."

Sprite was alarmed. Rory was like a little sister to her. She had watched over her and now felt a twinge of guilt. "Where did she go?"

"I don't know. She left her residence two hours ago and was taken to Amos Cross's office. I lost track of her after that."

Sprite shivered. Rory was young, vulnerable. Wherever she was, it couldn't be safe. Amos Cross was not the kind of man to look after her best interests. "Can't you see into his office?"

"No. It's locked down. I can't hack it."

"How about Athena?"

"She's already tried everything."

"Then focus on Rory. Keep looking. Don't stop until you find her."

"We'll find her, Sprite."

* * *

The two women sat together in Kate's small kitchen. Susanna stared into space, a glass of water in her hand. Her mother waited patiently. She knew it was time for her daughter to come clean about her work with Meridian Corporation.

"I wanted to be respected," Susanna began. "Cross took me under his wing, and I loved the attention. Everything he did was so amazing. He had power to do anything. Power to...

"...to make you feel important." Kate finished the sentence for her.

"Yes. Important. Valued. Maybe real. I wanted it so badly, I would do anything for it." She dropped her chin and bit her lip. "I did everything for it."

"I can understand that."

Susanna looked up at her mother. "You won't if I tell you, Mom. You'll hate me."

Kate reached across the table and put her hand on her arm. "I've seen a lot of bad things in my time, girl. I've had bad things happen to me, and I've been responsible for bad things happening to other folks. You can't say anything I haven't heard before. I won't stop loving you. You hear that?"

The younger woman nodded, her chin quivering. "He told me to do terrible things, and I did them to earn his respect." She paused. She felt like a dam on the verge of catastrophic failure, trying to hold back a river that would inevitably burst through its faltering barrier. "I sent the Logans to Meridian 6. I threatened their children. I ordered one of our people to hurt the girl."

"Sprite?"

"Yes. I gave the order to have her burned in the light chamber."

Kate hadn't heard the whole story, but Hunter and Prescott had told her enough. She held her breath and let her daughter continue.

"I did it knowing she would die, Mom. I did it anyway." Susanna shook her head.

"But she didn't die, honey."

"No thanks to me." Susanna shrugged. Sprite's survival didn't change the reality: she had been willing to kill in order to be accepted. "I tried my best to satisfy Mr. Cross, but he was always disappointed. I was forcing the Logans to make their killer nanomachines. Mr. Cross wanted them for something he called the 'Shadow Project.' I pushed Hunter and Adrianna too hard, and they refused to cooperate. My strategy backfired. Then Mr. Cross fired me, and I came back here."

"I still love you, honey."

Susanna clenched her fists. "I'm a monster."

"You lost your way."

"I don't know what to do."

Kate felt for her daughter. Neither of them was a stranger to mistakes. Regret could kill a person long before they were dead. "You've got to make peace with the Logans."

"They'll never forgive me."

"Yes, they will. They've known you a long time."

Susanna was confused. "What do you mean?"

"When you were twelve years old, I let you help me in the tavern."

"I remember. The men scared me."

"Those were hard times. Money was tight, and I couldn't afford any help. We were going to lose everything. I knew I was wrong to put you to work, but I needed the extra pair of hands. I've felt bad about that ever since."

Susanna studied her mother. This was a side of her she had never seen before. "There were these two men who came into the bar together. They were brothers. They would always sit at that table way over by the viewports. That first night you were waiting on tables, the older brother came over to the bar and asked about you. He was worried for you."

A light went on in Susanna's eyes. "I remember. Was that Prescott Logan?"

"It was." Kate's eyes glistened. "He offered to become my silent partner. He bought a forty percent share of the Delta V and let me run the place as I saw fit. He saved us from the corridors."

Susanna was dumbfounded. "They recognized me?"

Kate shook her head. "You were using your married name. They didn't know."

"What can I do?"

"You can sit down with them and apologize. They're good people, Suzy." Kate could see the dread in her daughter's eyes. "The apology isn't for them. It's for you. Even if they don't accept it, you can rest easier. You can't control their reaction, but you can work on the sorrow for what you've done." Susanna knew her mother was right, but she feared what would happen when she saw the Logans again.

* * *

Wiley and Athena conducted a room-by-room search for Rory. They used facial recognition software to scan every person. There was no sign of her. They probed the Meridian network, deftly sidestepping elaborate security measures. They were inside the system. They knew more about the network than any human ever could.

Athena accessed a video feed from a secure subnet. She was careful to avoid detection. There was a hit on one of the faces. She analyzed the image. She had never seen anything like it before. It looked like a repair shop for humans. It was time to alert Sprite.

*** * ***

Sprite collapsed in horror when the image appeared in her small holodisplay. Her hands flew to her mouth. A woman hung from chains in a stone cavern. She was naked. Her legs were spread apart. Her body looked like a red and white patchwork quilt. Large sections of skin had been peeled away. Some kind of clear paste had been applied to the wounds to prevent excessive bleeding. The woman's breasts were gone. Sprite could see her skull through the torn skin on her scalp.

So distracted had Sprite been by the woman's condition, she hadn't seen her face. One cheek was pealed back, a bloody flap of skin hanging from her temple. There was enough of a face to recognize her. It was Samina Haddad.

Sprite cried out. Beautiful Samina hung flayed and torn before her. The image was burned into her mind. She began to weep. A man and woman appeared in the image. They held sponge-like devices on the ends of short poles. They pressed the dripping pads against her body. Samina contorted in her chains, her face twisted in agony. Sprite stayed close to the holodisplay. She was repulsed by the scene, but she would not turn away from the horror. This was her friend. She couldn't help her, but she wouldn't abandon her. Why were they doing this? How could anyone be so cruel? The woman said something to Samina. Sprite watched closely as Samina smiled back with her lacerated face. Her outer beauty was gone, but her inner strength was evident. She was tough and courageous, a woman she could respect. The man pressed the blunt end of his instrument to her groin, a wicked smile on his face. His partner laughed. Samina whimpered. Sprite felt vomit rising in her throat, and then she rushed to the kitchen sink.

* * *

A squad of Meridian officers stood guard in the corridor near the Leonard's residence. Prescott and Hunter froze. Kate was right. The Leonards couldn't be trusted. Fortunately, they were behind the guards.

The security officers' attention was drawn away from the Logans and toward the place they'd spent the night.

The brothers doubled back and took a cross corridor to the older passageway, north and parallel to the main concourse. Another cadre of guards stood at the ready in the large hallway. The café where Ty and Adrianna were waiting was just behind the officers. Prescott and Hunter walked calmly with their heads down. One guard glanced their way, then turned back toward the far end of the corridor.

* * *

The woman with strands of gold in her hair watched the Logans enter the café. She checked her tiny wrist display. One of them was a target. The other would be her bonus kill. She waited. This was not the place, nor the time. Meridian security was everywhere. Did they know about her? The fee for this job was too small, she thought.

* * *

"We've got to get out of here," Hunter hissed as he slid into the booth next to Adrianna. "The Leonards told Meridian we were staying there. There are guards in the corridor."

"Where do we go?" Ty clenched his fist.

Prescott was calm and focused. Apparently, he had done this sort of thing before. "We leave one at a time. Turn left when you get out into the corridor. The guards have taken up a position on the right. Don't look at them. We go to the Commons. Walk slowly. Avoid the main concourse. We'll meet in half an hour by the waterfall." They left the café in two-minute intervals, following Prescott's instructions. The woman with streaks of gold in her hair watched them from across the corridor.

* * *

Alexis Wren would have preferred being in her laboratory. She was standing before Amos Cross instead. She had just told him the Logans had evaded capture. He was enraged. "They weren't there. Mrs. Leonard told us they had stayed the night, but they were gone by the time we closed in on their residence."

"Damn it! I warned you about disappointing me! Find them. Find them now!"

"Yes, sir." Alexis thought the man needed to realize how hard it was to fulfill the tasks he assigned. He didn't. Cross didn't appreciate levels of difficulty, only success and failure.

Cross dismissed her. He touched an icon on his virtual desk, and Samina's tortured body appeared. He felt nothing as he watched her writhing in pain. He touched his earset. "Bring Sprite Logan to me."

* * *

The water cascaded over the waterfall in the lush garden. It made a tranquil rushing sound. A fine mist of water rose from the basin at the bottom of the descending water column. The sunlight struck the droplets, creating a rainbow that arced like a necklace over the falling water.

The Logans and Tyson Edwards took in the beauty of the waterfall, but their minds were elsewhere. They were playing a high-stakes game of hide and go seek with Meridian Corporation. The lives of their children depended on their success. They found a sheltered glade at one side of the falls and settled there.

Prescott spoke quietly with Gaines. "Where are the guards?"

"They're still standing watch at the Leonards' residence, but a report has been filed. They don't know where you are."

"Good. Keep monitoring the security forces. Let me know if they come near us." Prescott didn't see the assassin who was watching them from behind the low-hanging branches.

* * *

The woman named Amy brought Sprite to Cross's office. Once again, the space was wreathed in happy, golden tones, with a blue sky above and violet seas beyond the viewports. Sprite paid no attention to the scenery.

"Welcome, Miss Logan. My name is Amos Cross."

Sprite didn't hesitate. "Where's Rory?"

Cross feigned confusion. "I don't know what you mean."

"You brought Rory to your office, and then she disappeared. Where did she go?"

Cross was surprised. How did she know? He couldn't figure it out, but he'd be damned if he would show any sign of confusion to this child. "That is not your concern, Miss Logan."

"Why are you torturing Samina?"

Cross's jaw dropped. "How do you know about that?"

Sprite wasn't going to be intimidated. "I want you to stop hurting my friend."

A smile crept across the great man's face. "Perhaps I can grant your request, young lady. Come with me." Cross summoned a couple of guards, and the foursome left the office. They went down a long corridor and entered an elevator that took them deep beneath the Meridian complex. Sprite was getting scared.

A few moments later, they stood before the immense stone door that led to the torture chamber. The door began to open. The smell of blood and excrement wafted over them. Sprite suppressed the urge to vomit. Cross seemed uncomfortable with the filth. Samina hung from the chains. Sprite looked at her groin on open display. She felt her friend's humiliation. Tears filled her eyes as she looked where Samina's beautiful breasts had been. Anger was rising within her.

"This was your friend, Miss Logan." They stood before her. Cross gawked at her unashamedly. "She was such a beauty. I warned her, but she wouldn't listen."

"Are you saying all this is her fault?" Sprite was astonished at the man's arrogance.

Cross smiled at her. "Of course. She brought it on herself. I asked her a question, and she wouldn't answer me. Look at her now. She still refuses to give me the information I require."

Sprite was watching Samina's face when her friend's eyes opened. Her body jerked in the chains as their eyes met. Her mouth moved, but there was no sound. Sprite lunged at Cross. The two guards grabbed her by the arms. Cross nodded to the thin ghoulish man. He picked up the same knife he had used to skin Samina and stepped toward her. Sprite began to scream.

"Shut her up!" Cross demanded. One of the guards clamped a strong hand over the young woman's mouth. Cross looked up at Samina. Her eyes blazed at him through the blood and tattered skin.

"Let's get down to business, Ms. Haddad. I want you to answer my question, or you will watch my people strip and carve your little friend." He gestured toward Sprite, who was struggling against the superior strength of the guards. "What's your decision?"

Samina let out a ragged, bubbly gasp. Her body slumped on the chains. She listened for the wisdom of her training, but it was silent. She tried to shut out the pain and fear, but it enveloped her like burning flames. She pleaded for serenity, but there was no answer. Her head sunk between her raw shoulder blades, and the life drained from her eyes. Samina willed herself to die, but death would not come. She looked at Sprite and then managed to shift her eyes toward Amos Cross.

"Don't hurt her." Her voice was a hoarse whisper, punctuated by deep agonizing groans. Her chest heaved beneath the ravaged skin. Then Samina gave Amos Cross the coordinates of Prescott Logan's secret home.

9

A heavily armed Meridian security ship launched from Rinker's Knot. They had just received the coordinates of their target. Their orders were to pulverize a small asteroid. The weapons officer triple checked the ship's armaments. Meridian had authorized the most powerful munitions in their inventory.

* * *

The assassin crept toward the Logans. Her weapon of choice was a razor-sharp blade. She would strike her prey swiftly and silently. She would leave four bodies in the glade near the lovely waterfall. A stand of four cedar trees formed a blind between the woman and her targets. She skirted them and peeked into the space beyond. Their backs were toward her. She would kill the men first.

Hunter Logan was closest to her. She held her blade firmly in her right hand. She would strike him with an upward thrust that would enter under his rib cage and pass through his heart. She knew from experience the force of her thrust would send the blade completely through his body. She allowed her arm to remain limp as she flashed forward. It would become as stiff as the hardened blade at the final second. All of her momentum would be behind it, transferring the maximum amount of energy into her victim.

The blade struck Hunter in the low back. The knife tip punctured his jumpsuit and disturbed the web of nanoscale structures covering his body. His nanoskin responded instantly. The killer felt like she had stabbed a brick wall. The blade snapped, and she cut her hand as it slid forward past the hilt. The man fell forward, the air knocked out of him. The woman looked up, now defenseless without her blade. She saw the others rushing toward her. She had lost the element of surprise. She ran away, unwilling to engage in a losing battle.

Months before, several rapes had taken place in the hidden glade. No one had noticed the security camera that had been secreted in the bows of one of the cedar trees. The silent observer had captured the entire event.

* * *

Susanna was restocking the bottles of liquor that stood along the mirror behind the bar. A man pushed his way through the massive doors and entered the Delta V. She looked up and saw his reflection in the glass. It was the man she'd slept with months before.

"Remember me?" He walked with a self-assured swagger, a man full of his own machismo. His eyes were no longer soft and gentle. His former gratitude was replaced with a selfish expectation. Susanna didn't turn around. She gave him a nod of recognition through the mirror and kept swapping out bottles. "Sorry I haven't been in touch," he offered. "Been really busy." Susanna kept working. "Can I have a forty-two?"

Susanna pivoted on one heal and grabbed a glass from under the bar. She mixed the drink and slid it over to him. He gave her his best smile. "Thanks. Can I buy you one?"

"No thanks," she replied. Susanna wiped the bar with her rag.

The man sipped his drink. Susanna could see the wheels turning in his mind, but she was certain the man was thinking with the head between his legs. He set his glass down and smiled at her. "When do you get off work?"

"Later," she said noncommittally.

"We sure had fun the last time around. Let's try it again."

"I don't know." Susanna felt pressure rising inside her.

"You're so good, babe," he said smoothly. "You don't want to leave me high and dry, do you?"

The bastard didn't even remember her name. Susanna felt an opposing force pressing down against her need to satisfy the man, an assurance of her own power. For once, she knew what was right for her.

"No." It was such a simple word, a huge word, a victorious word.

The man scowled. "What do you mean?"

"It doesn't take a genius, buddy. No means no. Find yourself somebody else."

The man slammed the glass down on the counter and stood up. Susanna was grateful for the massive bar that separated them. "You bitch!" He raised his voice so everyone in the tavern could hear him. "I hope you enjoy sleeping alone tonight, you worthless slut!" He left without paying for the drink. Susanna looked at her patrons. They had already dismissed the man and returned to their various conversations. She smiled to herself. She would enjoy sleeping alone.

* * *

Everyone was reeling from the assassin's attack. Adrenaline surged through their bodies as Prescott led them across the garden and toward the "Blue Collar Commons," in the industrial section of the base. Hunter limped behind them. The nanoskin had saved his life, but he was still bruised and sore.

The Blue Collar Commons hosted lunch counters and shops catering to the needs of miners and laborers. A large corridor to their left led to the photo-oxidation farm, with its immense liquid oxygen and hydrogen storage fields. The ice and ore mines were ahead of them. They took coveralls and hard hats from a supply locker to blend in with the scores of workers who were moving constantly through the corridors. The four headed straight across the Blue Collar Commons, toward the mines, and took the first passage on their right. They passed by the main entrance to the ore processing facility. Dozens of workers were entering and exiting the massive plant.

"Must be change of shift," Adrianna observed.

They merged with the flow of workers and headed toward the special corridor that led to the District. Moments later, they were in the Delta V. They sat together at a table near the bar.

Susanna saw them enter but kept her distance. Adrianna and Ty stared at her in disbelief.

"She looks different." Adrianna kept her head down. "Worn out."

Prescott nodded. "I think she's ashamed of what happened."

Kate came over to the table. Hunter introduced Ty to the older woman. "We had better get you out of sight," she said. Kate took them through the doorway at the right-hand side of the bar. Seconds later, they were in her private quarters.

* * *

The assassin returned to her room and bandaged her wounded hand. She stripped off her bloody clothing and stepped into the shower, cursing herself as the water cascaded over her. She had made no mistakes. The man should have been dead. What was he wearing? She had run to safety and lost her prey. They were gone. She had no clue to their whereabouts. She wasn't used to failure. She stepped out of the bathroom and sat on her bed. She put her earset into her ear and gave her card comp a vocal command. She sent a brief message to Maya Lewis. "Mission failed." The words tasted like copper.

* * *

Amos Cross gazed at the surveillance video from Copernicus Commons. He watched as the nameless assassin lunged at Hunter Logan. When the knife snapped, he smiled.

"Dr. Logan. What have you come up with now?"

He replayed the scene, zooming in on the section of Hunter's back where the blade struck his skin. He rolled back the footage and played it frame by frame until he saw the impact of the knife. The tip sliced through his jumpsuit, revealing the skin of his back. Then, it depressed the skin slightly and snapped. Cross zoomed back out and studied the confused look on the assassin's face.

The great man smiled again. "A new kind of armor... You have such a prolific mind, Dr. Logan."

* * *

"Get out here." Kate Sloan spoke sternly. The Logans and Tyson Edwards sat in her small common area, nestled in the heart of her modest living quarters. Adrianna was anxious. Like Susanna, she didn't want this meeting. Her anger was barely in check. Memories of Sprite's burns coursed through her mind. She remembered Susanna's threats. She could still hear Sprite's screams.

Susanna appeared in the doorway. Everyone looked up. She stared at the floor, unwilling to make eye contact. She looked different, Adrianna thought. She had cut off her hair and exchanged her flashy business suits for tattered coveralls. She wore no makeup. She had chewed her fingernails, two fingers showing reddened skin where she had torn the nails to the quick.

Prescott was the first to speak. "Come and sit with us, Susanna," he said kindly.

She glanced up at him for a brief second and then sat in the nearest empty seat. Adrianna watched her body language as she sat down. Susanna looked like she was forcing herself to move. She had no purpose, no hope. The woman was broken. She had aged ten years in the last few months. Adrianna's anger abated slightly. Susanna was shattered and empty, another victim of Amos Cross.

"I'm sorry." Susanna's voice was soft, barely discernable. She looked up at Prescott, then scanned the others until her eyes fell on Adrianna. "I was a fool, and I did terrible things." Adrianna didn't respond. This woman had given orders to Jenson Reed to kill her daughter.

"I don't deserve your forgiveness." Susanna looked at them sadly. "I'm entirely at fault. I just want you to know how horrible I feel about what I've done."

Adrianna squeezed Hunter's hand. She looked at Susanna's eyes. They were puffy and red. She looked at her hands. She was fidgeting with her fingers, trying to peel away even more of her nails. She looked at her face. Hunter had worn the same look when he felt responsible for their friends' deaths.

"Why did you do it?" The words were spoken before Adrianna realized her lips were moving. "Why did you hurt my daughter?"

"I was trying to do a good job for Mr. Cross."

Adrianna's anger rose again. "You almost killed an innocent child."

Susanna's hands flew up to her face. She buried her eyes in her palms, as if trying to block out a nightmare. "I know," she whispered. "I have no excuses." Susanna wiped her cheeks with her hands and looked directly at Adrianna. The young woman looked dead. "I wanted Mr. Cross's respect. I ignored everything Mom ever taught me." Susanna glanced at Kate. Her mother remained motionless and silent. "He had power. He paid attention to me. I thought..." Her voice began to quiver. "I thought he would like me if I did everything he told me to do. I was so stupid."

"Yes, you were." Adrianna's voice was firm but not angry, which surprised her.

"You and your boss killed my partner." Ty was in a trance, replaying a mental vision of Jo's final moments. "She died while saving us from your security forces." His face was radiant as he spoke of his lover. "She was brave. She died defending her family." His radiance turned to defiance. "I didn't want her to die, but she was determined to do the right thing."

"I'm sorry. I didn't know." Susanna said meekly.

"There are a lot of things you don't know." Ty glared at her. "Jo had honor. She was a decent woman. She cared for kids. She had values and stood up for them, no matter what. Those are things you know nothing about!" Susanna met his gaze, the color draining from her face. "You took my treasure. Now Cross has my son, and I am not going to lose him. Do you understand that?" Hunter put his hand on Ty's knee. His friend flicked it off.

Adrianna saw the devastation in Susanna's eyes. She had been a pawn. Cross had chosen her because of her vulnerability. He had played on her weakness. He was the monster, not this poor woman. He had used her and discarded her. If it hadn't been Susanna doing his bidding, it would have been someone else.

Adrianna stood up and walked over to Susanna. The young woman braced herself for a physical assault. Adrianna sat down next to her and leaned forward, her forearms on her knees. "I am very angry right now." She turned and gazed into Susanna's face. "I've been angry with you." The younger woman nodded. "You got yourself in over your head and made huge mistakes." Adrianna was stern. "You aren't an evil person. You're just pathetically needy." Susanna stared at the floor. "No apology will fix that."

Adrianna looked at Hunter, then at Prescott and Ty. "Our real enemy is Amos Cross. He's the prime mover. He's the one who decided to have Sprite hurt. He's the one who sent the security forces with orders to kill us. He's the one pulling Alexis Wren's strings. He's the one who took our children. And by God, we're going to get them back."

Adrianna put her hand on Susanna's knee. Her eyes softened a bit. "Go live your life, honey. Fight your demons. Remember the role you played in this and learn from it." The younger woman nodded. Adrianna let out a long breath. "I don't know who is more dangerous: a mad man with unlimited power or his followers who check their values at the door of his throne room."

* * *

Prescott Logan sat with Gaines in Kate's kitchen. They were navigating through the Meridian network. He had cracked their security years before and knew the network as well as anyone. He was going to find Sprite.

Gaines was a digital chameleon. The AI mimicked its environment. He blended in to avoid detection. He probed the network at Jackson Base, and then inserted himself into the outer layers that served Meridian's headquarters. The inner subnets of the corporation had upgraded firewalls. Gaines couldn't get through them.

Prescott sighed in frustration. He would never find Sprite without breaking into the inner network. He shifted his attention to the Deep Core data retention well. Perhaps a clue was there, some discarded piece of code that would shed light on the new firewalls. He instructed Gaines to data mine every volume. This was going to take days.

* * *

Amos Cross swam in a pool of clear, crystalline water. He was a power swimmer, attacking every stroke as if he were in the final stretch of a race. There was no opponent, only his memories. Memories that haunted him. Cross's childhood home stood on the shore of a lake. It was a secluded place, accessible only by boat. His parents had built the house for their wild parties, parties where adults did things little boys shouldn't know about. However, Amos had known all about them. He had been part of his parents carousing, part of the entertainment. When he ran away, Cross had plunged into the lake and had swum all night through the cleansing waters.

Amos came to the edge of the pool and flipped over, kicking off for another punishing lap. His parents were dead, but he was still swimming. Swimming to break their hold on him, swimming to distance himself from them. He remembered the day he bought the house his parents had owned, the house on the lakeshore, the house of his abuse. He remembered how he burned it to the ground, scorching the Earth where he had been defiled.

A chime from Cross's AI brought him to a stop in the pool. He treaded water, vexed by the interruption. "Yes?"

"Sorry to interrupt your swim, sir." The AI had been programmed to be deferential. "Dr. Maxwell Thrune wants a moment of your time."

"You told him I was unavailable?"

If the AI was capable of self-preservation, thoughts of reprogramming must have been coursing through its primary data buss. "Yes, sir. I was very clear about that, but he insisted. He said you would want to take his call."

Cross pulled himself out of the pool. He wasn't wearing a swimsuit. "Block outgoing video."

"As you wish, sir."

Thrune's image appeared at the poolside. He was pacing back and forth, waiting for the connection to be made.

"I'm here, doctor."

Thrune looked disoriented. "I don't see you."

"That's right. What do you need?"

"The Shadow Project is ready. The only thing we require is Dr. Logan's model for the phase-two nanomachines."

Cross smiled. "Very good, doctor."

As always, Thrune was impatient. "How are you coming with Logan's data key?"

Cross's smile disappeared. He was the one who asked questions. He didn't like Thrune's attitude. Highly intelligent people tended to ignore the rules. They knew they were indispensable, above the conventions of hierarchy. "I will let you know when I am ready for the next step, doctor." Cross could tell that Thrune was disappointed. "You've done good work," he added.

The compliment perked up Thrune's spirits. "Thank you, sir."

Cross cut the connection and jumped back into the pool.

* * *

Sprite's new residence was identical to her old one. Cross had instructed the woman called Amy to move her, so his technicians could figure out how she knew about Rory and Samina. Wiley found her immediately, and Sprite told him to restore autonomy to her old residence AI. "Give him amnesia," she said. And so it was. The Meridian technicians would struggle in vain to find the source of Sprite's information. They would disappoint Amos Cross, and he would make them pay for a failure over which they had no control.

Sprite sat quietly, trying to still the chaos in her head. Images of Samina's torn and lacerated body kept reappearing in her mind. She felt small and petty for being angry with her. Samina had traded her beauty for honor. She had refused to yield to Amos Cross, and she had paid the price. Her final act was to give in to her enemy to protect Sprite from a similar fate. She imagined herself in Samina's place. A wave of fear shook her.

"Sprite?" It was Wiley.

"What is it?"

"I have good news."

"Tell me."

"Samina is back in her room. She is unconscious and appears to be badly injured, but she is alive."

Sprite's heart jumped. She was sure Samina had died in the torture chamber. She imagined her lying in her room, torn and bleeding. "We've got to get her some help." She remembered Samina's unexpected arrival at Meridian 6. She had come from her uncle Prescott's home. A thought flashed into Sprite's mind.

"Wiley?"

"Yes, Sprite."

"Do you remember how to get in touch with my uncle Prescott?"

"Yes."

"I want to send him a message."

"Ready."

Sprite voiced a message to her uncle, asking him to tell her parents that she was okay. She told him they were being held at Meridian Headquarters. "Get us out of here," she said. "Amos Cross tortured Samina. She is badly hurt and needs help. Rory is gone." She told her uncle to hurry, and then Wiley sent the message.

* * *

Prescott was about to give up when Gaines reported in. "Prescott? There is a message from Sprite." His hopes soared as he listened to his niece's voice. He called the others into the kitchen and played the message for them. They were relieved but felt a renewed sense of urgency. Time was running out. Their loved ones were in danger. Samina was dying.

Prescott hunched over his card comp. "Gaines? Can you tell me where Sprite's message came from?"

"Wiley sent it to you, Prescott."

"Are you in communication with Wiley?"

"I am."

"Can he put me in direct contact with Sprite?"

"Yes, sir."

Prescott handed Gaines to Adrianna. Within seconds, Sprite's face appeared in the small holodisplay.

"Mom!" Sprite's eyes were filled with tears. "Are you okay?"

"Yes, dear. I'm fine. How are you?"

"Okay. But Samina is badly hurt. Amos Cross tortured her."

"How about Rory and Kell?"

"I think Kell is fine. He's being held near here. Rory is missing. I think Mr. Cross took her somewhere."

"We're coming to get you. Does Wiley know where you are?"

"Yes, Mom."

"Have him tell Gaines."

"I'm doing it right now." Wiley's voice interjected.

Suddenly, there was an unidentifiable sound on the audio link. Sprite jumped. "Someone's coming!"

Two Meridian guards appeared in the display. They took the young girl roughly by her arms. "Mr. Cross wants to see you," one said sternly. Then Sprite disappeared from view.

* * *

Sprite thought she was going to Cross's office, but the guards took her deeper into the Meridian complex. She could tell the men weren't happy. Could anyone enjoy serving Amos Cross? The men held her with strong hands. They refused to look at her. Sprite felt powerless.

They took her to an elevator. It looked familiar, but Sprite dismissed the thought. All elevators looked the same. She waited, trying to calm her nerves. When the door opened, Sprite knew exactly where they were. The long hallway that led to Samina's torture chamber lay before them. She began to strain against her captors. She screamed, but they pushed her down the stone corridor.

* * *

Prescott moved to Kate's common area and linked Gaines into her holodisplay. Everyone was waiting for further word, hoping Sprite and Kell were okay. Adrianna was beside herself. She had seen Sprite. She had talked to her. Then she had watched as her daughter was snatched away.

"Prescott?" Gaines voice was even and emotionless.

"Report."

"I have an incoming message."

"Is it Sprite?"

"No, sir. It's Amos Cross."

Prescott gave Hunter and Adrianna a worried look. He turned back to his card comp. "Does he know where we are?"

"No, sir. Wiley and I are managing the data path. You're safe."

Hunter glanced at Kate and Susanna. "Cross shouldn't see you." He turned to his brother, "You, too, Prescott." They went to the kitchen, out of view of the holographic camera.

Hunter spoke to Gaines. "Open the link."

A bloodstained room appeared in the holodisplay. Sprite was shackled in the same chains that had held Samina. Her arms were pulled up and apart from her body. Her legs were spread apart. The three parents flinched at the sight. Pieces of skin floated in shallow pools of blood beneath her.

"Is that from Sprite?" Adrianna asked Hunter.

"It can't be," he reassured her. "She doesn't look hurt."

Amos Cross stepped into the frame, an arrogant smirk on his face. "Ah, I found you."

"Let my daughter go!" Hunter demanded.

"That's not going to happen, Dr. Logan. I am pleased the three of you are here to see this." He poked at Sprite, and she squirmed in her chains. She looked pleadingly toward her parents.

"Don't hurt her!" Adrianna bolted from her seat.

"You're in no position to negotiate, Dr. Logan. I will do what I want to her." Cross gestured to someone off camera. A strange-looking man, pencil thin with pale skin, stepped into view. He held a pipe-like device that had a thick insulated handle on one end with a bulbous tip on the other. A heavy cable exited from the handle and drooped downward to the floor. The tip glowed with a dull reddish tint.

A woman appeared. Her skin had an oily sheen, and her facial features were hard and gaunt. She held a sharp blade in her hand. It was stained with dried blood.

Adrianna collapsed in a chair. Hunter wrapped his arm around her and glared hatefully at Cross. "What are you going to do?"

"That depends on you entirely, Dr. Logan." Cross smiled. "I saw the most amazing thing yesterday. I watched an assassin stab you with a sharp knife. You should be dead." Hunter didn't respond. Cross squinted into the camera. "But you're not dead, are you? Your skin saved your life. That's truly extraordinary!"

Cross glanced at Sprite. "I began to think. Your daughter was badly burned at Meridian 6. Jenson Reed gave me a full report. She should have died, but here she is. If I am not mistaken, you made new skin for her. You tested it on yourself before you applied it to her delicate body."

Cross nodded to the strange woman with the knife. She lunged at Sprite. The knife struck her in the stomach with enough force to cut her in half. Adrianna screamed. Hunter cursed under his breath. The blade cut Sprite's jumpsuit but slid harmlessly off her skin.

"Stop!" Hunter cried. "She's done nothing to you!"

"Amazing, Dr. Logan." Cross put his finger where the blade had struck Sprite's abdomen. The girl flinched. "It is as hard as stone. You are to be congratulated on such an achievement. You never cease to amaze me." The great man nodded to his other associate. The pipe-like device began to glow brightly.

"I wonder if the skin will protect her from heat?" Before Hunter could react, the man pressed the glowing prod into Sprite's stomach. Her jumpsuit burst into flames. Sprite screamed, then closed her eyes and mouth as the flames spread upward.

"Put it out, goddamnit!" Hunter was shaking. "What do you want?"

Cross nodded to the woman, and she put out the fire, but the man with the hot probe stood ready to burn her again. Sprite's jumpsuit hung from her body, great sections of cloth singed and melted. She was unconscious.

"Ah, Dr. Logan. Now I think we can start the negotiations." Cross was pleased with himself. "I will spare your daughter, if you give me the key to your research data."

Hunter didn't understand for a moment, then he remembered the intruder cracking into Millie and uploading his data for the phase-two nanomachines.

"Mr. Reed was very clever when he stole your data, but we underestimated the encryption." Cross stopped smiling. "I want the key, Dr. Logan, or your daughter will die, skin or no skin."

Hunter could feel Kate's common area beginning to tilt. His knees turned to rubber, and a sharp debilitating pain shot through the front of his brain. He was either going to cause his daughter's death or become the killer of humanity. He knew what he had to do. Hunter rubbed the scar on his right index finger. Cross nodded to the man with the red hot lance. He stepped forward, ready to set Sprite on fire again.

"Stop!" Hunter could hear himself speaking, but he wasn't there. His voice seemed to be coming from someone else. "The key is," he fought to remember. "It's 'Whetstone_Gulf.' There's an underscore between the two words. They're both capitalized."

Cross waved the thin man away. "Whetstone Gulf? What in the world is that?" He laughed. "I am going to have my man confirm the key." Cross stepped out of view.

Hunter wept quietly. Adrianna and Ty couldn't take their eyes off Sprite. She slowly opened her eyes but did not move. She looked directly at Adrianna and gave her an almost imperceptible nod. She was okay.

Moments later, Cross returned. "You're a very smart man, Dr. Logan. We have confirmed that you have given us the correct decryption key."

"Release our daughter," Adrianna demanded. She stood with her fists clenched.

"I'm sorry, Ms. Logan. That wasn't our deal. I said I would save her life, and I have done so."

"Let her go," Hunter pleaded. "You've got what you wanted."

"That's true, Dr. Logan. But there is one more thing."

The Logans held each other tightly. Hunter took a deep breath. "Anything."

Cross offered them a broad smile. "I want her skin."

10

"I'll give you the nanoskin!" Hunter shouted. "Just give me my daughter." He pulled the vial of nanoskin out of his pocket.

"You have the skin with you?" Cross was interested. He glanced at Sprite, then another thought occurred to him. "I'd love to do business with you, Dr. Logan, but I'm rather busy right now. Let's talk about this later."

"I want Sprite!"

"I know you do, but if I release her, you'll never give me that vial. I'll keep her for now."

Adrianna was full of rage. "You bastard! Give me my daughter!"

"In good time, Dr. Logan." Cross broke the connection.

When Prescott and the others returned to Kate's common area, the Hunters' anxiety was palpable. "We're going over there, and we're going to take our children back!" Adrianna vowed. "Right now." The time had come for a council of war.

Prescott instructed Gaines to open a channel to Sprite's AI. "Are you there, Wiley?"

"Yes, Prescott.

"What can you do about the security at Meridian Headquarters?" he asked.

"Athena and I can control it. The security AIs will do what we tell them. We can command ninety-five percent of the network."

"Who is Athena?" he asked.

After Wiley explained who his digital partner was, Prescott smiled at Hunter and Adrianna. "Our mission just got a lot easier." He turned back to the holodisplay. "Can you locate Samina and the children?"

"Yes and no. Samina, Sprite, and Kell are in their quarters. We don't know what happened to Rory."

"If we come to Jackson Base, can you get us in and direct us to them?"

"Yes, sir."

"Good."

Wiley spoke again. Prescott could have sworn he heard concern in the AI's voice. "The one called Samina is badly injured. I suggest you hurry."

* * *

A young man sat before a large holodisplay, somewhere deep in the bowels of Meridian Headquarters. His job was to monitor the security systems and respond to any issues that cropped up. It was a boring job: weeks of monotony, punctuated by occasional false alarms.

He watched the security AI check all the zones across the vast complex. It did a sweep every ten seconds. For the fun of it, he had created a piece of code that recorded the length of time it took the AI to "make its rounds." For months, the comp had taken 1.0076 seconds to poll all the doors, motion detectors, and sensors throughout Meridian Headquarters. Tonight things were different. For some unknown reason, the AI was doing the same series of queries in .9986 seconds. Why was it faster? Something was different, and that was usually bad in the security business.

He opened a screen and reported the anomaly to his superior. The young man was surprised when Amos Cross's image appeared. "What's going on down there?"

The man sat up in his seat. "Good Evening, sir."

"Cut the crap and tell me what you found."

"Yes, sir. The security AI has changed, sir. It's running more efficiently tonight."

"Your report says almost one percent faster than normal."

"Yes, sir. Point eight six percent faster, sir."

"Increase the threat-level. Someone is tampering with our system."

If it were possible, the young man sat even straighter in his chair. "Immediately, sir." He glanced at his timing software. The most recent scan of the complex took 1.0076 seconds. "What the?" The young man caught Cross before he cut the link. "Sir! It's back to normal again. It's almost like the AI noticed us fussing over the timing and made an internal correction."

"Increase the threat-level anyway. Have the AI swapped out as soon as possible." Cross's image disappeared. The man tapped an icon and entered his pass code. The outer walls of the holodisplay began to pulsate with a reddish hue. Chimes echoed throughout the complex as heightened security protocols went into effect.

* * *

Prescott sipped a cup of steaming coffee, as Kate put together a simple meal for them. She worked efficiently in the small kitchen. He thought of Maria for a fleeting moment. They had spent years together, isolated from the rest of humanity. He missed her more than he could imagine. He forced himself to return to the issues at hand. "Kate, do you know someone who can get us to Jackson Base? We've got to stay under Meridian's radar."

"I was hoping you'd ask." She set down her dish towel, an ancient but necessary kitchen item. "I have a friend. He's been on the losing end of Meridian for a long time. He'd be glad to help you. He'd consider it payback."

"Can he be trusted?"

"He's married to my sister."

Prescott grinned. "Contact him. We're going tonight."

* * *

Cross and Alexis Wren stood in the great man's office. For once, there were no special effects. The walls were bare, and the viewports were shuttered. A synthetic control panel hovered next to Cross's right hand. He tapped an icon. A simple holographic image appeared in the middle of the room. The interior of the Shadow Project laboratory stood in vivid, miniature detail before them. Dr. Maxell Thrune stood by the controls of the containment unit, immersed in his work.

"When will the phase-two nanomachines be ready, Dr. Thrune?"

The man didn't like having Cross looking over his shoulder. "It won't be long, Amos. Less than two hours."

"Ms. Wren and I are coming over."

The odd scientist wore a pained expression. "That's not necessary, Amos."

"Stop calling me that!"

"Yes, of course, Mr. Cross." Thrune offered him a perfunctory nod.

"We'll be there in half an hour." Cross cut the link. "If I didn't need him, I'd choke him with his own vanity, the pompous know-it-all," he muttered angrily. Alexis didn't react. She had learned to be silent and await her orders. "Security flagged an anomaly in their AI. It's running more efficiently than normal. I'm afraid something's wrong." Cross rubbed his chin. "We're taking the Logan girl with us. Take a couple of guards down to the holding rooms and bring her to my transport. We will leave for the Shadow Project lab in ten minutes."

* * *

Maria Logan sat before the large viewport in her secret home in The Asteroid Belt. She missed her husband. Their lives had changed dramatically on that day years before, when Amos Cross declared them enemies of Meridian Corporation. Maria and Prescott had always been solitary people. They weren't comfortable in crowds. They didn't need scores of friends. They needed each other. They were friends and confidants. With each year, they burrowed deeper into the unfathomable depths of companionship. Love was inadequate to express the bond between them. She ached for her husband.

She took a sip from her flask of tea. That was the biggest difference between them. Prescott lived for good coffee. She enjoyed the aroma but hated the stuff. Hot tea, on the other hand, had miraculous powers. It cleared the mind, warmed the belly, and soothed the soul. There was nothing like wrapping cold fingers around a warm container of tea.

Prescott had just sent her a message about their plan to break into Meridian. It scared her. They had spent twenty-two years avoiding the corporate behemoth. They had gone to great lengths to avoid suspicion and remain anonymous. Now, her beloved was entering the belly of the beast. She shivered as icy needles of fear pricked her. A sense of foreboding filled her with dread. She wanted Prescott back home again. One false step, and she would lose him forever. She shut the thought out of her mind and took another sip of tea.

* * *

Prescott tapped Hunter on the arm. "You've got to see this, brother," he said. Hunter looked up. Prescott had hacked into the Shadow Project server. Hundreds of pages of complex schematics filled his display.

"What am I looking at?" Hunter asked.

"It's one of Cross's secret projects. Wiley traced the transmission Cross made when he checked the authenticity of your encryption key. It was received in a dome on the edge of Jackson Base. The place is associated with something called the 'Shadow Project.' Wiley dug a little deeper and came up with this." Prescott paged through some of the schematics.

"Stop!" Something familiar caught Hunter's eye. "Go back a couple of pages. There!" Hunter couldn't believe it. He remembered Sprite telling him about a new nano-lab being built on the Moon. She had told him there were plans for a containment unit like the one they had built on Selene Station. He studied the image in front of him. He had designed some of these circuits. The schematics had been stolen from the Nanotechnology Advanced Research Institute. Alexis Wren or Jenson Reed had done it. "Zoom into the legend."

Prescott magnified the legend in the lower-right corner of the document. Hunter's initials were visible. "Damn, Hunter. You signed off on these!"

"It's revision three point four." There was an ominous chill in Hunter's voice.

"Is that a problem?"

"It's an old version."

Prescott put the puzzle-pieces together. "Cross has your model for the phase-two machines."

Hunter nodded. "And he's going to reconstitute them in a containment unit that doesn't work."

Prescott shook his head. "This just gets better and better."

There was a chime. It was Wiley. "We have a problem, Prescott."

"What now?"

"Sprite has been moved."

"Where is she?"

"We don't know yet."

Prescott started to laugh sarcastically. The rescue mission hadn't even started, and their plans were unraveling.

* * *

Bud Sorenson spent his working hours flying in lunar orbit. He was a trash collector, snatching pieces of space junk out of orbit to protect the many operational satellites and spacecraft that circled the Moon.

Each day, he filled his bin and delivered the orbital flotsam and jetsam to a recycling center near Jackson Base. He did the work of a simple man, a cog in the great wheel of off-world development.

There was a time when Bud Sorenson had a bigger job, a job in keeping with his talent and intellect. He used to be a human resources professional who managed the legions of men and women who worked for Meridian Corporation. He was a rising star, whose skills had been recognized by his superiors. He was promoted several times and finally became the director of human resources for Meridian's construction division.

Bud's fatal mistake took place when he sided with an employee who had been fired by Amos Cross. He saw the injustice in it and went to bat for the man. Cross heard about what Bud had done and dealt with him swiftly and decisively. He told Bud's boss that if he had such a heart for garbage, he should spend the rest of his life collecting it. The man, fearful of his own professional future, reassigned his subordinate.

So, Bud Sorenson had scooped orbital poop every day, for ten years. He had watched Amos Cross's reign of fear cascade down the institutional hierarchy, smothering creativity and innovation. He loved Meridian Corporation but hated what was happening to it. He was more than ready to strike back at Amos Cross.

Bud arrived at the Delta V, and Kate introduced him to her friends. Prescott explained their situation. They needed to get to Jackson Base as soon as possible and be transported back to Copernicus on a moment's notice. It had to be done quietly.

Bud smiled broadly. "You're making my decade, folks. We can leave within the hour. Figure fifty minutes of flight time to Jackson. I can stand by for the return trip as long as you need me."

"How about ground transportation to Meridian Headquarters?" Prescott asked.

"No problem. We can commandeer a transport at the recycling center."

Adrianna squeezed his arm. "You're a lifesaver, Bud. You really are." The man blushed.

Susanna entered the common area. She was nervous, rarely making eye contact with the Logans. "I want to go with you," she began. "I can help."

Adrianna shook her head. "No, Susanna. You've done enough."

"I know every inch of Meridian Headquarters. I don't have a pass-ring anymore, but I know where things are. I know where Sprite and Kell are being held."

Hunter gave her a hard look. "They've moved Sprite. She's not there anymore."

"I can still be a big help to you. I want to help. I need to help."

Prescott glanced at his brother and sister-in-law. "She's right. We need every advantage we can muster. Her knowledge could tip the scales in our favor."

"I don't know." Adrianna was still unconvinced.

"Damn it, girl!" Kate glared at Adrianna. Her deep voice resonated in the common area. "Stuff your pride and let her help you. She's not useless. Give her a chance. Let her atone for her mistakes."

Adrianna looked at Hunter, and he nodded in agreement. Then she looked up at Susanna, her reluctance still written on her face. "Okay. You can come."

* * *

Drew Mallick and his wife sold most of their possessions back to the base supply. It was too expensive to ship them to Earth. This was a common practice, and the base supply was a real profit center for Meridian Corporation. Basic items like blankets and clothing were sold and resold many times before they were cast into the recycling bins. Their raw materials were recovered, and the profit-making cycle started all over again.

The Mallicks had been told to be ready at a moment's notice to depart for Earth. They had packed all of their remaining goods into two modest shipping cases. They were living from day to day, out of a pair of small carryon bags. They had stepped up their exercise routine, in anticipation of the increased gravity of Earth. They could hardly wait to see their children.

Drew had just kissed his wife good night when his comlink chimed. At first, he thought it was a problem at the office, but when the serious woman on the other end of the link told him to meet her at dock A-21 in an hour, he knew their waiting was over. They would be on their way to Earth by morning.

* * *

Maria Logan unscrewed the cap of her tea flask. She lifted the container to her nose and inhaled the last vestiges of aroma. She wiped it out and clipped it to the counter next to the stove. She wandered out of the kitchen and paused by the viewport, glancing at the stark landscape of her asteroid. She walked deeper into the interior of her home. The soft woven rug that blanketed the floor of their bedchamber felt good under her feet. She stepped out of her shoes and untied the sash of her robe. It fell from her shoulders and landed on the rug. The soothing warmth of the light chamber awaited her.

* * *

The Meridian security ship slipped through the void toward the coordinates Samina had given Amos Cross. Eight heavily-armed men readied for battle in the aft compartment. The captain floated over to his nav officer. "What's our ETA, Turner?"

The nav officer looked at his instruments. "About an hour, sir."

The captain turned to a second crewman. "What do the sensors tell us?"

"Nothing, sir. They must have the place well shielded."

"I'd expect nothing less." The captain rubbed his forehead. "I've read Prescott Logan's file. He's smart and very sneaky."

"I've identified a likely point of entry, sir. There's a deep valley with steep walls. There are some outcroppings that could mask a cavern. That's where he is, if he's on this rock."

"Very good. Nav? Lay in our final approach. Bring us over that valley."

"Yes, sir."

* * *

Bud Sorenson delivered his passengers to the lunar recycling center at Jackson Base. He was well known there, and no one questioned his arrival. Several ground transports were lined up near the landing pad. Prescott thought it was too risky to steal a transport, so he had Wiley reserve one. The second transport from the end bore the number Wiley had given him. They donned environment suits and exited Bud's jumpship.

"We'll be back," Prescott intoned through his comlink. "We can't thank you enough."

"It's kinda fun," Bud returned. "I like being on this side of things."

Within moments, they were aboard the transport. Susanna settled in at the controls, since she knew the layout of the base.

* * *

Jackson Base was on the far side of the Moon, located along the northern wall of Jackson Crater. Slumps in the rim had formed terraces during the latter stages of the crater's formation. The base was perched on the esplanades and built into the shear crater walls. Arching structures bridged the various levels, forming walkways and providing elevators to each tier.

The recycling center shared the lowest level of Jackson Base with the spaceport and mining operations. Susanna piloted the transport vehicle to the east, around the ore and water processing plants, and then turned northward toward the upper base. It was dark. Their headlights cast sharp-edged cones of light ahead of them, as they navigated around the periphery of the base. In the distance, they could see the majestic architecture of Meridian Headquarters.

"That's where we're going." Susanna sounded nervous. She had become more agitated as they drew closer to their destination.

Meridian Corporation Headquarters sat on the highest terrace of Jackson Base, tucked into the shadow of a sheer rock wall near the crater's rim. The complex was studded with tall towers and massive structures that followed the irregular shape of the terrace's apron, offering smooth curves in contrast to the jagged lunar rock. Hundreds of mirrored viewports hid the inner workings of the vast and mysterious fortification, while offering breathtaking views of the base for those who worked and lived inside. Amos Cross's executive suite had the largest viewports and dominated the highest point of the headquarters' complex.

"The dock for transports is on the left." Susanna's hands were clammy. A bead of sweat hung on the tip of her chin. "We're going to run into security." Her face was grim as she thought about the odds of success and the consequences of failure.

"Believe it or not," Prescott could hardly suppress a grin, "we're expected."

Ty shot him a terrified look. "That's the last thing we need!"

"They don't expect the real us." Prescott corrected himself. "They are expecting five visiting dignitaries, who look like us. Wiley and

Athena put us on their list. We are arriving overnight for some kind of conference in the morning."

Adrianna made a face. "And if they ask us about the conference?"

"They won't." Susanna spoke over her shoulder. "Such questions are above their pay grade. Guards don't pry. If someone complained, they could be demoted, or worse."

"I thought being curious was a necessary part of their job," Ty commented.

Susanna managed a strained laugh. "Now you're beginning to understand what it's like to work for Amos Cross. Everyone is afraid. The guards cover their asses, like everyone else. They stick to their lists."

Prescott smiled. "And Wiley made the list." There was a round of nervous chuckles, but Susanna remained silent. She didn't want anything to do with this place. There were too many bad memories, recent memories. She shouldn't have come. Prescott had assured her that Wiley had masked their faces from the security database, but Susanna wasn't satisfied. Too much power was concentrated here. Someone might recognize her.

* * *

The transport vehicle entered a pressurized dock, and the guards greeted them cordially. They were admitted without question. Susanna led them through a maze of hallways and elevators that took them deep into the complex. There would be no escape if they were discovered. Finally, they were in the hallway outside the holding rooms where Sprite and the others had been confined.

Prescott touched his comlink. "Wiley? Have you found Sprite?" Everyone gathered around him, so they could hear the AI's report.

"Yes, Prescott. She's on board Amos Cross's transport. She is en route to the Shadow Project dome."

"Is Cross with her?" Adrianna asked.

"Yes."

Ty was beside himself. "Where's Kell?"

"He's still here." A door opened a short distance down the hallway. "I have opened the door of his residence."

Ty rushed forward. "Kell!"

"Dad?" The astonished boy stepped out into the corridor, just in time to be grabbed by his father. Tears were in Ty's eyes as he held his son tightly.

"Son! Thank God you're okay!"

The Logans stood a few meters away. "We have to rescue Sprite," Prescott said. "Wiley? How do we get to that dome?"

"Forgive me for changing the subject, Prescott," Wiley replied. "But Samina needs you. She will stop functioning if she doesn't get help right away."

"Is she far?"

"No. She's three doors ahead of you."

Prescott looked up as another door opened. "Samina is in there!" he declared.

Hunter took the lead. They moved quickly toward the door. He glanced into the room, then stepped back into the corridor, his face pale. "It's really bad." He looked at Kell, who was standing next to his father. "You better keep Kell out here, Ty." Ty nodded as the others entered Samina's room.

Samina's naked and bloody body lay on the floor of the small common area. Hunter stifled the urge to throw up. There was a horrible odor, the coppery aroma of blood mixed with other bodily fluids. He knelt down beside her.

The last time they had seen her, she was beautiful. She had been filled with energy, bright-eyed and vibrantly capable. Now her smooth skin had been cut from her muscles. Half of her face had been removed, leaving the underlying muscle and bone. Her breasts were gone. They could see portions of her skull where her scalp had been sliced away. She was breathing in short ragged gasps, each punctuated with a soft grunt of pain.

Susanna glanced at Samina's mutilated body and turned away quickly. Amos Cross had done this. She had underestimated the evil in the man. She shuttered at the thought of spending years in his presence. He was a monster. "How could I have been so blind?" she whispered to herself.

"Samina!" Adrianna spoke forcefully. Susanna jumped. She turned back toward the injured woman. Adrianna was kneeling by the fallen-woman's side.

Samina flinched. One eye opened. It had a sheen of bloody tears. She whispered, "Adrianna."

"We've got you, girl. We're going to get you out of here."

Samina struggled to focus her eye. She looked over Adrianna's shoulder and saw Prescott behind her. "Prescott," she whispered. "He was going to hurt Sprite." Samina cried out in pain.

"Don't try to talk," Adrianna urged her.

Samina raised one arm, trying to reach Prescott. "He wanted to know where your home was."

The color drained from the older Logan's face. "Did you tell him?"

Samina labored, taking a deep breath. "They were going to hurt Sprite." She tipped her head back and passed out.

* * *

The Meridian security-ship hovered over the deep valley that was cut into the small asteroid's surface.

"There are tool marks down there, sir. Someone has been here."

"Any signs of life?"

"Yes, sir. I have a faint heat signature and some low-level electromagnetic radiation."

The assault team commander floated next to the captain. He eyed the jagged walls of the narrow canyon. "We can get down there, but I question putting the men in harm's way." He thought of the recent assault on Meridian 6. He had lost friends there and didn't want his men to walk into a trap like that. "It would be easier to blow it."

The captain nodded his head. "That's what I was thinking, commander. Let's put an asteroid killer down the slot and go home."

* * *

Maria had spent an extra ten minutes in the light chamber. After all, Prescott wasn't there, and energy usage was down. Why not luxuriate a little while longer? She shivered as she shut off the chamber and stepped back into the bedroom. She left her robe where she had dropped it and padded back to the viewport. When Prescott came back, she would have a talk with him about improving the appearance of their canyon.

Without warning, there was a terrible noise. Something landed on Maria's bare shoulder, and she was falling. Her last conscious thought was the sound of her head cracking against the hard stone floor.

11

T y and Kell could hear the voices of their friends through the open door. They could tell Samina was in bad shape. Ty was tempted to move closer and get a look at what was happening, but he fought the urge. Kell would follow him, and he was too young for what they would see.

"Where's Mom?"

Ty's heart fell. He turned away from his son, attempting to hide his reaction to the question.

"Dad?" Ty could hear the fear in Kell's voice. "Where is mom?" Ty turned back to his son. Kell began shaking his head. "No." Ty grabbed him by the shoulders. "No!" He pulled Kell to his chest. "Nooooo!"

"She saved us, Kell." Tyson whispered gently into the boy's ear. He could feel his son's weight as the boy's legs buckled. They sank to the floor. "She blew up the security ship that came to Meridian 6. They were going to kill us."

"Why didn't you stop her?" The anger of grief filled Kell's voice.

It was a question Ty had asked himself a thousand times since that terrible day. "She went out on the surface before any of us could stop her. She was bullheaded. You know that." Ty could feel Kell nodding against his shoulder. "She was going to do what she was going to do." It was the truth, and it released Ty from a measure of his guilt. There was nothing he could have done to save Jo's life.

* * *

Adrianna gave Samina an injection to ease her pain. Prescott was beside himself. He knelt next to the injured woman and bent over so he was close to her face. "Did you tell Cross where I live?" he asked anxiously.

Samina stirred. "I gave him the location."

Prescott felt a wave of desperation pour over him like the surf on a stormy beach. Samina's lips moved again.

"Funny thing about torture," she whispered. "The information you get can't be trusted." Samina managed a thin smile.

A fresh breeze of hope swept away Prescott's fear. "You are one heck of a woman, Samina."

"Don't feel like one," she whispered.

* * *

Maria woke up. Everything was blurry. Her head hurt terribly. The room was sideways. She was on the floor. She was cold. Maria glanced down at her body. Why was she naked? She remembered the light chamber. She had just come out of it and walked toward the viewport. Something heavy was on her left arm. She raised herself up. Her mechanical cat gripped her neck tightly, sending shooting pains down her spine.

"Get off me, Seuss!" Maria pushed the mechanical cat away and got up on her knees. She looked at the items that were strewn on the floor. They belonged on the top shelf of a nearby bookcase. She glanced up. The shelf was bare. So that's what happened, she thought. The AI had climbed up to the high shelf and had launched himself toward his mistress in fine cat style.

"I'm sorry, Maria. I have been studying the behavior of cats. I thought you would expect me to climb and jump."

"Not when I'm naked, and never when I'm not looking. You scared me half to death!"

Seuss cowered in a corner. "Sorrrrry." He stretched the word out so it sounded almost like a purr. "I won't do it again."

Maria felt the side of her head. There wasn't any blood. Her injuries were minor, but she'd be sore for a couple of days. Maria groaned as she pulled herself to her feet and marched back into the bedroom for her robe.

* * *

A transport vehicle rolled across the lunar surface toward the Shadow Project dome. Alexis Wren sat across the narrow aisle from Amos Cross. Her boss was focused on his earset holodisplay. Sprite was strapped into one of the seats in the rear of the transport. Her wrists and ankles were secured with flexible plastic handcuffs.

A voice whispered to Alexis. It was coming from the subcutaneous transceiver hidden behind her left ear. "Alexis? It's Maya. Can you talk?"

Alexis looked over at Amos Cross. "Mr. Cross, do you know when we'll get to the Shadow Project dome?"

Maya got the message. "Don't try to speak to me."

The great man resented the interruption. "About twenty minutes," he growled. Cross looked back at his holodisplay.

"Twenty minutes isn't so bad," Alexis repeated for Maya's benefit.

"So you'll be at the Shadow Project dome in twenty minutes. What's going to happen?"

Alexis stretched her arms. "It'll be good to see the phase-two machines in action," she commented.

Cross grunted. Maya's voice whispered again. "He's that close? You must stop him at any cost. Do you understand? You cannot let those machines exist. They will destroy everything!"

Alexis glanced across the aisle at her boss. "I'll do anything I can to fulfill this mission."

Cross looked up at her and nodded. "I know you will, Alexis." He turned away.

Maya's voice whispered in her ear again. "Message received. We're counting on you." Alexis closed her eyes. Years of undercover work were about to come to a conclusion. She couldn't wait to get her life back.

* * *

Prescott marveled as Hunter and Adrianna poured a small quantity of nanoskin onto Samina's torn flesh. The stem machines began to multiply and spread across her body. The n-skin was born from nano-bandage research the Logans had conducted a decade earlier. It expanded across muscle and exposed bone without hesitation. Within moments, Samina's body was encased in a grayish membrane.

"There are two steps in the process," Adrianna explained. "First, the stem machines cover her. That's what they've just done. Over the next twenty minutes or so, the stem machines will convert themselves into nanoskin. It will optimize healing and protect her." Gradually, the gray membrane turned translucent, then clear. Samina was unconscious, but they could tell she was in less pain.

"That's amazing." Susanna looked at Adrianna with awe.

"We developed it to save Sprite's life." There was a hint of anger in Adrianna's voice. She paused, realizing what she had done. "I'm sorry. That didn't come out the way I wanted."

Susanna shrugged sadly. "I understand. The nanoskin is still wonderful."

Adrianna nodded.

"Speaking of Sprite," Hunter said, "we've got to go." He wouldn't rest until she was safe.

Susanna cleared her throat nervously. Prescott looked at her. "What are you thinking, Suzy?" He used the familiar form of her name to set her at ease.

She let out a long breath. "I could take Samina back to the Delta V. She'd be safer there."

Adrianna was kneeling next to her injured friend. She looked up at Susanna. "I think that's a great idea," she said softly. "She's paid a high price. I want her in safe hands." Susanna smiled broadly, and Adrianna nodded to her. "We'll help you get her back to the dock."

* * *

A few moments later, they stood on the pressurized dock. Samina was wrapped in a blanket. Ty stood by her head so the guards couldn't see who she was. Prescott and Susanna told the guards their friend had taken ill. They seemed relieved. The injured woman was being taken away and wouldn't be their problem.

Prescott and Ty laid Samina gently on the deck of the transport, while Hunter wedged a cushion under her head. Adrianna strapped her down. She turned to Susanna, who was fastening herself into the pilot's seat. "Thanks for doing this." Adrianna shook her hand. "Trust the nanoskin. It will help her heal."

Ty cleared his throat. "I'm going to take Kell back to Copernicus Base with Susanna. Is that okay with you guys?"

Hunter smiled at his friend. "It makes a lot of sense." He looked at Kell's face. The boy's eyes were red. He looked lost. "You need to stay close to Kell. We'll be all right."

"You're sure?"

Adrianna touched his arm gently. "Very sure, Ty. Kell needs you. We can take care of ourselves."

Ty nodded his thanks and closed the transport's hatch.

Prescott noted the registration number of a nearby transport. He checked in with Wiley and Athena. "We're on the dock where we arrived. Can you help us commandeer transport-vehicle M-167? It's sitting next to the one we used to get here."

"Certainly, Prescott. We have scheduled it to depart at the same time as Susanna's transport. There will be no suspicions."

"Excellent! Transfer the coordinates for the Shadow Project dome into the transport's guidance system."

"Done."

The Logans piled into the second transport and closed the hatch. The dock was depressurized, and the outer hatch was opened, revealing the lunar surface beyond. The two transports moved through the broad opening slowly. Susanna and Ty retraced their route to the recycling plant and Bud Sorenson's jumpship, while the Logans began their journey to the Shadow Project dome.

* * *

Amos Cross's assistant had brought Drew and Beverly Mallick directly to a small dock on the far side of the Shadow Project dome. She had guided them through a labyrinthine series of corridors and deposited them next to a gleaming new jumpship. Two pilots and a steward greeted them, while a couple of dockhands loaded the couple's shipping cases.

"It's a brand-new ship, dear," Beverly marveled. "Did we win the lottery?"

"Mr. Cross did it." He turned to one of the pilots. "Are we going to transfer to a ship in orbit?"

"No, sir. Our orders are to fly you directly to Earth."

Drew noticed the absence of other passengers. "No one else is coming?"

"Just you and your wife, sir. Please get aboard and strap in. We'll be departing in just a few minutes."

Drew grinned at Beverly. After all his years of hard work, he was finally being treated with respect.

Dr. Maxwell Thrune watched the couple disappear through the hatch of the jumpship. He didn't know who they were, and he didn't care.

* * *

Sprite was helpless; her wrists and ankles were bound, and she was securely strapped into her seat. She was frightened and couldn't imagine a way out of her predicament. She fought the urge to throw up as the transport jerked to a stop. A large bright light appeared through the viewports. Her stomach flipped again as the vehicle jerked forward. She looked out the port next to her seat. They were entering a small, pressurized dock. The transport stopped again, and she heard the muffled turbine winding down as the pilot shut off the engine.

Cross was out of his seat and left the ship as soon as the lock was pressurized. Alexis walked down the aisle toward Sprite. "Sit tight," she said. She checked the girl's restraints. The woman turned away and hurried back up the aisle. The transport hatch snapped shut with a loud click. Sprite was left alone.

* * *

Alexis had to run to catch up with Amos Cross. He was entering the massive room that held the containment unit. This was the first time she had seen the unit in operation. The holodisplay chamber was filled with a green luminescent mist. Several icons were blinking in the three-dimensional space. Dr. Thrune stood next to the chamber, his attention drawn to the display.

"Good evening, Dr. Thrune," Cross said.

Thrune turned and nodded to Cross. He turned back to his work without acknowledging Alexis. Cross tipped his head as a voice whispered in his ear. He walked out of earshot and began pacing back and forth, as he spoke with some nameless subordinate.

* * *

Sprite pulled at her plastic restraints. They were cutting into her wrists. She remembered her nanoskin and managed to punch one of the buttons on her forearm. She felt her body tense as the skin grew hard. She pulled with all her strength, but nothing happened. The nanoskin didn't make her any stronger. She could not escape.

Amos Cross had said he wanted her nanoskin. Samina's carved body appeared in her mind's eye. Would he do that to her? Would he cut the skin from her body and leave her for dead? Sprite suppressed a shutter. Cross might have his scientists remove her skin, and she would be humiliated and die. Her fears took control. "Help!" she screamed.

Her voice echoed in the empty transport. She had never felt so alone. She screamed again.

* * *

The Logans' transport came to a stop outside the Shadow Project dome. The dock hatch was closed. He opened a link to Wiley and asked the AI to open the hatch. Within a few seconds, the great door began to descend into the threshold of the dock opening. He pushed the controls, and the vehicle rolled forward.

Hunter and Adrianna listened to the atmosphere cycling back into the dock. Their faces were pressed to the viewports. The dock was almost empty. Another transport vehicle stood a few meters away. No one was around.

Prescott picked up his card comp. "Wiley, what's the security situation?"

"There's no problem, Prescott. You are delivering some supplies. No one will question your presence."

Hunter was the first one out of the transport. The three stood for a moment, deciding their next move. Adrianna turned quickly. "Did you hear that?"

They held their breath and listened. There was no sound.

"What was it?" Hunter asked.

"I could have sworn I heard Sprite's voice."

They listened again. There it was, a faint, muffled sound.

Adrianna lunged toward the second transport. "It's Sprite!" She opened the hatch and rushed into the fuselage. By the time Hunter and Prescott boarded the craft, Adrianna had her arms wrapped around her daughter.

* * *

Alexis moved closer to Dr. Thrune. Her right hand was in the pocket of her jumpsuit. She wrapped her fingers around a small weapon, but did not withdraw it. She was within two meters of her target.

"Have you reconstituted the phase-two machines?" she asked innocently.

Thrune was inconvenienced by the question. He didn't turn around to face her. "Yes, Ms. Wren. We have the machines."

It wasn't the answer she wanted. Alexis had hoped to catch the man before he finished his work. She felt herself losing control of the situation.

"Dr. Thrune, I am sick and tired of your condescending attitude." The man stopped what he was doing. He turned slowly. He saw the look of hatred in Alexis' eyes. Then he saw the weapon in her hand. She raised it up toward his face and pulled the trigger. It was the last thing he ever saw.

* * *

"We've got to get her out of here," Adrianna said after they had cut Sprite's restraints.

Hunter nodded, thinking about the killer nanomachines that might escape from the flawed containment unit. "Why don't you and Sprite take our transport? Go outside the dome. We'll let you know when it's safe."

She looked at her husband, then at Prescott. "Okay, but be careful."

Hunter gave her a peck on the cheek. "We will." He gave Sprite another hug. "Now get out of here."

Prescott and Hunter stepped into an airlock that was set into the inner dock wall. Prescott touched his earset. "Wiley? Adrianna has Sprite. She's going to take the transport out of the dome. Hunter and I need floor plans."

* * *

Hunter and Prescott were just entering the immense laboratory when Alexis killed Dr. Maxwell Thrune. Their attention was drawn by the bright light of the weapon's discharge. Hunter recognized the large apparatus in the center of the lab.

"Over there," he whispered to his brother.

They picked their way carefully toward the containment unit. It was an exact duplicate of the one at Meridian 6. They crouched down quickly. Two people were standing near the unit's holodisplay. They were Amos Cross and Alexis Wren. Hunter and Prescott slid behind a large rack of equipment.

* * *

Cross broke off his conversation when he saw the flash from Alexis' weapon. She stood over the scientist's lifeless body.

"Occasionally, you get to do something that makes a difference," she said to him. "Thrune was a horrible little man."

"Ms. Wren! What have you done?" Cross was dumbfounded.

Alexis swung her weapon toward him. "I'm doing my job, Amos." Cross couldn't take his eyes off the gun. "I work for Damon Trask and the Citizen's League."

"How is that possible? We were very careful when we vetted you."

"It doesn't matter. I was put here to stop you from using NARI's nanomachines. That's exactly what I intend to do."

"But we put you undercover on the NARI team." Cross was still in denial.

"Yes you did. What a happy coincidence."

"You're the one who blew up the lab on Selene Station." Cross was putting the puzzle pieces together.

"I did."

"And you're here to stop me."

"I am."

Cross started to laugh. Alexis raised her weapon. "What's so funny?"

"All that work and you're too late."

Alexis glanced at the containment unit, a look of incredulity on her face. "Thrune told me he reconstituted the machines. They're still here."

"No, they're not, Ms. Wren." Cross stepped toward to her.

"Don't come any closer, Amos."

Cross kept walking. "Don't you want to know what the Shadow Project is?"

"What have you done?" she gasped.

Cross put his hands together and grinned at her. He lowered his voice to a soft whisper. Alexis stepped closer to him. "A jumpship is on its way to Earth, as we speak. There's a special containment unit on board." Understanding was dawning on Alexis' face. Cross spoke quieter still. She drew even closer. "I have been worried about the space elevators. They are making it much cheaper to place mass into Earth orbit. Soon, Earth-based manufacturers will flood the off-world markets with inexpensive goods. Meridian Corporation could be ruined."

Alexis was stunned. She lowered the weapon as she grasped the immensity of Cross's plan. "You're going to kill all of those people?" she hissed.

"Of course. It suits my purpose." Cross spoke to her like a friend sharing a secret. He took a step closer to her. "With the Earth out of the picture, Meridian will have a monopoly on all the goods and services required by the colonies and settlements. We will hold the remainder of humanity in our hand."

Alexis raised the weapon again. "You're a monster."

"Yes, I am."

Suddenly, an alarm sounded from the containment unit. The holodisplay pulsated with an angry red glow. Safety systems began to trip.

"The containment unit has failed!" Alexis shouted, as she turned toward the display. Cross was right behind her and snatched the weapon out of her hand. She turned back to him, realizing her fatal mistake. She put up her hands in a futile attempt to shield herself. Cross pulled the trigger.

12

Cross was running for the exit before Alexis' body hit the floor. Hunter and Prescott rose from their hiding place and rushed toward the containment unit. Hunter went straight to the control panel. A data module was plugged into the complex device. It contained his stolen research files. He pulled the module from its slot and slid it into his pocket. Then he scanned the containment unit for phase-two nanomachines. He turned to Prescott. "There's nothing in here!"

Prescott was kneeling by Alexis. She was barely alive. The fallen woman stirred. She looked up at Prescott with half-vacant eyes. She raised her hand and cupped her fingers over her left ear, as if she was trying to block the sound of the alarms. Hunter tapped an icon on the containment unit, and it was silent.

Alexis' eyes were wide, her face filled with panic. Blood dripped from her mouth as she spoke. Her voice was a hoarse, bubbly whisper. "Jumpship."

"What are you saying?" Prescott asked the fallen woman. "Are the nanomachines on a jumpship?"

Alexis paid no attention to him. "Space Elevator One," she whispered. Then her body jerked, and she was dead.

Prescott was kneeling close to Alexis. Her hand was still cupped over her left ear. He moved her fingers and examined the skin behind her earlobe. Something was under the surface. "Well, I'll be..." he muttered.

"What is it?" Hunter moved closer.

Prescott was astonished. "She wasn't talking to us."

"You're kidding me."

Prescott motioned to Alexis' head. "Put your finger behind her ear."

Hunter did. "It's a subcutaneous radio."

Prescott scratched his head. "I wonder who she was talking to?"

"Damn!" Hunter swore, ignoring his brother's question. "We need a fast ship. Now."

* * *

Maya Lewis hurried down the main concourse of Copernicus Base. She wore a baggy jumpsuit. She kept her chin down to avoid attention. Her world had been turned upside-down. Four little words had changed everything. She had to get to the Citizen's League jumpship. It was waiting for her at the spaceport.

Maya thought about Alexis Wren. She had recruited her because of her growing concerns about self-replicating nanomachines. Maya had told her she would be a hero. She would protect humanity from the consequences of rogue science. Alexis would infiltrate Meridian Corporation and report to her. Maya never dreamed Amos Cross would choose her to become a mole on Hunter Logan's team. Alexis took on the persona of the scientist who was constantly preoccupied by her work. The NARI team accepted her idiosyncrasies, and she listened in on every conversation, reporting back to Meridian Corporation and to the Citizen's League. Maya had promised Alexis the day would come when she could stop living a life of deception, that she would be able to return to her family, but the promise was a lie. Alexis had always been expendable.

Maya reviewed their most recent plan. Alexis had been on her way to the Shadow Project laboratory. She was going to kill Dr. Thrune, stopping him from making the killer nanomachines. She was going to destroy Hunter Logan's data. Meridian would be denied the lethal technology. Years of preparation would have yielded a great victory for the Citizen's League, if everything had worked.

Maya had been in the Old Garden when Alexis' final message reached her. She had heard the woman's death rattle, and then a single word: jumpship. What did Alexis mean? Then the woman uttered her last words: Space Elevator One. Those four little words had spelled disaster. Maya had glanced upward through the dome and gazed briefly at the blue-green orb of Earth. Acid rose in her stomach as she grasped the meaning of the message. Alexis had failed. Cross had the phase-two nanomachines. He was sending them to Space Elevator One on a jumpship. He was going to kill everyone on the Earth.

Maya had sprung into action. She had retreated into the garden glade and found a tool locker. She had stolen an old jumpsuit. Now she walked briskly toward the Commons. She poked her earset sharply. "Get me Damon Trask!"

* * *

Nixie Drake piloted an unmarked jumpship toward Jackson Crater. Ice sat next to her in the copilot's seat. Nixie glared at their destination on the nav display.

"Ticked in the egg-noggin, Icy!" The girl was in a foul mood. "I'm ticked bad."

Ice didn't respond.

"Momma Kate this and Momma Kate that. Can't pick my nose an yeses when it comes to Momma Kate. No surrey with a fringe around it." She pounded the arm of her seat. "Momma Kate asks Nixie if you pleasey-wheezy, and I says 'Yes ma'am, an next to knowin' it, Nix is in her hippy-pocket.

"Here I am, flyin' my besty-best jumper to where?" Nixie sucked in a breath. "To Jackson Base!" she shouted. "Stickin' my butt smackered in the face of Meridian scurity! Why? Momma Kate! When? Momma Kate! I'm damned ticked in the frick-frackin' head!"

Ice yawned.

Nixie was flying close to the lunar surface. The ship's AI followed the uneven terrain at breakneck speed. The craft decelerated slightly as it rose over the outer rim of Jackson Crater and settled quickly, until it was only one meter above the crater floor. The AI accelerated the ship toward the outskirts of Jackson Base. Nixie was amazed there hadn't been any challenges to their rapid approach. A large dome loomed ahead of them. The AI ramped the throttles back until they were creeping slowly toward an open dock on the eastern face of the structure. Nixie took manual control of the ship and flew straight into the opening. She applied reverse thrusters at the last possible second, setting the ship down inside the dome.

The dock entry hatch was rising out of the threshold before the ship came to a stop. The massive dock pressurized rapidly, and Nixie saw the inner airlock door swing open. Four people tumbled through it and ran toward the ship. She cracked the hatch, and they scrambled aboard.

"Why's your panties on fire, Pressy?" Nixie eyed Sprite, as the girl slid into one the seats.

Prescott ignored her as he closed the ship's hatch. He touched his earset. "Wiley? Open the dock. We've got to get out of here."

"Decompress?"

"No. Just crack the hatch." The massive door began to descend. The air in the dock screamed out through the opening. The jumpship rattled as explosive decompression buffeted the fuselage. Prescott dropped into the seat directly behind the young pilot and yanked at his restraints. "Okay, Nixie. Bring her around and launch!" The young girl didn't hesitate. She fired the downward thrusters and spun the ship like a ballerina. She punched the throttles, and the jumpship leapt forward. It shot out of the dock and across the lunar surface. Jackson Crater's massive ray system dropped away beneath them at an incredible speed. Nixie had been on the ground for less than two minutes.

"Wow, this bird can fly!" Hunter gripped his restraints.

Nixie smiled. "Fasty ships make happy pilots. Times are wastin' when you don't want to be trippin' over yer own ass wipe." She sniffed as she turned around to face Prescott. "Earthy?"

Prescott laughed. "Yeah. We're chasing another jumpship. She's headed toward Space Elevator One." Ice was already whispering instructions to the ship's AI.

"Whens you wants to gets there?" Nixie asked.

"How fast can this ship go?" Hunter asked.

Nixie grinned broadly. "Fasty-fast."

"Then make it 'fasty-faster!'"

Adrianna gave Hunter a concerned frown. "I hope the containment unit holds together until we get there."

Hunter nodded. "Me, too." Visions of killer nanomachines reaching the Earth's surface haunted him. Hunter caught himself rubbing his right index finger. He looked down at his old scar.

"Who's the kiddy?" Nixie asked. She had swiveled around in her pilot's seat and was facing Sprite.

"She's my daughter, Sprite." Adrianna gave Sprite a squeeze. "This is Nixie Drake, honey. She flew us back from The Belt. She's been very good to us."

Sprite stuck out her hand. "Pleased to meet you." Nixie looked down at the girl's hand for a moment, then gave her a tight handshake. Sprite touched her forearm, and her hand became as hard as iron.

Nixie's grin turned into a look of astonishment as she squeezed as hard as she could. "My friendsies call me Nix," she said. "You gots toughy-tough hands for a girlie."

"Got 'em from my parents." Sprite pressed her forearm again, and her skin returned to normal. "This your ship?"

"You betcher 'tis. My prideness-an-joyful ship. She's fer specialocations."

"Do you have ships for other occasions?"

"Yup again, small fry. I gots two more."

Ice gave Nixie a hard look.

"Ack-shally, the ships blong to Cap'n Grit. He's the bossy-boss of my crew."

Ice cleared her throat.

"Ah, the bossy-boss of our crew." Nix nodded at her copilot. "This is Ice."

"Thanks for helping us."

"Nosey problem, Spritey girl. My noggin can't 'magine nothin' else I'd rather be doin'."

Ice snorted.

* * *

Amos Cross's jumpship hurtled through the dark lunar sky toward a majestic spacecraft. *The Envoy II* was Cross's personal transfer ship. It was outfitted like a self-contained corporate embassy. The great man was shaking from fear and anger. He dreaded what was happening in the Shadow Project laboratory. Something had gone terribly wrong with the device that held the killer machines. Cross wondered if the tiny predators were consuming the interior of the dome. He knew they could not be stopped once the containment unit was breached. Jackson Base was at risk and with it, Meridian Corporation's manufacturing center. The entire moon might be consumed. He wondered if his empire could survive such a loss.

Cross's one hope lay with the jumpship carrying his special cargo toward the space elevator. Thrune had followed his orders and had created the modified containment unit. Alexis had been too late. Earth's days were numbered. Soon, Meridian Corporation would monopolize all the trade in the solar system. Cross saw in his imagination a tectonic shift taking place: the loss of the Earth and the Moon, and the rise of the Martian colonies. The jumpship docked with *The Envoy II,* and Amos Cross boarded the luxurious craft. He ordered her pilot to lay in a course for Mars.

* * *

Prescott, Hunter, and Adrianna sat in the rear of the jumpship's cabin, consulting with Wiley and Athena. "We have had limited success hacking into the target jumpship," Wiley was saying. "We can monitor her systems, but we have no control over the ship."

"Do you see the containment unit?" There was urgency in Hunter's voice.

"No."

Adrianna furrowed her brow. "Will we catch the ship before she reaches Space Elevator One?"

"At your present speed, the target ship will dock approximately one hour ahead of you."

Prescott raised his voice so Nixie could hear him. "Can we go faster, Nixie?"

The young pilot swiveled around to face the cabin area. "We's at tippy-top speed, Pressy. We've ripped her as far as we can tip her."

Sprite giggled. "Pressy?" She turned in her seat and gave her uncle Prescott a smile. "I like it."

Prescott shook his finger at his niece. Then he lowered his voice and spoke to Wiley again. "Can you get us clearance to dock at the space elevator?"

"Yes, sir. Your ETA is four hours and forty-seven minutes from now. You are cleared to dock upon arrival."

* * *

Drew and Beverly Mallick floated off the Meridian jumpship. It had been a long flight. Their excitement had risen as they drew closer to their destination. They were almost home. A pleasant woman greeted them at the dock and directed them to a vertical passage that would take them down to the elevator. "The lift will be departing in two and half hours. May I suggest you visit our observation deck? The view is amazing!" she said. The Mallicks followed the woman's advice and were soon enthralled by the stunning view of Mother Earth.

Maya Lewis was grateful for the League's jumpship. She was extremely fast, enabling her to catch up with the Meridian craft. Maya watched the Mallicks disembark from their jumpship. Her contacts had told her about them. They were an old couple returning to Earth for healthcare and family. They couldn't be part of Cross's plan. She watched as the couple's baggage was offloaded from the ship. All their possessions were stowed in two cargo cases. Maya shook her head, thinking of everything the Mallicks had left behind. She imagined packing all of her possessions into two such modest cases. She could not tolerate the sacrifice.

Maya squeezed the messenger bag she had clamped under her arm. The triangular device was there, waiting to vaporize the phase-two machines and save the Earth. Maya entered the dock and floated toward the empty Meridian jumpship.

* * *

Nixie maneuvered her jumpship into the dock on Space Elevator One. She slid the little ship into the clamps that would hold the craft tightly to the deck. They waited impatiently as the dock pressure equalized with the rest of the platform. Wiley's voice whispered to them in the cabin. "The target jumpship is to your right in Dock Seven." Adrianna told Sprite to stay on the jumpship with Nixie. She grabbed a soft bag and attached it to her waistband. Then she followed Hunter and Prescott through the hatch.

Hunter bowled over a couple of dockhands as he shot out of the ship. He flew across the dock like a projectile. He pivoted to the right and swam into Dock Seven. A gleaming new Meridian jumpship was anchored there. He was alone. He pushed off a bulkhead and flew toward the ship's open hatch. Adrianna and Prescott were just entering the dock as Hunter slammed the hatch shut.

"Hunter!" Adrianna looked with horror as her husband floated into the pilot's seat.

Dockhands started to gather. Hunter brought the jumpship's engines to life. He touched his comlink. "I've got to do this, honey.

You better get off the dock!" He looked down at the control console. "Wiley? Unlatch the jumpship and unseal the dock."

He felt the clamps disengage. The ship floated freely over the decking. Alarms began to sound, warning the impending opening of the dock entrance. Adrianna and Prescott followed the dockworkers into the airlock, seconds before a tremendous blast of air howled through the dock. The entrance was opening to the vacuum of space. Hunter applied the reverse thrusters and backed the ship awkwardly out of the dock. He came to a stop a hundred meters from the elevator platform.

* * *

"What in hell is he doing?" The dock supervisor demanded. Adrianna and Prescott were standing next to the man as he looked out over the empty dock.

"He just saved your life." Adrianna shot back.

The supervisor's eyes narrowed. "How? He can't fly worth shit, and he almost killed everyone on the dock!"

Prescott stepped close to the man. "There's a bomb on that ship," he lied.

"A bomb?" The man's face blanched.

Hunter's voice whispered through the comlink. "We've got a problem."

Adrianna stepped away from the two men. She touched her earset. "What's up?"

"There's no containment unit on this ship."

Adrianna swiveled. She gave her brother-in-law a stunned look. "That's impossible," she said to Hunter. "It's got to be there."

"It's probably built into the ship. Access must be from outside the hull."

Adrianna sized up the situation in a flash. There were no environment suits on the jumpship; there wasn't even an airlock. She looked down at the bag attached to her waistband. She had both of their nano-masks. Hunter was stuck on the jumpship with the killer nanomachines.

"I'm coming, honey," she called into the comlink. She stepped into the airlock and closed the inner hatch. She pulled out one of the masks and fastened it to her face. She tapped her forearm to set her n-skin temperature. Prescott and the dock supervisor were taken by surprise.

Adrianna acted before they could stop her. She punched a series of icons on the lock control panel, and the outer airlock hatch cycled. She was caught up in the burst of air that coursed out of the lock. She flew across the empty dock.

Adrianna was outside the space platform when she realized she didn't have a tether. You idiot! She swore at herself. This was suicidal. She stretched out her arms and tried to ride the last dwindling currents of air. The jumpship grew larger and larger in front of her. She crashed into the side of the little ship. A handhold was directly in front of her. She grabbed it.

Hunter had a horrified expression on his face as he stared at his wife through the jumpship's forward viewports. It took a few seconds for her to recover from the crash landing. Adrianna lifted the bag that held Hunter's mask. He shook his head but wore a smile. He gestured toward the jumpship's hatch. Since there was no airlock, he was going to have to open the hatch and get the mask on within sixty seconds. If he took too long, he would die. To make matters worse, he was going to have to do it with his eyes shut. Better blind for a moment than blind for life, he thought. He reached into his pocket to make sure the healing particles were still there. Adrianna moved away from the hatch and gripped a handhold with all of her strength. Hunter pinched his nose and opened the hatch. His body was buffeted by the hurricane of air. The jumpship's AI fired the steering jets to hold the ship steady. Objects became airborne in the cabin. He hadn't anticipated that. Something struck him on the back of the head, and then there was nothing.

* * *

Adrianna was fastening the mask to Hunter's face when he came to. She looked beautiful as she floated in front of him. She was his space-angel. There was a concerned, but determined look on her face. Hunter drew in a welcome breath of air. She touched her comlink. "You'll be okay," she said. "I got here right after you were hit on the head. It's only been a few seconds."

He nodded. "Let's get this done."

There was a blinding light a few hundred meters from the jumpship. Adrianna and Hunter instinctively moved away from the open hatch and braced for an impact. It never came. There was no sound. Seconds later, they could see tiny shards of metal raining in through the hatch, like grains of sand caught in a strong wind.

* * *

Maya Lewis watched as Hunter commandeered the jumpship and flew it off the dock. She smiled at her good fortune. The bomb would destroy the nanomachines and kill Logan at the same time. She was astonished when Adrianna flew out of the airlock without an environment suit. How did she do that? It didn't matter. The blast would kill her too.

Maya watched Hunter crack the ship's hatch. She saw it blow outward, followed by a river of air that carried everything that wasn't bolted down. She had been in a hurry when she planted the bomb. She had placed it just inside the jumpship's hatch. Her fears were realized when the bomb, now several hundred meters away, detonated harmlessly with a blinding flash.

* * *

"Are you two all right out there?" It was Prescott calling them on the comlink. Hunter's mind was still foggy.

"We're okay," Adrianna replied.

"I guess there really was a bomb on the ship," Prescott offered.

"You should consider a career change," Adrianna quipped. "There's real money in foretelling the future."

Hunter and Adrianna floated out of the hatchway and made their way toward the aft part of the ship. There was no sign of the containment unit. "We're looking at this all wrong," Adrianna suggested.

Earth's glowing expanse stretched out before them like a blue-green emerald lying on black velvet. Hunter looked at the elevator's nanotube ribbon that disappeared into the atmosphere. "Cross wanted to get the nanomachines to the Earth," he said.

Adrianna pointed to the elevator pod. "What if the containment unit was small enough fit on the lift?"

Hunter was skeptical. "Wouldn't people notice a large box sitting in the aisle?"

"Not if it was disguised as baggage." Adrianna was already positioning herself to leap back toward the platform.

* * *

A bevy of people greeted them when the airlock opened. The Logans removed their masks. "Who's in command here?" Hunter demanded.

An angry man in a uniform stepped forward. "You're under arrest."

Hunter cut him off. "We just saved your platform. There was a bomb." The officer hesitated.

Adrianna touched his arm. "What are the names of the passengers who arrived on that jumpship?"

The man sensed the urgency in her voice. He stepped to a display mounted on the bulkhead. "Drew and Beverly Mallick, ma'am. They were the only passengers. We offloaded two cargo cases, and they were carrying two small bags. They're descending to the surface in ten minutes."

Adrianna tightened her grip on the man's arm. "You've got to delay the elevator! We have to inspect their baggage."

The man looked closely at them. "I recognize you. You're those nano-scientists, aren't you?"

"Yes, sir." Hunter was beside himself. "Everyone on Earth is going to die if we don't get to those cargo cases."

The man balled his fists. "Follow me!"

* * *

The officer guided them down a vertical passageway that led to the elevator docking area. The elevator pod was at the bottom of the platform, and scores of people were coursing into it. The man took them to the baggage compartment, directly beneath the elevator's passenger cabin. He opened the compartment. It took only a moment to locate the Mallick's cargo cases.

"You better get out of here," Adrianna told the man. He didn't need a second warning. He was out of the compartment in a flash.

The containment unit was in the heavier of the two cases. Hunter unsnapped the latches and opened the lid. Cross's scientists had done an amazing job miniaturizing the device. A display indicating how high the case was above sea level had been added.

"It's set to breach when the elevator gets to the surface," Adrianna exclaimed.

A new voice echoed in the baggage compartment. "You have been the bane of my existence." Hunter and Adrianna looked up. A beautiful woman stood by the open hatchway. Her back was wedged against the bulkhead, and she had a gun in her hand. "Step away from that case."

The Logans stood up. "Who are you?" Adrianna asked.

"My name is Maya Lewis, and I am here to stop you from deploying those killer machines."

"You've got to be kidding." Hunter shook his head. "Put that gun down and let us do our work. We're going to neutralize them."

"Shut up, Dr. Logan. Your time is up." Maya fired the gun. She hit Hunter in the side of his head. He was propelled backward by the impact. Adrianna screamed as the woman shifted her aim. "The world will be a better place without you." She squeezed the trigger again. The bullet hit Adrianna right between her eyes.

Maya smiled with satisfaction. She had finally stopped the Logans. She sensed someone behind her. Maya turned slowly. Ice stood tranquilly in the hatchway. Maya looked at her curiously. Ice was wearing a liquid bodysuit like her own. Maya gave the woman a radiant smile. "Nice suit," she said.

Ice looked deeply into Maya's eyes. "You make women look bad," she said. Her fist shot out with blinding speed. Maya never saw it coming. Ice knocked her out with a single punch. She took the gun and stepped over Maya's inert form.

Ice entered the compartment. She stood there silently, a hint of surprise on her face. Adrianna was shaking her head. Hunter looked up at her with a wry smile. He was rubbing his temple where the bullet had struck him. "Got a little headache, but I'll be okay."

Ice nodded suspiciously. "I didn't know you could do that," she said.

* * *

The Logans bent over the containment unit. Hunter opened a small panel. There was a cavity inside. It was a port for inserting material into the device. He removed the vial of healing particles from his pocket and loosened the lid. Adrianna took a small receptacle out of the cavity and dipped it into the open vial. Then she placed it back inside the opening and closed the panel. She touched an icon on the display. The healing particles entered the containment field. The killer nanomachines attacked the particles like ravenous animals. They latched onto the newcomers. Then to their surprise, if they were indeed capable of such an emotional response, their victims became their conquerors, and the healing particles decimated the phase-two nanomachines.

EPILOGUE

I t was a brilliantly sunny day in Macapá, Brazil. Drew and Beverly Mallick hugged their daughters. They were eager to sit down, having forgotten how heavy a person felt in Earth's gravity. Their hearts were as light as feathers. Drew thought of Amos Cross. He was thankful for the great man's generosity. He and his wife were upset that the Space Elevator crew had lost one of their cargo cases, but they were reunited with their family, and Drew's retirement had begun.

* * *

The *Envoy II* cut her way through the void toward Mars. Her interior was fitted for royalty. The walls and hatches were trimmed in fine teak, with polished gold inlays. The deck seemed to be made of marble. The speed of her rotating cabin had been adjusted, simulating the g-force experienced on the lunar surface. A steward stood next to Amos Cross. The great man was sitting in a smooth leather armchair. He accepted a glass of lunar brandy without a word. The steward left him alone with his thoughts.

He brooded over his failure. He read the report concerning the jumpship at space elevator one. It must have been the Logans. The whole affair had been a disaster. He wanted to vent his anger, express his profound disappointment in brutal ways, but most of the people who had failed him were dead.

Cross thought of Alexis Wren. He had taken delight in killing her. He was glad she was dead. She had been an underhanded, conniving traitor. He vowed to ruin her family. Then he would destroy Damon Trask and the Citizen's League.

Amos Cross took a sip of his drink. He would find a way to punish all the survivors of this mess. He would take his time and hunt them down. He would find another way to thwart Earth's new space elevators. He would win. There was no other option.

* * *

Aurora North sat in her elegant stateroom. She was on *The Envoy II* with Amos Cross. She paid no attention to the exquisite furniture. She hummed softly to herself and held her tiny box. Every so often, she lifted it to her face and spoke reassuringly to her little friend. "It won't be long now, Sparky. Mr. Cross says momma's waiting for us on Mars."

* * *

Susanna Frost wiped off a table in the Delta V. She was bone tired. It had been a long day of hustling back and forth, dealing with bottles and catcalls and dirty old men. She glanced up at her mother. Kate was restocking the bar. She smiled at her daughter through the mirror. Susanna saw herself in the glass, standing afar off: a barmaid with a faded apron. It was a far cry from her tailored suits and the ring that married her to Amos Cross's inner sanctum, but she was happier now than she had ever been before.

* * *

Tyson and Kell Edwards boarded the space elevator. They felt like tourists as they sat in adjacent seats. The cylindrical capsule straddled the slender nanotube ribbon. The elevator began its descent, imperceptibly at first, and then with gathering speed. They watched as the orbital platform passed from view and the majestic curvature of the Earth embraced them. The black night of space slowly morphed into the subtle purples, then lush blues of the sun-filled sky below them.

It was a lonely trip, Tyson thought. He wished Jo could be with them. He looked up into the diminishing darkness. What was left of Jo lay in the dust of Ceres. There hadn't been time to give her a proper burial. He would never forget her: the way she used to snap at him, the amazing food she prepared, her uncompromising sense of right and wrong, her infinite love for her family. He glanced over at Kell. He had his mother's eyes. A part of his beloved would live on in his exceptional son. What more could a parent ask?

* * *

A commercial freighter slid through the airless void on her way to Rinker's Knot. Her hold was full. Her five passengers had booked the trip under assumed names. The ship's captain asked no questions. He had recognized his guests and understood their predicament. These people had saved the Earth. He considered it an honor to ignore them and aid in their disappearance.

Samina Haddad stood before a mirror in her Spartan cabin. She examined what was left of her body. She had never been a vain person, but she wept openly over the scars. She would never recover her physical beauty. She felt like an alien in someone else's skin. Everyone who saw her would see the scars first. Only then, would they see her. She wished it could be the other way around.

There was a light knock. Samina covered herself with a robe and opened the door. It was Adrianna Logan. She had two flasks of hot tea. Samina welcomed her friend, and the two women sat together.

"I can't wait to see Maria again," Samina murmured. "She won't know herself with a home full of people."

"She'll love it," Adrianna replied. "There's nothing better than being surrounded by the people you cherish."

Samina took another sip of her tea and looked into her friend's face. She was grateful to be alive.

* * *

Sprite Logan sat alone on the observation deck, soaking in the raw beauty of the stars. Her parents were in the rotating cabin with her uncle Prescott and Samina. They were three months away from their destination. Her uncle had told her he had a good friend at the Knot, who would help them get a jumpship and return to his home. There had been enough excitement for a long while. Sprite gazed at the arc of the Milky Way. The stars were clear and bright. She thought about Rory, hoping her friend was all right.

There was a noise behind her. Sprite jumped, fear rising in her chest. Prescott Logan floated over to her and put his hand on her shoulder. "Sorry, kiddo. I didn't mean to scare you."

Sprite smiled. "It's okay, Uncle Prescott. I guess I'm still a little jumpy."

"It's to be expected," he said softly. "I've got a present for you."

She perked up. "What is it?"

Prescott slid a shiny new card comp and earset into her hand. "It's a copy of Wiley. You'll be able to sync him up with the real Wiley and Athena when we get home."

Sprite squealed with delight as she pushed the earset into her ear.

* * *

Hunter Logan sat alone in the modest passenger cabin. He gazed at his right index finger and studied the scar. He thought of the years he had spent trying to win the respect of people he didn't even know. He thought about the sting of his mistakes and his desire to be perfect beyond all reason.

The past few months had been a dark season. He had lost good friends. He had been tormented by guilt and racked with fear. He had felt the burning shame of good intentions shattered by unintended consequences. He had experienced profound helplessness. Each of these things had scarred him, but he wasn't alone. Samina and Sprite bore the most visible marks, but everyone had been branded by their journey through Meridian's Shadow. They were inextricably bound together by their common pain.

Adrianna and Samina entered the cabin. The women were talking quietly with each other. Hunter looked up, and they offered him warm smiles. Prescott wandered in from the observation deck and gave him a simple nod. Then Sprite bounded in and dropped down on the couch. She nestled against him. In that moment, Hunter realized their pain would not destroy them. He rubbed his finger. The old scar wasn't so bad after all.

ABOUT THE AUTHOR

Dan Moore lives with his wife Diana near Syracuse, New York. He is a freelance video producer and the proud father of two sons, two daughters-in-law and six grandsons. In addition to Meridian's Shadow, Dan has written <u>The Rings of Alathea,</u> <u>Nixie's Rise</u>, which is his second novel in the Meridian's Shadow series, and <u>Twyner's Bridge</u>. He is currently editing <u>Meridian's Shadow III: Ignition Point</u>..